It was hard not to laugh at what her and the Clones had said, especially as most of the class was giggling away. Becca and Cat may be right, I thought. Kaylie and her mates may be popular and trendy, but they're not very bright. I stared back at Kaylie, thinking, Two can play at this game and I'm not going to be intimidated by you. After a few minutes, she leaned back in her chair and whispered something to Fran behind her. Fran glanced over at me and laughed. I turned away. She wasn't worth it and I didn't want to get into playing stupid games. All I wanted was to go to school, do my lessons, and get on with everyone without any aggro. Sadly, though, by the look on Kaylie's face, she wasn't going to let that happen.

truth
or dare

Teen Queens and Has-Beens

Cathy Hopkins

Simon Pulse

New York   London   Toronto   Sydney

First Simon Pulse edition November 2004

Copyright © 2003 by Cathy Hopkins
Originally published in Great Britain in 2003 by
Picadilly Press Ltd. as *Truth, Dare, Kiss or Promise: Teen
Queens & Has Beens*

Published by arrangement with Piccadilly Press Ltd.

SIMON PULSE
An imprint of Simon & Schuster
Children's Publishing Division
1230 Avenue of the Americas
New York, NY 10020

Printed in the United States of America
2 4 6 8 10 9 7 5 3 1

Library of Congress Control Number 2004100036

ISBN 0-689-87129-5

Thanks as always to Brenda Gardner, Yasemin Uçar and the ever fab team at Piccadilly. To Rosemary Bromley at Juvenilia. And to Georgina Acar, Scott Brenman, Becca Crewe, Alice Elwes, Jenni Herzberg, Rachel Hopkins, and Olivia McDonnell for answering all my questions about what it's like being a teenager these days.

"POST IS HERE, Lia," Mum called as she went past my bedroom.

I looked out of the window to see the post van zooming away down the drive to the left of the house. It was a lovely clear day and the view from my window was stunning. Terraced lawns, then acres of fields leading down to the sea and our private beach. Although I've been officially living at home for almost eight months now, opening my curtains in the morning is still a thrill and such a change from the apartment block that I looked out on when I was at boarding school up in London.

"Be right down," I called back, then went into my bathroom to find my makeup bag. I wasn't in any great hurry to go downstairs. Not today. It was Friday, February 14. Valentine's Day. That meant cards and I knew there wouldn't be any for me.

As I slicked on some lip gloss, I thought back to

this time last year when I was still a boarder. I'd got loads of cards then. I had loads of boyfriends, too. Jason, Max, Elliott, Leo, Edward. None of them was major or soul mates or anything serious, just part of the gang that used to hang out together. But there had been dates. And cards. We'd send them to each other just for a laugh or so that no one missed out.

Life is so different since I moved down here to Cornwall. New school, new friends, new everything apart from romance. Not one single date since I changed schools. Hence the lack of expectation when it came to Valentine's cards.

I pottered around in my room getting ready for school; then my curiosity got the better of me. Maybe there'd be one card from some mysterious stranger who was secretly pining for me. An admirer who will later reveal himself to be the next best thing since pecan fudge ice cream. Yeah, and there's a yeti living in my fridge, I thought as I grabbed my rucksack and headed downstairs.

Mum was sorting through a pile of envelopes at the counter in the kitchen when I got down. She glanced up and by the look in her eyes, I could tell that I'd been right. Nothing for me.

"It's cool," I said. "I wasn't expecting any."

Mum shook her head. "They all need their heads examined, these boys down here." She pointed at a jug on the counter. "I've just made some juice. Beetroot, orange, and raspberry. Help yourself."

"Um, think I'll stick with plain orange," I said going to the fridge and helping myself to a carton.

Juicing is one of Mum's passions—partly for health reasons, partly for beauty. She's forty, but only looks thirty, which she puts down to juicing. She says it takes years off people and improves their skin no end. Some of her concoctions are fab, but some of them are strange with a capital *S*. I looked over at the dark crimson liquid in the juicer. "You're not going to serve that at the party tonight, are you?"

Mum laughed. "No. Course not. We'll be having Bellinis as the theme is Venetian."

"That's champagne and peach juice, isn't it?" I knew because my sister, Star, likes them. She always has a bottle of champagne and a carton of peach juice in the fridge in her tiny flat in Notting Hill. She makes me laugh as sometimes that's *all* she has in her fridge and, when I go to stay with her, I have to go and buy proper food myself. It's not that Star doesn't eat. She does, it's just that she eats out most of the time and is hardly ever home.

Mum nodded. "There's a place near St. Mark's Square in Venice called Harry's Bar. It's famous for its Bellinis."

"Harry's Bar? Doesn't sound very Italian. Sounds more like a café in the East End of London."

"I know," said Mum. "But then there's probably a famous café in the East End called La Dolce Vita that sells the best cup of tea in the city."

I laughed. Mum was in her element planning parties. If she ever had to work, that would be her perfect job as she's always throwing a do or planning the next. Always over the top. Always with a theme and always no expense spared. This time, the party planners have been here for weeks recreating Venice for a masked ball to be held in a marquee in the top acre of the garden. I felt like I was living in a hotel with all the catering vans outside and people buzzing about carrying vast flower arrangements, swathes of fabric, or lights.

"Any cards there for the Cornish Casanova?" I asked.

The Cornish Casanova is my elder brother, Ollie. He boards at school up in London, but he comes back about once a month and has a long list of admirers down here, including my mate Cat.

Mum counted the cards. "Three. But most girls know to send his to his school as he's there in the week."

"I guess," I said. "In fact, the post office probably had to hire an extra van to cope with the load addressed to him." Ollie's always been a girl magnet. He's got Mum's great bone structure and blue eyes but with dark hair like Dad, not blond like Mum and me. As I drank my juice, I wondered if Cat had sent a card to him. She and Ollie have had a bit of a "thing" since last summer. Nothing official, but you can see that they're really into each other whenever they're together. She knows that he's commitment-phobic so doesn't expect too much. I think that's one of the things that he likes about her and why she's lasted so long. She's cool about him, whereas other girls have virtually camped on his door to try and pin him down. Perfect way to get him to back off, which is why Cat is playing it just right.

"I got one from Dad." Mum smiled as she put an enormous flowery card on the kitchen counter. "And he's got his usual sack full."

My dad is Zac Axford, lead singer of the rock band Hot Snax. They were big in the eighties and he still has a bunch of faithful followers who never forget him, even though most of them are in their forties now. I tease him that he's like Cliff Richard with his middle-aged fan club, but with his faded rock star looks, his tatty jeans, leather jackets, and shoulder length hair, he's more Mick Jagger than Cliff.

I went out into the hall, grabbed my jacket, and went to wait outside for Meena, our housekeeper, to bring the Mercedes round to take me to school. Max and Molly, our mad red setters, came bounding up with their usual morning greeting of licks and paws on the shoulder. At least you love me, I thought as Max almost knocked me off my feet.

I couldn't help but feel disappointed that there wasn't one card for me even though I'd told myself that there wouldn't be. Get over it, it's no biggie, I told myself. So I haven't got a boyfriend down here, so what? At least I've made good mates—Cat,

Becca, Mac, and Squidge. They're really cool, though different to the London crowd in that their relationships seem to be more long-term. Becca has been going out with Mac for about six months, and Cat went out with Squidge for a few years until they broke up last summer, when she fell under the spell of the Cornish Casanova. The longest that I or any of my London mates ever lasted in a relationship was about three months. No one wanted to get tied down to one person.

Still, this new crowd have been brilliant and have made me feel really welcome. I felt petrified that first day of term last year and began to wonder if I'd made a huge mistake asking to change school. It wasn't that I didn't like my old school, I did, and I had great mates there—Tara, Athina, Gabby, Sienna, Isobel, Olivia, and Natalie. It was after Mum and Dad bought the house down here that everything changed. I had to be a boarder and as my mates were all day pupils, it was a bit lonely some evenings. On top of that, getting home at the weekend was a long way to travel. I felt like I never saw Mum and Dad properly, as I was forever on a train going back and forth. It didn't bother Ollie. He wanted to stay as a boarder, but I told Mum I'd like to go to a local school and live at home. She didn't object or try and talk me out of it, not even for a second, as I think she missed me as much as I missed her. She spoke to the headmistress down here and it was agreed. I'd move after Year Eight.

When I got to the new school, everyone seemed to know each other so well, all chatting and catching up after the summer, all totally familiar with where classes were, who the teachers were, who their mates were. And then there was me, the new girl in Year Nine, wondering where I fitted, if anywhere. All the cliques and friendships had clearly been established long ago and I wondered if I was destined to be a loner for the whole year, standing on the outside looking in. Not my favorite time, plus I really missed all the old gang back in London. Cat was my savior. She offered to show me around the school and we clicked immediately. She's one of the nicest, most genuine, unpretentious people I've ever met. Her mum died when she was nine and I think it made her grow up overnight. Whatever, it's made her sensitive to people when they're a bit lost, maybe on account of feeling lost herself when her mum first went.

I heard the car toot outside the garages, so I took a deep breath and prepared myself for the inevitable inquisition at school.

2

Mystery Admirer?

EVERYONE WAS hanging out in the corridor by the assembly hall when I got in. All the talk was about the school Valentine's disco and cards, with lots of whispering, giggling, and secret looks as people tried to guess who'd sent which card to who and who'd left which card in whose locker or rucksack.

"So, how many did you get?" asked Becca.

"Oh, way too many to count," I replied, trying to laugh it off. I started to count on my fingers. "One from Robbie Williams, one from Matt Damon, one from Eminem . . ."

Becca's eyes widened. "Really?"

Cat punched her arm. "No, she's kidding you."

I laughed. Becca was so gullible. She thinks that because Dad's in the music business that we know everyone. "How many cards did you get, Bec?"

"Just one. I guess it's from Mac," said Becca as she pulled her long red hair into a ponytail. "At least it better had be seeing as I sent him one. What about you, Cat?"

"One. Don't know who it's from. At first, I thought it was from Squidge as we've sent each other cards for years, but it's not his writing. I'd know his scrawl even if he tried to disguise it."

"I think people ought to sign Valentine's cards," said Becca. "It would save a lot of grief knowing who they were from."

"They do in some places," I said. "One of my mates at my old school was American and she said that sometimes they sign them there."

"Yeah, but it would take the mystery out of it," said Cat. "It's fun trying to guess."

"Did you send Squidge a card?" I asked.

Cat shook her head. "It's not like that with us anymore."

"Did you send Ollie one?"

"Nah. I reckon his head's big enough as it is and no doubt he'll get a sack load despite me. But seriously, Lia, how many did you get?"

I made my finger and thumb into an *0*.

"I don't get it," said Cat. "I mean, look at you. You're *stunning*, tall, long blond hair, silver-blue eyes . . . you're most boys' fantasy girl! Boys visibly dribble when you enter a room, and no, don't shake your head, I've *seen* them. By my reckoning, half the school is madly in love with you."

"Yeah, but some of the boys here like to act really hard," said Becca. "You know, they think that they'd look like soppy Sarahs if they did anything remotely romantic like send a card. Pathetic, isn't it? Doesn't mean that you haven't got loads of boys interested in you, though, Lia."

"So why haven't I had one single date since I got here, then?"

"Beneath the hard act, most boys are chickens," said Becca. "They're intimidated. You're beautiful, a five-star babe, and most of them know that they're not in your league. Boys hate rejection more than anything, so I reckon most of them daren't ask you out for fear of being turned down."

"I agree," said Cat. "Anyway, you're not missing much. Our school isn't exactly Talent City."

Becca punched Cat's arm. "Er, excuse me. Mac?"

"Yeah, course," said Cat. "And Squidge, but I don't count them. They're mates."

I didn't say anything, but privately, I think I

could fancy Squidge if I let myself. But I don't go there seeing as Cat and he were an item for ages and they're still really close mates. I don't know how she'd feel about me being into Squidge and I don't want to mess up anything between us. So I'm happy to just be good friends with him. Besides, I don't think I'm his type. I'm tall and blond and Cat is petite and dark, plus he's never given the slightest indication that he feels the same way about me.

"There's always Jonno Appleton," said Becca, glancing at a tall boy with spiky dark hair from Year Eleven, who was standing by the doors. "He's a nine out of ten in anybody's book."

"Yeah," I said, "I do fancy him, but who doesn't? Anyway, he's taken by Rosie Crawford, so it's hands off. Boyfriend stealing is against my rules."

"What do we care?" said Cat. "Isn't Ollie bringing that Michael guy down from London with him tonight?"

I felt my face flush. "Yeah. Michael Bradley."

"Does Ollie know that you like him?" asked Becca.

"No way," I said. "And you mustn't say anything. I'd die. No, I'd *never* tell Ollie as he might think he could do me a favor or something and try and fix us up. No, I want it to happen naturally."

I've known Michael since I was knee-high and had a crush on him since I was seven. Not that he's ever noticed me, not in a big way. I'm just Ollie's kid sister, someone to thrash at tennis and throw in the swimming pool in summer. But tonight I intend to change all that. We haven't seen each other for nearly a year and when Ollie told me that he was bringing him down for Mum's party, my imagination went into overdrive. My plan was to persuade Ollie to come with Michael to the school disco with the rest of us. That way, I could show Michael off a bit and prove to the school that I am not *totally* repulsive to boys. Then later at Mum's do . . . well, who knows what a romantic night in Venice might bring?

When the last bell went in the afternoon, school emptied in a flash. Doubtless everyone had their plans. Home, shower, dress, makeup, back to school. Our plan was to meet at Cat's, get dressed there, go to the school disco for an hour or so, then up to my house for Mum's latest extravaganza. She said that I could invite anyone I liked from school, but I'd only invited Becca, Cat, Squidge, and Mac.

It's funny, but since I came down here, sometimes I feel a bit awkward about how rich my family are. It's like I don't want anyone to think I'm showing off or flaunting it. All I've ever wanted was to be normal and be accepted and that was easy at my old school because most people's parents were loaded or famous. There was even a princess in Year Ten. Down here, though, people aren't as well off and sometimes all they see are the flash cars, the big house, and my dad's fame. What they don't know is that Mum and Dad lead very quiet lives most of the time. Both of them are real homebodies. Mum loves nothing better than pottering in the garden growing herbs and vegetables, and Dad is happiest in his studio listening to sounds or watching the telly. But that's not what the public sees. They see Dad on telly whenever he does interviews, which is rarely these days. Or in videos on MTV. They think that he's the wild man of rock and roll. The Cornish Ozzy Osbourne. I can't help being his daughter, and down here, I want to be Lia Axford—not Lia, Zac Axford, famous rock star's daughter. There's a difference, and sometimes it gets in the way of people's perception of me at my new school. I guess that's why I try to keep my family history quiet and in the background, so to speak.

I raced home to pick up my clothes to take to Cat's. It was complete pandemonium when I got there, with even more people dashing about than there had been in the morning. The Venetian theme had really taken shape. A trio of musicians were rehearsing in the hall and there were ornate candelabras in the corridor leading to the right of the house where the marquee had been set up for the party. It's going to look really fab, I thought as I spotted Mum giving a group of caterers some last-minute instructions.

"Is Ollie back?" I asked her.

She nodded her chin toward the stairs. "In his room with his friends, and oh, Lia, I'll leave a selection of masks in your room for you and your friends to put on when you're back from the school disco. Don't be back too late, okay?"

"Okay. Thanks, Mum," I said. Ollie's with his friends? Who else besides Michael, I wondered as I

16

took the stairs two at a time. Never mind, the more, the merrier. I made a quick dash up to my room to brush my hair and spritz some Cristalle on before going to say hello and hopefully get Michael to notice me properly for the first time.

As soon as I opened my door, I noticed a blue envelope on my bed. My name had been written on it in beautiful handwriting. I ripped it open. It was a card with a red rose on it. Inside, it read: *To the girl with silver eyes, from a distant admirer who's waiting until the time is right to reveal himself. Happy Valentine's.* Then three kisses.

I felt a rush of excitement as I studied the envelope for clues. No stamp, so it must have been either delivered by hand or come from someone in the house.

Hmmm. Interesting, I thought as I heard Ollie and Michael's voices in the corridor outside.

3

"HEY, IF it isn't little Lia," said Michael when I opened my bedroom door. Then he looked me up and down. "Only not so little anymore. You've shot up in the last year. You look great!"

"Thanks," I said, and gave him my best flirty look. So far, so good, I thought as he enveloped me in a huge hug. He looked as gorgeous as I remembered—tall and dark, with velvety brown eyes and amazing chiseled features.

"All ready for tonight?" asked Ollie. "Is Cat coming?"

"Yeah. Later with me. First we've got to go to our school disco. In fact, I wondered if you and Mich . . ." At that moment, I heard the door of one of the guest rooms open and close behind us and as I turned, a girl with long dark hair was coming toward us. She was very pretty—Indian-looking, with lovely high cheekbones. Oh *no*, I thought. Ollie's brought one of

18

his "girlfriends" with him. I hope Cat's not going to be upset. I felt a flash of annoyance. He *always* does this. Keeps himself surrounded with different girls, so that no one can get too close to him.

"Lia, this is Usha," said Ollie as the girl came to join us. "Michael's girlfriend."

As she slipped her hand into Michael's, I tried to smile and look friendly, but inside, I felt like my chest was made of glass and someone had just shattered it. "Oh . . . er, hi, Usha."

"So what were you just saying?" asked Ollie. "Something about a disco?"

"Yeah. Got to dash. Disco at school. Going there first. Be back later. See you then."

I ran back to my room, locked the door, dived onto my bed and put my pillow over my head. Girlfriend? He'd brought his *girlfriend*! Stinking finking. I never saw that coming. But, of course, someone as attractive as Michael was bound to have a girlfriend and Ollie wasn't to know that I fancied him. I lay on my bed for a while, stared at the ceiling, and ran through all the swear words I knew in my head. I daren't say them out loud as there were too many people in the house and someone might be passing my room and think I'd gone mad. Suddenly I wasn't in the mood for a disco, or a party. I wanted to hide under my bed and come out when it was all over.

A moment later, Cat phoned to ask if she could borrow my red beaded choker and it all came tumbling out.

". . . so, you see, I just can't come," I said. "I'd be lousy company and . . ."

"So what are you going to do? Hide in your bedroom all night? You know you can't do that. Your mum or someone's bound to come up and drag you out, then you'll have to spend the whole night watching Michael with Usha. No, come on, Lia, best get out of there. Take your mind off it. And you never know, we might have a good time at school, then later, at least Bec, Mac, Squidge, and I will be there with you."

The school disco was well underway by the time we got there. In the end, it wasn't me who held us up but Becca. She took six changes of clothes to Cat's and couldn't decide what to wear. She finally decided on black trousers and a black handkerchief top. She looked really sophisticated, more eighteen than fourteen.

Cat wore her short red dress and my choker and looked lovely as always. The name Cat suits her as she looks a bit like a cat—dark, glossy, and serene. Mum and I had picked out a silvery colored mini-dress with sparkles on it last time we were up in London, but it seemed a bit OTT for the school disco. I wasn't in the mood for dressing up, so I just put on my jeans and a pale blue halter-neck top instead.

"You'd look good whatever you wore," said Becca as we tried to apply lip gloss beneath the glaring fluorescent lights in the girls' cloakroom at school. I couldn't help thinking how different it looked to back home where Mum had put jasmine scented candles, flowers, and Floris soaps in all the cloakrooms. The only aroma here was the pong of disinfectant that the cleaners used to scour the loos with.

As we stood in front of the mirrors doing our hair, Kaylie O'Hara came in with one of her mates, Susie Cooke. Cat gave me an "Oh, here we go" look as Kaylie is one of those girls who takes over a place even if it's only the cloakroom. It's as if when she arrives, no one else is important. She has to be the center of attention and she's certainly very popular, especially with the boys. Becca says it's because boys are breast-fixated and she has the largest chest in our year. She always wears very tight tops that make her boobs look as though they're straining to escape. She's easily the prettiest of her group, in a baby-doll kind of way, and her mates are all clones of her. There are four of them. Kaylie, Susie, Jackie, and Fran. Becca calls them the Barbies. Cat calls them the Clones. All of them are really girlie girls who have blond-highlighted hair that they flick around a lot. They all wear loads of shiny lip gloss which they are always reapplying, even in the middle of math. And lately, they've all started talking in this lispy, breathy voice. Kaylie started it a few weeks ago and now they all do it. I guess they think it makes them sound sexy, but I think it makes them sound silly. Cat says Kaylie and her mates are as thick as two short planks. In her usual subtle way (not), Becca thinks that they will all probably marry some very rich but stupid men. "The type that likes arm candy, but doesn't care that the candy is brain-dead."

"Tonight's the night," sang Kaylie as she headed

for the mirror next to us and began to apply pink gloss to her lips.

"You look happy," said Becca.

Kaylie winked at Susie. "*Indeed.* Just heard some interesting news. Some *very* interesting news."

"Come on, then," said Becca, who never held back when she wanted to know something. "Spill."

Kaylie smiled. "Ah, well . . ." Then she began singing again. "Tonight's the night . . ."

Becca shrugged and headed for the door.

"Oh, all right," pouted Kaylie. "You'll find out soon enough anyway." She folded her arms and leaned back against the sink. "Jonno Appleton's broken up with Rosie."

"Is *that* all?" said Becca. "So what's the big deal?"

"He's free, you eejit," she said, then raised an eyebrow, "but not for long if I have my way."

Cat shot me a look as if to say, Yeah right, then turned to Kaylie. "But sometimes people need a bit of space when they've just split up with someone. He may not be ready yet."

Kaylie tapped the side of her nose. "Oh, don't worry. I know how to play it. I have it all worked out, in fact. I have an ickle plan."

I guess I must have let out a sigh when she said that, as she turned to look at me. "You don't think I can do it?" she asked in a tight voice.

"No, I . . . it wasn't that . . . ," I blustered. I didn't mean to dismiss her. I was just thinking that getting off with Michael had fizzled out despite all *my* plans. But I wasn't going to tell her about that. I felt intimidated by Kaylie. She's one of those girls who acts friendly, but you get the feeling that if you said the wrong thing, she could turn nasty. I've never crossed her, but I've seen her be really sarcastic to a couple of girls in our class. Luckily, she seemed to be in a good mood tonight.

"Whatever," she said as she took out a can of hairspray and sprayed liberally around her head. Some of the spray hit me in the eye. "Oh *sorry*, Lia, did I get you? Oops."

"S'okay," I said as I rubbed my eye. I swear she did it on purpose, but there was no way I was going to say anything.

Kaylie stood back and looked at her reflection. "Tonight, Mr. Appleton, you are mine, *all* mine."

Susie laughed and flicked her hair back. "He doesn't stand a chance, poor guy."

24

At that moment, Annie Peters came in and stood next to Kaylie at the sink. I like Annie. She's in Year Eleven and is a bit of an oddball. She does her own thing, has her own hippie style, and is brilliant at art, particularly photography.

"Hey, nice watch," she said to Kaylie as she applied some moss-green kohl to her eyes.

Kaylie beamed. "Thanks. It's a Cartier."

"For real?" asked Annie, taking Kaylie's wrist.

"Yeah, course. My brother brought it back from Thailand for me. Cool, huh?"

Annie examined the watch and nodded. "Yeah. Nice. There's one sure way to tell if it's real, though."

"How?" asked Kaylie as I headed for the door. Now would be a good time to leave, I thought, as I had the same watch on. My dad got it for me last Christmas and I've no doubt that mine's real, as I was with him when he bought it from the Cartier shop in London.

"Easy," said Annie. "My dad got my mum one for their twentieth wedding anniversary. She said that you can tell a real Cartier by looking at one of the numbers, I think it's the V, under a magnifying

25

glass. If it's genuine, you can see the word 'Cartier' written in minuscule writing."

I gave Becca the nod to say let's go, but she clearly wanted to stay and watch what was happening. Annie rummaged in her bag. "I've got a magnifying glass in here somewhere. Let's have a look."

She pulled out her glass, held it close to Kaylie's wrist, then screwed her eyes up to look at the watch. "Nope. Can't see any word."

I thought it was a bit mean of Annie to humiliate Kaylie like that, as she'd obviously been chuffed thinking that she had a real Cartier. To me, it's no big deal. A watch is a watch, main thing is that it tells the time, but I wanted to say something to make Kaylie feel better. "It looks real to me," I said. "It might just be on a particular model that the V has Cartier written on it." Big mistake as all eyes turned to me. Eagle-eyes Annie spotted my watch straightaway.

"Hey, same watch," she said, before I could hide my arm behind my back. "What a coincidence. Here. Let's have a look at yours, Lia."

Quick as a flash, she had my wrist in her hand and was scrutinizing my watch. "Yep," she said.

"Here it is. Tiny. 'Cartier.' Want to look, Kaylie?"

"Think I'll pass," she said sulkily as she flounced toward the door. "Little things for little minds."

"Good luck with Jonno," I called after her, in an attempt to break the sour atmosphere.

"Yeah, whatever," she said. Then she smiled back at me. But it was with her mouth not her eyes. She may be pretty, I thought, but there's something hard about her. She's clearly not someone to get on the wrong side of.

The music was thumping in the hall where the disco was being held. Already people were up, dancing and having a good time and the atmosphere was infectious. I soon forgot the incident in the cloakroom, as Becca and Cat pulled me out onto the floor and we began to dance. Mac and Squidge soon came to join us and after a while I began to really enjoy myself. Squidge is a brilliant dancer when he wants to be, but he was in the mood for looning about by doing Hawaiian dancing, then Greek, then Egyptian, then Russian—complete with knee bends and kicks. Then he fell over.

"And now, so that the teachers don't feel left out,

27

we'll have a golden oldie session," said the DJ. "Here's a blast from the past for the wrinklies with an old Beatles number: 'Can't Buy Me Love.'"

The group of teachers, who were standing by the drinks table, smiled wearily then carried on chatting.

As we danced to the words "Money can't buy me love," I thought, That's so true. Money can't buy a good time, either. Like there in the hall. The decorations looked really tatty. There were a few token balloons scattered around the walls and an old faded glitter ball catching light on the ceiling, and that was it, but it hadn't stopped anyone having a great time. Probably cost about five quid, I thought, whereas Mum's party must have cost thousands.

After a few dances, we went to get a drink and Becca nudged me. "Over there," she whispered. "Kaylie gets her man."

"Or not," said Cat as she looked over. "I think it's going to be a no score."

I glanced over to where they were looking and saw Kaylie at the other end of the drinks table. She was desperately trying to get Jonno's attention, but he seemed more interested in talking to one of his mates from the football team. She was flicking her hair and sticking her chest out for all she was worth, but he wasn't taking any notice. When another Beatles track began to play, she pulled on his arm and tried to get him to join her on the dance floor, but he shook his head and turned away to get a drink.

That makes two of us let down by love today, I thought, feeling sorry for her for a moment.

Cat, Becca, and I downed an orange juice then headed back onto the floor to join Mac and Squidge, who by now had moved on to sixties go-go dancing, à la Austin Powers style. We joined in and were having a real laugh when someone tapped me on the shoulder. I turned to see a handsome face smiling down at me.

"Want to dance?" asked Jonno Appleton.

Over his shoulder, I could see Kaylie watching from the drinks table. She didn't look pleased.

4

WE LEFT the disco around ten o'clock and piled into Squidge's dad's van. He was great at ferrying us all around when we needed a lift.

"You don't mind roughing it, do you?" asked Mr. Squires as he spread an old blanket that stank of petrol on the floor in the back.

I wedged myself in between a tool box and Becca. "No, course not. Rough is the new smooth, don't you know?"

"Bet you never traveled like this up in London," said Becca.

"Yeah, course I did," I lied. I didn't want Squidge or his dad to think I was snobby about the van. I wasn't bothered at all, but the truth was, at my old school, everyone used cabs to get about. One night, my friend Gabby's dad even had his chauffeur pick us up and take us to the theater in their Bentley. It was really cool. Her dad's a politician and the car had tinted windows and was bullet proof, at least Gabby said it was. Either way, we felt like we were in a Bond movie.

Mac jumped in and sat back against Becca pretending that she wasn't there. "Er, seats are a bit lumpy, mate," he joked to Squidge.

"Gerroff," said Becca, pushing him off and into Cat, who was squashed up in the corner.

"Gerroff yourself," she said, pushing him back at Becca.

Mac made his body go limp and lay over both of them. "Ah, poor me. At the mercy of cold-hearted women again."

"Get in the front beside me, nutter," Squidge said, laughing.

Mac climbed out, then closed the back door on us before getting in beside Squidge in the front.

What a strange night, I thought. In fact, what a strange day. No Valentine's card, then a card appears on my bed. I still don't know who sent it, but I guess Michael is off the list now. Probably Mum. It's the sort of thing she'd do. No boy interested in me, then the most popular boy in school makes a beeline for me. I had one dance with Jonno and he was really flirty, putting his arms around my waist and stuff, but I was so aware of Kaylie's eyes boring into me that I couldn't let go and enjoy it. In the end, I made an excuse and went back to mad dancing with my mates.

"You're bonkers," said Becca as the van reached our driveway and the gates swung open. "Jonno's *gorgeous*."

"I know," I said, "but I don't want any trouble. Kaylie bagged him in the loos. You heard her."

"So what? It doesn't mean that they're an item," continued Becca. "Anyone could see that he wasn't interested in her. He only had eyes for you."

I shook my head. "Not worth the aggro. I don't want to get on the wrong side of her."

Becca sighed. "Tough for her, I say. You can't let girls like Kaylie O'Hara run your life. Look at what *you* want to happen, not what she wants."

"Yeah . . . I will," I said. "In fact, at the disco, I invited a few boys from Year Eleven up to the party."

"Really?" said Cat. "Who? Jonno?"

"No. Not Jonno. Seth and Charlie from your class, Squidge."

"Yeah. They're okay," he said from the front. "Do you fancy one of them?"

"No. But I thought I ought to at least make an

effort to be friendly to some new boys. New start, new chapter, and all that." I'd decided back at the disco that it was time I got to know some of the local boys a bit better, especially as all my stupid dreams about Michael had fallen through.

"In that case," said Mac. "No better way to make a new start than with a quick round of truth, dare, kiss, or promise. . . ."

"Oh *nooo*," groaned Cat. "It always gets us into trouble of some sort."

"Oh, let's play," said Becca, then she grinned. "Only, because it's Valentine's day, you only have one option: Kiss. Sorry."

"So, who do we have to kiss, Cupid?" asked Cat.

"And don't say I have to kiss Seth or Charlie, please," I said.

"Well, Mac, you have to kiss me and I have to kiss you," said Becca. "Um, Cat, I'll make it easy for you. You have to kiss Ollie."

Cat smiled. "No problemo."

"Now. What about Squidge?" asked Becca.

"How about I choose for myself in my own time," he said. "I don't like to rush these things. Let me think about it."

I was about to say, Me too, I want to choose in my own time as well, when Becca piped up. "Okay, but Lia *has* to kiss Jonno Appleton."

"No, oh come on, don't be a wind-up," I said.

Becca shook her head. "Sorry, it's been decided. If you're going to be such a wimp as to be intimidated by Kaylie, then you need a push from us. All those in favor of Lia snogging Jonno, raise your hands."

Mac, Cat, and Becca raised their hands.

"You should let her choose herself," said Squidge as we reached the top of the drive.

"Sorry, you're out-voted, Squidge. Lia, did you or did you not say that you fancied Jonno Appleton?" demanded Becca.

"Yeah, but pick someone else, please. . . ."

"Well, who else do you fancy?" demanded Becca as Mr. Squires slowed the van down and parked between a Porsche and a BMW.

There was no way I was going to admit that I secretly liked Squidge. "No one, really."

"So the only boy you think is fanciable is Jonno, then?"

"I suppose," I said, then looked at Mac and Squidge, who are both very good looking in their own ways. Mac is blond, with fine features, and Squidge has brown, spiky hair, an open and friendly face, and a gorgeous, wide, smiley mouth. "Present company excepted, of course."

"So that's settled, then," said Becca. "Better to kiss someone you actually like than being dared to go and kiss some reject. It will be fine, Lia. Live dangerously."

"Okay, but I'll do it in my own time," I said.

"Fine," Becca said, then grinned. "You've got ten minutes. No, only joking. In your own time."

Cat gave me a half smile and looked at Becca as if to say, What can you do? I smiled back. Sometimes you can't argue with Becca. And it might not be so bad if I could get Jonno on his own sometime.

Mum had laid out some amazing masks on my bed for us.

"And there's more downstairs in the hall," I said. "Mum put a basket of them out by the fireplace for guests who didn't bring one."

"No, these are brilliant," said Becca, holding up a silver mask to her face in the mirror.

The girls chose the pretty ones. Becca opted for

one with a full white face with delicate gold sequined patterning on the cheeks, gold lips, and gold curls made out of paper around the head. Cat also went for a full face mask with red and gold diamond shapes painted on the cheeks, green rhinestones around the eyes, and a red feather plume. Squidge chose a black half mask with a hooked nose. As he was wearing his long black leather coat, the combination with the mask made him look pretty sinister. Not to be outdone, Mac picked a scary one as well—red with a bird's beak nose. It didn't look as effective as Squidge's, as Mac was wearing a fleece and jeans. I picked a Pierrot mask. White with sad eyes, red lips, and a tear painted on one cheek. Somehow it seemed to fit the mood of the day. It seemed I'd never be with a boy I liked. The beautiful Michael was attached, getting involved with the lovely Squidge was way too complicated, and to respond to Jonno would only cause trouble. Yes, the Pierrot mask would be perfect.

When we were ready, we headed down and out to join the party. Most of the guests had already arrived as it was almost eleven o'clock and as we made our way through them, it was hard to tell who was who.

"Woah," exclaimed Mac as he took in the sumptuous decorations in the marquee. It did look fabulous, like stepping into another world where everything was red and gold. Mum had really surpassed herself. Soft candlelight lit the tented room, and the trio of musicians dressed in eighteenth century costumes were playing classical music in a corner. Swathes of silk were draped around pillars and huge arrangements of flowers and grapes adorned every table. The whole effect was rich and romantic. There was even an ice sculpture of a lion with vodka coming out of its mouth.

The classical trio finished playing their pieces and it wasn't long before one of Dad's old hits from the eighties blasted through the speakers. Ollie appeared and swept Cat off to dance. Then, of course, Mac took off with Becca.

"You okay?" asked Squidge, who by now had his video camera out ready to film the proceedings.

Squidge wants to be a film director when he leaves school, and ever since I've known him, I've never seen him without his camera. He takes it everywhere and has a wall full of recorded material in his bedroom. Mum asked him to film our

Christmas party last year and she was so pleased with the results that she asked if he'd do this one as well.

I nodded. "Yeah, sure. You go ahead and start your filming."

After Squidge had gone, I sat at one of the tables and picked at some grapes. It looked like everyone was having a great time. Cat with Ollie, Mac with Becca, Mum with Dad, Michael and Usha, and Star, who was down from London with some new man. I felt like a spare part sitting there with no one to dance with, but it wasn't long before Dad spotted me and hauled me up onto the floor. After a few numbers, he had to go and greet some friends who had just arrived, so I sat down again. I was hoping Star would come and say hi, but she looked too busy with her new boyfriend. Like Ollie, she's never short of admirers. I guess I'm the odd one out in our family; in fact Dad even has a joke about it. He calls me the white sheep because, in comparison to the rest of them, I'm quiet whereas they're all outgoing and mega-confident. Sometimes I think I must be a disappointment to them. They're all so sociable and popular. Ollie with the girls, Star with the boys, and of course Dad, with his enormous fan club. And then me. It's not that I'm *not* sociable, it's just that I'm shyer than they are—until I get to know someone. That's part of the reason I liked hanging around in a large group at my old school. There were so many of us that people didn't notice that I was quieter than the rest.

I was just starting to feel self-conscious sitting there on my own, when I spied Seth and Charlie from school. At least they'd be someone to talk to, I thought. I was about to go over when someone tapped me on the shoulder. It was one of the magicians Mum had hired to circulate amongst the guests and do magic tricks. He was wearing a half mask and a cloak and produced a five pound note and a cigarette from his sleeve. He held up the note, lit the cigarette, then burned a hole in the money with the cigarette, only when I looked at the fiver, there was no trace of a hole. It was amazing.

"How did you do that?" I gasped. I *saw* him burn the hole in the fiver and I was so close, I would have seen if he'd replaced the note with another.

He grinned. "Magic."

Just at that moment, someone else in a full mask and cloak tapped him on the shoulder and said something. The first magician nodded and moved away.

"So, want to see another trick?" asked the man. I nodded. He got out a five pound note and a cigarette, then lit the cigarette.

"Er, your friend has just done that trick," I said.

Too late. The magician was pushing the cigarette through the fiver, but this time, it didn't go through. It set the fiver on fire!

"Oh *no*," he cried as he dropped the fiver on the floor and stamped on it. "Looks easier than it is."

I started to laugh as I recognized the voice. "Jonno," I said.

He peeled off his mask. "Hi, Lia. I knew it was you under your mask. Um, Seth and Charlie said you'd invited them. They're over by the ice sculpture; in fact, I think Seth may have got his tongue stuck to it. . . . Hope you don't mind me, er . . ."

"Gate-crashing?" I asked.

He looked sheepish. "Yeah, and almost burning down the marquee." Jonno gave me a cheeky smile. "Er, maybe I'd better go. . . ."

I glanced over at the dance floor, where by now everyone was slow dancing to one of Sting's ballads.

Shall I, shan't I? I asked myself. Jonno was still looking at me as if to gauge whether I minded him being there. He was very attractive in a Keanu Reeves kind of way. . . . Oh, why not? I thought. Kaylie's not here. Jonno is very cute, why shouldn't I enjoy myself with him? I got up, took his hand, and led him to the dance floor. He pulled me close and put his arms around my waist.

"Bit different here to the school disco." He smiled, then leaned in and kissed me gently on the lips. "Happy Valentine's Day," he whispered in my ear.

Over his shoulder, I could see Becca. She was standing with Mac and Charlie, who were trying to separate Seth from the ice sculpture. She looked over at me and gave me the thumbs-up.

5

IT WAS the following Monday at school that it all started.

I was in the corridor on my way to art class and Kaylie was coming the other way with Fran. She was walking toward class and she steered off course and straight into me, causing me to drop my books.

"Oh, *so* sorry, Ophelia," she said with a fake smile. "Wasn't looking where I was going."

"S'okay," I said as I picked up my things. "And please call me Lia. No one calls me Ophelia."

My parents christened me Ophelia Moonbeam. How naff is that? I never use that name as everyone calls me Lia and I certainly never tell anyone, but it was read out on the first day of registration last autumn. I didn't think anyone had taken much notice. Amazingly, Kaylie seemed to have remembered.

"But it *is* your name, isn't it?" insisted Kaylie.

"Yeah, but . . . ," I started, then I decided to confront what I thought was probably really bothering her. "Look, about Jonno. I didn't mean for anything to happen. He just kind of . . ."

"Yeah, yeah . . ."

"He came after me."

"That's not what I saw. You were all over him at the school disco."

"I *wasn't*. He came over to *me*. In fact, I purposely tried to stay out of his way, because I knew you liked him."

"Yeah, so that's why you were snogging him later at your parent's do," said Kaylie with a toss of her hair. "Anyway, it's his loss."

"Well, I just wanted you to know that I didn't set out to get him."

"Yeah, right. That's not what I heard. Oh, don't worry, everyone knows you begged him to go to your party."

"I didn't," I said. "He just turned up."

"That's not what Seth said."

"Seth? I did invite him and Charlie, but Jonno came along with them."

Kaylie put a finger under her chin and feigned surprise. "Oh and *what* a coincidence that they just happen to be Jonno's mates from the football team."

"Honestly, Kaylie, he just turned up."

"Whatever," said Kaylie again. "That's your story. But then we all know about you and your stories, don't we?"

"What do you mean?"

Kaylie shrugged and made a face at Fran. "Why you had to leave your old school."

"I don't know what you're talking about. What are you saying?"

Kaylie smiled one of her fake smiles. "Oh, nothing, Lia. Come *on*, we're just teasing you. Lighten up. Honestly, you're like . . . *so* intense." She put her hand on my shoulder and gave me a gentle shove. "Don't take things so seriously."

And with that, she flounced into class. I felt close to tears. And confused. Was I being oversensitive? Taking it all too seriously? It felt like she'd had a real go at me, but it was done with such a smile that I couldn't be sure. Maybe I was imagining things.

"Hey, Lia, everything all right?" asked a voice behind me.

I turned. It was Squidge.

"So what was all that about?" he asked. "I saw Kaylie walk into you. What's her problem?"

"Bad loser, I guess. I don't think she's too happy about the fact that I got off with Jonno and she didn't."

Squidge raised his eyes to the ceiling. "Sour grapes, huh? Well, you take no notice of her and if she gives you any trouble, you let me know, okay?"

I nodded.

"So," continued Squidge, "you and Jonno? You going out with him now?"

I grinned. "Well, it's still early days, but . . . so far, so good. We've got a proper date on Saturday. Going out somewhere, don't know where yet."

Squidge looked at me with concern for a moment, then turned to go. "Better get to class," he said. "Hope it all works out for you, Lia. You deserve a decent bloke, someone who really appreciates you. Don't let any stupid girl ruin it all for you."

"Thanks, Squidge. You're a mate."

As he took off down the corridor I took a deep breath and followed Kaylie and Fran into class. I hoped that they weren't going to make an issue of me going out with Jonno. It wasn't my fault that he'd chosen me and not Kaylie. And I didn't have any regrets. I'd had a great time with him at the party and we even saw each other again on Sunday. He came up to the house after breakfast and we talked for hours—about school and what music we like and what we want to do after we finish school. He wants to get into the music business, so he asked me loads of questions about what it was like having a rock star dad. He stayed and had lunch with us and was well impressed by Dad's gold records. Dad even showed him around his studio and that's not something he does with many people. I think he realized that Jonno was serious about pursuing music as a career. I really like him. He was clearly starstruck by Dad, but he still paid me loads of attention and seemed genuinely interested in what I was into.

No, stuff you, Kaylie O'Hara, I thought as I took my place at a table with Cat and Becca. I'm not going to let you run my life.

The next class was English and I made sure that I was out of the art room first and along the corridor so that Kaylie and the Clones couldn't "accidentally" bump into me again.

"You're in a hurry," said Cat, catching up with me. "What's the rush?"

"Oh nothing," I said. "Just wanted to go through some notes before the lesson starts."

Cat gave me a look like she didn't quite believe me, but she let it go. I didn't want to tell her about the run-in with Kaylie before art, because I hoped it would all blow over. If I told Cat and Becca about it, they'd take my side and stick up for me and maybe start something. No, best ignore it, I thought, and it will all go away.

"Right," said Mrs. Ashton, our English teacher, once we'd all taken our places. "First, I'll give you your essays back, then I thought we'd have a quick quiz to see who's remembered what from this term." She began to walk up and down the aisles, putting people's work in front of them on their desks. "Well done," she said when she got to me.

Cat caught my eye and grinned, but behind her, I saw Kaylie whisper something to Susie Cooke and they both looked over at me and giggled.

When she'd handed out the essays, Mrs. Ashton

went back to her desk. "Some of the work has been to a very high standard and I was impressed," she said. "George Gaynor, well done. Sunita Ahmed, also good. Lia Axford, excellent. Nick Thorn, keep up the good work. Becca Howard, an improvement. I'm glad to see you're putting your mind to your work at last." Then she paused. "Sadly, there were a number of essays that . . . how can I put it . . . ? Needed work, would be being polite. What has happened to some of you lately? I won't mention names, but you know who you are by your low grades and I'll be keeping an eye on you for the rest of the term." She gave Kaylie and the Clones a pointed look, but Kaylie just raised an eyebrow and looked away.

Mrs. Ashton adjusted her glasses and began to read from a sheet of paper in front of her. "Okay. Question one. Finish this sentence: King Solomon had three hundred wives and seven hundred what . . . ? Frances Wilton, maybe you'd like to stop staring out of the window and give us the answer?"

"Um . . . seven hundred porcupines, Miss."

The class cracked up laughing.

"Okay, what did she mean to say?" asked Mrs. Ashton, looking around.

Laura Johnson raised her hand. "Concubines," she said.

Mrs. Ashton looked over at Fran. "Exactly. What on earth would Solomon have done with hundreds of porcupines?"

Frances went bright red and looked at her desk as Mrs. Ashton went on to the next question. "Caesar was murdered on the Ides of March. His last words were . . ."

Mark Keegan stuck his hand up this time.

"Yes, Mark," said Mrs. Ashton.

"Tee hee, Brutus," said Mark.

Once again, the class started laughing, and Mark smiled broadly, pleased that his answer had got a laugh.

"I get the impression that you're not taking this quiz seriously, Mark," said Mrs. Ashton, then she looked around. "The attitude of some of the people in this class will have to change or else it will show on your end of term reports. So. Anyone like to tell me what Caesar's last words really were?"

She looked around the class. I knew the answer, but I didn't want to be a Norma Know-It-All. However, Mrs. Ashton looked over at me. "Lia?"

"Um, *et tu* Brute," I muttered.

"Correct. Without the 'um,' though. Well done, Lia."

Kaylie looked over at Fran Wilton and raised her eyebrows. I should have said I didn't know, I thought. Now they will think I'm a swotty nerd.

"Now," said Mrs. Ashton, going back to her quiz. "Kaylie O'Hara. Here's one for you. Shakespeare . . ." She adjusted her glasses and began to read. "When was William Shakespeare born?"

"On his birthday," said Kaylie as if it was absolutely obvious.

Once again, the class cracked up and I glanced over at Kaylie and noticed that she was blushing slightly. Unlike Mark who had given his answer for a laugh, I got the feeling that Kaylie thought that she'd given the right answer.

"Of *course* he was born on his *birth*day, Kaylie," said Mrs. Ashton. "Anybody like to give me the actual year?"

Joss Peters put his hand up. "1564," he said.

"Correct," said Mrs. Ashton, who then turned back to Kaylie. "Okay, Kaylie. Here's an easy one for you. We've been doing *Romeo and Juliet* this term. What was Romeo's last wish?"

"To be laid by Juliet," said Kaylie.

This got a huge laugh especially from the boys. Kaylie looked over at me with a hard expression in her eyes, as though daring me to join in the laughter. I kept my face straight.

"I think what you meant to say was that Romeo's last wish was to die alongside Juliet, Kaylie. Like Frances, try and pay more attention to how you express yourself."

Kaylie nodded and looked bored. "Yes, Miss," she drawled.

"And now for the last question," said Mrs. Ashton. "Jackie Reeves, I think you can have this one."

Kaylie looked over at her mate and sighed as though Mrs. Ashton's comments were all a great waste of time.

"The most famous composer in the world is?" asked Mrs. Ashton.

"Um . . . Bach. Um . . . Handel," drawled Jackie.

There was a snigger from the back of the class as

Mrs. Ashton sighed. "Anyone like to tell us what's wrong with that?" she asked.

This time I kept my head down. Luckily, Sunita Ahmed put her hand up. "It's got to be either one or the other, Miss. Either Bach is the most famous or Handel. Not both."

Jackie gave Sunita a really filthy look and I could see that, like me, Sunita suddenly felt as though she wished she'd kept her mouth shut.

"Exactly," said Mrs. Ashton with a weary sigh. "But I've heard worse. One pupil once told me that Handel was half German, half Italian, and half English. . . . Anyone like to comment?"

A few people tittered, but no one spoke. "Come on class, it's not difficult. Wake up. Who can tell me what's wrong with that? Cat Kennedy?"

"Um, the math isn't quite right. If he was half German, half Italian, and half English, he'd be one and a half people."

"Correct," said Mrs. Ashton. "Now all of you, I don't want to see any of you making these types of mistakes, not in my class. It shows you're not thinking. We have pupils like George, Sunita, Nick, and

Lia in the class setting a standard. Try and learn from them."

The Clones all started sniggering at this and Mrs. Ashton saw them. "Seeing as you find the whole thing so amusing, Susie Cooke, you can answer the next question. Who was it Salome danced naked in front of?"

Susie shrugged her shoulders like she didn't care.

"Come on, Susie," said Mrs. Ashton. "We only did it last week."

I could see Kaylie mouthing an answer to her mate. Susie screwed up her eyes to try and read Kaylie's lips then she nodded.

"Harrods," she said.

Mrs. Ashton looked up at the ceiling. "Herod, Susie. Not *Harrods*. Harrods is a shop in Knightsbridge."

I glanced over at Kaylie and she was staring at me again with narrowed eyes. It was hard not to laugh at what she and the Clones had said, especially as most of the class was giggling away. Becca and Cat may be right, I thought. Kaylie and her mates may be popular and trendy, but they're not very bright.

I stared back at Kaylie, thinking, Two can play at this game and I'm not going to be intimidated by you. After a few minutes, she leaned back in her chair and whispered something to Fran behind her. Fran glanced over at me and laughed. I turned away. She wasn't worth it and I didn't want to get into playing stupid games. All I wanted was to go to school, do my lessons, and get on with everyone without any aggro. Sadly, though, by the look on Kaylie's face, she wasn't going to let that happen.

A Turn for the Worse

6

THE NEXT day, I went into school determined not to let Kaylie and the Clones faze me. I'd tough it out, be all smiling and friendly. But they decided to try a new tactic. They just plain ignored me. When I saw them in the corridor before assembly, I said hi, and they all turned the other way like they'd smelled a bad smell. It was weird, I felt like I was invisible or something.

"What's up with them?" asked Becca, when she noticed them give me the cold shoulder.

"Oh nothing," I said. "I think Kaylie's got it in for me because of Jonno."

"God. How pathetic," said Becca, giving them a scornful look.

Suddenly Kaylie came bustling over and stood between Becca and me with her back to me. "I hear you're going to be helping Miss Segal produce the end-of-year show," she said.

"That's right," said Becca, moving to the right to include me in the conversation.

Kaylie moved, obscuring my view again. "Do you know what it's going to be yet?"

Becca nodded. "Nothing official, but I'm pretty sure we're going to be doing *The Rocky Horror Picture Show*."

"Oh, top!" said Kaylie then beckoned to her mates and began to sing, "Let's do the time warp again."

Fran, Susie, and Jackie came over to join us. "*Rocky Horror.* Excellent. Can we be in it?" asked Fran. I moved to stand with them, but Susie stepped to the left once again keeping me out of the circle.

Becca glanced at me with a worried expression. "Casting is in the main hall on Saturday afternoon," she said.

"Cool," said Kaylie, then she took a step back and stood on my toes.

"Ow!" I cried.

"Oh, *sooo* sorry, Ophelia. I didn't see you there." Then she gave me a snooty look and turned back to Becca. "I suppose *some* people wanting a part will be taking advantage of the fact that their mate is the producer."

"I doubt it," said Becca. "Best man wins, as always."

"Good," said Kaylie. "Because we don't want anyone getting in for the wrong reasons or because their dad is in the music business or anything."

"Knock it off, Kaylie," said Becca. "You know people get in because of their individual performances. Who's right for the part and so on."

"Yeah, right," said Kaylie. "Well, we'll see, shall we?"

"What's going on?" asked Becca when they'd gone. "They were, like, totally blanking you."

"I know," I said. "They were a bit weird with me yesterday as well, to be honest, but I'm not going to let it get to me."

"Good. They're not worth it. So you'll be at the casting session, won't you? I think it will be a total gas doing *The Rocky Horror Picture Show*. Mac will do the scenery and, of course, Squidge will film it, so it will be a laugh, all of us together."

I hesitated. I had no illusions about my singing so wouldn't expect to get a lead role, but I can dance and had hoped that maybe I could be in the chorus. Plus, Miss Segal is my favorite teacher. It's like she's really tuned in to people and can bring out the best in them. But if Kaylie was going to be there making jibes at me at every rehearsal, maybe it wouldn't be much fun.

"Not sure yet," I said.

Becca grimaced. "If you let them put you off, I'll . . . I'll . . ."

"You won't speak to me either," I laughed. "Then *no one* will be speaking to me."

Becca linked her arm through mine. "I'd never do that," she said.

I decided to confide in Becca. If anyone would understand how mean girls can be, it would be her. Recently, she'd had a run-in with Mac's sister, Jade, when both of them went up for a national singing competition to find a Pop Princess. Jade can be a total cow when she wants and she acted really unfriendly and unsupportive. She even tricked Becca into saying something negative on the phone about one of the competitors when, unaware to Becca, the girl was listening in on an extension.

"Only reason I'm hesitating is that . . . ," I started. "Look, I know people gossip about my dad and our house and stuff locally, but I don't want that to affect things here at school. I just want to be normal. To fit in with everyone else and for now, until Kaylie's got over whatever's bugging her, that's more important than having a role in the school show. Do you understand?"

Becca nodded, then shook her head. "I do, but don't let them walk all over you. I've seen them do it to girls in our year before. You have to stand up to them. Don't let them win. They don't bother me, I can tell you that. Do you want me to have a word with them?"

"*No,*" I said. "*Please.* That would only make an issue of it, and they'll get all sniffy about me talking to you about them. No. Please, don't get into it. Let me sort it my way, okay?"

"Okay," said Becca. "But you know that whatever they do, I'm on your side. Right?"

"Right," I said.

On my side, she said. Though I appreciated the support, I felt sad. Already, it was about taking sides. Oh, why can't I just fit in? Have my mates and not be noticed? All I want is to be accepted.

In the changing rooms on Wednesday, things took a turn for the worse. The Clones all stood in one corner and were whispering and looking at me as I was getting changed for gym. It was awful. Everyone seems to have got boobs except me. I've shot up to five-foot-seven, yet still have the shape of a nine-year-old boy. Becca's really sweet about it. She says I'm the perfect shape to be a model and she wishes she was like me, but I think she's just being kind. I wish I was more like her. She's got a great figure—really curvy, although she thinks she's fat. I guess no one's ever happy with their body. Even Cat, who is perfect, thinks she's too short.

As the Clones continued staring, I began to think I'd grown an extra breast or something. Then I remembered what Becca had said about standing up to them so I turned around and asked, "What are you looking at?"

Of course, they all turned away and looked at the floor or the wall—except Kaylie, that is. She leaned on her right hip, stuck her chin out at me, and said, "Think a lot of yourself, don't you?"

"No," I replied. "What do you mean?"

"Like, *why* would we be staring at you? You've a

problem, you know, Lia. You think everything is about you when it isn't. People do have their own lives you know."

I didn't know what to say, so I looked away. I felt confused again. They *had* been staring at me, I'm sure of it, but Kaylie had managed to turn everything around and make out that it was me who had the problem. Maybe she was right. Maybe I *am* getting obsessive about them. I had certainly spent a lot of time thinking about them and how to handle them over the past few days. Maybe I do spend too much time thinking about myself and what people think of me. Maybe it *is* me. Maybe I do have a problem.

As the week went on, I tried to tell myself that it didn't matter, but by Thursday, I felt more confused than ever and I dreaded going into school for fear of what they were going to do or say.

I've always been happy enough at school, but suddenly, it felt like some ordeal I had to endure. All I wanted was just to get to the end of the day so that I could go home. I tried my best to stay out of their way, but it's hard when we have so many classes together. I was sure I wasn't imagining it. Every time I saw the Clones, it seemed like they'd been busy chatting to people, but as soon as I arrived, everyone would go quiet for a moment in a guilty sort of way and sometimes they'd laugh. I wondered what they were saying about me, but I daren't ask for fear that Kaylie would tell me that I was self-obsessed again and that people had other things to talk about besides Lia Axford.

Friday was the final straw. At break, I met up with Cat and Becca and both of them were holding little pink invitation cards.

"Invite to Kaylie's tomorrow night," said Becca. "Shall we go after the casting session?"

"Dunno," said Cat. "I mean, those girls aren't exactly our best mates and she's never asked us before."

"All the more reason to go and see what it's like," said Becca. "I bet loads of people will be going and there's nothing else happening."

"I think that may be another reason that Kaylie is jealous of you, Lia," said Cat. "Before your family arrived, the do's at Kaylie's house were legendary. I think your mum's parties have stolen her thunder a bit."

"Understatement," said Becca. "I bet she's seething, mainly because you've never invited her. In fact, she's probably jealous of every aspect of your life. A glam rock star dad, an ex-model mum, a fab mansion to live in, latest clothes . . ."

"Gorgeous brother, gorgeous sister . . . ," said Cat. "The list is endless."

"But it's not my fault," I said. "I didn't choose my parents or my family. . . ."

"Yeah, but she would have, given half the chance," said Becca. "And she hasn't even got a look-in to any part of it."

"How come she holds so many parties?" I asked.

"Partly because she likes to be popular and being 'hostess with the mostest' gives her a chance to surround herself with people," said Becca. "Plus, her mum works night shifts in a hospital over in Plymouth, so she has a free reign of her house most evenings."

"What about her dad?" I asked. "Surely he's home."

Cat shook her head. "Disappeared years ago. Rumor has it he ran off with the barmaid from the

Crown and Anchor. Anyway, it's an empty house at the weekend and where else is there for teenagers to go round here in the winter? Weekends, a lot of people hang out at Kaylie's."

"I wonder if her mum knows that she uses the house," I said.

"Doubt it," said Becca. "She probably gets her little clones to tidy up for her afterward. So shall we go? It might be a laugh if we all go together. What do you think, Lia. You up for it?"

"She hasn't invited me," I said.

"Are you sure?" asked Becca. "Why would she invite us and not you? Look again. I saw her putting cards on everyone's desk. Maybe yours fell off. Go back and look."

I didn't have to. Not after the week I'd had. I had a feeling that she'd excluded me on purpose. It was weird, because she hadn't done anything major, not like when a boy bullies another boy. That might be simpler to deal with, I thought. If someone kicks or smacks you about, there's no doubt about it—you're being bullied. But this? I wasn't sure what was going on and wondered if it was all in my imagination. What had been happening was so subtle. Almost unseen. Secret looks between Kaylie and her mates, or whispers or sniggers, and now, no invite to her party. Plus, I felt there was no way I could go to the casting session. No big deal, not really. But inside, I felt like Kaylie had got it in for me and I felt miserable.

7

First Date

"PENNY FOR them," said Dad, making me jump as he came up behind me.

"Oh, sorry, I was miles away."

It was Saturday morning and I was sitting in the kitchen, gazing out of the window and going over the week in my mind.

"I could see that," said Dad. "So what's going on in that head of yours? How's your week been?"

"Oh . . . fine."

"Hmm. You sure? You don't look your usual bright self and you've been quieter than usual this week."

"No, honest. I'm great."

"Everything okay at school?"

"Yeah."

"Everything okay with Jonno?"

"Yeah. In fact, he's coming up tonight. We're going out somewhere."

"You don't sound too excited. Tonight's a first date, isn't it?"

I nodded. He was right. I wasn't too excited. It was as if, in putting up a wall in my head to keep Kaylie out, I'd kept everything else out as well.

"So what is it, pet?" asked Dad. "Come on, spill. You don't live in the same house as someone and not notice when something's going on."

"Honest, Dad. It's nothing. Just . . . do you think I'm self-obsessed?"

Dad laughed. "What kind of question is that? What do you mean?"

"You know, always thinking about myself?"

Dad laughed again. "All teenagers are self-obsessed. It's part of the package. And, to a degree, so is everyone else. I mean, you live in your body, in your world. You're the only one who sees things through your eyes, so you're bound to be a little self-obsessed."

I laughed.

"Maybe we need another word," said Dad. "Not 'obsessed' . . . um, self-motivated. That sounds better, more positive. But why did you ask that, Lia? Is something worrying you?"

I sighed and tried to decide how much to tell him. Sometimes if you get parents involved, they worry. Then they end up becoming more of a problem than the problem itself. I decided to tell him part of the story.

"It's like . . . well, there's this girl and her mates at school, and I don't think they like me very much. I haven't ever done anything bad to them, but they seem to have it in for me."

Dad pulled up a stool, took my hand, and looked me directly in the eye. "Are you being bullied, Lia?"

"*No.* No. That's exactly it. I'm not. But it almost feels like I am. But then, I don't know if it's me being paranoid or self-obsessed. Thinking too much about what other people think of me, when they're not even thinking about me at all. . . . Oh, I don't know. It's okay, Dad, really. I know I'm not even making any sense. It's just, I want to fit in. You know, new school. But it's like some people won't even give me a chance."

"Could be they're jealous," said Dad, indicating our vast, top-of-the-range kitchen with his hand. "We do live very well compared to most. And you are a very pretty girl. . . ."

"Yeah, yeah . . ."

"Seriously. It could be that."

"I don't think these girls are jealous. I'm not sure. I mean, one of them was a bit miffed that I got off with Jonno, but these girls are popular and very pretty. The Teen Queens. It's not like I'm any kind of threat to their position in the school."

Dad nodded. "Yes, but you got Jonno and they didn't. They might think, first you get him, what's next?"

"Nothing. I just want to be ordinary."

"Then sorry, Lia, can't help you. You'll never be ordinary, not with your looks and personality. And you're a clever girl. So you'll always do well at school if you keep working. And our life, well, no one can ever say that that's ordinary, can they? Sometimes you just have to accept your lot and get on with it."

"I know. Sorry. I'm going on about nothing. And I may be imagining it all anyway."

"So these girls who are giving you a hard time. . . . How, exactly? Calling you names? What?"

My brain felt numb for a moment as I tried to think about it. There wasn't actually anything I could say that sounded so bad. So someone stared at me and didn't say hi back. Big deal. It sounds so pathetic.

"I'm pretty sure that they're all talking about me, but not in a nice way. Sometimes they ignore me, but sometimes, like when I go into a class, everyone shuts up like they've been talking about me . . . that sort of thing."

Dad got up to fill the coffee grinder with beans. "What do Cat and Becca think?"

"Becca says stand up to them, and I haven't really talked to Cat about it much. To tell the truth, I don't want them to get into it. You know, they might feel that they have to take sides and all that. . . . I just want it all to go away."

Dad came over and squeezed my shoulder. "I know just how you feel, love."

"You do? How can you? Did someone give you a hard time at school?"

"Bully me? No way. I'd have thumped anyone back who tried. But it's different with lads. If someone's a bully and tries to kick your head in, it's pretty clear what's happening. No. It was later when I first began to make a name for myself in the music business that I got bullied, but in a different kind of way to what goes on in schools."

"Who by?"

Dad went to the fridge and got some milk. "The press," he said with a grim expression. "First, they're all, Oh, the new golden boy, and they can't get enough of you. But they can turn, and when they do, boy, do you feel it! I tell you, Lia, the press can be the biggest bullies of all and they can make or break someone."

"So what happened?"

"I was on tour in the States and there was some story about a girl I was supposed to be having an affair with. All nonsense. I sat next to her in a club and the next day it was all over the papers over here. Course, your mum got to hear about it and was livid. Didn't know what or who to believe. The more I defended my position, the more guilty I looked. I had to learn fast, believe me. No, the best way to deal with them, or those girls at your school, is not to waste any energy on them. Don't rise to the challenge. Don't engage. Don't try to defend yourself as sometimes you can't win."

"So what can you do?"

"Decide who's important in your life and be honest

with them. Keep them close. But keep them out of it—gossip, rumour mongering, all of it. I've learned to keep my head down where the press are involved. But at the time, when I was younger, I used to get so mad at some of the things they'd write. Total fiction, but I had sleepless nights, thinking, What will people think? I must put the story straight, and so on. Dignified silence, that's the best. Now I know who I can count on and they're the people who matter. They know the score and the rest of them can go to hell and believe what they want. Fame is fickle. The press are fickle. Sounds like these girls at your school are fickle. It sounds like you wouldn't want them as friends anyway, would you?"

I shook my head.

"So, there's your answer. Don't waste your energy letting them bother you. Enjoy your date tonight. And you have some great mates that care about you and they're the ones who matter. There will always be other people who won't like you, no matter what you do. Don't even give them the time of day. Okay, pal?"

"Okay," I said.

"So how's about one of my cappuccino specials with extra chocolate on top?"

"Sure," I said. I felt a lot better after talking to Dad. He was right. I'd been stupid letting it all get to me so much. In the future, Kaylie and the Clones could do what they liked. I had my friends and my family, and they're the ones that counted. "Thanks, Dad."

Later, I went upstairs to have a bath and get ready for my date. I was really looking forward to it and wondered where Jonno would suggest going. There weren't that many places open nearby apart from pubs, so maybe he planned on going into Plymouth. I decided to make a real effort and spent ages trying on different outfits and doing my makeup. My first proper date since London. I couldn't wait.

Jonno arrived at seven o'clock, full of gossip about the casting session for *The Rocky Horror Picture Show* that had taken place at school in the afternoon.

"Did you get it?" I asked as I took him into the red sitting room. He'd played Danny Zucko in *Grease* in the Christmas show, so everyone was expecting that he'd play the lead again.

He shook his head and flopped on to a sofa. "No, the role of Dr. Frank-N-Furter went to Adam Hall."

"Do you mind?"

"Nah. I'm cool with it. It can be a bit time-consuming playing the lead, and actually, I could do with some time to concentrate on other things."

"So who got the other parts?"

"Do you know the story?"

"Vaguely. Some kids end up in a castle with a load of weirdos."

Jonno laughed. "That's about the gist of it. Dan Archer is playing Brad Majors and Jessica Moon is playing Janet. They're the geeky kids whose car breaks down and who end up at Frank-N-Furter's castle. Ryan Nolan is Riff Raff, the hunchback henchman, and Jade Macey is playing his sister, Magenta."

"What about Cat?"

"I think she's playing the tap dancing groupie, Columbia. But where were you? I thought you'd be there."

"Um, I decided to give it a miss this time. As you said, being in a show can be a bit full on. Did Kaylie and her mates get parts?"

Jonno nodded. "Chorus, I think. Good job, because I doubt if they'd be able to remember their lines if they got bigger parts. They're not exactly the brightest coins in the collection, are they? Once when I was asked to coach the netball team, I said I wanted to discuss tactics. One of them, I think it was Jackie, thought I was talking about mints."

I laughed, but wasn't quite sure if he was just joking.

"By the way, did you get the invite to Kaylie's?" he asked.

I shook my head. I hadn't thought of her party as an option and hoped that Jonno hadn't planned on taking me there. "No. But . . . but you go if you want."

"No, thanks," he said getting up and going over to look at a painting on the wall opposite. "Nice painting. Picasso, isn't it? My mum's got the same print."

"Er, yeah, Picasso." I didn't tell him that ours was the original, in case he thought I was showing off.

"Nah," he continued, "Kaylie's dos are not my scene. I find her crowd a bit too . . ." He mimicked a girlie girl walking on high heels and flicking her hair. "You know, lipstick, handbags, and pointy shoes—that's all they think about."

Yeah, I thought, and how to ruin my life. "So what shall we do this evening?" I asked.

Jonno came and sat next to me and took my hand. "Ah well. I wanted to talk to you about this. . . ."

At that moment, Dad came in. "Watcha, Jonno," he said as he turned on the television. "Don't mind me."

Jonno glanced at me, then looked longingly at the telly. "Er, how about we stay here? Hang out. It's raining outside and I missed this afternoon's game . . . because of the casting session . . . and now, well, there's the . . ."

"Highlights of the Arsenal versus Man United game," said Dad, rubbing his hands together, then bouncing onto the sofa.

Fifteen minutes later, Dad and Jonno were ensconced, shoes off, feet up, Cokes in hand, watching the football.

"*Whoa*," cried Dad as both of them rose in unison from the sofa when there was a near miss goal. As they settled back down again, Dad turned to look at me with one of his cheeky grins. "Think we need another after that," he said pointing at his Coke can.

This wasn't quite my romantic fantasy, I thought as I got up to go to the kitchen for fresh supplies. Mum was in the kitchen feeding the dogs when I went over to the fridge.

She smiled up at me. "Not going out?"

"Arsenal versus Man United," I said. "I think Dad and Jonno have just discovered that they're soul mates."

"Ah," sighed Mum. "Some things you just can't compete with."

"Why did Dad have to watch in the red room? There's five other televisions in the house."

"But that's where the biggest telly is. He got it specially for the footie. Digital sound, wide screen . . . he says he feels like he's actually there."

"I just don't get it," I said. "How men can get so excited about kicking a bit of leather around a field."

"Welcome to the club," said Mum. "Want to hear a joke about football?"

I nodded.

"What's the similarity between a boy and a football player?" she asked.

"Dunno."

"They both dribble when they're trying to score."

I laughed, then turned my head toward the door. I could hear singing. It sounded like the "I–I–yippee" song. Mum laughed. "Better get used to it. Men tend to behave like kids when their beloved football's on. It can get very emotional."

We went and stood in the hall by the red room door and, sure enough, they were both singing their hearts out. "We're the best behaved supporters in the land, we're the best behaved supporters in the land, the best behaved supporters, best behaved supporters, the best behaved supporters in the land . . . when we win. We're a right bunch of bastards when we lose, we're a right bunch of bastards when we lose, we're a right bunch of bastards, right bunch of bastards, right bunch of bastards when we lose."

"Hmm," said Mum. "Fancy a game of backgammon in the library?"

"Anything to get away from this," I laughed, putting my hands over my ears.

I spent the evening in the library with Mum while Jonno bonded with my dad in the red room. At one point, I crept in to catch up, but they were deeply absorbed in conversation, analyzing the game so far. As the second half of their program started up, they burst into song again. This time it was to the tune of "Glory, Glory Hallelujah." "Glory, Glory, Man United. Glory, Glory, Man

United," they sang. "Glory, Glory, Man United. When the Reds keep marching on, on, on."

"Ah, the famous rock star and the aspiring music student," I teased from the door. "I wish your fans could see you now, Dad."

"I've had a *top* time," said Jonno later when I saw him to the door. "We must do it again soon."

"Yeah, right," I said as he leaned in to kiss me good night.

"Next week for Man United and Liverpool," called Dad as he went up the stairs.

"Absolutely," said Jonno, giving Dad a wave. Somehow the moment for snogging had been ruined, so I stepped back inside. Jonno didn't even seem to have noticed and went off smiling.

So much for my first date, I thought later as I wiped off my makeup.

8

Junk Mail?

THE FOLLOWING week at school, to my relief, the Clones seemed to have lost interest in me and life got back to normal. Sort of. At home, some rather strange things were starting to happen.

On Monday, when I got back from school, I had post. A catalog advertising Tea Tree oil products for people who suffer from bad perspiration and BO. I didn't think anything of it, as so much junk mail comes through the door, so I chucked it in the bin.

Tuesday, I got a catalog about padded bras for women who had flat chests. Quite useful, I thought, seeing as I'm as flat as a pancake. Again, I didn't think anything of it, only that our address must have gone on some mailing list somewhere. Although it was strange that it was addressed to me, as I wasn't the home owner.

Wednesday, a catalog came for me from a company selling gravestones. It couldn't be Kaylie, could it? I wondered. Surely she wouldn't go to all the trouble of getting these things sent to me? A shiver went down my spine when I thought over the things that had been sent. A catalog for people with BO, a catalog for padded bras, and now one for gravestones. The insinuations were horrible. That I smelled, had no chest, and soon might need a gravestone. No, *no*, I told myself, *no one* would be that horrible.

By the time the evening came, I had to believe that my earlier suspicions about Kaylie were right. At eight o'clock, two nettuna cheese pizzas arrived for me and I definitely hadn't ordered them. The delivery boy insisted that I had—he had my name, phone number, and everything. Mum phoned the restaurant and, sure enough, they had all my details. She paid the boy, then turned to me in the hall.

"What's going on, Lia? Were you still hungry after supper and didn't want to say?"

"No. Course not. I'd tell you if I wanted pizza, you know that."

"So who ordered these if you didn't?"

Kaylie O'Hara and her mates, I thought. And I'm pretty sure that they arranged for the catalogs to be sent as well. Mum saw me hesitate.

"Do you think you might know who ordered these?" she asked.

"Maybe . . ."

"Come on, let's go and sit down and try and get to the bottom of this."

I followed Mum into the red room and we sat on the sofa. My mind was whirring round and round like a washing machine on spin. What to say? I couldn't be sure it was Kaylie. It might just be a mistake on the computer at the pizza restaurant. There was only one locally and we had ordered from there before, so I know they had our details on record. It was possible that they'd made a mistake. But a nagging feeling told me otherwise, although I couldn't prove anything. I felt miserable. If Kaylie was doing these things, she was doing them in a way that didn't obviously point the finger back at her. It could be her being vindictive, but it also could be me being paranoid and imagining things.

"So?" asked Mum.

"I'm not sure," I said. "Just at school lately, this girl has kind of got it in for me. I thought she'd dropped it as she's been pretty cool this week. Sort of back to normal, but maybe not."

Mum nodded. "Your dad did mention that someone had upset you. You do know that you can come to either of us, don't you?"

I nodded. "Yeah. I . . . I didn't want to make a big deal out of it."

"Has anything else arrived out of the ordinary, Lia? I noticed that there's been a lot of post for you this week."

"Catalogs," I admitted. "At first I thought they were junk mail, but now . . ."

"What sort of catalogs?"

"One for people with BO, one for people with flat chests, and one for gravestones."

"Oh, Lia," gasped Mum. "Why didn't you say anything?"

"Because I'm not a hundred percent sure. You know how much rubbish comes through the door—people advertising everything from windows to life insurance."

"Yes, but all that stuff comes to me or your father. There's no reason why mail-order firms would have your name. If it *is* this girl, then she has to be stopped. Do you want me to have a word with your class teacher?"

"*No!*" I cried. "God *no*, that would be the worst thing ever. What if it wasn't her? Maybe it's just coincidence. She's already accused me of being self-obsessed. . . ."

"One coincidence I could buy," said Mum softly, "but not this many."

The thought of Mum going into the school filled me with horror. I imagined the teachers ticking Kaylie off, then she'd spread it around that I'd ratted on her, then there'd be even more talking about me behind my back and sniggering behind hands. No, Mum mustn't go in. I decided to try and make light of the situation.

"It's not a big deal, Mum. Not really. I thought it would all blow over and maybe it has. But if it *was* Kaylie who ordered the pizzas and you went and talked to the teachers, then I'd be labeled as a sneak."

"But, Lia, darling, you can't let her get away with this."

"I know."

"So what do you want to do?"

"Don't know," I sighed. "I really don't know."

"Do I know this girl?" asked Mum, putting her arm around me.

I shook my head. "Doubt it."

"What's her name?"

"Kaylie. But please, Mum, don't do anything about it. I can handle it."

"Well, you'll keep me informed as to what's going on, won't you?"

"Sure," I said. It was good to know I had her support, but another part of me felt like I was letting her down. Star was so popular at school and Ollie is at his. And it's not that I wasn't popular. Lots of people thought I was okay, but I knew that could change if Kaylie carried on poisoning people's minds about me. Already, I was noticing that people in our class weren't being quite as friendly as they had been. God, I hate this, I thought. I really, really hate it. Why can't Kaylie just leave me alone? Heaven knows what people are thinking.

I had to make sure that Mum didn't make things worse. "I'll talk to her. Please, Mum, let me deal with it."

The next morning before school, Meena called me down into the hall. She was holding a huge bunch of tulips.

"Who are they for?" I asked.

"For you. See, here your name. No message, though."

Oh, not Kaylie again, I thought, but then she wouldn't send me flowers. Must be from Jonno, I decided as I took the bouquet. How sweet. He must have felt bad about neglecting me Saturday. I went to phone him immediately.

"But . . . but they're not from me," he said. "Sorry. Should be, I suppose. I just didn't think of it. Looks like you have another admirer. Hmm . . . don't know if I like that. No message, you say?"

"Not an admirer," I said. "I think I might know who sent them and believe me, you've got no competition. Er, see you at school later."

Just as I was about to leave for school, Mum called me into her room. "I've just had a call from the florists, Lia. They say that you called yesterday and ordered some flowers. They called to ask if I wanted to change my usual weekly order of white lilies to tulips from now on."

I shook my head. "Sorry, Mum. I think it might be Kaylie stirring it again."

Mum sighed. "Darling, we have to do something."

"I know, I know," I said. I could kill Kaylie, I thought. But then that's probably just what she wanted—a confrontation so that she can deny everything and make me look like a fool. But now this was getting out of hand. She was involving Mum. I wondered what else she'd ordered in my name that Mum would have to pay for.

When I got to school, Kaylie, Jackie, Susie, and Fran were all standing in their usual spot near the radiators in the hall. I saw them look over when I walked in, and Kaylie said something and they all giggled.

How to play it, I thought. I guess they're waiting for me to be upset or mad. Well, I'm not going to be.

I smiled as I went by. "Hi. Lovely day, isn't it?"

Ha. A puzzled expression flashed across Kaylie's face. She couldn't ask if I'd got the post or flowers, as that would identify her as the person sending things. And she'd never know if I got them or not if I didn't react. Yes, that was how to play it. She could deny sending me things and I could deny ever getting anything.

Sadly, though, my lack of reaction only made Kaylie react more. It was just after RE at the end of

the day and most of the class had filed out. I asked
Cat if I could borrow a book. "Yeah, sure. In my
bag," she said, pointing to her rucksack. But then
she suddenly tried to grab it before I did. "Er, *no*, let
me get it for you."

I was instantly suspicious. There was something
in her bag she didn't want me to see. Maybe another
invite to one of Kaylie's little weekend parties. I
didn't mind that, but I did mind Cat hiding stuff
from me.

I looked into her bag before she could stop me
and saw a piece of pink paper folded up next to the
books. Kaylie always wrote on pink. I quickly
pulled it out and began to read it.

"Oh no," said Cat. "*Please* don't read that. I *so*
didn't want you to see it."

My face must have fallen, because Cat put her
arm around me. "Lia, she's not worth it. Nobody's
going to believe what she's written."

It said:

To Year Nine,
If you ever wondered why Lia Axford left her last
school, this is why. She was expelled for lying and

making up stories about classmates to try and make
out that they were doing bad things. Be very careful
what she says about anyone, as it will be lies. She
twists events to make people think that everything is
about her. Remember—Lia equals LIAR.

I felt tears sting my eyes. "It's not true!" I blurted. "I left my old school because I wanted to live at home. That's all."

Cat put her arms around me. "We know that, Lia. That's why I didn't want you to see the note."

"*Why* has she got it in for me? I don't understand."

"Because she's a mean, spiteful cow," said Cat. "And she's jealous because you've got everything that she wants."

I glanced up and saw Susie peering through the glass pane at the classroom door. I didn't even bother to try and hide that I was crying. Okay, result, I thought. You got me. Made me cry. Now go and tell your leader. Let her know Lia's in tears and I hope you'll all be very happy.

9

I DECIDED I had to take action. Put a stop to it. And there was only one way to do it. Cat had said that I had everything that Kaylie wanted, and that included Jonno. So the solution was simple.

"What do you mean you don't want to meet up later? Why?" he asked, when I saw him outside the gates after school.

"Look, it's not you, it's me . . . ," I started.

"It's because I watched the game with your dad last week, isn't it? I *knew* it was a mistake. Girls always hate it when blokes watch the footie. Look, I won't do it again if you don't want me to."

"It's not that, Jonno. I didn't mind. Not really."

"So what is it, then?"

This was proving more difficult than I'd thought. I couldn't come up with a logical reason. I did like him.

"It doesn't make sense, Lia. Come on, talk to me.

We get on really well, so what's the problem?"

"Just . . . things are a bit awkward at the moment. Maybe we could go out at a later date. In a month or so?"

Jonno looked bewildered. "Now you're really not making sense. Unless . . . is there someone else you've been seeing and you have to finish with him?"

"No. No one else."

"So *what*, then? Come on. This is crazy."

At that moment, Becca walked past. "Phone me later, Lia," she called.

"Sure," I said.

Jonno waved her over. "Hey, Becca. Lia doesn't want to see me anymore and won't tell me why. You're her mate. Can you enlighten me?"

Becca looked surprised and glanced at me, then back at Jonno. "Kaylie O'Horrible," she said.

"What's she got to do with it?" asked Jonno.

Becca nudged me. "I think you should tell him, Lia. She can't rule people's lives like this."

"What is going on?" asked Jonno, who by now looked really confused. "What do you mean, Kaylie can't rule people's lives?"

"She's been giving Lia a hard time," Becca blurted out, "because you're going out with Lia and not with her."

Jonno narrowed his eyes and his expression turned to thunder. "A hard time? Like how?"

"Telling lies about Lia, for a start," said Becca. "Spreading rumors."

Jonno turned to face me. "Why didn't you tell me?"

I felt at a loss to say anything. I felt so mixed up. Part of me felt relieved, as I'd been worried that he might have heard something about the note and wondered if it was true, if I really was a liar. Another part just wanted to escape from everything. It was all happening too fast. My head suddenly felt vacant, like someone had sucked all the air out of it. I saw Jonno glance behind Becca and me at a crowd coming out of school. Kaylie and the Clones were amongst them. Jonno took one look at them and went straight over.

"Oh hell, now what have you started, Becca?" I asked.

Becca looked hurt. "Look, I told you I'm on your side. Girls like her can't be allowed to get away with it. I saw that note she sent round class. You—*we*—have to stand up to them."

I strained to hear what Jonno was saying to Kaylie. Whatever it was, it looked heated and a small crowd gathered to see what was going on. Jonno is easily the most popular boy in school and Kaylie wouldn't like the fact that he was yelling at her in public. She was shifting about on her feet and looking at the pavement as though she wanted it to swallow her. Jonno finished what he was saying, then turned to leave. As he walked back toward us, he turned back. "Just stay out of my business and grow up, Kaylie. I'll see who I choose and it wouldn't be you even if you were the last girl on the planet."

"You'd be so lucky," she called after him. But she looked upset.

Oh finking stinking, I thought as my stomach twisted into a knot. What now? I know Becca meant well. I know Jonno meant well, but now it was all out in the open, in front of the whole school. Jonno came back to me and put his arm around my shoulder. I glanced back at Kaylie as he began to lead me away and she gave me the filthiest look. If looks could kill, I thought, I'd be six foot under. It was awful. Everyone was staring and I knew it would be all around the school in half an hour. So much for fitting in and lying low, I thought. She's never going to let that happen now.

Jonno seemed to think that his "conversation" with Kaylie had put an end to the idea of finishing with him. And quite honestly, it didn't seem to matter anymore. Whether I was with Jonno or not, it was too late. Kaylie had been humiliated in public. War had been declared, and though not directly by me, I was in the front line whether I liked it or not.

Jonno and Becca stayed with me as I waited for Meena to pick me up. Only when they saw Kaylie and the Clones pile on the bus with the other school kids, did they go off on their various ways, Jonno to football practice and Becca to a production meeting with Miss Segal.

This is ridiculous, I thought. Now they think I need bodyguards.

As Meena drove me home, I had a good long hard think. The situation couldn't continue like this. I didn't want to fight with Kaylie or any of her mates. Or argue with them. I just wanted to get on.

"What would you do if someone waged war on you, Meena?" I asked.

"Hmmm," she said as she drove down the windy roads toward our house. "I no like war. I think is big waste of time, money, and innocent lives. Best not have war."

"Yes, but if someone starts a war against you, even though you don't want it, what then?"

"Once I read book by Mahatma Gandhi. He leader of India for long time. He had good philosophy. He say that before resorting to war, one should always try the peaceful approach. Make effort to negotiate."

I hadn't thought of taking that approach. I'd thought my only two options were to back off or fight. Hmm. Negotiate. Maybe I should give it a try. Plus, Mum's always saying that there's good in everyone. Kaylie must have feelings; she's only human. There's bound to be a heart in there somewhere. Maybe I could appeal to her better nature.

When I got home, I went straight to my room and turned on my computer. I opened my Outlook Express and looked for the folder of old e-mails. There was one in particular I was looking for. It was from before Christmas, before everything went weird with Kaylie. It was one of those chain letters that tells you to send it on to ten people immediately or else something awful will happen to you. It had been sent around to just about everyone in the school and before you got to the actual message, there were about five pages of people's e-mail addresses. I vaguely remembered Kaylie's being on the list. It was blondebombshell.co.uk or something. I scrolled down the list. Bingo, there it was. Barbiebombshell@info.co.uk.

I opened a page for a new message and began to write:

```
Dear Kaylie,
I wanted to ask why you are being so
horrible to me. These last few weeks
have been the worst of my life and
I've been really miserable . . .
```

I deleted that. It sounded too much like I was a victim.

```
Dear Kaylie,
Mahatma Gandhi said that in times of
```

```
war, one should try the peaceful meth-
ods  of  finding  a  solution  before
resorting to fighting . . .
```

Definitely not. For one thing, Kaylie wouldn't know who Mahatma Gandhi was and would proba-bly think that I was trying to be clever. Delete.

```
Dear Kaylie,
As you know these last few weeks have
been rather strained . . .
```

Rather *strained*? Understatement! When did I get to be so polite? I sounded like the blooming queen! May husboind and A have been rather strained lately . . . it has been my annus horribilis. No. Definitely the wrong tone. Delete.

```
Dear Kaylie,
You finking stinking cow. You're mak-
ing my life hell—to the point that I
don't  want  to  come  to  school  any
more. But I suppose that would make
you very happy, so you can stuff it.
```

```
You're not going to win, you rotten
bitch. I don't know why you've got it
in for me, but LEAVE ME ALONE. You
stink, your hair's dyed and . . . and
you've got a big bum and short legs.
And I bet that they're hairy.
```

Hmmm. I *knew* I couldn't send that, but it did
make me feel slightly better writing it. I quickly
deleted it. With my luck, I'd press the wrong button and send it off by mistake!

After about twenty more versions, I finally
wrote:

```
Dear Kaylie,
I don't understand why you have been
so mean to me the last few weeks or
why you sent that blatantly untrue
note around our year. However, I'm
prepared to put it all behind me if
you are. Can we start again, make an
effort to get on, and be friends?
Li@
```

There, I thought. Simple, to the point, and not too emotional. I pressed the send button before I could change my mind and off it went. I felt lighter than I had in days.

Half an hour later, Cat phoned.

"Are you on your own?" she asked.

"Yes. Why?"

There was a silence. Then Cat said, "I don't know how to tell you this . . ."

I felt my chest tighten and the knot in my stomach twist. "What?"

"I was just on the computer and I got mail. From Kaylie. I think she's sent the same message to everyone."

"*What?* What did she say?"

"I wanted it to come from me and not anyone else."

"I understand. What did she say?"

"She's written: *Ha ha, look at this. How pathetic. Poor little rich girl's got no friends.* Then she's pasted an e-mail from you asking if you could be friends with her. Did you write that?"

I felt sick. "Yeah. Yeah, I did. I . . . I thought . . . oh, I don't know what I thought."

"I'm so sorry, Lia. She's such a cow."

"Yeah."

"You *do* have friends. *I'm* your friend—you know that, don't you? And Becca. And Mac and Squidge. You don't need people like her. Or her approval."

I knew she was right, but her words didn't console me. I didn't understand. Why were some people so horrible?

Two hours later, Becca phoned to tell me about the message. Apparently Mac and Squidge had got it as well.

"It looks like she's sent it to everyone from our school that has a computer," said Becca.

"And that's just about everyone."

"I'm going to kill her," said Becca.

"Be my guest," I said. "I can't deal with it any-more."

Teen Queens and Has-Beens

10

I CRIED myself to sleep that night and the next day woke with the now familiar knot in my stomach. I didn't want to go into school, but I daren't tell Mum. She'd soon realize why and storm in and have it out with the teachers. Another person waging war on my behalf was the last thing I needed. But then, my methods of trying to resolve things hadn't worked either. I felt ill. I didn't want to eat, didn't want to do anything but hide under the duvet and come out when it was all over and someone appeared at my bedside to tell me that it had all been a bad dream.

I made myself get up and get dressed, and then hoped that Mum and Dad would go out somewhere for the day and not notice that I hadn't gone in.

At half past eight, the doorbell rang. It was Squidge.

"Hey," he said.

"Hey. What are you doing here?"

"Thought you might like someone to go into school with," he said.

"But you've come right out of your way."

"No problem," he said.

"And Meena usually drives me."

"Cool. I'll arrive in style."

"Not if Max and Molly have their way," I laughed. "They'll be covered in mud." The dogs had just spotted us from one of the lawns below the house and were running as fast as they could toward us. Squidge and I made a dive for the car, which was waiting outside one of the garages, ready to take me to school. We only just made it in time and couldn't help laughing at the disappointed looks on their faces as they put their paws up to the windows.

A few moments later, Meena appeared and we were on our way, leaving Max and Molly behind on the drive. As we got closer to school, I asked if he'd seen the message that Kaylie had sent round.

"Oh that." He shrugged. "That's what the delete button is for."

Then he asked about what I was doing at the weekend and filled me in on the film he was making about the school show. We talked about music, what movies were coming out . . . everything apart from Kaylie and the Clones. By the time we got to school, the knot in my tummy had loosened a bit. Only when we got out of the car did he refer to it.

"Don't let them wear you down, Lia," he said. "And you know where I am if you need me."

As I walked toward class, Jackie came up behind me.

"Hey, Lia," she said.

"Uh," I replied, wondering what nastiness she had in store.

"How are you?"

What does she mean, how am I? I thought. She must know the effect that they've had on me these last two weeks.

"Look, Jackie, I don't know what you want, but if you want the truth, I've been very freaked out. I don't know why you and your mates are being so horrid to me. I've never done anything to you and I've had about as much as I can take."

Jackie shook her head. "I know. I feel rotten about it."

I felt shocked. "You do?"

"Yeah, course. Not everyone agrees with Kaylie all the time and I think she's been really mean to you. I'm sorry."

This was the last thing I expected. "Oh," was all I could say.

"Yeah, a few of us feel bad about it. She can be a Class A bitch, can Kaylie."

"Really," I agreed. "A total bitch."

She gave me a friendly smile, then took off down the corridor. Strange, I thought. Not at all what I expected, but then maybe some of the Clones have got minds of their own after all. I made my way to the girls' cloakroom to sit for a minute on my own before facing everyone who had no doubt got Kaylie's e-mail the night before. I'd only been in there a few minutes when I heard the door open and voices. One of them was Kaylie's. I quickly lifted my feet off the floor so that she wouldn't know that I was in there.

"And did you see the way she wrote her name? Lia with an at symbol, like you use on e-mail addresses," Kaylie was saying. "I suppose she thinks she's pretty cool, doing that."

"You thought it was cool before," said Susie.

"I never did," said Kaylie. "Whose side are you on?"

"Yours, of course," said Susie. "I've always thought that she was full of herself, so stuck up. She makes me sick."

"Yeah, with her designer clothes and her private chauffeur," said Jackie.

That's Jackie's voice! I thought. But she was just so friendly to me and now she's slagging me off with the rest of them. What's going on?

But they weren't finished yet.

"And I bet her hair is dyed," said Fran. "No one has hair that blond without spending some serious money on it."

"Which we all know darling daddy has," said Jackie. "She probably thinks she can buy friends as well."

"And she's such a show-off," said Kaylie. "With her *real* Cartier watch. Like who cares? And why does she have to get driven to school every day in a Mercedes? Just to rub our noses in it. Like, look what I've got and you haven't. I mean, she could get the bus with the rest of us, but oh no, she wouldn't mix with us, would she?"

"I don't think she's that pretty anyway," said Fran.

"No, me neither," said Susie. "Only in a really obvious way. Honestly, Kaylie, I couldn't believe that e-mail she sent you. What a cheek. Let's be friends—like, who'd want to be her friend?"

"And she didn't mean it," said Jackie. "I spoke to her two minutes ago in the hall and she said she thought you were a total bitch, Kaylie."

"Really?" said Kaylie.

"Really. Her very words. 'A total bitch.' She was trying so hard to be friendly with me and get me on her side, but course, I wasn't having any of it."

I felt my shoulders sag and I hung my head. So it was all an act from Jackie. Talk about two-faced! And to think for a moment, I'd thought she might be okay.

"No one will be her friend," said Kaylie. "Like, it's *so* obvious that Cat and Becca only hang out with her because they wanted to get in with a famous family. If she wasn't Zac Axford's daughter, I bet they'd have nothing to do with her."

"Yeah," said Fran, "everyone knows that Cat only spends time with her because she wants to get off with her brother, Ollie."

"And Mac and Squidge," said Susie, "they're such

hangers-on. Wanting to be part of a glam lifestyle."

"I bet she left her old school because she had no friends there, either," said Jackie.

"Yeah."

"Yeah."

"Poor little rich girl," said Fran. "I wonder if she knows she's a has-been."

"We're the Teen Queens and she's the has-been," said Kaylie, and they all started laughing.

Then I heard the door open and close again. I felt like I'd been stabbed in the stomach and the tears I'd been holding back started to fall. There was no way I could go into class after what I'd heard, especially with red, swollen eyes. I waited five minutes, until I heard the first bell go when I knew that they'd all be in assembly, then I ran for the door and out the school gates.

I went straight down to the Cremyl ferry, then caught the bus into Plymouth. I knew what I had to do next. They'd left me no option.

11

Becoming Invisible

"WHAT DO you mean, you don't want Meena to drive you to school anymore?" asked Mum on Saturday morning as we had breakfast.

"There's a bus," I said.

"But you'd have to walk about half a mile to get it. Don't be ridiculous, Lia. Meena's always taken you to school. What's this really about?"

I took a deep sigh and got ready to explain. My new tactic: I was going to do everything I could to fit in and *not* stand out, and that meant some things had to go. First, the chauffeur-driven lift to school. Second, my watch. I'd bought a new one at the market in Plymouth yesterday—cheap, pink strap, plastic. Third, my clothes. I'd got some new outfits from a discount warehouse—all for under a tenner. From now on, I'd wear my hair scraped back and no makeup. No one would be able to accuse me of showing off. I'd be gray, blend with the crowd. I was going to fit in if it killed me. In fact, more than that; I was going to be invisible so that no one would notice me at all.

"It's really important that I don't stand out in any way, Mum. Being the only one at school who is chauffeur-driven in a Mercedes makes me stand *way* out."

"But loads of the kids get dropped off or picked up."

"Yeah, but not in this year's Mercedes. And the others get picked up by their mums and dads—not by the housekeeper."

"Are you saying you want me to drive you in?"

"Yes. *No.*" Mum drives a silver Porsche. Imagine what they'd make of that! "No. But how about Meena drives me in in her car? Her old Ford wouldn't stand out so much."

"Has that girl been getting at you again?"

"No," I lied. "I just want to fit in, and it's so different to my old school, that's all."

Mum didn't look like she believed me. "Well, you're going to have to wear a paper bag over your head, Lia. You're a stunning girl, and I'm not just saying that because I'm your mum. You'll always stand out in a crowd."

"Not if I dress down and don't wear any makeup."

"Lia, have you looked in the mirror lately? You look just as good without makeup as you do with it on."

"I have to blend in, Mum. It's really important. Please support me on this."

Mum sighed. "I'm not happy about this, Lia. Something's not right and I get the feeling that you're not telling me the whole story, but . . . if that's what you want, then fine. I do understand how important it is at your age not to feel like the odd one out. So Meena will take you in her car from now on. And you're going to wear drab clothes . . . I don't get it, but fine."

It seemed to work to a degree. Nothing major happened. The Clones just ignored me or sniggered if I ever said anything within their earshot. I could deal with that. I no longer wore anything to school that would draw attention to me. I stopped putting my hand up in class when a teacher asked a question. Meena picked me up in her old banger. I made sure I saw Jonno out of school and kept out of his way in school. If I saw Kaylie or one of the Clones coming,

I'd turn and walk the other way. They'd won, they knew it, and they seemed to lose interest.

As the weeks went on and life settled down, I carried on seeing Jonno. However, as I began to feel slightly better, I also began to feel that Jonno and I didn't have much in common. I found I was making excuses so that I could hang out with the old crowd—Mac, Becca, Squidge, and Cat. Jonno preferred coming up to the house to going out, so he could watch the footie with Dad, and it just wasn't fun like it was with my mates.

We did spend a little time on our own, though—going for a pizza, to a movie, round the Old Town in Plymouth. Those were the times when I began to realize that it wasn't really happening for me with him. We didn't talk in the way that I've been able to talk with boyfriends in the past and, some of the time, I felt like Jonno was just agreeing with me and not really listening when I tried to share some of my ideas or views about things. There were only two topics of conversation that Jonno was interested in: sports and music. And it was getting boring.

That and his new joke collection, which had made me laugh in the beginning, but was starting to wear a bit thin. Every time I saw him, he had a new one for me.

"How do you make Kaylie's eyes light up? Shine a torch in her ear."

"Why does Kaylie hate Smarties? Because they're hard to peel."

"What's the difference between a Kaylie Clone and a supermarket trolley? A supermarket trolley has a mind of its own."

"What does a Kaylie Clone do when someone shouts, 'There's a mouse in the room!'? Checks her highlights."

"What's the similarity between a Brazilian rainforest and Kaylie O'Hara? They're both dense."

And on and on they went. I think he got the jokes from the Internet, then adapted them. I think the jokes were his way of being supportive, but as the weeks went on, I was beginning to wish he'd just shut up about Kaylie. I didn't even want to hear her name.

Thank God for Squidge. He phoned one Saturday afternoon when Dad and Jonno were ensconced in their usual positions on the sofa and asked if I'd go up to Rame Head with him.

I leaped at the chance. We took the dogs with us and had one of the best afternoons I've had in ages. Cat told me that Squidge plans to do a film about the tiny church up there. It's right on the peninsula, on top of a small hill that looks out over the sea. There's something about the place. It's magical. I always feel so peaceful there, like nothing in the world matters.

"So how's it going with lover boy?" he asked as we made our way up the steps to the church.

"Och, he's football crazy," I sang in a Scottish accent. "Football mad."

Squidge laughed. "Not your scene, huh?"

"No thanks. I think he should be dating my dad—they're clearly madly in love."

"It must be hard for you sometimes. . . ."

"What do you mean?"

"All the trappings that come with you. Fab house. Your dad. You must get hangers-on."

"Yeah. In fact, I overheard Kaylie and the Clones saying that you and Mac were only interested in me because of the glam lifestyle."

I expected him to laugh it off, but Squidge looked serious. "Just be careful, Lia," he said. "Sometimes you don't know who your real friends are."

I wasn't sure who he was talking about, but I didn't want to pursue it and ruin our afternoon. It did make me wonder, though. Cat? Becca? Mac? Who was he referring to?

Gutted

12

THE FOLLOWING Tuesday morning, I was going into school as normal and spotted Cat and Becca just inside the gates. They were deeply engrossed in conversation about something and didn't see me until I'd almost got up to them.

Becca jumped as soon as she saw me and nudged Cat to shut her up.

"Oh," said Cat, looking awkward. "Lia."

"What were you talking about?" I asked. "You looked totally absorbed."

Becca glanced guiltily at Cat. "Oh, nothing," she said.

"Um, we were talking about the show," said Cat.

Yeah right, I thought. My heart sank. I knew they were lying.

As we walked into school together, I felt gutted, even more so when I saw Cat look at Becca and make a face, as if to say, Oh dear, she almost caught us. I felt like turning around and running. It was the last betrayal. Cat and Becca, my two best friends. And now even they were talking about me in secret.

It was too much. I no longer knew who to trust. I was beginning to think that maybe changing schools had been the worst idea of my whole life. I resolved that when I got home, I'd speak to Mum about going back to my old school. I had my friends up there and even though it would mean being away from home again and I'd miss Mum and Dad, at least Star and Ollie were in London and I'd be away from this nightmare.

In the break, I went off to find Squidge. At first, I thought that I wouldn't say anything to him as I know that Cat and Becca are his friends too, but somehow I felt I could trust him. He had tried to warn me about who my real friends were.

"I just don't understand it," I said after I explained what I'd seen. "I really thought that there were no secrets between Cat, Bec, and me, and now . . . I don't know what to think. They were clearly talking about me."

Squidge shook his head. "No. You've got it

wrong. They *are* your mates. Honest. Look, they were probably trying to protect you."

"Against what?"

"Same ole, same ole. Kaylie."

"No," I said. "She's been okay lately. Lost interest."

"I don't think so. . . ."

"Why?"

Squidge bit his lip.

"Oh, please Squidge. If they're doing something I don't know about, please tell me. Please."

"Look, promise you won't say that I told you. . . ."

"Promise."

"Apparently Kaylie's still trying to stir it about you. She told Cat and Becca that you'd been slagging them off to her."

"*What?* I never even speak to Kaylie. That's mad!"

Squidge shrugged. "Well, she is, isn't she?"

"How do you know this? When did it happen?"

"Last night at rehearsal. I saw her talking to Cat and Becca, then Becca told me what she'd said."

My stomach tightened into the familiar knot. "And what did she say?"

"Something about you saying that you only hung out with Cat and Becca because they were nice to you when you first arrived and now you can't shake them off. Then she told them that really you wanted to be in with Kaylie and her lot and that's why you've been so upset about them not accepting you."

"But surely they wouldn't believe her? I'd never slag them off. Why didn't they phone and ask me? Why didn't they tell me about it this morning?"

Squidge faced me squarely and put his hands on my shoulders. "Because they didn't believe a word of it and didn't want to upset you. Look, Lia. They're your best mates. They know what Kaylie's like."

"Do they? *Do* they? But they were whispering about me this morning. I just don't know who to trust anymore. And . . . and on Saturday, you said to be careful about who my real friends were."

"I didn't mean *them*, you doofus," said Squidge.

"Then who?"

This time it was Squidge's turn to look uncomfortable.

"Who?" I insisted.

Squidge hesitated for what seemed like ages. "Okay. Jonno," he said finally.

"Why? He's not in with Kaylie," I said. "He doesn't even like her."

"I know," said Squidge. "Look, forget I even said anything. It's probably just me coming over all big brothery about you."

"Oh, tell me, Squidge. Do you know something about Jonno that I don't?"

Squidge glanced around the playground to make sure no one was listening. "Not exactly. Just . . . you know what we were talking about on Saturday. About hangers-on. Well, sorry, but I think that's what Jonno might be doing. When you talk about him, it sounds like he used you to get in with your dad. You know he's desperate to get into the music business when he leaves here. He must know that your dad could help him and it sounds like he spends more time with him than you."

I couldn't deny it. It had begun to really annoy me lately, and privately, I had been thinking of calling it a day with him. Not so much because I thought he was a hanger-on, but because I didn't think I really fancied him anymore. There was no chemistry—not on my side, anyway. Even though he was good looking and nice, I wanted more than that. I preferred to be with someone I could really talk to and have a laugh with, and if I had a boyfriend, I wanted one who made me feel tingly when he kissed me. Snogging Jonno was like eating porridge. A bit dull.

"I hope I haven't spoken out of turn," said Squidge anxiously. "In fact, take no notice of me. Deep down, I'm probably jealous."

"Jealous?"

Now Squidge looked *really* awkward. "Look, got to go. Class starts in a minute." And with that, he turned and fled.

Squidge jealous? That stopped me in my tracks for a minute. Could he possibly fancy me? I felt my brain do a gear shift, as I'd never let myself imagine being with him. But we do get on well. He's so funny and full of life and new ideas, and he has the most amazing brown eyes, with thick black lashes and a lovely wide mouth. . . . Hmm. Jealous? Maybe he felt the same about me. Yes, interesting. Very interesting.

Vicars and Tarts

13

"SO PLEASE, no secrets," I said to Cat and Becca when I caught up with them at lunchtime. "I know that Kaylie was stirring it again, but please, tell me when she tries a stunt like that."

"We didn't want you getting upset," said Becca. "And it wasn't as if we took any notice. In fact, Cat asked how many times she'd have to flush before Kaylie would go away."

I laughed. "I'd be more upset if I thought you weren't my mates anymore. I knew something was going on when I saw you this morning. I felt awful. I thought I'd lost you. I'm sorry, I guess I'm getting paranoid with everything that's been going on, so please, no secrets from each other."

Cat looked at Becca questioningly and Becca gave her a nod.

"We were talking about you, Lia," she said. "It's true. But not what you think. We weren't talking about Kaylie—I wouldn't waste my breath. No. We were trying to think of a surprise for you. We know you've had a rough time lately, and we wanted to do something to cheer you up."

"Just be my friends and always tell me what's going on. That's the best thing you could ever do."

"Yeah, but we wanted to do *something* . . . I don't know," sighed Becca. "It's like you haven't been yourself lately. You've been sort of defeated, like a shadow of yourself. You're so quiet. You can even see it in your posture. You've stooped in on yourself—it's as though you're trying to disappear."

"I am," I said. "I don't want anyone to notice me."

"But that's not you," said Cat. "It's like Kaylie's rubbing you out somehow. We wanted to do something to bring the old Lia back. Make you laugh again."

"Like what?"

"Well, that's what we were trying to decide. A movie, a sleepover . . . dunno. We didn't know if you'd like to do something on your own or whether you'd want Jonno along."

"Okay, seeing as we're being totally honest, I don't think I want to go out with Jonno anymore."

"Why?" asked Becca.

I shrugged. "Don't know. I mean, he's a really nice guy and cute and everything, but I don't think we've got a lot in common."

"This isn't part of your campaign to be invisible, is it?" asked Becca. "You've ditched the watch, the nice clothes, the Mercedes, and now you're going to ditch the cutest boy in school, all so that Kaylie O'Horrible won't give you a hard time. . . ."

Speak of the devil. At that very moment, Kaylie came out of the loos and made a beeline for us. In her hand, she had a pile of envelopes. Oh, here we go, I thought. Invites to one of her dos.

"Hi." She smiled at us all, then turned to me and handed me an invite. "Look, Lia, I just wanted to say, let's bury the hatchet and start again. I've been thinking about that e-mail you sent and you're right, we should try to get on. So, bygones be bygones, et cetera, and please come to my party on Saturday."

I think my mouth fell open. "Oh . . . right. Thanks," I said as I took the envelope from her.

She gave invites to Cat and Becca as well. "I thought I'd have a theme party this time," she said, "so it's fancy dress. Vicars and Tarts. All the boys are coming as vicars, so all the girls are coming as tarts. Should be a right laugh."

Becca pulled a face at her as she went off. "What a cheek! I don't believe it. At rehearsal, she fed us a pack of lies about you and now she swans in and gives us invites as though nothing was said. Huh! Bury the hatchet? Her? More like she wants to bury it in our backs. So no. No way I'm going to one of her stupid parties. Not if you paid me."

"Me neither," said Cat. "She might think she can just wave and we'll all come running. No way. No, let's put these invites in the bin."

"No, wait," I said. "I think we should go. She's put out the hand of friendship and I bet that wasn't easy for someone like her. Please. I don't want to go on my own, so please come with me. I . . . I want to give it a try."

Becca looked at Cat.

"Why is getting on with Kaylie so important to you, Lia?" asked Becca. "She's a Class A bitch. You don't need people like that in your life."

I felt a moment's panic. I didn't want them to think that there was any truth in what Kaylie had said to them about me wanting to get in with her and shake them off.

"I don't want to be a close friend of hers, I don't. I just want it to be all right between us. Like, no stuff . . . no bad vibes. If she is on the level and I don't go to her do, she might think I'm being snooty or something. I'd like to go and show that I simply want to get on with everyone. Then maybe we can put this whole mad thing behind us all and get on with our lives."

"All right," sighed Becca. "But only for you."

On the night of the party, we had a great laugh getting dressed. Being Queen Party Planner, Mum's got a dressing-up chest full of weird and wonderful costumes from Venetian wigs to Japanese kimonos to Roman togas. At the bottom of the chest, we found some wonderful tarty gear: rubber skirts, feather boas, blond wigs, high strappy shoes. . . . Becca put on a tiny black leather skirt and black lace bra with a see-through black blouse over it. Cat chose a white see-through top with a black bra underneath—very trashy. And I went for a short, low cut, pink strappy dress, fishnet tights, and a magenta pink feather boa. We plastered our faces with makeup and back-combed our hair as high as we could. By the time we'd finished we looked like a right bunch of slappers.

Dad's eyes almost came out on stalks when he saw us totter down the stairs in our high heels. "And just where on earth do you think you're going, dressed like that?" he asked.

"Party," said Cat.

"I don't think so . . . ," Dad began.

"Fancy dress," I said. "Vicars and Tarts, and I think you can tell that we're not the vicars."

He still didn't seem too happy about it. "Put your coats on until you get there and I'll drive you." He glanced anxiously at the three of us again. "*And* pick you up!"

I asked Dad to drop us on the corner of Kaylie's road, as I didn't want to draw attention to his Ferrari. As soon as he drove off, we whipped off our coats, applied a bit more rouge and red lipstick, then tottered up to Kaylie's front door. Becca rang the bell.

A few moments later, a middle-aged lady with

frizzy blond hair answered the door. She was wearing a tracksuit and smoking a cigarette. She looked horrified to see us standing there, giggling, on her doorstep.

She took a drag of her cigarette. "Yeah?"

Suddenly I had a sense of foreboding. There was no sound of music coming from inside or people's voices. The house was quiet and I could see a flicker of light from a TV through the window at the front.

Becca and Cat began suspect something was up at the same time. "I . . . er, we thought there was a party here," said Becca.

"Well, you thought wrong," said Mrs. O'Hara, looking us up and down with disapproval. "And do your parents know that you're out dressed like this?"

"Um, we thought it was fancy dress," muttered Cat. "Sorry. Wrong house. Sorry to have bothered you."

Mrs. O'Hara shut the door without another word. She doesn't look like a very friendly person, I thought, walking down the path toward the gate. Suddenly, I was blinded by a flash of light as someone leaped out of nowhere.

"Smile for the camera," called Kaylie. As my eyes adjusted back to the dark, I could see that behind her were the Clones—Jackie, Fran, and Susie. They were all laughing their heads off. Becca put her hand up to her face so that they couldn't get another picture, but it was too late, Kaylie was clicking away as fast as she could.

Suddenly Becca made a bolt for her, but she wasn't quick enough to get the camera. Kaylie ran for her front door and in a second, disappeared inside. The Clones raced down the road to the left and were out of sight in a minute.

"Come on," cried Becca, setting off after them, "let's get them."

Cat and I tried to follow them, but in three-inch high heels, running was an impossibility. Cat collapsed into a privet hedge in someone's front garden and starting laughing.

"I can't even walk in these things, never mind run," she moaned.

Becca came back to check that Cat was okay, then looked in the direction that the Clones had gone. "Oh, stuff them," said Becca. "They're not worth it."

"Yeah," I said. "Stuff them." She put her arm around me. "It doesn't matter, Lia. Who needs Kaylie or her stupid friends anyway?"

"Yeah," said Cat. "So she got us to dress up—like, very funny, ha ha."

"Yeah, pathetic," I agreed.

"Let's go back to yours, Lia, and have our own party," said Cat.

We all sat on the wall and, as I got out my mobile to call Dad, a green Fiesta drove past. It slowed down when the driver saw us.

"Whey *hey*," called a boy in the passenger seat as he wound down his window. "Want to spend the rest of your lives with me, darlin's?"

"You couldn't afford my dry cleaning, *darling*," Cat called back in a very posh voice.

When they realized that we weren't interested, they drove off, thankfully. Cat and Becca began to laugh and I tried to join in, but my earlier sense of foreboding had deepened. Somehow I felt that this wasn't the end of it.

14

The Last Straw

THE FOLLOWING Monday, when I got into school, there was a crowd of people around the notice board in the corridor outside the assembly hall. There seemed to be a lot of giggling going on, so I went to see what the joke was. People often posted jokes that they'd found on the Internet, although they didn't last long up there, as usually one of the teachers saw them and took them down. As I approached, one of the boys in the crowd spotted me and nudged the person next to him. Suddenly, everyone went quiet. Kaylie, I thought immediately. Oh no, what has she done now? The crowd parted like a wave and I peered at the board to see what they'd all been looking at. Up on the board was a blown-up Polaroid of Cat, Becca, and me, dressed in our tarts outfits. Underneath it, was written: *The real Lia Axford and her mates. How the little Miss Perfects are out of school. We vote for Ophelia Axford as Slag of the Week.*

Sign here if you agree. There was a whole list of names and a few messages with boys' phone numbers with invitations to call them.

Jerry Robinson from Year Eight whistled and winked. "Hey, Ophelia, I'll have afeelofya. Get it?" he started laughing. "Ophelia, a feel of ya. And you look so quiet in school. Call me." Then he laughed. "No, on second thoughts, I'll call you. Maybe."

I tried to smile and make light of it, but inside I felt frozen. I couldn't even cry. This was the last straw. I felt numb except for the knot in my stomach that felt tighter than ever. Suddenly, I couldn't breathe. As the crowd dispersed, I reached up to take down the photo. Just as I reached out, someone put a hand on my shoulder. It was Miss Segal.

"I'll take that," she said with a grim expression. She took the photo from the board and walked off without a second glance at me.

That's it, I thought as I watched her walk away. My favorite teacher and now even *she* is going to think badly of me. I ran for the girls' cloakrooms and luckily they were empty. The bell went for assembly and I could hear everyone outside heading for the hall. I went into the last cubicle and locked the door. I'd reached the end. I didn't know how to be anymore.

First, the boys here thought I was aloof, and now they thought that I was a slag. I'd tried standing up for myself. I'd tried being invisible. None of it had worked and now Kaylie had even got it in for Cat and Becca and it was all because of me. If I hadn't come to this school, I thought, their photo wouldn't be up on the notice board for the whole world to see. I felt a total failure. I'd let everyone down. I didn't fit in here. And it was probably my fault. So that was it. I would definitely, *definitely* talk to Mum about leaving this horrible school and going back to my old one in London.

I decided to hide in the cubicle until assembly got going, then I would go home and beg Mum to let me leave here and never come back.

It was only a minute later that I heard the cloak-room door open then close. Like before, when Kaylie and her mates came in, I lifted my feet up so that no one would know I was in there. This is insane, I thought. I can't stay at this school any longer. I can't spend the rest of my school years hiding in the loos.

Whoever it was that had come in was looking in

each cubicle. Oh, *please* don't be Kaylie, I prayed. I didn't think I could take any more of her abuse.

"Lia, I know you're in here."

It was Squidge's voice! What should I do? I asked myself. Maybe if I'm really quiet, he'll go away. He reached the cubicle I was in and tried the door.

"Lia?"

I tried not to breathe.

"Lia. I know you're in there. Look. No one takes Kaylie and her mob seriously. You mustn't take it to heart. Honestly, no one gives a toss. Please come out."

A moment later, the cloakroom doors opened again and I heard more footsteps.

"Is she in here?" asked Mac.

"Lia?" called Becca.

"I think she's in there," said Squidge.

It wasn't that I didn't want to speak to them—I just couldn't. I felt numb.

"Hey, Lia," said Cat softly. "We know you've seen the photo. So they think they've made fools of us. It's no biggie. We're in this together. Please come out."

"Yeah, in fact," said Becca, "most people think

she's a sad loser, stooping to this last stunt. Come on, come out."

I didn't reply.

"We're not going to go away," said Squidge.

I heard footsteps go into the cubicle next door and it sounded like someone was hoisting herself up. Suddenly there was Becca's face peering over the partition. She smiled. "Hey, we've got to stop meeting like this."

"Is she in there?" asked Cat.

"Yeah," said Becca. "Come on, Lia, come out. We can deal with this. Together. Come on."

I felt so ashamed. So stupid and weak that I couldn't be like them and just laugh it off.

"Come on," said Becca. "You can't sit in here all day. Assembly will be over in a minute and people will start coming in before class."

"I'm so sorry," I whispered. I got up and unlocked the door. I still didn't feel like going out, but on hearing the lock open, Cat pushed the door and came in and put her arm around me.

"You're bigger than this," she said. "Come on. We have to show them that it hasn't got to us. We can't let her win."

"I'm so sorry," I said again. "I wish I could be like you, but . . . I'm sorry. It's like I've just, I dunno . . . I'm going to go back to my old school. I can't take it here anymore . . ."

Suddenly Mac stiffened and jerked his thumb toward the door. We all held our breath for a moment as we listened to the footsteps outside in the corridor. Click clack on the floor. Quick footsteps. Alert. Efficient. Not the footsteps of a schoolgirl or boy sauntering to or from assembly. The door opened. It was the headmistress.

"Becca Howard. Why aren't you in assembly? Jack Squires and Tom Macey! *What* are you doing in the girls' cloakrooms? And who's in that cubicle?" She marched forward. "Cat Kennedy. Lia Axford." She sniffed the air. "You've not been smoking, have you?"

"No, Miss," said Becca.

Mrs. Harvey looked us all up and down. "I don't expect this sort of behavior from any of you lot. Don't let me see it again!"

Then she turned on her spiky heels and left.

I was still ready to make a bolt for home, but Squidge wouldn't let me leave.

"You know that saying. Take a twig on its own and it's easy to snap. Bind a few twigs together, not so easy to break. Five twigs, even more difficult. There's you, me, Mac, Cat, and Becca. They won't break us if we stick together. You're not alone in this. Okay?"

"Okay . . . ," I said, with an attempt at a smile. Dear Squidge, I thought. He's trying his best, and maybe even thought he fancied me, but he doesn't know what I'm like. Pathetic. A loser. Can't fight my own battles. Whingey, wet, and full of self-pity. It's best I'm out of here and out of all their lives.

Cat and Becca wouldn't let me go. They marched me, one on either side, to the first class. Although Kaylie and the Clones sniggered when we walked in, it didn't matter anymore. I'd decided. Her, her clones, and this horrible episode were soon going to be nothing more than a bad memory. Three classes to sit through: double English, then drama with Miss Segal. Then at lunch, I'd slip away. I'd go back to my old school and, at last, the nightmare would be over for good.

Role-Play Nightmare

15

"OKAY, CLASS," said Miss Segal, looking around the room. I tried not to meet her eyes as I felt embarrassed about the photo she'd taken from the board. "Today I want to do something a bit different. I know we've done scripts in the past, we've looked at other people's words, other people's ideas. Today, we're going to free things up a bit."

I was hardly listening. In my head, I was calling my old mates in London—Tara, Athina, Gabby, Sienna, Olivia, Isobel, and Natalie. I hoped they would still be my friends when I went back to my old school, and that they'd still like me and accept me and not pick up on the fact that, somehow, I'd become a loser.

"Lia?" asked Miss Segal. "Are you with us today?"

I nodded. "Sorry. Yes. Just thinking."

Kaylie sniggered. It didn't bother me. You're history, I thought. I only have to get through this last class, then I'll never ever have to see you or your stupid friends ever again.

"Right," continued Miss Segal. "We're going to do some role-play situations. I'll need a couple of volunteers, then I'll set the scene and we'll see where it takes us. The idea is to improvise. I'm not going to tell you what to say or do, just see what comes into your head."

Count me out, I thought. One thing I will not be doing today is volunteering for anything like that. Sounds like my worst nightmare.

"Okay. First scenario," said Miss Segal. "Two people who have some kind of a relationship. What it is, our volunteers have to decide. It can be sisters, family, business partners, whatever. It can be at home, in an office, school . . . you choose, and the rest of us will try and work out what the relationship is. Okay. Who's up?"

Mary Andrews and Mark Keegan put their hands up. I watched as though from a distance as they enacted a scene in a bank. It was quite clear. Mark was the manager and Mary was a customer. I wasn't really interested. I looked at my watch. Thirty-five minutes to go until lunchtime. Then I was out of here.

After Mark and Mary had done their role-play, Miss Segal stood up again. "Good," she said. "Now let's make it more interesting. The essence of all good drama is conflict. And how do you create that?"

"Fight, Miss," said Joanne Nesbitt.

"Arguments," said Bill Malloy.

"Yes, but what causes those arguments in the first place?" asked Miss Segal.

No one answered.

"Conflict of some sort," said Miss Segal. "By putting opposites together we can create that. For example, put two non-smokers on a train. What do we have?"

"People with something in common," said David Alexander.

"Okay. Two smokers together?" asked Miss Segal.

"A smoky compartment," said Mark Keegan.

Miss Segal laughed. "Yes, but again, we have two people who get on. Now. Put a smoker and a non-smoker in a room together and what do we have?"

Becca gave Kaylie a dirty look. "Conflict," she said.

"That's right. Can anyone think of any other opposites?"

"Vegetarian and meat-eater," said Sunita Ahmed.

"Good. Any others?"

"Different religions, different politics . . . ," said Laura Johnson.

"That's it. Now you're getting it."

"Rich and poor," said Cat.

"Popular and not popular," sneered Kaylie, with a side glance at me.

"Winner and loser," said Susie.

"Excellent. So, for our next scenario," continued Miss Segal, "I want two boys."

Peter Hounslow and Scott Parker got up and went to the front.

"Okay, boys, this time I want you to play opposites. You choose who and where. Let it evolve and let's see what happens."

Despite myself, I couldn't help but be interested. In front of me, Pete and Scott began to size each other up, then call each other names. Pete started mocking Scott's voice and laughing at him. It wasn't long before the boys were fighting. I knew it wasn't serious as they're best friends out of school, but it reminded me that when a boy is a bully, then it's obvious. Pete was playing the bully and Scott was his victim.

When they'd finished, Miss Segal clapped. "Excellent, and did you see, as they got into their roles, Pete became stronger and Scott became weaker? Great body language, boys. Scott, you really looked weary and defeated by the end. Okay. I think that was pretty clear—the bully and his victim."

She looked around class and fixed her gaze on me. "Okay. Now let's see how two girls might play out that situation."

I felt myself stiffen. This was getting a bit close to home and I felt like I wanted to disappear. No way. Look somewhere else, I thought as I stared at the floor, avoiding Miss Segal's eyes. I felt myself getting hot. I looked at my watch. Only twenty more minutes to go.

Miss Segal's gaze moved on. "Any volunteers?"

To my amazement, Cat nodded at Becca, then the two of them were up like a shot.

"Okay, girls," said Miss Segal. "Off you go."

Cat started to say something and Becca started rolling her eyes and looking away as if she was really bored. She flicked her hair and sniggered to an invisible person. Cat shut up. Then Becca started acting really friendly to a group of invisible people and pretended to hand out cards. She stopped at Cat. "Oh sorry, not you," she said, with a toss of her hair. "You're not pretty enough."

Someone at the back laughed. I was stunned. She was doing the most perfect imitation of Kaylie. Then Becca walked into Cat. "Oh *sorry*, wasn't looking where I was going," she said, with a really false smile. Cat started looking miserable. "Oh, lighten up, Cat," teased Becca. "You're too serious."

I glanced over at Kaylie. She was looking daggers at Becca. I wanted to die. Becca was on a roll. She spoke to her invisible friends, sniggered, whispered, gave Cat filthy looks.

Finally she stood in front of Cat with her hand on her hip. "Whatever kind of style you were going for," she said, "you missed." Then she started laughing again.

When they'd finished, Miss Segal clapped. "Well done," she said. "And very interesting. I'll tell you why. Because with the first scenario, the boys, it was clear. Pete was the bully, Scott was the victim. But with Cat and Becca, it felt different. Can anyone tell me why?"

A hush had fallen over the class. A few girls glanced nervously at Kaylie.

Miss Segal looked around. I think she felt the tension in the air. "It's suddenly gone very quiet in here. Come on, class. Why did it feel different?"

Sunita put up her hand. "With the boys, the bullying was physical. With the girls, it was more subtle. Like, Scott would have had a bruise or a broken arm to show for it. All Cat had was a broken ego. The aggression toward her was almost unseen, as Becca made it all look so casual. Like walking into her accidentally on purpose. Cat might think that she was imagining it."

"So, what's the solution?" asked Miss Segal.

"There isn't one," said Sunita. "You can't tell your parents, as it's not like you've got a black eye or anything, and if you make a fuss, they might make things worse by causing a scene at school and *no one* wants that."

"So why not go to a teacher?" asked Miss Segal.

"No way," said Laura Johnson. "What are you going to say? They might think, What's the big deal? So someone walked into you or didn't invite you to their party. So what. Deal with it. Then you'd feel like a fool. Or maybe the teacher would talk to the bully girl and then the girl might act all sugary-nice to you for a while, but you'd know it was totally false. No, best leave teachers out of it."

I had the feeling that Sunita and Laura were talking from experience and wondered whether they had once been subject to Kaylie's methods as well.

"So what *do* you do?" asked Miss Segal.

No one spoke for a few moments, then a voice from the back of the classroom started up. It was Tina Woods, a really quiet girl who hardly ever said anything. "You, er . . ." She nervously adjusted her glasses. "You cry at home on your own. You hide your feelings and try and get through each day without anyone noticing you. . . . You try to be invisible."

At that moment, the bell went for lunch and people began to shuffle at their desks, anxious to get out, but I was riveted to my seat. Tina had described my experience exactly, as had Laura and Sunita.

"Just before you go," said Miss Segal, "I'd like to say that there *are* things that you can do. Most bullies are cowards at heart and must be stood up to, one way or another. Expose them. Because if they're doing it to one person, they're probably doing it to someone else as well. And if not now, they will in another year. I should know. I was bullied at school and it took me a long time to realize that I had to be myself and not to let others define who I was. Okay, you can go now, but I'm here if anyone wants to talk about this further."

As the class made a dash for the door, I noticed that Tina Woods was hovering in the background. I got up and followed Cat and Becca out the door. I felt stunned.

16

Real Friends

"YOU WERE totally brilliant, Becca," said Laura as we sat eating our sandwiches in the hall at lunchtime. "You had you-know-who down to a T."

Everyone was talking about Miss Segal's class. It seemed that loads of people had stories about being bullied. Tina, Sunita, Laura—even some of the boys had been subject to forms of exclusion, name calling, and general nastiness.

"Well, I'm not afraid to say her name," said Cat. "You mean Kaylie. And it's the first time I've ever seen her look so uncomfortable in class. And I noticed she scarpered pretty fast when the bell went. Doesn't want a taste of her own medicine."

"She and her mates made my life miserable last term, just because I wore the wrong kind of trainers," said Sunita. "But my parents couldn't afford to buy me the trendy ones."

"So what did you do?" asked Cat.

"I begged my mum and she saved up and got me some new ones for Christmas," said Sunita, "but that didn't work either. Kaylie accused me of being a copycat and dressing like her."

"You can't win with people like her," said Becca. "Best just leave them to rot in their own poison."

"It's amazing," I said, "because there were times when I thought it was just me. That it was my fault."

"No way," said Becca. "There are just some girls who are really mean. Who knows the reason. Like Jade Macey. We could have been real mates. But no, she didn't want anyone else from our school going for that Pop Princess competition. And she was just plain horrible to anyone she saw as a threat."

"I hate all that," I said. "Why can't people just see each other as equals, not as rivals."

"Way too liberal for someone like Kaylie," said Cat. "She sees you as a threat, especially as you took Jonno from under her nose. . . ."

"Well, she can have him back." I laughed. "Actually, no. Even though I don't want to go out with him, he's still too nice for Kaylie."

"Still want to leave, Lia?" asked Cat.

I looked at my watch and shook my head. It was

ten to one. My plan to run as soon as morning classes ended had been forgotten. Miss Segal's class had changed everything. I realized that I wasn't alone.

"So, what are we going to do to stop her antics from now on?" asked Becca. "She's made the best part of this term a misery for Lia, and for Tina, Laura, Sunita, and probably a load of others, too."

"Confront her, Lia," said Cat. "I bet there's enough people to back you up. She'd run a mile. She's okay if she can get you on your own or if she's got her little gang with her, but I bet she wouldn't be so sure of herself if she realized that she's outnumbered."

I shook my head. "After this morning, I honestly don't think it's going to be necessary. There's no doubt that everyone in our class knew what was going on. Her behavior has been exposed all right, and I doubt if she'll be able to get away with it in future."

"I guess," said Cat. "In fact, I think everyone can see what a spiteful cow she is and always has been. I think you'll be surprised at how much anti-Kaylie feeling there is."

"Count me in," said Laura.

"And me," said Sunita, taking a seat next to me and offering me a piece of her Kit Kat.

I felt hugely relieved, as until today I'd thought that Sunita and Laura didn't like me either. I thought no one did. And now I saw that it wasn't that they didn't like me. Kaylie had a hold over a good number of people and they were afraid to go against her. What a waste. All that time worrying what these girls thought about me and we might have been friends all along.

I took a deep breath. "And do you know, the fact that I let it all get to me so much suddenly seems mad. I don't even like Kaylie. . . ."

"Neither do we," said Laura and Sunita in unison.

"So why have I been so bothered about whether I fit in with her crowd or not?" I said. "I don't want her as a friend. It's weird—it seemed so important to win her over, but I see now I'll never win her over. And you know what? I *don't* care."

"That's exactly what I realized with Jade," said Becca. "I have some really good mates—you and Cat and the boys—and there I was, getting all strung out about some stupid girl who was just mean. Not someone I wanted to hang out with anyway. It *is* weird, you're right. It can get all out of proportion. We spend so much time wanting to be liked by people who we don't even like ourselves."

Laura started laughing.

"It's true," said Laura. "It's because they're popular. . . ."

"Not so popular after today, I don't think," said Cat. "And who said they were popular, anyway? I think it's a myth they started themselves."

"It worked," said Laura. "Because they didn't like me, I thought no one did. Just because I don't dress and behave like them, they made me feel like I was a weirdo. I wish they could accept that everyone is different and just let people be."

"Yeah, there's room for all of us," said Sunita, then she laughed. "Not everyone wants to be a Barbie and it's not a look I could ever really do—not unless I bleached my skin and dyed my hair."

"Yeah," said Laura. "We don't all have to be like her to have friends. There are plenty of people in our year, and only four of them."

"Exactly," said Becca. "I think it's important to invest in the people you do like—your real friends. It's what they think that counts."

I nodded. "That's what my dad said, but I didn't really appreciate it at the time. He was right. There will always be people for and against you and it's pointless wasting time trying to win over some of the people who are against. Spend time with the people who are *for* you. Those relationships are worth it."

"And that means being totally honest so that we always know that we can trust each other," said Cat. "Even if what we say upsets the other. I think trust is the most important thing there is."

"No hiding anything," said Becca.

"And no unspoken grievances, as that's how it all starts," I added. "So no secrets."

I felt happier than I had in weeks, like a huge weight had been lifted. At that moment, Squidge appeared at the end of the table and I suddenly found myself blushing. Ohmigod, I thought. Here's me going on about trust and honesty and I have the biggest secret of all. Squidge. I've fancied Squidge for ages and never told anyone.

"To real friends," Cat said, putting her hand on the table.

Becca put hers over Cat's. "To real friends," she said.

I put my hand over theirs. "To real friends."

"So things are better since before assembly?"

asked Squidge, sitting down at our table and smiling at me. I felt myself blush even more. Totally honest, I thought. . . . That means I have to tell Cat that I fancy her ex-boyfriend. Arghh.

A wave of anxiety flooded through me. How would she react? Maybe best if I keep it quiet and not get into it. I glanced over at her and she gave me a big smile back. What am I thinking? I asked myself. She's not Kaylie. She hasn't got a nasty streak. I can trust her, I know I can. And I have to let her know, by being totally honest with her, that she can trust me.

"So what's all this hand stuff about?" asked Squidge.

"A pledge," Cat replied. "To friendship, trust, honesty, no secrets, and saying what you really feel to the people you care about."

Squidge looked deeply into my eyes. I knew he was thinking what I was thinking, and once again, I blushed furiously.

In the afternoon break, I saw Cat go into the girls' cloakrooms. It's now or never, I told myself, and dived in after her.

She was washing her hands at the sink and looked

up when I burst in. "Hey," she said. "It's been a good day, hasn't it?"

"Yeah. But . . . Cat, I have something to tell you," I blustered.

She dried her hands and leaned back against the sink, ready to listen.

"Er, um . . . I know we said we've got to be honest and stuff, so I'm just going to come out and say it, and if there's even the slightest objection, you have to say. Promise?"

"Yeah. Promise. What is it?"

I took a deep breath. "Well, it's like . . . there was probably something there the first time. No, um . . . how can I put this? Would you mind if . . . ? No. Er . . ."

Cat laughed. "Lia, what are trying to say?"

"Um, Squidge."

Cat looked at me, waiting for me to continue. "Yeah, Squidge?"

"I like him," I said.

"Yeah. Everyone likes Squidge."

"No. I mean, I *like* like him."

"You like like him? Oh! You *like* like him? As in, fancy?"

"Yeah."

Cat grinned. "But that's brilliant. I always knew he liked you. I mean, *like* liked you."

"Really? And you don't mind?"

"Me? No, course not! No. Me and Squidge, we're long over. It's funny. Even at the beginning, I had a sneaky feeling that he fancied you. Ages ago, he said he thought you were stunning. So, has anything happened?"

I shook my head.

"Has he said anything?"

"Not exactly."

Suddenly Cat slapped her forehead. "D'oh. Stupid me. I bet it was Squidge who sent you that Valentine card! Have you got it with you?"

I shook my head.

"Bring it into school tomorrow and I'll tell you. I know his handwriting, even when he tries to disguise it."

"But really, really, really, you wouldn't mind if I got off with him?"

"Really, really, really," said Cat. "In fact, it would make things a lot easier for me, as although he's cool and stuff, I've always been worried about hurting his feelings. I didn't want him to be on his own. I'd love it if he found someone, and even better if it was you. If he was seeing you, I could date other boys without feeling guilty."

"Date other boys? But what about Ollie?"

"Yeah, Ollie . . . ," said Cat. "I'll see him when he's down here, but I think we both know that he's not one for the big serious relationship. I'm sure he sees other girls when he's up in London, and I'm not going to get all possessive. I'm not going to let myself go there. I don't want to get burned."

"He really does like you," I said, then grinned. "He always asks after you whenever he phones."

"Yeah, but does he *like* like me?" teased Cat.

"Yeah, I think he's got a bad case of *like* liking you."

Cat grinned. "Good. Let's keep it that way. I know if I got all heavy with him and started demanding that he tells me what's going on with other girls and stuff, he'd be off. No, I want to keep it casual."

"Treat 'em mean to keep 'em keen?" I asked.

"Sort of. Though I could never be mean to Ollie."

"I know what you mean," I said.

Then we both started laughing. "What do you

mean, you know what I mean? That I'm mean, or are you suggesting some other meaning?"

"You're mad, Cat."

"Mean, mad . . . is there no end to your insults?" She put her fists up in mock fight just as Kaylie came in. "Hey, Kaylie, do you mean to be mean, or . . . ?"

Kaylie took one look at us, turned on her heel and fled. Cat and I burst out laughing.

Cat shrugged her shoulders. "I didn't *mean* anything. . . ."

"Don't start that again," I said.

As we made our way back to class, I realized that I hadn't looned about like that for ages. I'd been so careful about everything I said and how I came across, analyzing every look and gesture from everyone and wondering if there was anything behind it. It felt so good to feel carefree again. Plus, now I knew that Cat wouldn't mind about Squidge. The future was beginning to look very promising.

White Flag

17

AFTER SCHOOL, we all piled back to Cat's house.

"I think we should celebrate," said Cat, going into their kitchen and straight to the fridge. "Who wants a scone, and oh . . . there's a tub of Cornish cream. Who wants a cream tea?"

"Well, we do live in Cornwall," said Becca. "When in Cornwall, do as the Cornish do."

"Do you have strawberrry jam?" I asked.

Cat rummaged in the fridge and produced a pot of jam, which she put on the table. "We do."

Becca read the label. "Straight from Widdecombe's Farm and onto our hips. Oh, what the hell? It's a celebration."

Cat rolled her eyes. "I don't know why you worry about your weight so much. You're just right."

"Just right for the Teletubbies, you mean."

I laughed. Becca looks great, but thinks that she's big. She's mad. She's got a great figure.

Five minutes later, just as we were tucking into freshly baked scones oozing with jam and cream, my mobile bleeped that there was a text message. I wiped the crumbs off my hands and checked the message.

"It's from Kaylie. It says, if I dare go to any of the teachers about her, my life won't be worth living." I laughed. "How pathetic is that?"

"Oooh scary," said Cat, putting her hand on her heart and feigning a faint. "Bite me."

"Hmm," said Becca. "Warning you off going to the teachers. She was obviously rattled by Miss Segal's class. What should we do?"

"Nothing," I said. "I honestly don't think it's worth it. She knows what she's done and so does most of our class now. In fact, I wouldn't be surprised if the table turns and she finds people ganging up against her now that they realize that they're not alone."

"Serve her right if they do," said Becca.

"Yeah. But you know what, life's too short. I should have listened to Dad. He told me that at one point in his life, the press gave him a hard time. He said it took him years to learn just to leave it. Not retaliate, not to try and put the story straight, just leave it. That's what I'd like to do. She probably only wants a reaction—you know, to see that she's upset me or scared me. That's what gives her the power. But if she doesn't get the reaction she expects, no power. Anyway, I've really had enough of it all. . . ."

"Oh, you mustn't leave, Lia," said Cat. "Please don't talk about going back to your old school again."

"Don't worry, I won't. No. Enough of all the bad feelings. I don't want revenge or to get back at her, or to give her a taste of her own medicine, or anything. I just want it all to stop. She leaves me alone, I leave her alone."

"So, what do we do, then? Wave a white flag to say we don't want to do battle?"

I thought for a moment. "Actually, that's not a bad idea. Let's send her one more e-mail," I said.

"What?! After what happened last time?" asked Becca. "You're mad."

"What kind of e-mail?" asked Cat.

"Sort of last chance kind of thing . . ."

Becca sighed. "You're far too forgiving, Lia."

"No, I'm not. Not forgiving. I'll never forget what she's done, but I do want this to be the end of it now. *Finito. Kaput.*"

"Suit yourself," said Becca. "But I think you're mad. You just said what your dad said. Don't engage. Don't have anything to do with bullies."

"I won't after today, but I just want it to end on a positive note—not with her having the last word with that stupid threat of hers. I want to let her know that I'm not scared and that I'm not in to waging some stupid battle either. We've got years left at school. I want her to be clear about the way it's going to be with me."

Cat looked at Becca. "Makes sense."

After we'd finished tea, we went into Cat's dad's study and turned on the computer.

"Sign it from all of us so that she knows that we're here with you," said Cat. "But what shall we say?"

"Dear Kaylie, get lost, you stupid loser," said Becca.

"Tempting," I said, "but . . . can I write it, then if you agree, we'll send it?"

"Course," said Cat, then made way for me to sit down.

Dear Kaylie,

First, your threats don't scare me. In fact, I think they're pretty pathetic. Second, I'm well aware that you might send this round our class again, but who cares? Do what you like. I never wanted any trouble between us and I'm prepared to put it all behind me. I know that after today, a lot of girls are ready to gang up against you, but I think this whole thing should stop here, for good. I propose that tomorrow morning, we meet before assembly and we go in together and show our year that we are all okay and have resolved our differences. I'm not suggesting that we become friends, as that will never happen, but I don't want any more crap at school.

I'll be outside the school gate at 8:55. The choice is yours.

Li@ @xford.

Cat leaned over my shoulder and typed in: And C@t and Becc@.

"You sure you want to send it?" asked Becca when she'd finished reading it.

I nodded.

Cat leaned over and pressed the "Send" button.

Kiss

18

THE NEXT morning, I got up early and put on my favorite CD track. It's called "Don't Panic," by Coldplay, and it always makes me feel really up and in a good mood. I haven't played it for weeks, but as the words to the song echoed around my bedroom, I found myself singing along. "We live in a beautiful world . . ."

Mum knocked on my door, then came in and sat on the end of the bed. "You're feeling happy today. What's happening?"

"I have decided to be myself," I said.

"Ah," said Mum. "Good. At least, I think it is. And what exactly does this entail?"

I sat next to her. "It means that I'm no longer going to hide who I am or who my family are. In fact, I wondered if you could give me a lift to school today?"

"In Meena's car?"

"Nope. In your gorgeous Porsche."

Mum laughed. "So what happened to low-key?"

"Not me," I said. "That was last month. I've realized we are what we are. I am who I am. I can't spend my whole life pretending to be something I'm not. I'm Lia Axford, my dad's a rock star, and I'm proud of it. I've spent so much time apologizing for the fact that we live well and I have nice things. Well, I'm going to enjoy it from now on. Why not?"

"Why not, indeed," said Mum. "So what's brought on this change?"

"Long story. Just . . . I've realized that I might be quiet, but I'm not invisible. Nope. I'm going to be who I am and happy about it."

Mum smiled. "Excellent. Now get a move on or we're going to be late."

When she'd gone, I got my Cartier watch out of its box and put it back on my wrist. Then I found my Valentine's card and put it in my rucksack ready to show Cat. I picked my best pair of jeans and DKNY T-shirt and put them on. Then I applied a little mascara, a little lip gloss, and a squirt of Cristalle, and I was ready.

* * *

Cat and Becca were waiting for me at the school gates when Mum and I drew up. Cat whistled when I got out of the car.

"Hubba hubba," she said as Mum hooted, then drove off. "You look great. You haven't worn your hair loose like that for ages."

"Thanks . . . ," I said as I looked around. "Any sign of Kaylie?"

"Not yet," said Becca.

I pulled out the Valentine's card and showed it to Cat. She took one look and grinned. "Definitely," she said. "Squidge always was rubbish at trying to disguise his handwriting."

I smiled back at her. I was really chuffed that it was from Squidge. All that time he'd liked me and had never said a word.

"Hmmm, you and Squidge, huh?" said Becca. "Cat told me all about it. I think it's brilliant."

I grinned. "So do I."

After that, we stood and waited. And waited. Finally the school bell went for assembly.

"She's not going to show, is she?" I said.

Becca shook her head. "Didn't think she would."

"Do you mind?" asked Cat.

"Not at all," I said, and I meant it. "Her loss. Now we'd better run."

We made it into the hall just in time and lined up with the others in our class. There was no sign of Kaylie. It was only when we were going into our first lesson that Cat spotted her. With the Clones as usual, and they were going into class. It didn't bother me one bit that she hadn't shown up at the gates. I'd waved the white flag and she'd chosen to ignore it. Fine by me. While we waited for Mr. Riley, our math teacher, to arrive, Cat, Becca, and I went over to chat to Laura, Sunita, and Tina on the opposite side of the room from the Clones.

"Cat told us about the e-mail, Lia," said Sunita. "Good for you. But no show, huh?"

"No show. But no worries, either," I said. "I couldn't give a toss."

"I think she could," said Laura, glancing over at Kaylie. "She looks dreadful, like she hasn't slept for a week."

"Good," said Tina. "Now she knows how it feels."

"I think you're right, though," said Laura. "It's not that I'm scared of her or anything anymore, but I don't want to get into a revenge thing. Like you, I want to leave it and get on with life. Stick with the friends I've got and not think about her. I hate all that bad vibe stuff."

Excellent, I thought as I looked around. There are some really nice girls in our year and I resolved to invite them over and get to know them better.

"Okay, take your places," said Mr. Riley as he came in through the door.

As the morning classes went on, I glanced over at Kaylie a few times, but she kept her head down through the whole lesson, like she didn't want to look at anyone. She did look terrible, but it was her choice not to have turned up at the gates and go into assembly with us. I felt totally indifferent about it. No loss. She didn't want to change, but I did. I felt like the whole ordeal had made me stronger, firmer in my resolve to be true to myself and to my friends, and to spend time getting to know people I actually liked. For the time being, Kaylie's campaign was over and if she ever started up again, she couldn't touch me.

When school ended that day, I went out to wait for my lift home as usual. As I was standing at the pick-up point, my mobile bleeped. Oh, here we go, I thought as I checked the text message. Maybe Kaylie wants to have one last go at me. . . . But it wasn't from her. It was from Squidge.

Do u want to meet l8r? it said.

I texted back. Yes.

Meet me at the bttm of ur drive at 7.

OK.

An amazing feeling of anticipation fluttered in my stomach as I tried to envisage what he might want.

He arrived to pick me up on his battered old moped.

"So, where are we going?" I asked as I climbed on the back.

"Rame Head," he answered.

"But it's dark."

"I know."

We rode up the lanes in silence and I wondered why he'd want to go up there at this time. We wouldn't be able to see the amazing view. Not that I really minded. I was alone with Squidge and that was enough for me.

Ten minutes later, Squidge parked his moped in the field near the peninsula, then he unhooked his rucksack from the back.

"What's in there?" I asked. "It looks really heavy."

"You'll see," he said, pulling out a parka jacket. "Here, put this on. It might be cold up there."

I put on the coat over my jacket and Squidge led the way with his torch. We trudged across the field that led to the small hill where the church was, then began the ascent up the wooden steps to the church at the top.

"Careful," said Squidge, shining his torch so that I could see. "Hold on to the banister."

"Don't worry, I am," I said. Apart from the torch light, it was very black out there, as there are no electric lights or lampposts, but strangely, I didn't feel frightened—only intrigued. I looked up at the sky. It was a clear night and I could see a million stars.

When we got to the top, Squidge led me to the side of the church. "Okay, stay here and close your eyes, and I'll tell you when to open them."

I did as I was told. "Good job I trust you," I said.

Squidge did a maniacal laugh, then I heard him

walk into the church. What on earth could he be doing? I wondered.

A short time later, he came back out and took my hand. "Okay, you can come now, but don't open your eyes yet."

He led me around the side of the church, then inside. "Okay," he said, "you can open your eyes now."

I opened my eyes and gasped. "Wow! It's beautiful."

The church is tiny—only three meters by four, with three gaps in the walls where once there were probably windows. Inside, it is all gray stone—even the floor. If there was ever any tiling on the floor, it's long gone. Usually it's cold and damp in there, but this night, it looked like the most magical place on earth. What Squidge had been carrying in his bag were candles and nightlights. Loads of them. He'd placed them all around the floor and on the window ledges and they glowed a soft, golden light.

"This is what it must have been like in ancient times," said Squidge. "Imagine coming up to a service here from the village before there was any electric lighting."

"Amazing," I said. "An amazing atmosphere. Like Christmas."

Squidge produced a flask from his bag. "And supplies," he said. "I thought we might want something warm, so, cup of tea, vicar?"

I laughed and took the cup he was offering me.

"Actually, it's hot chocolate," he said. "Much nicer than tea."

"So what made you do this, Squidge?"

He shrugged. "Every time I come here, it feels special. Energizing. The locals say that a lot of very powerful ley lines converge here. . . ."

"What are ley lines?"

"They're supposed to be prehistoric tracks, joining prominent points on the landscape—like churches and burial grounds. Stonehenge is on a ley line; so are the Stone Circles and the Standing Stones. I suppose you could say that in the same way that rivers carry water, these ley lines carry good energy, which is probably why people used to come to them to worship in ancient times. You know, to soak up the good vibes. Anyway, I always wanted to come up here at night. I've often tried to imagine how it must have been in the old days, so I thought I'd recreate it."

I looked around at the tiny church bathed in the

soft glow of the candles and nightlights. "Totally magical," I said. "Very good energy. I've always felt that too whenever I've come up here. It's like my battery gets charged, if you know what I mean."

He nodded. "I plan to film something up here one day. Maybe some scene from the past. You can have a lead role if you like."

"God. I can't act for toffee. In fact, the only time I got a lead part was when I was five. I was in the nativity play as Mary and totally forgot my lines. Since then I've been out of the way in the chorus."

"Well, you *were* only five," said Squidge. "And I bet you were very cute. I was in a nativity play as well when I was little. I played a donkey."

I laughed. "Have you always been so sure of what you want to do? You know, to direct films?"

Squidge nodded again. "Sort of. I mean, I started out taking photos, then Dad got me a video camera and it evolved from there."

"You've never wanted to act, then—always direct?"

"Oh yes, that way I get to cast the movie and pick the locations and so on. Location is so important, it has to be the right place for the right moment in a film."

"And what is this kind of location right for?" I asked. In my mind, it was perfect for a romantic scene. I wondered if he thought the same.

Squidge smiled a half-smile, looked full into my eyes, and leaned closer to me. I felt my chest tighten and for a moment I thought he was going to kiss me. But he leaned away and the moment was over. "Something and someone very special," he said. "But it's not just for films that you choose locations."

"What do you mean?"

"I guess having got interested in making films has made me think about a lot of things. The parallels in life. Life is what you make it, just as a film is what the director makes it."

"Explain."

"I see my life like I'm making a film. It's like, the camera starts rolling the moment you're born and it films your perspective on life—a view that's totally unique in the universe. Your view. But that's not all. In a film there's a leading lady, a leading man, sometimes a baddie, parts for extras, and so on. In your life, you're making *your* film. You've got the lead part, like I've got the lead part in mine. You had a baddie in yours, Kaylie O'Horrible. Thing is, we can choose how the script goes. I'm realizing it more and more. Whether we're going to play a hero, a heroine, or someone who loses it all. It's choice, just as it is in a script. You make up your own dialogue, your own responses, and so on. In your own film, you are the writer, the . . ."

I laughed. "I get it—the writer, director, and producer. At the end, the credits will come up: *My life, starring Lia Axford, Cat Kennedy, Becca Howard . . .*"

"Yeah, exactly. You chose to cast them as friends," said Squidge. "You choose the locations as well, the plot lines, the love interests, the lot."

"I like that. Creator of my own movie."

"And the cameras are rolling now," continued Squidge, "behind your eyes, seeing it all from your point of view, so you get to be cameraman as well. You choose what to focus on, what details to zoom in and out on, et cetera."

Well, I'm zooming in on your mouth at the moment, I thought. Everyone at school thinks that Jonno is the best-looking boy in school—well, I prefer Squidge. His face is far more interesting. But it's not just his face, I thought, watching him. It's the way his face lights up when he talks. And he has great style. I love the long black leather coat he wears. It makes him look so cool. Choice, he said. Was it my choice that Kaylie was so horrible to me? Maybe it was, partly, because I fell into playing a part in *her* film and she had chosen me to play the part of a victim. Not any more, pal. I'm taking back control of *my* movie and I want a better role.

"You're staring at me," said Squidge, smiling.

"Oh, sorry, I was just thinking. . . ."

"About what?"

"About choice. I've had such a weird time lately. I was thinking that I didn't feel I had much choice in it. But you're right, I did. I chose how I responded to things. Like that saying—you can either sink or swim. I was sinking for a while back there and now I've chosen to swim. I was letting Kaylie have a major part in my movie, and now," I laughed, "she's sacked. I don't want her in the film at all. She can be an extra in the background school scenes. And definitely *no* dialogue."

"Good," said Squidge.

"It's funny, because the whole thing with her

started after that game of truth, dare, kiss, or promise," I said. "Remember on Valentine's Day, when Becca told us all we had to kiss someone and she told me I had to kiss Jonno?"

Squidge's face clouded for a moment. "Oh yeah, your leading man. How's that going?"

"Ah. I think I'm going to do a recast. I'm the director of my movie. I can do that, can't I?"

Squidge smiled again. "Sure. Does Jonno know that he's been made redundant yet?"

I shook my head. "Haven't written the dialogue for that scene yet, but I'm going to work on it over the next few days and tell him next time I see him."

After this evening, I was more sure than ever that I had to end it with Jonno. I'd only been with Squidge a short while, but he was so interesting. He really thought about things. And not *one* mention of football.

"But forget Jonno for a moment. Thinking back to Valentine's night, you never fulfilled the kiss dare. You said you were going to do it in your own time."

Squidge was quiet for a moment. "I will when the time is right."

I *really* wanted him to kiss me, like I've never felt before. "And when do you think that will be?"

Squidge did this amazing thing. He smiled with his eyes, then he looked at the floor. "Right girl, right time," he said, then looked up into my eyes. "You can't hurry it. It's like an avocado pear—if you bite into it too soon, it doesn't taste as good as when it's ripened."

I felt my stomach flip over. If he'd been waiting for me, then I was ready. No doubt about it—I'd never felt this way about a boy, *ever*—not even Ollie's friend Michael. This felt different. Special. I felt so alive. Hyper, like I'd drunk ten cups of coffee, yet strangely calm at the same time. Life is what you make it, Squidge had said. You make the choices about how you want your movie to turn out. Well, I choose not to be so timid anymore, I thought. I want a more fun role in my own film. But is *he* ready to play the next scene? As Squidge continued to look into my eyes, I wondered how to speed up the process.

"Well, winter's over," I said. "Spring is on its way, then summer. Good times for things to ripen, I'd say."

I took a deep breath, took a step toward him and gently put my arms around his neck. He slid his hands around my waist and pulled me close, then . . .

Cue slushy soundtrack as the camera pulls away to fade out.

The end.

Well, it's my film. I can do that. And I think most people can guess what happened next. . . .

Don't miss the next round of Truth or Dare!

Turn the page for an excerpt of . . .

Truth or Dare!

starstruck

Cathy Hopkins

I AM A DEAD MAN, I thought. How will I ever be able to tell Mum and Dad?

I left the shop and went to look for Mac, who had taken off to another street to buy some oil pastels from an artist's supply shop. He wants to be a cartoonist when he leaves school. He can paint, draw, do illustrations, but really cartooning is his thing. He can capture anyone with just a few strokes of his pen. Takes talent, that does. You need an eye for the absolute essentials. It's a bit like photography; you have to have an eye for that too. It's one of the things we have in common as mates. We might go to the same college if we can find one that does film studies as well as cartooning and animation.

I crossed the road and as I went round the corner, I spotted Mac looking in the window of the art shop. He looked up and beckoned me over to him.

"Hey, come and look at this," he said, then he saw my face. "Not good news?"

I shook my head. "Think I'm going to need a small miracle this time. It'll cost a fortune to fix. Guy in the shop said I may as well get a new one, but no way can I afford one and I can't go to Cousin Ed or Jo to get it repaired, as word will get back to Dad."

"Maybe you should just bite the bullet and tell him," said Mac. "Accidents happen. He'll understand, won't he?"

"Yeah," I said. "And that's exactly way I don't want to tell him. Him being understanding would make it even worse. I know Mum and Dad really went out on a limb to get me that camcorder. I don't want to disappoint them. Let them down like a stupid kid who breaks his toy on Christmas morning. No, what I'll do is get a Saturday job. I'll work in the Easter holidays. I'll sort it."

Mac started grinning like an idiot.

"It's not funny, Mac."

"I know. I'm not smiling because of that. I'm smiling because someone up there must be looking after you."

"Yeah, right. And exactly where were they when I tripped over Rupert the Bear?"

"Look in the window," said Mac.

"What at?" I asked.

"At the notices," said Mac pointing to a noticeboard on the left of the window. "One small miracle, I do believe."

There were loads of notices on postcards: flat to

rent; bicycle for sale; cleaner needed.

"What?" I asked. "You suggesting I leave home and become a cleaner? I suppose I could sell my bike. Yeah. I guess that's an option. . . ."

Mac shook his head and pointed to a notice to the left of the others. "There, you dufus."

Then I saw it.

Ever wanted to work in the movies? Now is your chance.

Needed: extras, drivers, runners, cleaners, caterers.

Must be local.

Must be available between April 14 and May 5.

Want to know more? Call 07365 88921 and ask for Sandra.

The answer to my prayers, I thought. "That's in the Easter holidays," I gasped. "I wonder where exactly they're going to film."

I turned to Mac, but he was already on his mobile asking for someone named Sandra.

See what the girls are up to this time!
Turn the page for a sneak-peak of . . .

Mates, Dates, and Tempting Trouble

Cathy Hopkins

After the tour, we went and sat outside the Coffee Cup café in the village and chatted about what we'd learned and what we might put in our presentation. It was then I started to feel uncomfortable. Walking round with Luke had been okay, but sitting opposite him and looking straight into his eyes and he into mine, I felt strange, like my brain was going to fuse and I was sure I was blushing madly. I didn't want to be feeling what I was feeling, and the more I tried to push the sensations to the back of my head, the more they seemed to want to be in the front. I the end, I didn't look at him. Instead I watched the passersby as Luke continued talking and World War Three started in my head.

You're in danger of becoming like Sian, said one voice at the back of my mind, and you know what Luke thinks of her. A mixed-up kid. Someone with a sad crush on him. You'll be another on a long list.

But he is very attractive, said another voice. Not

only looking, but personality-wise, as well. There's nothing wrong in appreciating beauty. It would be mad not too. Chill.

And on the voices went:

But he's Nesta's boyfriend.

So? You're not planning to steal him or anything.

No. I'm not. But I shouldn't flirt either.

Don't kid yourself that he'd flirt with you. Someone like Luke would never look twice at someone like you, not in a fancying kind of way.

But I think he does like me.

So? There's a difference between liking someone and fancying them.

Erk! How many people are there inside my head?

"Are you listening to me, T. J.?" Asked Luke. "You look like you're miles away. What are you thinking about?"

"Oh! Nothing. Er. Sorry," I said, getting up. "Look. Better go. Just realized the time."

He looked disappointed. "Sorry," he said. "I've been boring you, haven't I? Was I going on?"

"No, no . . . just have to go."

Luke didn't look convinced. "Okay. See you Tuesday, then, and we'll compare notes."

I started to head off.

"Hey, sure you don't want a lift?" Luke called after me.

"Nope. Thanks. Gotta run," I said over my shoulder, then hurried on. I must be mad, I thought. A lift would have been brilliant. Now I have to make my own way home. But I needed time on my own to think. Blow away the madness that seemed to be taking me over.

Okay, I told myself as I made my way home, okay, so Luke is class A, five star attractive. So is Orlando Bloom. Fine. I can appreciate them. It's fine. That's okay. Only looking. It would be insane not to acknowledge beauty and appreciate that someone is nice and interesting. Yeah. Madness not to. So no big deal. No problem. Maybe I'm getting a bug. Yeah. That's it. Probably a virus going round making me feel funny. Being out in the cold with all those strangers. Lot of bugs going round at this time of year. Flu, colds, fevers. Nothing more than that.

By the time I reached home, I felt calmer. More rational.

Got a bug. Sorted. Yes. No prob.

THE
FOREVER
WAR

BY
JOE HALDEMAN

A Del Rey Book

BALLANTINE BOOKS • NEW YORK

For Ben and, always, for Gay

PRIVATE
MANDELLA

"Tonight we're going to show you eight silent ways to kill a man." The guy who said that was a sergeant who didn't look five years older than me. So if he'd ever killed a man in combat, silently or otherwise, he'd done it as an infant.

I already knew eighty ways to kill people, but most of them were pretty noisy. I sat up straight in my chair and assumed a look of polite attention and fell asleep with my eyes open. So did most everybody else. We'd learned that they never scheduled anything important for these after-chop classes.

The projector woke me up and I sat through a short tape showing the "eight silent ways." Some of the actors must have been brainwipes, since they were actually killed.

After the tape a girl in the front row raised her hand. The sergeant nodded at her and she rose to parade rest. Not bad looking, but kind of chunky about the neck and shoulders. Everybody gets that way after carrying a heavy pack around for a couple of months.

"Sir"—we had to call sergeants "sir" until graduation—"most of those methods, really, they looked . . . kind of silly."

"For instance?"

"Like killing a man with a blow to the kidneys, from an entrenching tool. I mean, when would you *actually* have only an entrenching tool, and no gun or knife? And why not just bash him over the head with it?"

"He might have a helmet on," he said reasonably.

"Besides, Taurans probably don't even *have* kidneys!"

He shrugged. "Probably they don't." This was 1997, and nobody had ever seen a Tauran; hadn't even found any pieces of Taurans bigger than a scorched chromosome. "But their body chemistry is similar to ours, and we have to assume they're similarly complex creatures. They *must* have weaknesses, vulnerable spots. You have to find out where they are.

3

"That's the important thing." He stabbed a finger at the screen. "Those eight convicts got caulked for your benefit because you've got to find out how to kill Taurans, and be able to do it whether you have a megawatt laser or an emery board."

She sat back down, not looking too convinced.

"Any more questions?" Nobody raised a hand.

"OK. Tench-hut!" We staggered upright and he looked at us expectantly.

"Fuck you, sir," came the familiar tired chorus.

"Louder!"

"FUCK YOU, SIR!" One of the army's less-inspired morale devices.

"That's better. Don't forget, pre-dawn maneuvers tomorrow. Chop at 0330, first formation, 0400. Anybody sacked after 0340 owes one stripe. Dismissed."

I zipped up my coverall and went across the snow to the lounge for a cup of soya and a joint. I'd always been able to get by on five or six hours of sleep, and this was the only time I could be by myself, out of the army for a while. Looked at the newsfax for a few minutes. Another ship got caulked, out by Aldebaran sector. That was four years ago. They were mounting a reprisal fleet, but it'll take four years more for them to get out there. By then, the Taurans would have every portal planet sewed up tight.

Back at the billet, everybody else was sacked and the main lights were out. The whole company'd been dragging ever since we got back from the two-week lunar training. I dumped my clothes in the locker, checked the roster and found out I was in bunk *31*. Goddammit, right under the heater.

I slipped through the curtain as quietly as possible so as not to wake up the person next to me. Couldn't see who it was, but I couldn't have cared less. I slipped under the blanket.

"You're late, Mandella," a voice yawned. It was Rogers.

"Sorry I woke you up," I whispered.

" 'Sallright." She snuggled over and clasped me spoon-fashion. She was warm and reasonably soft.

I patted her hip in what I hoped was a brotherly fashion. "Night, Rogers."

4

"G'night, Stallion." She returned the gesture more pointedly.

Why do you always get the tired ones when you're ready and the randy ones when you're tired? I bowed to the inevitable.

2.

"Awright, let's get some goddamn *back* inta that! Stringer team! Move it up—move your ass up!"

A warm front had come in about midnight and the snow had turned to sleet. The permaplast stringer weighed five hundred pounds and was a bitch to handle, even when it wasn't covered with ice. There were four of us, two at each end, carrying the plastic girder with frozen fingertips. Rogers was my partner.

"Steel!" the guy behind me yelled, meaning that he was losing his hold. It wasn't steel, but it was heavy enough to break your foot. Everybody let go and hopped away. It splashed slush and mud all over us.

"Goddamnit, Petrov," Rogers said, "why didn't you go out for the Red Cross or something? This fucken thing's not that fucken heavy." Most of the girls were a little more circumspect in their speech. Rogers was a little butch.

"Awright, get a fucken *move* on, stringers—epoxy team! Dog 'em! Dog 'em!"

Our two epoxy people ran up, swinging their buckets. "Let's go, Mandella. I'm freezin' my balls off."

"Me, too," the girl said with more feeling than logic.

"One—two—heave!" We got the thing up again and staggered toward the bridge. It was about three-quarters completed. Looked as if the second platoon was going to beat us. I wouldn't give a damn, but the platoon that got their bridge built first got to fly home. Four miles of muck for the rest of us, and no rest before chop.

We got the stringer in place, dropped it with a clank, and fitted the static clamps that held it to the rise-beams. The female half of the epoxy team started slopping glue on it before we even had it secured. Her partner was waiting for the stringer on the other side. The floor team

5

was waiting at the foot of the bridge, each one holding a piece of the light, stressed permaplast over his head like an umbrella. They were dry and clean. I wondered aloud what they had done to deserve it, and Rogers suggested a couple of colorful, but unlikely, possibilities.

We were going back to stand by the next stringer when the field first (name of Dougelstein, but we called him "Awright") blew a whistle and bellowed, "Awright, soldier boys and girls, ten minutes. Smoke 'em if you got 'em." He reached into his pocket and turned on the control that heated our coveralls.

Rogers and I sat down on our end of the stringer and I took out my weed box. I had lots of joints, but we were ordered not to smoke them until after night-chop. The only tobacco I had was a cigarro butt about three inches long. I lit it on the side of the box; it wasn't too bad after the first couple of puffs. Rogers took a puff, just to be sociable, but made a face and gave it back.

"Were you in school when you got drafted?" she asked.

"Yeah. Just got a degree in physics. Was going after a teacher's certificate."

She nodded soberly. "I was in biology . . ."

"Figures." I ducked a handful of slush. "How far?"

"Six years, bachelor's and technical." She slid her boot along the ground, turning up a ridge of mud and slush the consistency of freezing ice milk. "Why the fuck did this have to happen?"

I shrugged. It didn't call for an answer, least of all the answer that the UNEF kept giving us. Intellectual and physical elite of the planet, going out to guard humanity against the Tauran menace. Soyashit. It was all just a big experiment. See whether we could goad the Taurans into ground action.

Awright blew the whistle two minutes early, as expected, but Rogers and I and the other two stringers got to sit for a minute while the epoxy and floor teams finished covering our stringer. It got cold fast, sitting there with out suits turned off, but we remained inactive on principle.

There really wasn't any sense in having us train in the cold. Typical army half-logic. Sure, it was going to be cold where we were going, but not ice-cold or snow-cold. Almost by definition, a portal planet remained within a degree or two of absolute zero all the time—since collapsars don't shine—and the first chill you felt would mean that you were a dead man.

Twelve years before, when I was ten years old, they had discovered the collapsar jump. Just fling an object at a collapsar with sufficient speed, and out it pops in some other part of the galaxy. It didn't take long to figure out the formula that predicted where it would come out: it travels along the same "line" (actually an Einsteinian geodesic) it would have followed if the collapsar hadn't been in the way—until it reaches another collapsar field, whereupon it reappears, repelled with the same speed at which it approached the original collapsar. Travel time between the two collapsars . . . exactly zero.

It made a lot of work for mathematical physicists, who had to redefine simultaneity, then tear down general relativity and build it back up again. And it made the politicians very happy, because now they could send a shipload of colonists to Fomalhaut for less than it had once cost to put a brace of men on the moon. There were a lot of people the politicians would love to see on Fomalhaut, implementing a glorious adventure rather than stirring up trouble at home.

The ships were always accompanied by an automated probe that followed a couple of million miles behind. We knew about the portal planets, little bits of flotsam that whirled around the collapsars; the purpose of the drone was to come back and tell us in the event that a ship had smacked into a portal planet at .999 of the speed of light.

That particular catastrophe never happened, but one day a drone limped back alone. Its data were analyzed, and it turned out that the colonists' ship had been pursued by another vessel and destroyed. This happened near Aldebaran, in the constellation Taurus, but since "Aldebaranian" is a little hard to handle, they named the enemy "Tauran."

Colonizing vessels thenceforth went out protected by an armed guard. Often the armed guard went out alone, and finally the Colonization Group got shortened to

UNEF, United Nations Exploratory Force. Emphasis on the "force."

Then some bright lad in the General Assembly decided that we ought to field an army of footsoldiers to guard the portal planets of the nearer collapsars. This led to the Elite Conscription Act of 1996 and the most elitely conscripted army in the history of warfare.

So here we were, fifty men and fifty women, with IQs over 150 and bodies of unusual health and strength, slogging elitely through the mud and slush of central Missouri, reflecting on the usefulness of our skill in building bridges on worlds where the only fluid is an occasional standing pool of liquid helium.

3.

About a month later, we left for our final training exercise, maneuvers on the planet Charon. Though nearing perihelion, it was still more than twice as far from the sun as Pluto.

The troopship was a converted "cattlewagon" made to carry two hundred colonists and assorted bushes and beasts. Don't think it was roomy, though, just because there were half that many of us. Most of the excess space was taken up with extra reaction mass and ordnance.

The whole trip took three weeks, accelerating at two gees halfway, decelerating the other half. Our top speed, as we roared by the orbit of Pluto, was around one-twentieth of the speed of light—not quite enough for relativity to rear its complicated head.

Three weeks of carrying around twice as much weight as normal . . . it's no picnic. We did some cautious exercises three times a day and remained horizontal as much as possible. Still, we got several broken bones and serious dislocations. The men had to wear special supporters to keep from littering the floor with loose organs. It was almost impossible to sleep; nightmares of choking and being crushed, rolling over periodically to prevent blood pooling and bedsores. One girl got so fatigued that she almost slept through the experience of having a rib push out into the open air.

I'd been in space several times before, so when we finally stopped decelerating and went into free fall, it was nothing but relief. But some people had never been out, except for our training on the moon, and succumbed to the sudden vertigo and disorientation. The rest of us cleaned up after them, floating through the quarters with sponges and inspirators to suck up the globules of partly-digested "Concentrate, High-protein, Low-residue, Beef Flavor (Soya)."

We had a good view of Charon, coming down from orbit. There wasn't much to see, though. It was just a dim, off-white sphere with a few smudges on it. We landed about two hundred meters from the base. A pressurized crawler came out and mated with the ferry, so we didn't have to suit up. We clanked and squeaked up to the main building, a featureless box of grayish plastic.

Inside, the walls were the same drab color. The rest of the company was sitting at desks, chattering away. There was a seat next to Freeland.

"Jeff—feeling better?" He still looked a little pale.

"If the gods had meant for man to survive in free fall, they would have given him a castiron glottis." He sighed heavily. "A little better. Dying for a smoke."

"Yeah."

"*You* seemed to take it all right. Went up in school, didn't you?"

"Senior thesis in vacuum welding, yeah. Three weeks in Earth orbit." I sat back and reached for my weed box for the thousandth time. It still wasn't there. The Life Support Unit didn't want to handle nicotine and THC.

"Training was bad enough," Jeff groused, "but *this* shit—"

"Tench-hut!" We stood up in a raggedy-ass fashion, by twos and threes. The door opened and a full major came in. I stiffened a little. He was the highest-ranking officer I'd ever seen. He had a row of ribbons stitched into his coveralls, including a purple strip meaning he'd been wounded in combat, fighting in the old American army. Must have been that Indochina thing, but it had fizzled out before I was born. He didn't look that old.

9

"Sit, sit." He made a patting motion with his hand. Then he put his hands on his hips and scanned the company, a small smile on his face. "Welcome to Charon. You picked a lovely day to land, the temperature outside is a summery eight point one five degrees Absolute. We expect little change for the next two centuries or so." Some of them laughed halfheartedly.

"Best you enjoy the tropical climate here at Miami base; enjoy it while you can. We're on the center of sunside here, and most of your training will be on darkside. Over there, the temperature stays a chilly two point zero eight.

"You might as well regard all the training you got on Earth and the moon as just an elementary exercise, designed to give you a fair chance of surviving Charon. You'll have to go through your whole repertory here: tools, weapons, maneuvers. And you'll find that, at these temperatures, tools don't work the way they should; weapons don't want to fire. And people move v-e-r-y cautiously."

He studied the clipboard in his hand. "Right now, you have forty-nine women and forty-eight men. Two deaths on Earth, one psychiatric release. Having read an outline of your training program, I'm frankly surprised that so many of you pulled through.

"But you might as well know that I won't be displeased if as few as fifty of you, half, graduate from this final phase. And the only way not to graduate is to die. Here. The only way anybody gets back to Earth—including me—is after a combat tour.

"You will complete your training in one month. From here you go to Stargate collapsar, half a light away. You will stay at the settlement on Stargate 1, the largest portal planet, until replacements arrive. Hopefully, that will be no more than a month; another group is due here as soon as you leave.

"When you leave Stargate, you will go to some strategically important collapsar, set up a military base there, and fight the enemy, if attacked. Otherwise, you will maintain the base until further orders.

"The last two weeks of your training will consist of constructing exactly that kind of a base, on darkside. There you will be totally isolated from Miami base: no

10

communication, no medical evacuation, no resupply. Sometime before the two weeks are up, your defense facilities will be evaluated in an attack by guided drones. They will be armed."

They had spent all that money on us just to kill us in training?

"All of the permanent personnel here on Charon are combat veterans. Thus, all of us are forty to fifty years of age. But I think we can keep up with you. Two of us will be with you at all times and will accompany you at least as far as Stargate. They are Captain Sherman Stott, your company commander, and Sergeant Octavio Cortez, your first sergeant. Gentlemen?"

Two men in the front row stood easily and turned to face us. Captain Stott was a little smaller than the major, but cut from the same mold: face hard and smooth as porcelain, cynical half-smile, a precise centimeter of beard framing a large chin, looking thirty at the most. He wore a large, gunpowder-type pistol on his hip.

Sergeant Cortez was another story, a horror story. His head was shaved and the wrong shape, flattened out on one side, where a large piece of skull had obviously been taken out. His face was very dark and seamed with wrinkles and scars. Half his left ear was missing, and his eyes were as expressive as buttons on a machine. He had a moustache-and-beard combination that looked like a skinny white caterpillar taking a lap around his mouth. On anybody else, his schoolboy smile might look pleasant, but he was about the ugliest, meanest-looking creature I'd ever seen. Still, if you didn't look at his head and considered the lower six feet or so, he could have posed as the "after" advertisement for a body-building spa. Neither Stott nor Cortez wore any ribbons. Cortez had a small pocket-laser suspended in a magnetic rig, sideways, under his left armpit. It had wooden grips that were worn smooth.

"Now, before I turn you over to the tender mercies of these two gentlemen, let me caution you again:

"Two months ago there was not a living soul on this planet, just some leftover equipment from the expedition of 1991. A working force of forty-five men struggled for a month to erect this base. Twenty-four of them, more than half, died in the construction of it. This is the most

11

dangerous planet men have ever tried to live on, but the places you'll be going will be this bad and worse. Your cadre will try to keep you alive for the next month. Listen to them . . . and follow their example; all of them have survived here much longer than you'll have to. Captain?" The captain stood up as the major went out the door.

"Tench-*hut*!" The last syllable was like an explosion and we all jerked to our feet.

"Now I'm only gonna say this *once* so you better listen," he growled. "We *are* in a combat situation here, and in a combat situation there is only *one* penalty for disobedience or insurbordination." He jerked the pistol from his hip and held it by the barrel, like a club. "This is an Army model 1911 automatic *pistol,* caliber .45, and it is a primitive but effective weapon. The Sergeant and I are authorized to use our weapons to kill to enforce discipline. Don't make us do it because we will. We *will.*" He put the pistol back. The holster snap made a loud crack in the dead quiet.

"Sergeant Cortez and I between us have killed more people than are sitting in this room. Both of us fought in Vietnam on the American side and both of us joined the United Nations International Guard more than ten years ago. I took a break in grade from major for the privilege of commanding this company, and First Sergeant Cortez took a break from sub-major, because we are both *combat* soldiers and this is the first *combat* situation since 1987.

"Keep in mind what I've said while the First Sergeant instructs you more specifically in what your duties will be under this command. Take over, Sergeant." He turned on his heel and strode out of the room. The expression on his face hadn't changed one millimeter during the whole harangue.

The First Sergeant moved like a heavy machine with lots of ball bearings. When the door hissed shut, he swiveled ponderously to face us and said, "At ease, siddown," in a surprisingly gentle voice. He sat on a table in the front of the room. It creaked, but held.

"Now the captain talks scary and I look scary, but we both mean well. You'll be working pretty closely with me, so you better get used to this thing I've got hanging in front of my brain. You probably won't see the captain much, except on maneuvers."

He touched the flat part of his head. "And speaking of brains, I still have just about all of mine, in spite of Chinese efforts to the contrary. All of us old vets who mustered into UNEF had to pass the same criteria that got you drafted by the Elite Conscription Act. So I suspect all of you are smart and tough—but just keep in mind that the captain and I are smart and tough *and* experienced."

He flipped through the roster without really looking at it. "Now, as the captain said, there'll be only one kind of disciplinary action on maneuvers. Capital punishment. But normally *we* won't have to kill you for disobeying; Charon'll save us the trouble.

"Back in the billeting area, it'll be another story. We don't much care what you do inside. Grab ass all day and fuck all night, makes no difference. . . . But once you suit up and go outside, you've gotta have discipline that would shame a Centurian. There will be situations where one stupid act could kill us all.

"Anyhow, the first thing we've gotta do is get you fitted to your fighting suits. The armorer's waiting at your billet; he'll take you one at a time. Let's go."

4.

"Now I know you got lectured back on Earth on what a fighting suit can do." The armorer was a small man, partially bald, with no insignia of rank on his coveralls. Sergeant Cortez had told us to call him "sir," since he was a lieutenant.

"But I'd like to reinforce a couple of points, maybe add some things your instructors Earthside weren't clear about or couldn't know. Your First Sergeant was kind enough to consent to being my visual aid. Sergeant?"

Cortez slipped out of his coveralls and came up to the little raised platform where a fighting suit was standing, popped open like a man-shaped clam. He backed into it and slipped his arms into the rigid sleeves. There was a click and the thing swung shut with a sigh. It was bright green with CORTEZ stenciled in white letters on the helmet.

"Camouflage, Sergeant." The green faded to white, then dirty gray. "This is good camouflage for Charon and most of your portal planets," said Cortez, as if from a deep well. "But there are several other combinations available." The gray dappled and brightened to a combination of greens and browns: "Jungle." Then smoothed out to a hard light ochre: "Desert." Dark brown, darker, to a deep flat black: "Night or space."

"Very good, Sergeant. To my knowledge, this is the only feature of the suit that was perfected after your training. The control is around your left wrist and is admittedly awkward. But once you find the right combination, it's easy to lock in.

"Now, you didn't get much in-suit training Earthside. We didn't want you to get used to using the thing in a friendly environment. The fighting suit is the deadliest personal weapon ever built, and with no weapon is it easier for the user to kill himself through carelessness. Turn around, Sergeant.

"Case in point." He tapped a large square protuberance between the shoulders. "Exhaust fins. As you know, the suit tries to keep you at a comfortable temperature no matter what the weather's like outside. The material of the suit is as near to a perfect insulator as we could get, consistent with mechanical demands. Therefore, these fins get *hot*—especially hot, compared to darkside temperatures—as they bleed off the body's heat.

"All you have to do is lean up against a boulder of frozen gas; there's lots of it around. The gas will sublime off faster than it can escape from the fins; in escaping, it will push against the surrounding 'ice' and fracture it . . . and in about one-hundredth of a second, you have the equivalent of a hand grenade going off right below your neck. You'll never feel a thing.

"Variations on this theme have killed eleven people in the past two months. And they were just building a bunch of huts.

"I assume you know how easily the waldo capabilities can kill you or your companions. Anybody want to shake hands with the sergeant?" He paused, then

14

stepped over and clasped his glove. "He's had lots of practice. Until *you* have, be extremely careful. You might scratch an itch and wind up breaking your back. Remember, semi-logarithmic response: two pounds' pressure exerts five pounds' force; three pounds' gives ten; four pounds', twenty-three; five pounds', forty-seven. Most of you can muster up a grip of well over a hundred pounds. Theoretically, you could rip a steel girder in two with that, amplified. Actually, you'd destroy the material of your gloves and, at least on Charon, die very quickly. It'd be a race between decompression and flash-freezing. You'd die no matter which won.

"The leg waldos are also dangerous, even though the amplification is less extreme. Until you're really skilled, don't try to run, or jump. You're likely to trip, and that means you're likely to die."

"Charon's gravity is three-fourths of Earth normal, so it's not too bad. But on a really small world, like Luna, you could take a running jump and not come down for twenty minutes, just keep sailing over the horizon. Maybe bash into a mountain at eighty meters per second. On a small asteroid, it'd be no trick at all to run up to escape velocity and be off on an informal tour of intergalactic space. It's a slow way to travel.

"Tomorrow morning, we'll start teaching you how to stay alive inside this infernal machine. The rest of the afternoon and evening, I'll call you one at a time to be fitted. That's all, Sergeant."

Cortez went to the door and turned the stopcock that let air into the airlock. A bank of infrared lamps went on to keep air from freezing inside it. When the pressures were equalized, he shut the stopcock, unclamped the door and stepped in, clamping it shut behind him. A pump hummed for about a minute, evacuating the airlock; then he stepped out and sealed the outside door.

It was pretty much like the ones on Luna.

"First I want Private Omar Almizar. The rest of you can go find your bunks. I'll call you over the squawker."

"Alphabetical order, sir?"

"Yep. About ten minutes apiece. If your name begins with Z, you might as well get sacked."

That was Rogers. She probably was thinking about getting sacked.

5.

The sun was a hard white point directly overhead. It was a lot brighter than I had expected it to be; since we were eighty AUs out, it was only one 6400th as bright as it is on Earth. Still, it was putting out about as much light as a powerful streetlamp.

"This is considerably more light than you'll have on a portal planet." Captain Stott's voice crackled in our collective ear. "Be glad that you'll be able to watch your step."

We were lined up, single-file, on the permaplast sidewalk that connected the billet and the supply hut. We'd practiced walking inside, all morning, and this wasn't any different except for the exotic scenery. Though the light was rather dim, you could see all the way to the horizon quite clearly, with no atmosphere in the way. A black cliff that looked too regular to be natural stretched from one horizon to the other, passing within a kilometer of us. The ground was obsidian-black, mottled with patches of white or bluish ice. Next to the supply hut was a small mountain of snow in a bin marked OXYGEN.

The suit was fairly comfortable, but it gave you the odd feeling of simultaneously being a marionette and a puppeteer. You apply the impulse to move your leg and the suit picks it up and magnifies it and moves your leg *for* you.

"Today we're only going to walk around the company area, and nobody will *leave* the company area." The captain wasn't wearing his .45—unless he carried it as good luck charm, under his suit—but he had a laser-finger like the rest of us. And his was probably hooked up.

Keeping an interval of at least two meters between each person, we stepped off the permaplast and followed the captain over smooth rock. We walked carefully for about an hour, spiraling out, and finally stopped at the far edge of the perimeter.

"Now everybody pay close attention. I'm going out to that blue slab of ice"—it was a big one, about twenty

16

meters away—"and show you something that you'd better know if you want to stay alive."

He walked out in a dozen confident steps. "First I have to heat up a rock—filters down." I squeezed the stud under my armpit and the filter slid into place over my image converter. The captain pointed his finger at a black rock the size of a basketball, and gave it a short burst. The glare rolled a long shadow of the captain over us and beyond. The rock shattered into a pile of hazy splinters.

"It doesn't take long for these to cool down." He stopped and picked up a piece. "This one is probably twenty or twenty-five degrees. Watch." He tossed the "warm" rock onto the ice slab. It skittered around in a crazy pattern and shot off the side. He tossed another one, and it did the same.

"As you know, you are not quite *perfectly* insulated. These rocks are about the temperature of the soles of your boots. If you try to stand on a slab of hydrogen, the same thing will happen to you. Except that the rock is *already* dead.

"The reason for this behavior is that the rock makes a slick interface with the ice—a little puddle of liquid hydrogen—and rides a few molecules above the liquid on a cushion of hydrogen vapor. This makes the rock or *you* a frictionless bearing as far as the ice is concerned, and you *can't* stand up without any friction under your boots.

"After you have lived in your suit for a month or so you *should* be able to survive falling down, but right *now* you just don't know enough. Watch."

The captain flexed and hopped up onto the slab. His feet shot out from under him and he twisted around in midair, landing on hands and knees. He slipped off and stood on the ground.

"The idea is to keep your exhaust fins from making contact with the frozen gas. Compared to the ice they are as hot as a blast furnace, and contact with any weight behind it will result in an explosion."

After that demonstration, we walked around for another hour or so and returned to the billet. Once through the airlock, we had to mill around for a while, letting the suits get up to something like room tempera-

17

ture. Somebody came up and touched helmets with me.

"William?" She had MCCOY stenciled above her face-plate.

"Hi, Sean. Anything special?"

"I just wondered if you had anyone to sleep with to-night."

That's right; I'd forgotten. There wasn't any sleeping roster here. Everybody chose his own partner. "Sure, I mean, uh, no . . . no, I haven't asked anybody. Sure, if you want to. . . ."

"Thanks, William. See you later." I watched her walk away and thought that if anybody could make a fighting suit look sexy, it'd be Sean. But even she couldn't.

Cortez decided we were warm enough and led us to the suit room, where we backed the things into place and hooked them up to the charging plates. (Each suit had a little chunk of plutonium that would power it for several years, but we were supposed to run on fuel cells as much as possible.) After a lot of shuffling around, everybody finally got plugged in and we were allowed to unsuit—ninety-seven naked chickens squirming out of bright green eggs. It was *cold*—the air, the floor and especially the suits—and we made a pretty disorderly exit toward the lockers.

I slipped on tunic, trousers and sandals and was still cold. I took my cup and joined the line for soya. Everybody was jumping up and down to keep warm.

"How c-cold, do you think, it is, M-Mandella?" That was McCoy.

"I don't, even want, to think, about it." I stopped jumping and rubbed myself as briskly as possible, while holding a cup in one hand. "At least as cold as Missouri was."

"Ung . . . wish they'd, get some, fucken, heat in, this place." It always affects the small women more than any-body else. McCoy was the littlest one in the company, a waspwaist doll barely five feet high.

"They've got the airco going. It can't be long now."

"I wish I, was a big, slab of, meat like, you."

I was glad she wasn't.

6.

We had our first casualty on the third day, learning how to dig holes.

With such large amounts of energy stored in a soldier's weapons, it wouldn't be practical for him to hack out a hole in the frozen ground with the conventional pick and shovel. Still, you can launch grenades all day and get nothing but shallow depressions—so the usual method is to bore a hole in the ground with the hand laser, drop a timed charge in after it's cooled down and, ideally, fill the hole with stuff. Of course, there's not much loose rock on Charon, unless you've already blown a hole nearby.

The only difficult thing about the procedure is in getting away. To be safe, we were told, you've got to either be behind something really solid, or be at least a hundred meters away. You've got about three minutes after setting the charge, but you can't just sprint away. Not safely, not on Charon.

The accident happened when we were making a really deep hole, the kind you want for a large underground bunker. For this, we had to blow a hole, then climb down to the bottom of the crater and repeat the procedure again and again until the hole was deep enough. Inside the crater we used charges with a five-minute delay, but it hardly seemed enough time—you really had to go it slow, picking your way up the crater's edge.

Just about everybody had blown a double hole; everybody but me and three others. I guess we were the only ones paying really close attention when Bovanovitch got into trouble. All of us were a good two hundred meters away. With my image converter turned up to about forty power, I watched her disappear over the rim of the crater. After that, I could only listen in on her conversation with Cortez.

"I'm on the bottom, Sergeant." Normal radio procedure was suspended for maneuvers like this; nobody but the trainee and Cortez was allowed to broadcast.

"Okay, move to the center and clear out the rubble. Take your time. No rush until you pull the pin."

"Sure, Sergeant." We could hear small echoes of rocks clattering, sound conduction through her boots. She didn't say anything for several minutes.

"Found bottom." She sounded a little out of breath.

"Ice or rock?"

"Oh, it's rock. Sergeant. The greenish stuff."

"Use a low setting, then. One point two, dispersion four."

"God darn it, Sergeant, that'll take forever."

"Yeah, but that stuff's got hydrated crystals in it—heat it up too fast and you might make it fracture. And we'd just have to leave you there, girl. Dead and bloody."

"Okay, one point two dee four." The inside edge of the crater flickered red with reflected laser light.

"When you get about half a meter deep, squeeze it up to dee two."

"Roger." It took her exactly seventeen minutes, three of them at dispersion two. I could imagine how tired her shooting arm was.

"Now rest for a few minutes. When the bottom of the hole stops glowing, arm the charge and drop it in. Then *walk* out, understand? You'll have plenty of time."

"I understand, Sergeant. Walk out." She sounded nervous. Well, you don't often have to tiptoe away from a twenty-microton tachyon bomb. We listened to her breathing for a few minutes.

"Here goes." Faint slithering sound, the bomb sliding down.

"Slow and easy now. You've got five minutes."

"Y-yeah. Five." Her footsteps started out slow and regular. Then, after she started climbing the side, the sounds were less regular, maybe a little frantic. And with four minutes to go—

"Shit!" A loud scraping noise, then clatters and bumps. "Shit-shit."

"What's wrong, private?"

"Oh, shit." Silence. "Shit!"

"Private, you don't wanna get shot, you *tell me what's wrong!*"

"I . . . shit, I'm stuck. Fucken rockslide . . . shit. . . .

20

DO SOMETHING! I can't move, shit I can't move I, I—"

"Shut up! How deep?"

"Can't move my, shit, my fucken legs. HELP ME—"

"Then goddammit use your arms—push! You can move a ton with each hand." Three minutes.

She stopped cussing and started to mumble, in Russian, I guess, a low monotone. She was panting, and you could hear rocks tumbling away.

"I'm free." Two minutes.

"Go as fast as you can." Cortez's voice was flat, emotionless.

At ninety seconds she appeared, crawling over the rim. "Run, girl. . . .You better run." She ran five or six steps and fell, skidded a few meters and got back up, running; fell again, got up again—

It looked as though she was going pretty fast, but she had only covered about thirty meters when Cortez said, "All right, Bovanovitch, get down on your stomach and lie still." Ten seconds, but she didn't hear or she wanted to get just a little more distance, and she kept running, careless leaping strides, and at the high point of one leap there was a flash and a rumble, and something big hit her below the neck, and her headless body spun off end over end through space, trailing a red-black spiral of flash-frozen blood that settled gracefully to the ground, a path of crystal powder that nobody disturbed while we gathered rocks to cover the juiceless thing at the end of it.

That night Cortez didn't lecture us, didn't even show up for night-chop. We were all very polite to each other and nobody was afraid to talk about it.

I sacked with Rogers—everybody sacked with a good friend—but all she wanted to do was cry, and she cried so long and so hard that she got me doing it, too.

7.

"Fire team *A*—move out!" The twelve of us advanced in a ragged line toward the simulated bunker. It was about a kilometer away, across a carefully prepared obstacle course. We could move pretty fast, since all of the ice had been cleared from the field, but even with ten days' experience we weren't ready to do more than an easy jog.

I carried a grenade launcher loaded with tenth-microton practice grenades. Everybody had their laser-fingers set at a point oh eight dee one, not much more than a flashlight. This was a *simulated* attack—the bunker and its robot defender cost too much to use once and be thrown away.

"Team *B,* follow. Team leaders, take over."

We approached a clump of boulders at about the halfway mark, and Potter, my team leader, said, "Stop and cover." We clustered behind the rocks and waited for Team *B.*

Barely visible in their blackened suits, the dozen men and women whispered by us. As soon as they were clear, they jogged left, out of our line of sight.

"Fire!" Red circles of light danced a half-klick downrange, where the bunker was just visible. Five hundred meters was the limit for these practice grenades; but I might luck out, so I lined the launcher up on the image of the bunker, held it at a forty-five degree angle and popped off a salvo of three.

Return fire from the bunker started before my grenades even landed. Its automatic lasers were no more powerful than the ones we were using, but a direct hit would deactivate your image converter, leaving you blind. It was setting down a random field of fire, not even coming close to the boulders we were hiding behind.

Three magnesium-bright flashes blinked simultaneously about thirty meters short of the bunker. "Mandella! I thought you were supposed to be good with that thing."

"Damn it, Potter—it only throws half a klick. Once we get closer, I'll lay 'em right on top, everytime."

"Sure you will." I didn't say anything. She wouldn't be team leader forever. Besides, she hadn't been such a bad girl before the power went to her head.

Since the grenadier is the assistant team leader, I was slaved into Potter's radio and could hear *B* team talk to her.

"Potter, this is Freeman. Losses?"

"Potter here—no, looks like they were concentrating on you."

"Yeah, we lost three. Right now we're in a depression about eighty, a hundred meters down from you. We can give cover whenever you're ready."

"Okay, start." Soft click: "*A* team, follow me." She slid out from behind the rock and turned on the faint pink beacon beneath her powerpack. I turned on mine and moved out to run alongside of her, and the rest of the team fanned out in a trailing wedge. Nobody fired while *A* team laid down a cover for us.

All I could hear was Potter's breathing and the soft *crunch-crunch* of my boots. Couldn't see much of anything, so I tongued the image converter up to a log two intensification. That made the image kind of blurry but adequately bright. Looked like the bunker had *B* team pretty well pinned down; they were getting quite a roasting. All of their return fire was laser. They must have lost their grenadier.

"Potter, this is Mandella. Shouldn't we take some of the heat off *B* team?"

"Soon as I can find us good enough cover. Is that all right with you? Private?" She'd been promoted to corporal for the duration of the exercise.

We angled to the right and lay down behind a slab of rock. Most of the others found cover nearby, but a few had to hug the ground.

"Freeman, this is Potter."

"Potter, this is Smithy. Freeman's out; Samuels is out. We only have five men left. Give us some cover so we can get—"

"Roger, Smithy." *Click.* "Open up, *A* team. The *B*'s are really hurtin'."

I peeked out over the edge of the rock. My rangefinder said that the bunker was about three hundred fifty meters away, still pretty far. I aimed a smidgeon high and popped three, then down a couple of degrees, three more. The first ones overshot by about twenty meters; then the second salvo flared up directly in front of the bunker. I tried to hold on that angle and popped fifteen, the rest of the magazine, in the same direction.

I should have ducked down behind the rock to reload, but I wanted to see where the fifteen would land, so I

23

kept my eyes on the bunker while I reached back to unclip another magazine—

When the laser hit my image converter, there was a red glare so intense it seemed to go right through my eyes and bounce off the back of my skull. It must have been only a few milliseconds before the converter overloaded and went blind, but the bright green afterimage hurt my eyes for several minutes.

Since I was officially "dead," my radio automatically cut off, and I had to remain where I was until the mock battle was over. With no sensory input besides the feel of my own skin (and it ached where the image converter had shone on it) and the ringing in my ears, it seemed like an awfully long time. Finally, a helmet clanked against mine.

"You okay, Mandella?" Potter's voice.

"Sorry, I died of boredom twenty minutes ago."

"Stand up and take my hand." I did so and we shuffled back to the billet. It must have taken over an hour. She didn't say anything more, all the way back—it's a pretty awkward way to communicate—but after we'd cycled through the airlock and warmed up, she helped me undo my suit. I got ready for a mild tongue-lashing, but when the suit popped open, before I could even get my eyes adjusted to the light, she grabbed me around the neck and planted a wet kiss on my mouth.

"Nice shooting, Mandella."

"Huh?"

"Didn't you see? Of course not. . . . The last salvo before you got hit—four direct hits. The bunker decided it was knocked out, and all we had to do was walk the rest of the way."

"Great." I scratched my face under the eyes, and some dry skin flaked off. She giggled.

"You should see yourself. You look like—"

"All personnel, report to the assembly area." That was the captain's voice. Bad news, usually.

She handed me a tunic and sandals. "Let's go." The assembly area-chop hall was just down the corridor. There was a row of roll-call buttons at the door; I pressed the one beside my name. Four of the names were covered with black tape. That was good, only four. We hadn't lost anybody during today's maneuvers.

The captain was sitting on the raised dais, which at least meant we didn't have to go through the tench-hut bullshit. The place filled up in less than a minute; a soft chime indicated the roll was complete.

Captain Stott didn't stand up. "You did *fairly* well today. Nobody killed, and I expected some to be. In that respect you exceeded my expectations but in *every* other respect you did a poor job.

"I am glad you're taking good care of yourselves, because each of you represents an investment of over a million dollars and one-fourth of a human life.

"But in this simulated battle against a *very* stupid robot enemy, thirty-seven of you managed to walk into laser fire and be killed in a *sim*ulated way, and since dead people require no food *you* will require no food, for the next three days. Each person who was a casualty in this battle will be allowed only two liters of water and a vitamin ration each day."

We knew enough not to groan or anything, but there were some pretty disgusted looks, especially on the faces that had singed eyebrows and a pink rectangle of sunburn framing their eyes.

"Mandella."

"Sir?"

"You are far and away the worst-burned casualty. Was your image converter set on normal?"

Oh, shit. "No, sir. Log two."

"I see. Who was your team leader for the exercises?"

"Acting Corporal Potter, sir."

"Private Potter, did you order him to use image intensification?"

"Sir, I . . . I don't remember."

"You don't. Well, as a memory exercise you may join the dead people. Is that satisfactory?"

"Yes, sir."

"Good. Dead people get one last meal tonight and go on no rations starting tomorrow. Are there any questions?" He must have been kidding. "All right. Dismissed."

I selected the meal that looked as if it had the most calories and took my tray over to sit by Potter.

"That was a quixotic damn thing to do. But thanks."

"Nothing. I've been wanting to lose a few pounds any-

25

way." I couldn't see where she was carrying any extra.

"I know a good exercise," I said. She smiled without looking up from her tray. "Have anybody for tonight?"

"Kind of thought I'd ask Jeff. . . ."

"Better hurry, then. He's lusting after Maejima." Well, that was mostly true. Everybody did.

"I don't know. Maybe we ought to save our strength. That third day . . ."

"Come on." I scratched the back of her hand lightly with a fingernail. "We haven't sacked since Missouri. Maybe I've learned something new."

"Maybe you have." She tilted her head up at me in a sly way. "Okay."

Actually, she was the one with the new trick. The French corkscrew, she called it. She wouldn't tell me who taught it to her though. I'd like to shake his hand. Once I got my strength back.

8.

The two weeks' training around Miami base eventually cost us eleven lives. Twelve, if you count Dahlquist. I guess having to spend the rest of your life on Charon with a hand and both legs missing is close enough to dying.

Foster was crushed in a landslide and Freeland had a suit malfunction that froze him solid before we could carry him inside. Most of the other deaders were people I didn't know all that well. But they all hurt. And they seemed to make us more scared rather than more cautious.

Now darkside. A flyer brought us over in groups of twenty and set us down beside a pile of building materials thoughtfully immersed in a pool of helium II.

We used grapples to haul the stuff out of the pool. It's not safe to go wading, since the stuff crawls all over you and it's hard to tell what's underneath; you could walk out onto a slab of hydrogen and be out of luck.

I'd suggested that we try to boil away the pool with our lasers, but ten minutes of concentrated fire didn't drop the helium level appreciably. It didn't boil, either; helium II is a "superfluid," so what evaporation there was had to take place evenly, all over the surface. No hot spots, so no bubbling.

We weren't supposed to use lights, to "avoid detection." There was plenty of starlight with your image converter cranked up to log three or four, but each stage of amplification meant some loss of detail. By log four the landscape looked like a crude monochrome painting, and you couldn't read the names on people's helmets unless they were right in front of you.

The landscape wasn't all that interesting, anyhow. They were half a dozen medium-sized meteor craters (all with exactly the same level of helium II in them) and the suggestion of some puny mountains just over the horizon. The uneven ground was the consistency of frozen spiderwebs; every time you put your foot down, you'd sink half an inch with a squeaking crunch. It could get on your nerves.

It took most of a day to pull all the stuff out of the pool. We took shifts napping, which you could do either standing up, sitting or lying on your stomach. I didn't do well in any of those positions, so I was anxious to get the bunker built and pressurized.

We couldn't build the thing underground—it'd just fill up with helium II—so the first thing to do was to build an insulating platform, a permaplast-vacuum sandwich three layers thick.

I was an acting corporal, with a crew of ten people. We were carrying the permaplast layers to the building site—two people can carry one easily—when one of "my" men slipped and fell on his back.

"Damn it, Singer, watch your step." We'd had a couple of deaders that way.

"Sorry, Corporal. I'm bushed. Just got my feet tangled up."

"Yeah, just watch it." He got back up all right, and he and his partner placed the sheet and went back to get another.

I kept my eye on Singer. In a few minutes he was practically staggering, not easy to do in that suit of cybernetic armor.

"Singer! After you set the plank, I want to see you."

"OK." He labored through the task and mooched over.

"Let me check your readout." I opened the door on his chest to expose the medical monitor. His temperature was two degrees high; blood pressure and heart rate both elevated. Not up to the red line, though.

"You sick or something?"

"Hell, Mandella, I feel OK, just tired. Since I fell I been a little dizzy."

I chinned the medic's combination. "Doc, this is Mandella. You wanna come over here for a minute?"

"Sure, where are you?" I waved and he walked over from poolside.

"What's the problem?" I showed him Singer's readout.

He knew what all the other little dials and things meant, so it took him a while. "As far as I can tell, Mandella . . . he's just hot."

"Hell, I coulda told you that," said Singer.

"Maybe you better have the armorer take a look at his suit." We had two people who'd taken a crash course in suit maintenance; they were our "armorers."

I chinned Sanchez and asked him to come over with his tool kit.

"Be a couple of minutes, Corporal. Carryin' a plank."

"Well, put it down and get on over here." I was getting an uneasy feeling. Waiting for him, the medic and I looked over Singer's suit.

"Uh-oh," Doc Jones said. "Look at this." I went around to the back and looked where he was pointing. Two of the fins on the heat exchanger were bent out of shape.

"What's wrong?" Singer asked.

"You fell on your heat exchanger, right?"

"Sure, Corporal,—that's it. It must not be working right."

"I don't think it's working at *all*," said Doc.

Sanchez came over with his diagnostic kit and we told him what had happened. He looked at the heat exchanger, then plugged a couple of jacks into it and got a digital readout from a little monitor in his kit. I didn't know what it was measuring, but it came out zero to eight decimal places.

28

Heard a soft click, Sanchez chinning my private frequency. "Corporal, this guy's a deader."

"What? Can't you fix the goddamn thing?"

"Maybe . . . maybe I could, if I could take it apart. But there's no way——"

"Hey! Sanchez?" Singer was talking on the general freak. "Find out what's wrong?" He was panting.

Click. "Keep your pants on, man, we're working on it." *Click*. "He won't last long enough for us to get the bunker pressurized. And I can't work on the heat exchanger from outside of the suit."

"You've got a spare suit, haven't you?"

"Two of 'em, the fit-anybody kind. But there's no place . . . say . . ."

"Right. Go get one of the suits warmed up." I chinned the general freak. "Listen, Singer, we've gotta get you out of that thing. Sanchez has a spare suit, but to make the switch, we're gonna have to build a house around you. Understand?"

"Huh-uh."

"Look, we'll make a box with you inside, and hook it up to the life-support unit. That way you can breathe while you make the switch."

"Soun's pretty compis . . . compil . . . cated t'me."

"Look, just come along——"

"I'll be all right, man, jus' lemme res'. . . ."

I grabbed his arm and led him to the building site. He was really weaving. Doc took his other arm, and between us, we kept him from falling over.

"Corporal Ho, this is Corporal Mandella." Ho was in charge of the life-support unit.

"Go away, Mandella, I'm busy."

"You're going to be busier." I outlined the problem to her. While her group hurried to adapt the LSU—for this purpose, it need only be an air hose and heater—I got my crew to bring around six slabs of permaplast, so we could build a big box around Singer and the extra suit. It would look like a huge coffin, a meter square and six meters long.

We set the suit down on the slab that would be the floor of the coffin. "OK, Singer, let's go."

No answer.

"Singer, let's go."

29

No answer.

"Singer!" He was just standing there. Doc Jones checked his readout.

"He's out, man, unconscious."

My mind raced. There might just be room for another person in the box. "Give me a hand here." I took Singer's shoulders and Doc took his feet, and we carefully laid him out at the feet of the empty suit.

Then I lay down myself, above the suit. "OK, close 'er up."

"Look, Mandella, if anybody goes in there, it oughta be me."

"Fuck you, Doc. *My* job. My man." That sounded all wrong. William Mandella, boy hero.

They stood a slab up on edge—it had two openings for the LSU input and exhaust—and proceeded to weld it to the bottom plank with a narrow laser beam. On Earth, we'd just use glue, but here the only fluid was helium, which has lots of interesting properties, but is definitely not sticky.

After about ten minutes we were completely walled up. I could feel the LSU humming. I switched on my suit light—the first time since we landed on darkside—and the glare made purple blotches dance in front of my eyes.

"Mandella, this is Ho. Stay in your suit at least two or three minutes. We're putting hot air in, but it's coming back just this side of liquid." I watched the purple fade for a while.

"OK, it's still cold, but you can make it." I popped my suit. It wouldn't open all the way, but I didn't have too much trouble getting out. The suit was still cold enough to take some skin off my fingers and butt as I wiggled out.

I had to crawl feet-first down the coffin to get to Singer. It got darker fast, moving away from my light. When I popped his suit a rush of hot stink hit me in the face. In the dim light his skin was dark red and splotchy. His breathing was very shallow and I could see his heart palpitating.

First I unhooked the relief tubes—an unpleasant business—then the bio-sensors; and then I had the problem of getting his arms out of their sleeves.

It's pretty easy to do for yourself. You twist this way and turn that way and the arm pops out. Doing it from the outside is a different matter: I had to twist his arm and then reach under and move the suit's arm to match —it takes muscle to move a suit around from the outside.

Once I had one arm out it was pretty easy; I just crawled forward, putting my feet on the suit's shoulders, and pulled on his free arm. He slid out of the suit like an oyster slipping out of its shell.

I popped the spare suit and after a lot of pulling and pushing, managed to get his legs in. Hooked up the biosensors and the front relief tube. He'd have to do the other one himself; it's too complicated. For the nth time I was glad not to have been born female; they have to have two of those damned plumber's friends, instead of just one and a simple hose.

I left his arms out of the sleeves. The suit would be useless for any kind of work, anyhow; waldos have to be tailored to the individual.

His eyelids fluttered. "Man . . . della. Where . . . the fuck . . ."

I explained, slowly, and he seemed to get most of it. "Now I'm gonna close you up and go get into my suit. I'll have the crew cut the end off this thing and I'll haul you out. Got it?"

He nodded. Strange to see that—when you nod or shrug inside a suit, it doesn't communicate anything.

I crawled into my suit, hooked up the attachments and chinned the general freak. "Doc, I think he's gonna be OK. Get us out of here now."

"Will do." Ho's voice. The LSU hum was replaced by a chatter, then a throb. Evacuating the box to prevent an explosion.

One corner of the seam grew red, then white, and a bright crimson beam lanced through, not a foot away from my head. I scrunched back as far as I could. The beam slid up the seam and around three corners, back to where it started. The end of the box fell away slowly, trailing filaments of melted 'plast.

"Wait for the stuff to harden, Mandella."

"Sanchez, I'm not that stupid."

"Here you go." Somebody tossed a line to me. That

31

would be smarter than dragging him out by myself. I threaded a long bight under his arms and tied it behind his neck. Then I scrambled out to help them pull, which was silly—they had a dozen people already lined up to haul.

Singer got out all right and was actually sitting up while Doc Jones checked his readout. People were asking me about it and congratulating me, when suddenly Ho said "Look!" and pointed toward the horizon.

It was a black ship, coming in fast. I just had time to think it wasn't fair, they weren't supposed to attack until the last few days, and then the ship was right on top of us.

9.

We all flopped to the ground instinctively, but the ship didn't attack. It blasted braking rockets and dropped to land on skids. Then it skied around to come to a rest beside the building site.

Everybody had it figured out and was standing around sheepishly when the two suited figures stepped out of the ship.

A familiar voice crackled over the general freak. "Ev-ery *one* of you saw us coming in and not *one* of you responded with laser fire. It wouldn't have done any good but it would have indicated a certain amount of fighting spirit. You have a week or less before the real thing and since the sergeant and *I* will be here *I* will insist that you show a little more will to live. Acting Sergeant Potter."

"Here, sir."

"Get me a detail of twelve people to unload cargo. We brought a hundred small robot drones for *target* practice so that you might have at least a fighting chance when a live target comes over.

"Move *now*. We only have thirty minutes before the ship returns to Miami."

I checked, and it was actually more like forty minutes.

Having the captain and sergeant there didn't really

make much difference. We were still on our own; they were just observing.

Once we got the floor down, it only took one day to complete the bunker. It was a gray oblong, featureless except for the airlock blister and four windows. On top was a swivel-mounted gigawatt laser. The operator— you couldn't call him a "gunner"—sat in a chair holding dead-man switches in both hands. The laser wouldn't fire as long as he was holding one of those switches. If he let go, it would automatically aim for any moving aerial object and fire at will. Primary detection and aiming was by means of a kilometer-high antenna mounted beside the bunker.

It was the only arrangement that could really be expected to work, with the horizon so close and human reflexes so slow. You couldn't have the thing fully automatic, because in theory, friendly ships might also approach.

The aiming computer could choose among up to twelve targets appearing simultaneously (firing at the largest ones first). And it would get all twelve in the space of half a second.

The installation was partly protected from enemy fire by an efficient ablative layer that covered everything except the human operator. But then, they *were* dead-man switches. One man above guarding eighty inside. The army's good at that kind of arithmetic.

Once the bunker was finished, half of us stayed inside at all times—feeling very much like targets—taking turns operating the laser, while the other half went on maneuvers.

About four klicks from the base was a large "lake" of frozen hydrogen; one of our most important maneuvers was to learn how to get around on the treacherous stuff.

It wasn't too difficult. You couldn't stand up on it, so you had to belly down and sled.

If you had somebody to push you from the edge, getting started was no problem. Otherwise, you had to scrabble with your hands and feet, pushing down as hard as was practical, until you started moving, in a series of little jumps. Once started, you'd keep going until you ran out of ice. You could steer a little bit by digging in, hand and foot, on the appropriate side, but you

33

couldn't slow to a stop that way. So it was a good idea not to go too fast and wind up positioned in such a way that your helmet didn't absorb the shock of stopping.

We went through all the things we'd done on the Miami side: weapons practice, demolition, attack patterns. We also launched drones at irregular intervals, toward the bunker. Thus, ten or fifteen times a day, the operators got to demonstrate their skill in letting go of the handles as soon as the proximity light went on.

I had four hours of that, like everybody else. I was nervous until the first "attack," when I saw how little there was to it. The light went on, I let go, the gun aimed, and when the drone peeped over the horizon— zzt! Nice touch of color, the molten metal spraying through space. Otherwise not too exciting.

So none of us were worried about the upcoming "graduation exercise," thinking it would be just more of the same.

Miami base attacked on the thirteenth day with two simultaneous missiles streaking over opposite sides of the horizon at some forty kilometers per second. The laser vaporized the first one with no trouble, but the second got within eight klicks of the bunker before it was hit.

We were coming back from maneuvers, about a klick away from the bunker. I wouldn't have seen it happen if I hadn't been looking directly at the bunker the moment of the attack.

The second missile sent a shower of molten debris straight toward the bunker. Eleven pieces hit, and, as we later reconstructed it, this is what happened:

The frist casualty was Maejima, so well-loved Maejima, inside the bunker, who was hit in the back and the head and died instantly. With the drop in pressure, the LSU went into high gear. Friedman was standing in front of the main airco outlet and was blown into the opposite wall hard enough to knock him unconscious; he died of decompression before the others could get him to his suit.

Everybody else managed to stagger through the gale and get into their suits, but Garcia's suit had been holed and didn't do him any good.

By the time we got there, they had turned off the LSU and were welding up the holes in the wall. One man was trying to scrape up the unrecognizable mess that had been Maejima. I could hear him sobbing and retching. They had already taken Garcia and Friedman outside for burial. The captain took over the repair detail from Potter. Sergeant Cortez led the sobbing man over to a corner and came back to work on cleaning up Maejima's remains, alone. He didn't order anybody to help and nobody volunteered.

10.

As a graduation exercise, we were unceremoniously stuffed into a ship—*Earth's Hope,* the same one we rode to Charon—and bundled off to Stargate at a little more than one gee.

The trip seemed endless, about six months subjective time, and boring, but not as hard on the carcass as going to Charon had been. Captain Stott made us review our training orally, day by day, and we did exercises every day until we were worn to a collective frazzle.

Stargate 1 was like Charon's darkside, only more so. The base on Stargate 1 was smaller than Miami base—only a little bigger than the one we constructed on darkside—and we were due to lay over a week to help expand the facilities. The crew there was very glad to see us, especially the two females, who looked a little worn around the edges.

We all crowded into the small dining hall, where Submajor Williamson, the man in charge of Stargate1, gave us some disconcerting news:

"Everybody get comfortable. Get off the tables, though, there's plenty of floor.

"I have some idea of what you just went through, training on Charon. I won't say it's all been wasted. But where you're headed, things will be quite different. Warmer."

He paused to let that soak in.

"Aleph Aurigae, the first collapsar ever detected, revolves around the normal star Epsilon Aurigae in a twenty-seven year orbit. The enemy has a base of operations, not on a regular portal planet of Aleph, but on a planet in orbit around Epsilon. We don't know much about the planet, just that it goes around Epsilon once every 745 days, is about three-fourths the size of Earth, and has an albedo of 0.8, meaning it's probably covered with clouds. We can't say precisely how hot it will be, but judging from its distance from Epsilon, it's probably rather hotter than Earth. Of course, we don't know whether you'll be working . . . fighting on lightside or darkside, equator or poles. It's highly unlikely that the atmosphere will be breathable—at any rate, you'll stay inside your suits.

"Now you know exactly as much about where you're going as I do. Questions?"

"Sir," Stein drawled, "now we know where we're goin' . . . anybody know what we're goin' to do when we get there?"

Williamson shrugged. "That's up to your captain—and your sergeant, and the captain of *Earth's Hope*, and *Hope*'s logistic computer. We just don't have enough data yet to project a course of action for you. It may be a long and bloody battle; it may be just a case of walking in to pick up the pieces. Conceivably, the Taurans might want to make a peace offer,"—Cortez snorted—"in which case you would simply be part of our muscle, our bargaining power." He looked at Cortez mildly. "No one can say for sure."

The orgy that night was amusing, but it was like trying to sleep in the middle of a raucous beach party. The only area big enough to sleep all of us was the dining hall; they draped a few bedsheets here and there for privacy, then unleashed Stargate's eighteen sex-starved men on our women, compliant and promiscuous by military custom (and law), but desiring nothing so much as sleep on solid ground.

The eighteen men acted as if they were compelled to try as many permutations as possible, and their performance was impressive (in a strictly quantitative sense, that is). Those of us who were keeping count led a cheering section for some of the more gifted members. I think that's the right word.

The next morning—and every other morning we were on Stargate 1—we staggered out of bed and into our suits, to go outside and work on the "new wing." Even-

36

tually, Stargate would be tactical and logistic headquarters for the war, with thousands of permanent personnel, guarded by half-a-dozen heavy cruisers in *Hope*'s class. When we started, it was two shacks and twenty people; when we left, it was four shacks and twenty people. The work was hardly work at all, compared to darkside, since we had plenty of light and got sixteen hours inside for every eight hours' work. And no drone attack for a final exam.

When we shuttled back up to the *Hope,* nobody was too happy about leaving (though some of the more popular females declared it'd be good to get some rest). Stargate was the last easy, safe assignment we'd have before taking up arms against the Taurans. And as Williamson had pointed out the first day, there was no way of predicting what *that* would be like.

Most of us didn't feel too enthusiastic about making a collapsar jump, either. We'd been assured that we wouldn't even feel it happen, just free fall all the way.

I wasn't convinced. As a physics student, I'd had the usual courses in general relativity and theories of gravitation. We only had a little direct data at that time— Stargate was discovered when I was in grade school— but the mathematical model seemed clear enough.

The collapsar Stargate was a perfect sphere about three kilometers in radius. It was suspended forever in a state of gravitational collapse that should have meant its surface was dropping toward its center at nearly the speed of light. Relativity propped it up, at least gave it the illusion of being there . . . the way all reality becomes illusory and observer-oriented when you study general relativity. Or Buddhism. Or get drafted.

At any rate, there would be a theoretical point in space-time when one end of our ship was just above the surface of the collapsar, and the other end was a kilometer away (in our frame of reference). In any sane universe, this would set up tidal stresses and tear the ship apart, and we would be just another million kilograms of degenerate matter on the theoretical surface, rushing headlong to nowhere for the rest of eternity or dropping to the center in the next trillionth of a second. You pays your money and you takes your frame of reference.

But they were right. We blasted away from Stargate 1,

made a few course corrections and then just dropped, for about an hour.

Then a bell rang and we sank into our cushions under a steady two gravities of deceleration. We were in enemy territory.

11.

We'd been decelerating at two gravities for almost nine days when the battle began. Lying on our couches being miserable, all we felt were two soft bumps, missiles being released. Some eight hours later, the squawk-box crackled: "Attention, all crew. This is the captain." Quinsana, the pilot, was only a lieutenant, but was allowed to call himself captain aboard the vessel, where he outranked all of us, even Captain Stott. "You grunts in the cargo hold can listen, too.

"We just engaged the enemy with two fifty-gigaton tachyon missiles and have destroyed both the enemy vessel and another object which it had launched approximately three microseconds before.

"The enemy has been trying to overtake us for the past 179 hours, ship time. At the time of the engagement, the enemy was moving at a little over half the speed of light, relative to Aleph, and was only about thirty AU's from *Earth's Hope*. It was moving at .47c relative to us, and thus we would have been coincident in space-time"—rammed!—"in a little more than nine hours. The missiles were launched at 0719 ship's time, and destroyed the enemy at 1540, both tachyon bombs detonating within a thousand klicks of the enemy objects."

The two missiles were a type whose propulsion system was itself only a barely-controlled tachyon bomb. They accelerated at a constant rate of 100 gees, and were traveling at a relativistic speed by the time the nearby mass of the enemy ship detonated them.

"We expect no further interference from enemy vessels. Our velocity with respect to Aleph will be zero in another five hours; we will then begin the journey back. The return will take twenty-seven days." General moans

38

and dejected cussing. Everybody knew all that already, of course; but we didn't care to be reminded of it.

So after another month of logy calisthenics and drill, at a constant two gravities, we got our first look at the planet we were going to attack. Invaders from outer space, yes sir.

It was a blinding white crescent waiting for us two AU's out from Epsilon. The captain had pinned down the location of the enemy base from fifty AU's out, and we had jockeyed in on a wide arc, keeping the bulk of the planet between them and us. That didn't mean we were sneaking up on them—quite the contrary; they launched three abortive attacks—but it put us in a stronger defensive position. Until we had to go to the surface, that is. Then only the ship and its Star Fleet crew would be reasonably safe.

Since the planet rotated rather slowly—once every ten and one-half days—a "stationary" orbit for the ship had to be 150,000 klicks out. This made the people in the ship feel quite secure, with 6,000 miles of rock and 90,000 miles of space between them and the enemy. But it meant a whole second's time lag in communication between us on the ground and the ship's battle computer. A person could get awful dead while that neutrino pulse crawled up and back.

Our vague orders were to attack the base and gain control, while damaging a minimum of enemy equipment. We were to take at least one enemy alive. We were under no circumstances to allow ourselves to be taken alive, however. And the decision wasn't up to us; one special pulse from the battle computer, and that speck of plutonium in your power plant would fiss with all of .01% efficiency, and you'd be nothing but a rapidly expanding, very hot plasma.

They strapped us into six scoutships—one platoon of twelve people in each—and we blasted away from *Earth's Hope* at eight gees. Each scoutship was supposed to follow its own carefully random path to our rendezvous point, 108 klicks from the base. Fourteen drone ships were launched at the same time, to confound the enemy's anti-spacecraft system.

The landing went off almost perfectly. One ship suffered minor damage, a near miss boiling away some of the ablative material on one side of the hull, but it'd still be able to make it and return, keeping its speed down while in the atmosphere.

We zigged and zagged and wound up first ship at the rendezvous point. There was only one trouble. It was under four kilometers of water.

I could almost hear that machine, 90,000 miles away, grinding its mental gears, adding this new bit of data. We proceeded just as if we were landing on solid ground: braking rockets, falling, skids out, hit the water, skip, hit the water, skip, hit the water, sink.

It would have made sense to go ahead and land on the bottom—we were streamlined, after all, and water just another fluid—but the hull wasn't strong enough to hold up a four kilometer column of water. Sergeant Cortez was in the scoutship with us.

"Sarge, tell that computer to *do* something! We're gonna get—"

"Oh, shut up, Mandella. Trust in th' lord." "Lord" was definitely lower-case when Cortez said it.

There was a loud bubbly sigh, then another, and a slight increase in pressure on my back that meant the ship was rising. "Flotation bags?" Cortez didn't deign to answer, or didn't know.

That was it. We rose to within ten or fifteen meters of the surface and stopped, suspended there. Through the port I could see the surface above, shimmering like a mirror of hammered silver. I wondered what it would be like to be a fish and have a definite roof over your world.

I watched another ship splash in. It made a great cloud of bubbles and turbulence, then fell—slightly tail-first—for a short distance before large bags popped out under each delta wing. Then it bobbed up to about our level and stayed.

"This is Captain Stott. Now listen carefully. There is a beach some twenty-eight klicks from your present position, in the direction of the enemy. You will be proceeding to this beach by scoutship and from there will mount your assault on the Tauran position." That was *some* improvement; we'd only have to walk eighty klicks.

We deflated the bags, blasted to the surface and flew in a slow, spread-out formation to the beach. It took several minutes. As the ship scraped to a halt, I could hear pumps humming, making the cabin pressure equal to the air pressure outside. Before it had quite stopped moving, the escape slot beside my couch slid open. I rolled out onto the wing of the craft and jumped to the ground. Ten seconds to find cover—I sprinted across loose gravel to the "treeline," a twisty bramble of tall sparse bluish-green shrubs. I dove into the briar patch and turned to watch the ships leave. The drones that were left rose slowly to about a hundred meters, then took off in all directions with a bone-jarring roar. The real scoutships slid slowly back into the water. Maybe that was a good idea.

It wasn't a terribly attractive world but certainly would be easier to get around in than the cyrogenic nightmare we were trained for. The sky was a uniform dull silver brightness that merged with the mist over the ocean so completely it was impossible to tell where water ended and air began. Small wavelets licked at the black gravel shore, much too slow and graceful in the three-quarters Earth-normal gravity. Even from fifty meters away, the rattle of billions of pebbles rolling with the tide was loud in my ears.

The air temperature was 79 degrees Centigrade, not quite hot enough for the sea to boil, even though the air pressure was low compared to Earth's. Wisps of steam drifted quickly upward from the line where water met land. I wondered how a lone man would survive exposed here without a suit. Would the heat or the low oxygen (partial pressure one-eighth Earth normal) kill him first? Or was there some deadly microorganism that would beat them both . . . ?

"This is Cortez. Everybody come over and assemble on me." He was standing on the beach a little to the left of me, waving his hand in a circle over his head. I walked toward him through the shrubs. They were brittle, unsubstantial, seemed paradoxically dried-out in the steamy air. They wouldn't offer much in the way of cover.

"We'll be advancing on a heading .05 radians east of

41

north. I want Platoon One to take point. Two and Three follow about twenty meters behind, to the left and right. Seven, command platoon, is in the middle, twenty meters behind Two and Three. Five and Six, bring up the rear, in a semicircular closed flank. Everybody straight?" Sure, we could do that "arrowhead" maneuver in our sleep. "OK, let's move out."

I was in Platoon Seven, the "command group." Captain Stott put me there not because I was expected to give any commands, but because of my training in physics.

The command group was supposedly the safest place, buffered by six platoons: people were assigned to it because there was some tactical reason for them to survive at least a little longer than the rest. Cortez was there to give orders. Chavez was there to correct suit malfunctions. The senior medic, Doc Wilson (the only medic who actually had an M.D.) was there, and so was Theodopolis, the radio engineer, our link with the captain, who had elected to stay in orbit.

The rest of us were assigned to the command group by dint of special training or aptitude that wouldn't normally be considered of a "tactical" nature. Facing a totally unknown enemy, there was no way of telling what might prove important. Thus I was there because I was the closest the company had to a physicist. Rogers was biology. Tate was chemistry. Ho could crank out a perfect score on the Rhine extrasensory perception test, every time. Bohrs was a polyglot, able to speak twenty-one languages fluently, idiomatically. Petrov's talent was that he had tested out to have not one molecule of xenophobia in his psyche. Keating was a skilled acrobat. Debby Hollister—"Lucky" Hollister—showed a remarkable aptitude for making money, and also had a consistently high Rhine potential.

12.

When we first set out, we were using the "jungle" camouflage combination on our suits. But what passed for jungle in these anemic tropics was too sparse; we looked like a band of conspicuous harlequins trooping through the woods. Cortez had us switch to black, but that was just as bad, as the light of Epsilon came evenly from all parts of the sky, and there were no shadows except ours. We finally settled on the dun-colored desert camouflage.

The nature of the countryside changed slowly as we walked north, away from the sea. The thorned stalks—I guess you could call them trees—came in fewer numbers but were bigger around and less brittle; at the base of each was a tangled mass of vine with the same blue-green color, which spread out in a flattened cone some ten meters in diameter. There was a delicate green flower the size of a man's head near the top of each tree.

Grass began to grow some five klicks from the sea. It seemed to respect the trees' "property rights," leaving a strip of bare earth around each cone of vine. At the edge of such a clearing, it would grow as timid blue-green stubble, then, moving away from the tree, would get thicker and taller until it reached shoulderhigh in some places, where the separation between two trees was unusually large. The grass was a lighter, greener shade than the trees and vines. We changed the color of our suits to the bright green we had used for maximum visibility on Charon. Keeping to the thickest part of the grass, we were fairly inconspicuous.

We covered over twenty klicks each day, buoyant after months under two gees. Until the second day, the only form of animal life we saw was a kind of black worm, finger-sized, with hundreds of cilium legs like the bristles of a brush. Rogers said that there obviously had to be some larger creature around, or there would be no reason for the trees to have thorns. So we were doubly on guard, expecting trouble both from the Taurans and the unidentified "large creature."

Potter's second platoon was on point; the general freak was reserved for her, since her platoon would likely be the first to spot any trouble.

"Sarge, this is Potter," we all heard. "Movement ahead."

"Get down, then!"

"We are. Don't think they see us."

"First platoon, go up to the right of point. Keep
43

down. Fourth, get up to the left. Tell me when you get in position. Sixth platoon, stay back and guard the rear. Fifth and third, close with the command group."

Two dozen people whispered out of the grass to join us. Cortez must have heard from the fourth platoon.

"Good. How about you, first? . . . OK, fine. How many are there?"

"Eight we can see." Potter's voice.

"Good. When I give the word, open fire. Shoot to kill."

"Sarge, . . . they're just animals."

"Potter—if you've known all this time what a Tauran looks like, you should've told us. Shoot to kill."

"But we need . . ."

"We need a prisoner, but we don't need to escort him forty klicks to his home base and keep an eye on him while we fight. Clear?"

"Yes. Sergeant."

"OK. Seventh, all you brains and weirds, we're going up and watch. Fifth and third, come along to guard."

We crawled through the meter-high grass to where the second platoon had stretched out in a firing line.

"I don't see anything," Cortez said.

"Ahead and just to the left. Dark green."

They were only a shade darker than the grass. But after you saw the first one, you could see them all, moving slowly around some thirty meters ahead.

"Fire!" Cortez fired first; then twelve streaks of crimson leaped out and the grass wilted black, disappeared, and the creatures convulsed and died trying to scatter.

"Hold fire, hold it!" Cortez stood up. "We want to have something left—second platoon, follow me." He strode out toward the smoldering corpses, laser-finger pointed out front, obscene divining rod pulling him toward the carnage. . . . I felt my gorge rising and knew that all the lurid training tapes, all the horrible deaths in training accidents, hadn't prepared me for this sudden reality . . . that I had a magic wand that I could point at a life and make it a smoking piece of half-raw meat; I wasn't a soldier nor ever wanted to be one nor ever would want—

"OK, seventh, come on up." While we were walking toward them, one of the creatures moved, a tiny shidder,

44

and Cortez flicked the beam of his laser over it with an almost negligent gesture. It made a hand-deep gash across the creature's middle. It died, like the others, without emitting a sound.

They were not quite as tall as humans, but wider in girth. They were covered with dark green, almost black, fur—white curls where the laser had singed. They appeared to have three legs and an arm. The only ornament to their shaggy heads was a mouth, wet black orifice filled with flat black teeth. They were thoroughly repulsive, but their worst feature was not a difference from human beings, but a similarity. . . .Whenever the laser had opened a body cavity, milk-white glistening veined globes and coils of organs spilled out, and their blood was dark clotting red.

"Rogers, take a look. Taurans or not?"

Rogers knelt by one of the disemboweled creatures and opened a flat plastic box, filled with glittering dissecting tools. She selected a scalpel. "One way we might be able to find out." Doc Wilson watched over her shoulder as she methodically slit the membrane covering several organs.

"Here." She held up a blackish fibrous mass between two fingers, a parody of daintiness through all that armor.

"So?"

"It's grass, Sergeant. If the Taurans eat the grass and breathe the air, they certainly found a planet remarkably like their home." She tossed it away. "They're animals, Sergeant, just fucken animals."

"I don't know," Doc Wilson said. "Just because they walk around on all fours, threes maybe, and eat grass . . ."

"Well, let's check out the brain." She found one that had been hit in the head and scraped the superficial black char from the wound. "Look at that."

It was almost solid bone. She tugged and ruffled the hair all over the head of another one. "What the hell does it use for sensory organs? No eyes, or ears, or . . ." She stood up.

"Nothing in that fucken head but a mouth and ten centimeters of skull. To protect nothing, not a fucken thing."

"If I could shrug, I'd shrug," the doctor said. "It doesn't prove anything—a brain doesn't have to look like a mushy walnut and it doesn't have to be in the head. Maybe that skull isn't bone, maybe *that's* the brain, some crystal lattice . . ."

"Yeah, but the fucken stomach's in the right place, and if those aren't intestines I'll eat—"

"Look," Cortez said, "this is real interesting, but all we need to know is whether that thing's dangerous, then we've gotta move on; we don't have all—"

"They aren't dangerous," Rogers began. "They don't—"

"Medic! DOC!" Somebody back at the firing line was waving his arms. Doc sprinted back to him, the rest of us following.

"What's wrong?" He had reached back and unclipped his medical kit on the run.

"It's Ho. She's out."

Doc swung open the door on Ho's biomedical monitor. He didn't have to look far. "She's dead."

"Dead?" Cortez said. "What the hell—"

"Just a minute." Doc plugged a jack into the monitor and fiddled with some dials on his kit. "Everybody's biomed readout is stored for twelve hours. I'm running it backwards, should be able to—there!"

"What?"

"Four and a half minutes ago—must have been when you opened fire—Jesus!"

"Well?"

"Massive cerebral hemorrhage. No . . ." He watched the dials. "No . . .warning, no indication of anything out of the ordinary; blood pressure up, pulse up, but normal under the circumstances . . . nothing to . . . indicate—" He reached down and popped her suit. Her fine oriental features were distorted in a horrible grimace, both gums showing. Sticky fluid ran from under her collapsed eyelids, and a trickle of blood still dripped from each ear. Doc Wilson closed the suit back up.

"I've never seen anything like it. It's as if a bomb went off in her skull."

"Oh fuck," Rogers said, "she was Rhine-sensitive, wasn't she."

"That's right," Cortez sounded thoughtful. "All right, everybody listen up. Platoon leaders, check your platoons and see if anybody's missing, or hurt. Anybody else in seventh?"

"I . . . I've got a splitting headache, Sarge," Lucky said.

Four others had bad headaches. One of them affirmed that he was slightly Rhine-sensitive. The others didn't know.

"Cortez, I think it's obvious," Doc Wilson said, "that we should give these . . . monsters wide berth, especially shouldn't harm any more of them. Not with five people susceptible to whatever apparently killed Ho."

"Of course, God damn it, I don't need anybody to tell me that. We'd better get moving. I just filled the captain in on what happened; he agrees that we'd better get as far away from here as we can, before we stop for the night.

"Let's get back in formation and continue on the same bearing. Fifth platoon, take over point; second, come back to the rear. Everybody else, same as before."

"What about Ho?" Lucky asked.

"She'll be taken care of. From the ship."

After we'd gone half a klick, there was a flash and rolling thunder. Where Ho had been came a wispy luminous mushroom cloud boiling up to disappear against the gray sky.

13.

We stopped for the "night"—actually, the sun wouldn't set for another seventy hours—atop a slight rise some ten klicks from where we had killed the aliens. But they weren't aliens, I had to remind myself—*we* were.

Two platoons deployed in a ring around the rest of us, and we flopped down exhausted. Everybody was allowed four hours' sleep and had two hours' guard duty.

Potter came over and sat next to me. I chinned her frequency.

"Hi, Marygay."

"Oh, William," her voice over the radio was hoarse and cracking. "God, it's so horrible."

"It's over now—"

"I killed one of them, the first instant, I shot it right in the, in the . . ."

I put my hand on her knee. The contact had a plastic click and I jerked it back, visions of machines embracing, copulating. "Don't feel singled out, Marygay; whatever guilt there is, is . . . belongs evenly to all of us, . . . but a triple portion for Cor—"

"You privates quit jawin' and get some sleep. You both pull guard in two hours."

"OK, Sarge." Her voice was so sad and tired I couldn't bear it. I felt if I could only touch her, I could drain off the sadness like ground wire draining current, but we were each trapped in our own plastic world—

"G'night, William."

"Night." It's almost impossible to get sexually excited inside a suit, with the relief tube and all the silver chloride sensors poking you, but somehow this was my body's response to the emotional impotence, maybe remembering more pleasant sleeps with Marygay, maybe feeling that in the midst of all this death, personal death could be very soon, cranking up the procreative derrick for one last try . . . lovely thoughts like this. I fell asleep and dreamed that I was a machine, mimicking the functions of life, creaking and clanking my clumsy way through a world, people too polite to say anything but giggling behind my back, and the little man who sat inside my head pulling the levers and clutches and watching the dials, he was hopelessly mad and was storing up hurts for the day—

"Mandella—wake up, goddammit, your shift!"

I shuffled over to my place on the perimeter to watch for god knows what . . . but I was so weary I couldn't keep my eyes open. Finally I tongued a stimtab, knowing I'd pay for it later.

For over an hour I sat there, scanning my sector left, right, near, far, the scene never changing, not even a breath of wind to stir the grass.

Then suddenly the grass parted and one of the three-legged creatures was right in front of me. I raised my finger but didn't squeeze.

48

"Movement!"

"Movement!"

"Jesus Chri—there's one right—"

"HOLD YOUR FIRE! f' shit's sake don't shoot!"

"Movement."

"Movement." I looked left and right, and as far as I could see, every perimeter guard had one of the blind, dumb creatures standing right in front of him.

Maybe the drug I'd taken to stay awake made me more sensitive to whatever they did. My scalp crawled and I felt a formless *thing* in my mind, the feeling you get when somebody has said something and you didn't quite hear it, want to respond, but the opportunity to ask him to repeat it is gone.

The creature sat back on its haunches, leaning forward on the one front leg. Big green bear with a withered arm. Its power threaded through my mind, spiderwebs, echo of night terrors, trying to communicate, trying to destroy me, I couldn't know.

"All right, everybody on the perimeter, fall back, slow. Don't make any quick gestures. . . . Anybody got a headache or anything?"

"Sergeant, this is Hollister." Lucky.

"They're trying to say something . . . I can almost . . . no, just . . ."

"All I can get is that they think we're, think we're . . . well, *funny.* They're not afraid."

"You mean the one in front of you isn't—"

"No, the feeling comes from all of them, they're all thinking the same thing. Don't ask me how I know, I just do."

"Maybe they thought it was funny, what they did to Ho."

"Maybe. I don't feel they're dangerous. Just curious about us."

"Sergeant, this is Bohrs."

"Yeah."

"The Taurans've been here at least a year—maybe they've learned how to communicate with these . . . overgrown teddy bears. They might be spying on us, might be sending back—"

"I don't think they'd show themselves if that were the

case," Lucky said. "They can obviously hide from us pretty well when they want to."

"Anyhow," Cortez said, "if they're spies, the damage has been done. Don't think it'd be smart to take any action against them. I know you'd all like to see 'em dead for what they did to Ho, so would I, but we'd better be careful."

I didn't want to see them dead, but I'd just as soon not have seen them in any condition. I was walking backwards slowly, toward the middle of camp. The creature didn't seem disposed to follow. Maybe he just knew we were surrounded. He was pulling up grass with his arm and munching.

"OK, all of you platoon leaders, wake everybody up, get a roll count. Let me know if anybody's been hurt. Tell your people we're moving out in one minute."

I don't know what Cortez had expected, but of course the creatures followed right along. They didn't keep us surrounded; just had twenty or thirty following us all the time. Not the same ones, either. Individuals would saunter away, and new ones would join the parade. It was pretty obvious that *they* weren't going to tire out.

We were each allowed one stimtab. Without it, no one could have marched an hour. A second pill would have been welcome after the edge started to wear off, but the mathematics of the situation forbade it; we were still thirty klicks from the enemy base, fifteen hours' marching at the least. And though you could stay awake and energetic for a hundred hours on the tabs, aberrations of judgment and perception snowballed after the second one, until *in extremis* the most bizarre hallucinations would be taken at face value, and a person could fidget for hours deciding whether to have breakfast.

Under artificial stimulation, the company traveled with great energy for the first six hours, was slowing by the seventh, and ground to an exhausted halt after nine hours and nineteen kilometers. The teddy bears had never lost sight of us and, according to Lucky, had never stopped "broadcasting." Cortez's decision was that we would stop for seven hours, each platoon taking one hour of perimeter guard. I was never so glad to have been in the seventh platoon, as we stood guard the last

50

shift and thus were able to get six hours of uninterrupted sleep.

In the few moments I lay awake after finally lying down, the thought came to me that the next time I closed my eyes could well be the last. And partly because of the drug hangover, mostly because of the past day's horrors, I found that I really didn't give a shit.

14.

Our first contact with the Taurans came during my shift.

The teddy bears were still there when I woke up and replaced Doc Jones on guard. They'd gone back to their original formation, one in front of each guard position. The one who was waiting for me seemed a little larger than normal, but otherwise looked just like all the others. All the grass had been cropped where he was sitting, so he occasionally made forays to the left or right. But he always returned to sit right in front of me, you would say *staring* if he had had anything to stare with.

We had been facing each other for about fifteen minutes when Cortez's voice rumbled:

"Awright everybody, wake up and get hid!"

I followed instinct and flopped to the ground and rolled into a tall stand of grass.

"Enemy vessel overhead." His voice was almost laconic.

Strictly speaking, it wasn't really overhead, but rather passing somewhat east of us. It was moving slowly, maybe a hundred klicks per hour, and looked like a broomstick surrounded by a dirty soap bubble. The creature riding it was a little more human-looking than the teddy bears, but still no prize. I cranked my image amplifier up to forty log two for a closer look.

He had two arms and two legs, but his waist was so small you could encompass it with both hands. Under the tiny waist was a large horseshoe-shaped pelvic structure nearly a meter wide, from which dangled two long skinny legs with no apparent knee joint. Above that waist his body swelled out again, to a chest no smaller

51

than the huge pelvis. His arms looked suprisingly human, except that they were too long and undermuscled. There were too many fingers on his hands. Shoulderless, neckless. His head was a nightmarish growth that swelled like a goiter from his massive chest. Two eyes that looked like clusters of fish eggs, a bundle of tassles instead of a nose, and a rigidly open hole that might have been a mouth sitting low down where his adam's apple should have been. Evidently the soap bubble contained an amenable environment, as he was wearing absolutely nothing except his ridged hide, that looked like skin submerged too long in hot water, then dyed a pale orange. "He" had no external genitalia, but nothing that might hint of mammary glands. So we opted for the male pronoun by default.

Obviously, he either didn't see us or thought we were part of the herd of teddy bears. He never looked back at us, but just continued in the same direction we were headed, .05 rad east of north.

"Might as well go back to sleep now, if you can sleep after looking at *that* thing. We move out at 0435." Forty minutes.

Because of the planet's opaque cloud cover, there had been no way to tell, from space, what the enemy base looked like or how big it was. We only knew its position, the same way we knew the position the scoutships were supposed to land on. So it too could easily have been underwater, or underground.

But some of the drones were reconnaissance ships as well as decoys: and in their mock attacks on the base, one managed to get close enough to take a picture. Captain Stott beamed down a diagram of the place to Cortez—the only one with a visor in his suit—when we were five klicks from the bases's "radio" position. We stopped and he called all the platoon leaders in with the seventh platoon to confer. Two teddy bears loped in, too. We tried to ignore them.

"OK, the captain sent down some pictures of our objective. I'm going to draw a map; you platoon leaders copy." They took pads and styli out of their leg pockets, while Cortez unrolled a large plastic mat. He gave it a shake to randomize any residual charge, and turned on his stylus.

"Now, we're coming from this direction." He put an arrow at the bottom of the sheet. "First thing we'll hit is this row of huts, probably billets or bunkers, but who the hell knows. . . . Our initial objective is to destroy these buildings—the whole base is on a flat plain; there's no way we could really sneak by them."

"Potter here. Why can't we jump over them?"

"Yeah, we could do that, and wind up completely surrounded, cut to ribbons. We take the buildings.

"After we do that . . . all I can say is that we'll have to think on our feet. From the aerial reconnaissance, we can figure out the function of only a couple of buildings—and that stinks. We might wind up wasting a lot of time demolishing the equivalent of an enlisted-men's bar, ignoring a huge logistic computer because it looks like . . . a garbage dump or something."

"Mandella here," I said. "Isn't there a spaceport of some kind—seems to me we ought to . . ."

"I'll *get* to that, damn it. There's a ring of these huts all around the camp, so we've got to break through somewhere. This place'll be closest, less chance of giving away our position before we attack.

"There's nothing in the whole place that actually looks like a weapon. That doesn't mean anything, though; you could hide a gigawatt laser in each of those huts.

"Now, about five hundred meters from the huts, in the middle of the base, we'll come to this big flower-shaped structure." Cortez drew a large symmetrical shape that looked like the outline of a flower with seven petals. "What the hell this is, your guess is as good as mine. There's only one of them, though, so we don't damage it any more than we have to. Which means . . . we blast it to splinters if I think it's dangerous.

"Now, as far as your spaceport, Mandella, is concerned—there just isn't one. Nothing.

"That cruiser the *Hope* caulked had probably been left in orbit, like ours has to be. If they have any equivalent of a scoutship, or drone missiles, they're either not kept here or they're well hidden."

"Bohrs here. Then what did they attack with, while we were coming down from orbit?"

"I wish we knew, Private.

53

"Obviously, we don't have any way of estimating their numbers, not directly. Recon pictures failed to show a single Tauran on the grounds of the base. Meaning nothing, because it *is* an alien environment. Indirectly, though . . . we count the number of broomsticks, those flying things.

"There are fifty-one huts, and each has at most one broomstick. Four don't have any parked outside, but we located three at various other parts of the base. Maybe this indicates that there are fifty-one Taurans, one of whom was outside the base when the picture was taken."

"Keating here. Or fifty-one officers."

"That's right—maybe fifty thousand infantrymen stacked in one of these buildings. Now way to tell. Maybe ten Taurans, each with five broomsticks, to use according to his mood.

"We've got one thing in our favor, and that's communications. They evidently use a frequency modulation of magahertz electromagnetic radiation."

"Radio!"

"That's right, whoever you are. Identify yourself when you speak. So it's quite possible that they can't detect our phased-neutrino communications. Also, just prior to the attack, the *Hope* is going to deliver a nice dirty fission bomb; detonate it in the upper atmosphere right over the base. That'll restrict them to line-of-sight communications for some time; even those will be full of static."

"Why don't . . . Tate here . . . why don't they just drop the bomb right in their laps. Save us a lot of—"

"That doesn't even deserve an answer, Private. But the answer is, they might. And you better hope they don't. If they caulk the base, it'll be for the safety of the *Hope*. *After* we've attacked, and probably before we're far enough away for it to make much difference.

"We keep that from happening by doing a good job. We have to reduce the base to where it can no longer function; at the same time, leave as much intact as possible. And take one prisoner."

"Potter here. You mean, at least one prisoner."

"I mean what I say. One only. Potter . . . you're relieved of your platoon. Send Chavez up."

"All right, Sergeant." The relief in her voice was unmistakable.

Cortez continued with his map and instructions. There was one other building whose function was pretty obvious; it had a large steerable dish antenna on top. We were to destroy it as soon as the grenadiers got in range.

The attack plan was very loose. Our signal to begin would be the flash of the fission bomb. At the same time, several drones would converge on the base, so we could see what their antispacecraft defenses were. We would try to reduce the effectiveness of those defenses without destroying them completely.

Immediately after the bomb and the drones, the grenadiers would vaporize a line of seven huts. Everybody would break through the hole into the base . . . and what would happen after that was anybody's guess.

Ideally, we'd sweep from that end of the base to the other, destroying certain targets, caulking all but one Tauran. But that was unlikely to happen, as it depended on the Taurans' offering very little resistance.

On the other hand, if the Taurans showed obvious superiority from the begining, Cortez would give the order to scatter. Everybody had a different compass bearing for retreat—we'd blossom out in all directions, the survivors to rendezvous in a valley some forty klicks east of the base. Then we'd see about a return engagement, after the *Hope* softened the base up a bit.

"One last thing," Cortez rasped. "Maybe some of you feel the way Potter evidently does, maybe some of your men feel that way . . . that we ought to go easy, not make this so much of a bloodbath. Mercy is a luxury, a weakness we can't afford to indulge in at this stage of the war. *All* we know about the enemy is that they have killed seven hundred and ninety-eight humans. They haven't shown any restraint in attacking our cruisers, and it'd be foolish to expect any this time, this first ground action.

"*They* are responsible for the lives of all of your comrades who died in training, and for Ho, and for all the others who are surely going to die today. I can't *understand* anybody who wants to spare them. But that doesn't make any difference. You have your orders and, what the hell, you might as well know, all of you have a post-hypnotic suggestion that I will trigger by a phrase, just before the battle. It will make your job easier."

"Sergeant . . ."

"Shut up. We're short on time; get back to your platoons and brief them. We move out in five minutes."

The platoon leaders returned to their men, leaving Cortez and ten of us—plus three teddy bears, milling around, getting in the way.

15.

We took the last five klicks very carefully, sticking to the highest grass, running across occasional clearings. When we were 500 meters from where the base was supposed to be, Cortez took the third platoon forward to scout, while the rest of us laid low.

Cortez's voice came over the general freak: "Looks pretty much like we expected. Advance in a file, crawling. When you get to the third platoon, follow your squad leader to the left or right."

We did that and wound up with a string of eighty-three people in a line roughly perpendicular to the direction of attack. We were pretty well hidden, except for the dozen or so teddy bears that mooched along the line, munching grass.

There was no sign of life inside the base. All of the buildings were windowless and a uniform shiny white. The huts that were our first objective were large feature-less half-buried eggs some sixty meters apart. Cortez assigned one to each grenadier.

We were broken into three fire teams: team *A* consisted of platoons two, four, and six; team *B* was one, three, and five; the command platoon was team *C*.

"Less than a minute now—filters down!—when I say 'fire,' grenadiers, take out your targets. God help you if you miss."

There was a sound like a giant's belch, and a stream of five or six iridescent bubbles floated up from the flow-er-shaped building. They rose with increasing speed until they were almost out of sight, then shot off to the south, over our heads. The ground was suddenly bright, and for the first time in a long time, I saw my shadow, a long one pointed north. The bomb had gone off prematurely. I just had time to think that it didn't make too much difference; it'd still make alphabet soup out of their communications—

"Drones!" A ship came screaming in just about tree level, and a bubble was in the air to meet it. When they contacted, the bubble popped and the drone exploded into a million tiny fragments. Another one came from the opposite side and suffered the same fate.

"FIRE!" Seven bright glares of 500-microton grenades and a sustained concussion that surely would have killed an unprotected man.

"Filters up." Gray haze of smoke and dust. Clods of dirt falling with a sound like heavy raindrops.

"Listen up:

> 'Scots, wha hae wi' Wallace bled;
> Scots, wham Bruce has aften led,
> Welcome to your gory bed,
> Or to victory!' "

I hardly heard him for trying to keep track of what was going on in my skull. I knew it was just post-hypnotic suggestion, even remembered the session in Missouri when they'd implanted it, but that didn't make it any less compelling. My mind reeled under the strong pseudo-memories: shaggy hulks that were Taurans (not at all what we now knew they looked like) boarding a colonists' vessel, eating babies while mothers watched in screaming terror (the colonists never took babies; they wouldn't stand the acceleration), then raping the women to death with huge veined purple members (ridiculous that they would feel desire for humans), holding the men down while they plucked flesh from their living bodies and gobbled it (as if they could assimilate the alien protein) . . . a hundred grisly details as sharply remembered as the events of a minute ago, ridiculously overdone and logically absurd. But while my conscious mind was rejecting the silliness, somewhere much deeper, down in that sleeping animal where we keep our real

57

motives and morals, something was thirsting for alien blood, secure in the conviction that the noblest thing a man could do would be to die killing one of those horrible monsters. . . .

I knew it was all purest soyashit, and I hated the men who had taken such obscene liberties with my mind, but I could even *hear* my teeth grinding, feel my cheeks frozen in a spastic grin, blood-lust . . . A teddy bear walked in front of me, looking dazed. I started to raise my laser-finger, but somebody beat me to it and the creature's head exploded in a cloud of gray splinters and blood.

Lucky groaned, half-whining, "Dirty . . . filthy fucken bastards." Lasers flared and crisscrossed, and all of the teddy bears fell dead.

"Watch it, goddamnit," Cortez screamed. *"Aim* those fuckin things—they aren't toys!

"Team *A,* move out—into the craters to cover *B.*"

Somebody was laughing and sobbing. "What the fuck is wrong with *you,* Petrov?" Strange to hear Cortez cussing.

I twisted around and saw Petrov, behind and to my left, lying in a shallow hole, digging frantically with both hands, crying and gurgling.

"Fuck," Cortez said. "Team *B!* Ten meters past the craters, get down in a line. Team *C*—into the craters with *A.*"

I scrambled up and covered the hundred meters in twelve amplified strides. The craters were practically large enough to hide a scoutship, some ten meters in diameter. I jumped to the opposite side of the hole and landed next to a fellow named Chin. He didn't even look around when I landed, just kept scanning the base for signs of life.

"Team *A*—ten meters, past team *B,* down in line." Just as he finished, the building in front of us burped, and a salvo of the bubbles fanned out toward our lines. Most people saw it coming and got down, but Chin was just getting up to make his rush and stepped right into one.

It grazed the top of his helmet and disappeared with a faint pop. He took one step backwards and toppled over the edge of the crater, trailing an arc of blood and brains. Lifeless, spreadeagled, he slid halfway to the bottom, shoveling dirt into the perfectly symmetrical hole where the bubble had chewed indiscriminately through plastic, hair, skin, bone and brain.

"Everybody hold it. Platoon leaders, casualty report . . . check . . . check, check . . . check, check, check . . . check. We have three deaders. Wouldn't be *any* if you'd have kept low. So everybody grab dirt when you hear that thing go off. Team *A*, complete the rush."

They completed the maneuver without incident. "OK. Team *C*, rush to where *B* . . . hold it! Down!"

Everybody was already hugging the ground. The bubbles slid by in a smooth arc about two meters off the ground. They went serenely over our heads and, except for one that made toothpicks out of a tree, disappeared in the distance.

"*B*, rush past *A* ten meters. *C*, take over *B*'s place. You *B* grenadiers, see if you can reach the Flower."

Two grenades tore up the ground thirty or forty meters from the structure. In a good imitation of panic, it started belching out a continuous stream of bubbles—still, none coming lower than two meters off the ground. We kept hunched down and continued to advance.

Suddenly, a seam appeared in the building and widened to the size of a large door. Taurans came swarming out.

"Grenadiers, hold your fire. *B* team, laser fire to the left and right—keep'm bunched up. *A* and *C*, rush down the center."

One Tauran died trying to run through a laser beam. The others stayed where they were.

In a suit, it's pretty awkward to run and keep your head down at the same time. You have to go from side to side, like a skater getting started; otherwise you'll be airborne. At least one person, somebody in *A* team, bounced too high and suffered the same fate as Chin.

I was feeling pretty fenced-in and trapped, with a wall of laser fire on each side and a low ceiling that meant death to touch. But in spite of myself, I felt happy, euphoric, finally getting the chance to kill some of those villainous baby-eaters. Knowing it was soyashit.

They weren't fighting back, except for the rather ineffective bubbles (obviously not designed as an anti-personnel weapon), and they didn't retreat back into the building, either. They milled around, about a hundred of them, and watched us get closer. A couple of grenades would caulk them all, but I guess Cortez was thinking about the prisoner.

"OK, when I say 'go,' we're going to flank 'em. *B* team will hold fire. . . . Second and fourth platoons to the right, sixth and seventh to the left. *B* team will move forward in line to box them in.

"Go!" We peeled off to the left. As soon as the lasers stopped, the Taurans bolted, running in a group on a collision course with our flank.

"*A* team, down and fire! Don't shoot until you're sure of your aim—if you miss you might hit a friendly. And fer Chris' sake save me one!"

It was a horrifying sight, that herd of monsters bearing down on us. They were running in great leaps—the bubbles avoiding them—and they all looked like the one we saw earlier, riding the broomstick; naked except for an almost transparent sphere around their whole bodies, that moved along with them. The right flank started firing, picking off individuals in the rear of the pack.

Suddenly a laser flared through the Taurans from the other side, somebody missing his mark. There was a horrible scream, and I looked down the line to see someone—I think it was Perry—writhing on the ground, right hand over the smoldering stump of his left arm, seared off just below the elbow. Blood sprayed through his fingers, and the suit, its camouflage circuits scrambled, flickered black-white-jungle-desert-green-gray. I don't know how long I stared—long enough for the medic to run over and start giving aid—but when I looked up the Taurans were almost on top of me.

My first shot was wild and high, but it grazed the top of the leading Tauran's protective bubble. The bubble disappeared and the monster stumbled and fell to the ground, jerking spasmodically. Foam gushed out of his mouth-hole, first white, then streaked red. With one last jerk he became rigid and twisted backwards, almost to the shape of a horseshoe. His long scream, a high-pitched whistle, stopped just as his comrades trampled over him. I hated myself for smiling.

It was slaughter, even though our flank was outnumbered five to one. They kept coming without faltering, even when they had to climb over the drift of bodies and parts of bodies that piled up high, parallel to our flank. The ground between us was slick red with Tauran blood —all God's children got hemoglobin—and like the teddy bears, their guts looked pretty much like guts to my untrained eye. My helmet reverberated with hysterical laughter while we slashed them to gory chunks, and I almost didn't hear Cortez:

"Hold your fire—I said HOLD IT, goddammit! *Catch* a couple of the bastards, they won't hurt you."

I stopped shooting and eventually so did everybody else. When the next Tauran jumped over the smoking pile of meat in front of me, I dove to try to tackle him around those spindly legs.

It was like hugging a big, slippery balloon. When I tried to drag him down, he popped out of my arms and kept running.

We managed to stop one of them by the simple expedient of piling half-a-dozen people on top of him. By that time the others had run through our line and were headed for the row of large cylindrical tanks that Cortez had said were probably for storage. A little door had opened in the base of each one.

"We've *got* our prisoner," Cortez shouted. *"Kill!"*

They were fifty meters away and running hard, difficult targets. Lasers slashed around them, bobbing high and low. One fell, sliced in two, but the others, about ten of them, kept going and were almost to the doors when the grenadiers started firing.

They were still loaded with 500-mike bombs, but a near miss wasn't enough—the concussion would just send them flying, unhurt in their bubbles.

"The buildings! Get the fucken buildings!" The grenadiers raised their aim and let fly, but the bombs only seemed to scorch the white outside of the structures until, by chance, one landed in a door. That split the building just as if it had a seam; the two halves popped away and a cloud of machinery flew into the air, accompanied by a huge pale flame that rolled up and disappeared in an instant. Then the others all concentrated on the doors, except for potshots at some of the Taurans, not so much to get them as to blow them away before they could get inside. They seemed awfully eager.

All this time, we were trying to get the Taurans with laser fire, while they weaved and bounced around trying to get into the structures. We moved in as close to them as we could without putting ourselves in danger from the grenade blasts, yet too far away for good aim.

Still, we were getting them one by one and managed to destroy four of the seven buildings. Then, when there were only two aliens left, a nearby grenade blast flung one of them to within a few meters of a door. He dove in and several grenadiers fired salvos after him, but they all fell short or detonated harmlessly on the side. Bombs were falling all around, making an awful racket, but the sound was suddenly drowned out by a great sigh, like a giant's intake of breath, and where the building had been was a thick cylindrical cloud of smoke, solid-looking, dwindling away into the stratosphere, straight as if laid down by a ruler. The other Tauran had been right at the base of the cylinder; I could see pieces of him flying. A second later, a shock wave hit us and I rolled helplessly, pinwheeling, to smash into the pile of Tauran bodies and roll beyond.

I picked myself up and panicked for a second when I saw there was blood all over my suit—when I realized it was only alien blood, I relaxed but felt unclean.

"Catch the bastard! Catch him!" In the confusion, the Tauran had gotten free and was running for the grass. One platoon was chasing after him, losing ground, but then all of *B* team ran over and cut him off. I jogged over to join in the fun.

There were four people on top of him, and a ring around them of about fifty people, watching the struggle.

"Spread out, damnit! There might be a thousand more of them waiting to get us in one place." We dispersed, grumbling. By unspoken agreement we were all sure that there were no more live Taurans on the face of the planet.

Cortez was walking toward the prisoner while I backed away. Suddenly the four men collapsed in a pile on top of the creature. . . . Even from my distance I could see the foam spouting from his mouth-hole. His bubble had popped. Suicide.

"Damn!" Cortez was right there. "Get off that bastard." The four men got off and Cortez used his laser to slice the monster into a dozen quivering chunks. Heartwarming sight.

"That's all right, though, we'll find another one—everybody! Back in the arrowhead formation. Combat assault, on the Flower."

Well, we assaulted the Flower, which had evidently run out of ammunition (it was still belching, but no bubbles), and it was empty. We scurried up ramps and through corridors, fingers at the ready, like kids playing soldier. There was nobody home.

The same lack of response at the antenna installation, the "Salami," and twenty other major buildings, as well as the forty-four perimeter huts still intact. So we had "captured" dozens of buildings, mostly of incomprehensible purpose, but failed in our main mission, capturing a Tauran for the xenologists to experiment with. Oh well, they could have all the bits and pieces they'd ever want. That was something.

After we'd combed every last square centimeter of the base, a scoutship came in with the real exploration crew, the scientists. Cortez said, "All right, snap out of it," and the hypnotic compulsion fell away.

At first it was pretty grim. A lot of the people, like Lucky and Marygay, almost went crazy with the memories of bloody murder multiplied a hundred times. Cortez ordered everybody to take a sed-tab, two for the ones most upset. I took two without being specifically ordered to do so.

Because it *was* murder, unadorned butchery—once we had the anti-spacecraft weapon doped out, we hadn't been in any danger. The Taurans hadn't seemed to have any conception of person-to-person fighting. We had just herded them up and slaughtered them, the first encounter between mankind and another intelligent species. Maybe it was the second encounter, counting the teddy bears. What might have happened if we had sat down and tried to communicate? But they got the same treatment.

I spent a long time after that telling myself over and over that it hadn't been *me* who so gleefully carved up those frightened, stampeding creatures. Back in the twentieth century, they had established to everybody's satisfaction that "I was just following orders" was an inadeqaute excuse for inhuman conduct . . . but what can you do when the orders come from deep down in that puppet master of the unconscious?

Worst of all was the feeling that perhaps my actions weren't all that inhuman. Ancestors only a few generations back would have done the same thing, even to their fellow men, without any hypnotic conditioning.

I was disgusted with the human race, disgusted with the army and horrified at the prospect of living with myself for another century or so. . . . Well, there was always brainwipe.

A ship with a lone Tauran survivor had escaped and had gotten away clean, the bulk of the planet shielding it from *Earth's Hope* while it dropped into Aleph's collapsar field. Escaped home, I guessed, wherever that was, to report what twenty men with hand-weapons could do to a hundred fleeing on foot, unarmed.

I suspected that the next time humans met Taurans in ground combat, we would be more evenly matched. And I was right.

SERGEANT
MANDELLA
2007-2024 A. D.

Scared? Oh yes, I was scared—and who wouldn't be? Only a fool or a suicide or a robot. Or a line officer.

Submajor Stott paced back and forth behind the small podium in the assembly room-chop-hall-gymnasium of the *Anniversary*. We'd made our final collapsar jump, from Tet-38 to Yod-4. We were decelerating at $1\frac{1}{2}$ gravities, and our velocity relative to that collapsar was a respectable .90c. We were being chased.

"I wish you people would relax for a while and trust the ship's computer. The Tauran vessel at any rate will not be within strike range for another two weeks, and if you keep moping around for two weeks neither you nor your men will be in any condition to fight when the time comes. Fear is a contagious disease. Mandella!"

He was always careful to call me "Sergeant" Mandella in front of the company. But everybody at this briefing was a squad leader or more; not a private in the bunch. So he dropped the honorifics. "Yes, sir."

"Mandella, you are responsible for the psychological as well as the physical efficiency of the men and women in your squad. Assuming that you are aware of the morale problem building aboard this vessel, *and* assuming that your squad is not immune . . . what have you done about it?"

"As far as my squad is concerned, sir?"

He looked at me for a long moment. "Of course."

"We talk it out, sir."

"And have you arrived at any dramatic conclusion?"

"Meaning no disrespect, sir, I think the major problem is obvious. My people have been cooped up in this ship, hell, everybody has, for fourteen—"

"Ridiculous. Every one of us has been adequately conditioned against the pressures of living in close quarters, *and* the enlisted men have the privilege of confraternity." That was a delicate way of putting it. "Officers must remain celibate and yet *we* have no morale problem."

67

If he thought his officers were celibate, he should have sat down and had a long talk with Lieutenant Harmony. Maybe he just meant line officers, though, Cortez and himself. Fifty percent right, probably. Cortez was rather friendly with Corporal Kamehameha.

"The therapists reinforced your conditioning in this regard," he continued, "while they were working to erase the hate-conditioning—everybody knows how *I* feel about that—and they may be misguided but they are skilled."

"Corporal Potter." He called her by rank to remind everybody why she hadn't been promoted along with the rest of us. Too soft. "Have you 'talked it out' with your people, too?"

"We've discussed it. Sir."

The submajor could "glare mildly" at people. He glared mildly at Marygay until she continued.

"I don't think Sergeant Mandella was finding fault with the condi—"

"Sergeant Mandella can speak for himself. I want your opinion. Your observations." He said it in a way that indicated he didn't want them much.

"Well, I don't think it's the fault of the conditioning either, sir. We don't have any trouble living together. Everybody is just impatient, tired of doing the same thing week after week."

"They're anxious for combat, then?" No sarcasm in his voice.

"They want to get off the ship, sir, out of the routine."

"They *will* get off the ship," he said, allowing himself a small mechanical smile. "And then they'll probably be just as impatient to get back on."

It went back and forth like that for a long time. Nobody wanted to put words to the basic fact that our men and women had had over a year to brood on the upcoming battle; they could only become more and more apprehensive. And now a Tauran cruiser closing on us—we'd have to take our chances with it before we were within a month of the ground assault.

The prospect of hitting the portal planet and playing soldier was bad enough. But at least you have a chance,

TABLE OF ORGANIZATION:

Strike Force Alpha

Yod-4 Campaign

First Platoon

COMMANDING:	SM Stott	CMD Martinez
2ECHN:	1LT Cortez	
3ECHN:	FFSGT (vac)	
		FIELD MEDIC
4ECHN:	2LT (vac)	2LT Wilson MD
5ECHN:	PSgt Rogers	

6ECHN:	Sgt Mandella	Sgt Ching	Cpl Potter
	Cpl Tate	Cpl Petrov	Cpl Struve
	Cpl Yukawa	Pvt Luthuli	Pvt Kurosawa
	Pvt Hofstadter	Pvt Herz	Pvt Alexandrov
	Pvt Mulroy	Pvt Heyrovksy	Pvt Bergman
	Pvt Shockley	Pvt Katawba	Pvt Demy
	Pvt Rabi	Pvt Pauling	Pvt Stiller
		Pvt Renault	

SPECIALISTS: 1LTs Bok (CK), Levine (CPR), Pastori (PSY), Winebrenner (MED); 2LTs Harmony (MED), Princewell (DAT); 3LTs Stonewell (ARM), Theodopolis (RAD); Esg Singhe (NAV); PSgts Dalton (MAIN), Namgyal (SUP).

ISSUED STARGATE TACBD/1003-9674-1300/20 Mar 2007 SG:

BY AUTH STFCOM Commander

DIST. PRIM: All Personnel 1 PLT/STFALPHA
      SEC: All Personnel STFALPHA 6ECHN and above
      TRT: Personnel STFCOM 5ECHN and above NTK basis

By and for 4GEN Mubutu Ngako COMM

FOR THE COMMANDER
Arlathea Lincoln BGEN STFCOM
20 Mar 2007 SG

TACBD/1003/9674/1300/100 cop

fighting on the ground, to influence your own fate. This bullshit of sitting in a pod, part of the target, while the *Anniversary* played mathematical games with the Tauran ship . . . To be alive one nanosecond and dead the next because of an error in somebody's thirtieth decimal place, *that's* what was giving me trouble. But try to tell that to Stott. I'd finally had to admit to myself that he wasn't putting on a grisly little act. He actually couldn't understand the difference between fear and cowardice. Whether he'd been purposefully conditioned into that viewpoint—which I doubted—or was just plain crazy, it no longer mattered.

He was raking Ching over the coals, the same old song and dance. I fingered the fresh T/O they had given us.

I knew most of the people from the Aleph massacre. The only new ones in my platoon were Demy, Luthuli and Heyrovsky. In the company (excuse me, the "strike force") as a whole, we had twenty replacements for the nineteen people we'd lost during the Aleph raid. One amputation, four deaders and fourteen psychotics, casualties of overzealous hate-conditioning.

I couldn't get over the "20 Mar 2007" at the bottom of the T/O. I'd been in the army ten years, though it felt like less than two. Time dilation, of course. Even with the collapsar jumps, traveling from star to star eats up the calendar.

After this raid, I would probably be eligible for retirement with full pay—if I lived through the raid, and if they didn't change the rules on us. A twenty-year veteran, and only twenty-five years old.

Stott was summing up when there was a knock on the door, a single loud rap. "Enter," he said.

An ensign I vaguely knew walked in casually and handed Stott a slip of paper without saying a word. He stood there while Stott read it, slumping with just the right degree of insolence. Technically, Stott was out of his chain of command; everybody in the Navy disliked him anyhow.

Stott handed the paper back to the ensign and looked through him.

"You will alert your squads that preliminary evasive maneuvers will commence at 2010, fifty-eight minutes from now." He hadn't looked at his watch. "All personnel will be in acceleration shells by 2000. Tench . . . hut!"

We rose and, without enthusiasm, chorused, "Fuck you, sir." Idiotic.

Stott strode out of the room and the ensign followed, smirking.

I turned my ring to position *4*, my assistant squad leader's channel, and talked into it: "Tate, this is Mandella." Everyone else in the room was doing the same.

A tinny voice came out of the ring. "Tate here. What's up?"

"Get ahold of the men and tell them we have to be in the shell by 2000. Evasive maneuvers."

"Shit. They told us it'd be days."

"I guess something new came up. Maybe the Commodore has a bright idea."

"The Commodore can stuff it. You up in the lounge?"

"Yeah."

"Bring me back a cup when you come, OK? Little bit of sugar?"

"OK. Be down in about half an hour."

"Thanks. I'll start rounding 'em up."

There was a general movement toward the soya machine. I got in line behind Corporal Potter.

"What do you think, Marygay?"

"I'm just a corporal, Sarge. I'm not paid to—"

"Sure, sure. Seriously."

"Well, it doesn't have to be very complicated. Maybe the Commodore just wants us to try out the shells again."

"Once more before the real thing."

"Mm-hm. Maybe." She picked up a cup and blew into it. She looked worried, a tiny line bisecting the space between her eyebrows. "Or maybe the Taurans had a ship 'way out, waiting for us. I've wondered why they don't do it like we do at Stargate."

I shrugged. "Stargate's a different thing. It takes seven or eight cruisers, moving all the time, to cover the most probable exit angles. We can't afford to cover more than one collapsar, and neither can they."

"I don't know." She didn't say anything while she filled her cup. "Maybe we've stumbled on their version

71

of Stargate. Or maybe they have ten times as many ships. A hundred times. Who knows?"

I filled and sugared two cups, sealed one. "No way to tell." We walked back to a table, careful with the rapid sloshing of the soya in the high gravity.

"Maybe Singhe knows something," she said.

"Maybe he does. But I'd have to get to him through Rogers and Cortez. Cortez would jump down my throat if I tried to bother him now."

"Oh, I can get to Singhe directly. We . . ." She looked at me very seriously and dimpled a little bit. "We've been friends."

I sipped some scalding soya and tried to sound nonchalant. "That's where you disappeared to Wednesday night?"

"I'd have to check my roster," she said and smiled. "I think it's Mondays, Wednesdays and Fridays during months with an *r* in them. Why? You disapprove?"

"Well . . . damn it, no, of course not. But—but he's an officer! A *Navy* officer!"

"He's attached to us, and that makes him part army." She twisted her ring and said "Directory." To me: "What about you and cuddly little Miss Harmony?"

"That's not the same thing." She was whispering a directory code into the ring.

"Yes, it is. You just wanted to do it with an officer. Pervert." The ring bleated twice. Busy. "How was she?"

"Adequate." I was recovering.

"Besides, Ensign Singhe is a perfect gentleman. And not the least bit jealous."

"Neither am I," I said. "If he ever hurts you, tell me and I'll break his ass."

She smiled at me across her cup. "If Lieutenant Harmony ever hurts you, tell me and I'll break *her* ass."

"It's a deal." We shook on it solemnly.

2.

The acceleration shells were something new, installed while we rested and resupplied at Stargate. They enable us to use the ship at closer to its theoretical efficiency, the tachyon drive boosting it to over twenty-five gravities' acceleration.

Tate was waiting for me in the shell area. The rest of the squad was milling around talking. I gave him his soya.

"Thanks. Find out anything?"

"Afraid not. Except that the swabbies don't seem to be scared, and it's their show. Probably just another practice run."

He slurped some soya. "What the hell. It's all the same to us, anyhow. Sit there and get squeezed half to death. God, I hate those things."

"Oh, I don't know. They might make the infantry obsolete. Then we can all go home."

"Sure thing." The medic came by and gave me my shot.

I waited until 1950 and hollered to the squad: "Let's go. Strip down and zip up."

The shell is like a flexible space suit; at least the fittings on the inside are pretty similar. But instead of a life support package, there's a hose going into the top of the helmet and two coming out of the heels, as well as two relief tubes per suit. They're crammed in shoulder-to-shoulder on light acceleration couches; getting to your shell is like picking your way through a giant plate of olive-drab spaghetti.

When the lights in my helmet showed that everybody was suited up, I pushed the button that flooded the room. No way to see, of course, but I could imagine the pale blue solution—ethylene glycol and something else—foaming up, around and over us. The suit material, cool and dry, collapsed in to touch my skin at every point. I knew that my internal body pressure was increasing rapidly to match the increasing fluid pressure outside. That's what the shot was for: keep your cells from getting squished between the devil and the pale blue sea. You could still feel it, though. By the time my meter read 2 (external pressure equivalent to a column of water two nautical miles deep), I felt that I was at the same time being crushed and bloated. By 2005 it was at 2.7 and holding steady. When the maneuvers began at 2010, I couldn't feel the difference. I thought I saw the needle fluctuate a tiny bit, though, and wondered how much acceleration it took to make that barely visible wobble.

The major drawback of the system is that, of course, anybody caught outside of his shell when the *Anniversary* hits twenty-five gees would be just so much strawberry jam. So the guiding and the fighting have to be done by the ship's tactical computer—which does most of it anyway, but it's nice to have a human overseer.

Another small problem is that if the ship gets damaged and the pressure drops, you'll explode like a dropped melon. If it's the internal pressure, you'd be crushed to death in a microsecond.

It takes ten minutes, more or less, to get depressurized, and another two or three to get untangled and dressed. Not exactly something you can hop out of and come up fighting. Only four people have any mobility while the rest of us are trapped in our shells; that's the Navy maintenance crew. They essentially carry the whole acceleration chamber apparatus around with them, their suits becoming twenty-ton vehicles. And even they have to remain in one place while the ship is maneuvering.

The accelerating was over at 2038. A green light went on and I chinned the button to depressurize.

Marygay and I were getting dressed outside. The residual fumes from the pressurizing fluid made me unpleasantly giddy and a little nauseous.

"How'd that happen?" I pointed to an angry purple welt that ran from beneath her right breast to the opposite hipbone.

"That's the second time," she said, pinching the skin angrily. "The first one was on my rear—I think that shell doesn't fit right, gets creases."

"Maybe you've lost weight."

"Wise guy."

Our caloric intake and exercise had been rigorously monitored and controlled since suit-fitting at Stargate. You can't use a fighting suit unless the sensor-skin inside fits like a film of oil.

A wall speaker drowned out the rest of her comment. "Attention, all personnel. Attention. All army personnel echelon 6 and above and all naval personnel echelon 4 and above will report to the briefing room at 2130. Attention—"

It repeated the message twice. I went off to lie down for a few minutes while Marygay showed her bruise—and all the rest of herself—to the medic and the armorer. For the record, I didn't feel a bit jealous.

The Commodore began the briefing. "There's not much to tell, and what there is, is not good news.

"Six days ago, the Tauran vessel that is pursuing us released a drone missile. The initial acceleration was on the order of eighty gravities." He paused.

"After blasting for approximately a day, its acceleration suddenly jumped to 148 gravities." Collective gasp.

"Yesterday, it jumped again. 203 gravities. I shouldn't need to tell you that this is twice the accelerability of the enemy drones in our last encounter.

"We launched a salvo of drones, four of them, intersecting what the computer predicted to be the four most probable future trajectories of the enemy drone. One of them paid off, very near, while we were doing evasive maneuvers. We contacted and destroyed the Tauran weapon about ten million kilometers from here."

That was practically next door. "The only encouraging thing we learned from the encounter was from spectral analysis of the blast. It was no more powerful than ones we have observed in the past, so we might infer that at least their progress in explosives has not matched their progress in propulsion. Or perhaps they just didn't feel a more powerful blast to be necessary.

"This is the first manifestation of a very important effect that has heretofore been of interest only to theorists. Tell me, soldier," he pointed at Negulesco. "How long has it been since we first fought the Taurans, at Aleph?"

"That depends on your frame of reference," she answered dutifully. "To me, it's been about eight months, Commodore."

"Exactly. You've lost about nine years, though, to time dilation, while we maneuvered between collapsar jumps. In an engineering sense, as we haven't done any important research and development during that period, . . . the enemy vessel comes from our future!" He stopped to let that sink in.

"As the war progresses, this can only become more and more pronounced. The Taurans don't have any cure for relativity, though, so it will be to our benefit as often as to theirs.

"For the present, however, it is *we* who are operating with a handicap. As the Tauran pursuit vessel draws closer, this handicap will become more severe. They can simply outshoot us.

"We're going to have to do some fancy dodging. When we get within five hundred million kilometers of the enemy ship, everybody gets into his shell and we have to trust the logistic computer. It will put us through a rapid series of random changes in direction and velocity.

"I'll be blunt. As long as they have one more drone than we, they can finish us off. They haven't launched any more since that first one. Perhaps they are holding their fire"—he mopped his forehead nervously—"or maybe they only *had* one. In that case, it's we who have them.

"At any rate, all personnel will be required to be in their shells with no more than ten minutes' notice. When we get within a thousand million kilometers of the enemy, you are to stand *by* your shells. By the time we are within five hundred million kilometers, you will be in them, and all shell compounds will be flooded and pressurized. We cannot wait for anyone.

"That's all I have to say. Sub-major?"

"I'll speak to my people later, Commodore. Thank you."

"Dismissed." And none of this "fuck you, sir" nonsense. The navy thought that was a bit beneath their dignity. We stood at attention—all except Stott—until he had left the room. Then some other swabbie said "dismissed" again, and we left. I went to the NCO room for some soya, company, and maybe a little information.

There wasn't much happening but idle speculation, so I took Rogers and went off to bed. Marygay had disappeared again, hopefully trying to wheedle something out of Singhe.

3.

We had our promised get-together with the sub-major the next morning, when he more or less repeated what the commodore had said, in infantry terms and in his staccato monotone. He emphasized the fact that all we knew about the Tauran ground forces was that if their naval capability was improved, it was likely they would be able to handle us better than last time.

But that brings up an interesting point. Eight months or nine years before, we'd had a tremendous advantage: they had seemed not quite to understand what was going on. As belligerent as they has been in space, we'd expected them to be real Huns on the ground. Instead, they practically lined themselves up for slaughter. One escaped and presumably described the idea of old-fashioned in-fighting to his fellows.

But that, of course, didn't mean that the word had necessarily gotten to this particular bunch, the Taurans guarding Yod-4. The only way we know of to communicate faster than the speed of light is to physically carry a message through successive collapsar jumps. And there was no way of telling how many jumps there were between Yod-4 and the Tauran home base—so these might be just as passive as the last bunch, or might have been practicing infantry tactics for most of a decade. We would find out when we got there.

The armorer and I were helping my squad pull maintenance on their fighting suits when we passed the thousand million kilometer mark and had to go up to the shells.

We had about five hours to kill before we had to get into our cocoons. I played a game of chess with Rabi and lost. Then Rogers led the platoon in some vigorous calisthenics, probably for no other reason than to get their minds off the prospect of having to lie half-crushed in the shells for at least four hours. The longest we'd gone before was half that.

Ten minutes before the five hundred million kilometer mark, we squad leaders took over and supervised

77

buttoning everybody up. In eight minutes we were zipped and flooded and at the mercy of—or safe in the arms of—the logistic computer.

While I was lying there being squeezed, a silly thought took hold of my brain and went round and round like a charge in a superconductor: according to military formalism, the conduct of war divides neatly into two categories, tactics and logistics. Logistics has to do with with moving the troops and feeding them and just about everything except the actual fighting, which is tactics. And now we're fighting, but we don't have a *tactical* computer to guide us through the attack and defense, just a huge, super-efficient pacifistic cybernetic grocery clerk of a logistic, mark that word, *logistic* computer.

The other side of my brain, perhaps not quite as pinched, would argue that it doesn't matter what name you give to a computer, it's a pile of memory crystals, logic banks, nuts and bolts . . . If you program it to be Ghengis Khan, it is a tactical computer, even if its usual function is to monitor the stock market or control sewage conversion.

But the other voice was obdurate and said by that kind of reasoning, a man is only a hank of hair and a piece of bone and some stringy meat; no matter what kind of man he is, if you teach him well, you can take a Zen monk and turn him into a slavering bloodthirsty warrior.

Then what the hell are you, we, am I, answered the other side. A peace-loving, vacuum-welding specialist *cum* physics teacher snatched up by the Elite Conscription Act and reprogrammed to be a killing machine. You, I have killed and liked it.

But that was hypnotism, motivational conditioning, I argued back at myself. They don't do that any more.

And the only reason, I said, they don't do it is that they think you'll kill better without it. That's logic.

Speaking of logic, the original question was, why do they send a logistic computer to do a man's job? Or something like that . . . and we were off again.

The light blinked green and I chinned the switch automatically. The pressure was down to 1.3 before I real-

78

ized that it meant we were alive, we had won the first skirmish.

I was only partly right.

4.

I was belting on my tunic when my ring tingled and I held it up to listen. It was Rogers.

"Mandella, go check squad bay 3. Something went wrong; Dalton had to depressurize it from Control."

Bay 3 —that was Marygay's squad! I rushed down the corridor in bare feet and got there just as they opened the door from inside the pressure chamber and began straggling out.

The first out was Bergman. I grabbed his arm. "What the hell is going on, Bergman?"

"Huh?" He peered at me, still dazed, as everyone is when they come out of the chamber. "Oh, s'you. Mandella. I dunno. Whad'ya mean?"

I squinted in through the door, still holding on to him. "You were late, man, you depressurized late. What happened?"

He shook his head, trying to clear it. "Late? Whad' late. Uh, how late?"

I looked at my watch for the first time. "Not too—" Jesus Christ. "Uh, we zipped in at 0520, didn't we?"

"Yeah, I think that's it."

Still no Marygay among the dim figures picking their way through the ranked couches and jumbled tubing. "Um, you were only a couple of minutes late . . . but we were only supposed to be under for four hours, maybe less. It's 1050."

"Um." He shook his head again. I let go of him and stood back to let Stiller and Demy through the door.

"Everybody's late, then," Bergman said. "So we aren't in any trouble."

"Uh—" Non sequiturs. "Right, right—Hey, Stiller! You seen—"

From inside: "Medic! MEDIC!"

Somebody who wasn't Marygay was coming out. I pushed her roughly out of my way and dove through the door, landed on somebody else and clambered over to

79

where Struve, Marygay's assistant, was standing over a pod and talking very loud and fast into his ring.

"—and blood God yes we need—"

It was Marygay still lying in her suit she was

"—got the word from Dalton—"

covered every square inch of her with a uniform bright sheen of blood

"—when she didn't come out—"

it started as an angry welt up by her collarbone and was just a welt as it traveled between her breasts until it passed the sternum's support

"—I came over and popped the—"

and opened up into a cut that got deeper as it ran down over her belly and where it stopped

"—yeah, she's still—"

a few centimeters above the pubis a membraned loop of gut was protruding . . .

"—OK, left hip. Mandella—"

She was still alive, her heart palpitating, but her blood-streaked head lolled limply, eyes rolled back to white slits, bubbles of red froth appearing and popping at the corner of her mouth each time she exhaled shallowly.

"—tattooed on her left hip. Mandella! Snap out of it! Reach under her and find out what her blood—"

"TYPE O RH NEGATIVE GOD damn . . . it. Sorry—Oh negative." Hadn't I seen that tattoo ten thousand times?

Struve passed this information on and I suddenly remembered the first-aid kit on my belt, snapped it off and fumbled through it.

Stop the bleeding—protect the wound—treat for shock, that's what the book said. Forgot one, forgot one . . . *clear air passages.* She was breathing, if that's what they meant. How do you stop the bleeding or protect the wound with one measly pressure bandage when the wound is nearly a meter long? Treat for shock, that I could do. I fished out the green ampoule, laid it against her arm and pushed the button. Then I laid the sterile side of the bandage gently on top of the exposed intestine and passed the elastic strip under the small of her back, adjusted it for nearly zero tension and fastened it.

"Anything else you can do?" Struve asked.

I stood back and felt helpless. "I don't know. Can you think of anything?"

"I'm no more a medic that you are." Looking up at the door, he kneaded a fist, biceps straining. "Where the hell are they? You have morph-plex in that kit?"

"Yeah, but somebody told me not to use it for internal—"

"William?"

Her eyes were open and she was trying to lift her head. I rushed over and held her. "It'll be all right, Marygay. The medic's coming."

"What . . . all right? I'm thirsty. Water."

"No, honey, you can't have any water. Not for a while, anyhow." Not if she was headed for surgery.

"Why is all the blood?" she said in a small voice. Her head rolled back. "Been a bad girl."

"It must have been the suit," I said rapidly. "Remember earlier, the creases?"

She shook her head. "Suit?" She turned suddenly paler and retched weakly. "Water . . . William, please."

Authoritative voice behind me: "Get a sponge or a cloth soaked in water." I looked around and saw Doc Wilson with two stretcher bearers.

"First half-liter femoral," he said to no one in particular as he carefully peeked under the pressure bandage. "Follow that relief tube down a couple of meters and pinch it off. Find out if she's passed any blood."

One of the medics ran a ten-centimeter needle into Marygay's thigh and started giving her whole blood from a plastic bag.

"Sorry I'm late," Doc Wilson said tiredly. "Business is booming. What'd you say about the suit?"

"She had two minor injuries before. Suit doesn't fit quite right, creases up under pressure."

He nodded absently, checking her blood pressure. "You, anybody, give—" Somebody handed him a paper towel dripping water. "Uh, give her any medication?"

"One ampoule of No-shock."

He wadded the paper towel up loosely and put it in Marygay's hand. "What's her name?" I told him.

"Marygay, we can't give you a drink of water but you can suck on this. Now I'm going to shine a bright light in your eye." While he was looking through her pupil with a metal tube, he said, "Temperature?" and one of the medics read a number from a digital readout box and withdrew a probe. "Passed blood?"

"Yes. Some."

He put his hand lightly on the pressure bandage. "Marygay, can you roll over a little on your right side?"

"Yes," she said slowly, and put her elbow down for leverage. "No," she said and started crying.

"Now, now," he said absently and pushed up on her hip just enough to be able to see her back. "Only the one wound," he muttered. "Hell of a lot of blood."

He pressed the side of his ring twice and shook it by his ear. "Anybody up in the shop?"

"Harrison, unless he's on a call."

A woman walked up, and at first I didn't recognize her, pale and disheveled, bloodstained tunic. It was Estelle Harmony.

Doc Wilson looked up. "Any new customers, Doctor Harmony?"

"No," she said dully. "The maintenance man was a double traumatic amputation. Only lived a few minutes. We're keeping him running for transplants."

"All those others?"

"Explosive decompression." She sniffed. "Anything I can do here?"

"Yeah, just a minute." He tried his ring again. "God damn it. You don't know where Harrison is?"

"No . . . well, maybe, he might be in Surgery *B* if there was trouble with the cadaver maintenance. Think I set it up all right, though."

"Yeah, well, hell you know how . . ."

"Mark!" said the medic with the blood bag.

"One more half-liter femoral," Doc Wilson said. "Estelle, you mind taking over for one of the medics here, prepare this gal for surgery?"

"No, keep me busy."

"Good—Hopkins, go up to the shop and bring down a roller and a liter, uh, two liters isotonic fluorocarb with the primary spectrum. If they're Merck they'll say 'abdominal spectrum.'" He found a part of his sleeve with no blood on it and wiped his forehead. "If you find Harrison, send him over to surgery *A* and have him set up the anesthetic sequence for abdominal."

82

"And bring her up to *A?*"

"Right. If you can't find Harrison, get somebody"—he stabbed a finger in my direction—"this guy, to roll the patient up to *A;* you run ahead and start the sequence."

He picked up his bag and looked through it. "We could start the sequence here," he muttered. "But hell, not with paramethadone—Marygay? How do you feel?"

She was still crying. "I'm . . . hurt."

"I know," he said gently. He thought for a second and said to Estelle, "No way to tell really how much blood she lost. She may have been passing it under pressure. Also there's some pooling in the abdominal cavity. Since she's still alive I don't think she could've bled under pressure for very long. Hope no brain damage yet."

He touched the digital readout attached to Marygay's arm. "Monitor the blood pressure, and if you think it's indicated, give her five cc's vasoconstrictor. I've gotta go scrub down."

He closed his bag. "You have any vasoconstrictor besides the pneumatic ampoule?"

Estelle checked her own bag. "No, just the emergency pneumatic . . . uh . . . yes, I've got controlled dosage on the 'dilator, though."

"OK, if you have to use the 'constrictor and her pressure goes up too fast—"

"I'll give her vasodilator two cc's at a time."

"Check. Hell of a way to run things, but . . . well. If you're not too tired, I'd like you to stand by me upstairs."

"Sure." Doc Wilson nodded and left.

Estelle began sponging Marygay's belly with isopropyl alcohol. It smelled cold and clean. "Somebody gave her No-shock?"

"Yes," I said, "about ten minutes ago."

"Ah. That's why the Doc was worried—no, you did the right thing. But No-shock's got some vasoconstrictor. Five cc's more might run up an overdose." She continued silently scrubbing, her eyes coming up every few seconds to check the blood pressure monitor.

"William?" It was the first time she'd shown any sign of knowing me. "This wom—, uh, Marygay, she's your lover? Your regular lover?"

"That's right."

83

"She's very pretty." A remarkable observation, her body torn and caked with crusting blood, her face smeared where I had tried to wipe away the tears. I suppose a doctor or a woman or a lover can look beneath that and see beauty.

"Yes, she is." She had stopped crying and had her eyes squeezed shut, sucking the last bit of moisture from the paper wad.

"Can she have some more water?"

"OK, same as before. Not too much."

I went out to the locker alcove and into the head for a paper towel. Now that the fumes from the pressurizing fluid had cleared, I could smell the air. It smelled wrong. Light machine oil and burnt metal, like the smell of a metalworking shop. I wondered whether they had overloaded the airco. That had happened once before, after the first time we'd used the acceleration chambers.

Marygay took the water without opening her eyes.

"Do you plan to stay together when you get back to Earth?"

"Probably," I said. *"If* we get back to Earth. Still one more battle."

"There won't be any more battles," she said flatly. "You mean you haven't heard?"

"What?"

"Don't you know the ship was hit?"

"Hit!" Then how could any of us be alive?

"That's right." She went back to her scrubbing. "Four squad bays. Also the armor bay. There isn't a fighting suit left on the ship . . . and we can't fight in our underwear."

"What—squad bays, what happened to the people?"

"No survivors."

Thirty people. "Who was it?"

"All of the third platoon. First squad of the second platoon."

Al-Sadat, Busia, Maxwell, Negulesco. "My God."

"Thirty deaders, and they don't have the slightest notion of what caused it. Don't know but that it may happen again any minute."

"It wasn't a drone?"

"No, we got all of their drones. Got the enemy vessel, too. Nothing showed up on any of the sensors, just *blam!* and a third of the ship was torn to hell. We were lucky it wasn't the drive or the life support system." I was hardly hearing her. Penworth, LaBatt, Smithers. Christine and Frida. All dead. I was numb.

She took a blade-type razor and a tube of gel out of her bag. "Be a gentleman and look the other way," she said. "Oh, here." She soaked a square of gauze in alcohol and handed it to me. "Be useful. Do her face."

I started and, without opening her eyes, Marygay said, "That feels good. What are you doing?"

"Being a gentleman. And useful, too—"

"All personnel, attention, all personnel." There wasn't a squawk-box in the pressure chamber, but I could hear it clearly through the door to the locker alcove. "All personnel echelon 6 and above, unless directly involved in medical or maintenance emergencies, report immediately to the assembly area."

"I've got to go, Marygay."

She didn't say anything. I didn't know whether she had heard the announcement.

"Estelle," I addressed her directly, gentleman be damned. "Will you—"

"Yes. I'll let you know as soon as we can tell."

"Well."

"It's going to be all right." But her expression was grim and worried. "Now get going," she said, softly.

By the time I picked my way out into the corridor, the 'box was repeating the message for the fourth time. There was a new smell in the air, that I didn't want to identify.

5.

Halfway to the assembly area I realized what a mess I was, and ducked into the head by the NCO lounge. Corporal Kamehameha was hurriedly brushing her hair.

"William! What happened to you?"

"Nothing." I turned on a tap and looked at myself in the mirror. Dried blood smeared all over my face and tunic. "It was Marygay, Corporal Potter, her suit . . . well, evidently it got a crease, uh . . ."

85

"Dead?"

"No, just badly, uh, she's going into surgery—"

"Don't use hot water. You'll just set the stain."

"Oh. Right." I used the hot to wash my face and hand, dabbed at the tunic with cold. "Your squad's just two bays down from Al's, isn't it?"

"Yes."

"Did you see what happened?"

"No. Yes. Not *when* it happened." For the first time I noticed that she was crying, big tears rolling down her cheeks and off her chin. Her voice was even, controlled. She pulled at her hair savagely. "It's a mess."

I stepped over and put my hand on her shoulder. "DON'T touch me!" she flared and knocked my hand off with the brush. "Sorry. Let's go."

At the door to the head she touched me lightly on the arm. "William . . ." She looked at me defiantly. "I'm just glad it wasn't me. You understand? That's the only way you can look at it."

I understood, but I didn't know that I believed her.

"I can sum it up very briefly," the commodore said in a tight voice, "if only because we know so little.

"Some ten seconds after we destroyed the enemy vessel, two objects, very small objects, struck the *Anniversary* amidships. By inference, since they were not detected and we know the limits of our detection apparatus, we know that they were moving in excess of nine-tenths of the speed of light. That is to say, more precisely, their velocity vector *normal* to the axis of the *Anniversary* was greater than nine-tenths of the speed of light. They slipped in behind the repeller fields."

When the *Anniversary* is moving at relativistic speeds, it is designed to generate two powerful electromagnetic fields, one centered about five thousand kilometers from the ship and the other about ten thousand klicks away, both in line with the direction of motion of the ship. These fields are maintained by a "ramjet" effect, energy picked up from interstellar gas as we mosey along.

Anything big enough to worry about hitting (that is, anything big enough to see with a strong magnifying glass) goes through the first field and comes out with a very strong negative charge all over its surface. As it enters the second field, it's repelled away from the path of the ship. If the object is too big to be pushed around this way, we can sense it at a greater distance and maneuver out of its way.

"I shouldn't have to emphasize how formidable a weapon this is. When the *Anniversary* was struck, our rate of speed with respect to the enemy was such that we traveled our own length every ten-thousandth of a second. Further, we were jerking around erratically with a constantly changing and purely random lateral acceleration. Thus the objects that struck us must have been guided, not aimed. And the guidance system was self-contained, since there were no Taurans alive at the time they struck us. All of this in a package no larger than a small pebble.

"Most of you are too young to remember the term *future shock*. Back in the seventies, some people felt that technological progress was so rapid that people, normal people, couldn't cope with it; that they wouldn't have time to get used to the present before the future was upon them. A man named Toffler coined the term *future shock* to describe this situation." The commodore could get pretty academic.

"We're caught up in a physical situation that resembles this scholarly concept. The result has been disaster. Tragedy. And, as we discussed in our last meeting, there is no way to counter it. Relativity traps us in the enemy's past; relativity brings them from our future. We can only hope that next time, the situation will be reversed. And all we can do to help bring that about is try to get back to Stargate, and then to Earth, where specialists may be able to deduce something, some sort of counterweapon, from the nature of the damage.

"Now we could attack the Tauran's portal planet from space and perhaps destroy the base without using you infantry. But I think there would be a very great risk involved. We might be . . . shot down by whatever hit us today, and never return to Stargate with what I consider to be vital information. We could send a drone with a message detailing our assumptions about this new enemy weapon . . . but that might be inadequate. And

87

the Force would be that much further behind, technologically.

"Accordingly, we have set a course that will take us around Yod-4, keeping the collapsar as much as possible between us and the Tauran base. We will avoid contact with the enemy and return to Stargate as quickly as possible."

Incredibly, the Commodore sat down and kneaded his temples. "All of you are at least squad or section leaders. Most of you have good combat records. And I hope that some of you will be rejoining the Force after your two years are up. Those of you who do will probably be made lieutenants, and face your first real command.

"It is to these people I would like to speak for a few moments, not as your . . . as one of your commanders, but just as a senior officer and advisor.

"One cannot make command decisions simply by assessing the tactical situation and going ahead with whatever course of action will do the most harm to the enemy with a minimum of death and damage to your own men and materiel. Modern warfare has become very complex, especially during the last century. Wars are won not by a simple series of battles won, but by a complex interrelationship among military victory, economic pressures, logistic maneuvering, access to the enemy's information, political postures—dozens, literally dozens of factors."

I was hearing this, but the only thing that was getting through to my brain was that a third of our friends' lives had been snuffed out less than an hour before, and he was sitting up there giving us a lecture on military theory.

"So sometimes you have to throw away a battle in order to help win the war. This is exactly what we are going to do.

"This was not an easy decision. In fact, it was probably the hardest decision of my military career. Because, on the surface at least, it may look like cowardice.

"The logistic computer calculates that we have about a 62 percent chance of success, should we attempt to destroy the enemy base. Unfortunately, we would have only a 30 percent chance of survival—as some of the scenarios leading to success involve ramming the portal planet with the *Anniversary* at light speed." Jesus Christ.

"I hope none of you ever has to face such a decision. When we get back to Stargate, I will in all probability be court-martialed for cowardice under fire. But I honestly believe that the information that may be gained from analysis of the damage to the *Anniversary* is more important then the destruction of this one Tauran base." He sat up straight. "More important than one soldier's career."

I had to stifle an impulse to laugh. Surely "cowardice" had nothing to do with his decision. Surely he had nothing so primitive and unmilitary as a will to live.

The maintenance crew managed to patch up the huge rip in the side of the *Anniversary* and to repressurize that section. We spent the rest of the day cleaning up the area; without, of course, disturbing any of the precious evidence for which the Commodore was willing to sacrifice his career.

The hardest part was jettisoning the bodies. It wasn't so bad except for the ones whose suits had burst.

I went to Estelle's cabin the next day, as soon as she was off duty.

"It wouldn't serve any good purpose for you to see her now." Estelle sipped her drink, a mixture of ethyl alcohol, citric acid and water, with a drop of some ester that approximated the aroma of orange rind.

"Is she out of danger?"

"Not for a couple of weeks. Let me explain." She set down her drink and rested her chin on interlaced fingers. "This sort of injury would be fairly routine under normal circumstances. Having replaced the lost blood, we'd simply sprinkle some magic powder into her abdominal cavity and paste her back up. Have her hobbling around in a couple of days.

"But there are complications. Nobody's ever been injured in a pressure suit before. So far, nothing really unusual has cropped up. But we want to monitor her innards very closely for the next few days.

89

"Also, we were very concerned about peritonitis. You know what peritonitis is?"

"Yes." Well, vaguely.

"Because a part of her intestine had ruptured under pressure. We didn't want to settle for normal prophylaxis because a lot of the, uh, contamination had impacted on the peritoneum under pressure. To play it safe, we completely sterilized the whole shebang, the abdominal cavity and her entire digestive system from the duodenum south. Then, of course, we had to replace all of her normal intestinal flora, now dead, with a commercially prepared culture. Still standard procedure, but not normally called for unless the damage is more severe."

"I see." And it was making me a little queasy. Doctors don't seem to realize that most of us are perfectly content not having to visualize ourselves as animated bags of skin filled with obscene glop.

"This in itself is enough reason not to see her for a couple of days. The changeover of intestinal flora has a pretty violent effect on the digestive system—not dangerous, since she's under constant observation. But tiring and, well, embarrassing.

"With all of this, she would be completely out of danger if this were a normal clinical situation. But we're decelerating at a constant 1-1/2 gees, and her internal organs have gone through a lot of jumping around. You might as well know that if we do any blasting, anything over about two gees, she's going to die."

"But . . . but we're *bound* to go over two on the final approach! What—"

"I know, I know. But that won't be for a couple of weeks. Hopefully, she will have mended by then.

"William, face it. It's a miracle she survived to get into surgery. So there's a big chance she won't make it back to Earth. It's sad; she's a special person, *the* special person to you, maybe. But we've had so much death . . . you ought to be getting used to it, come to terms with it."

I took a long pull at my drink, identical to hers except for the citric acid. "You're getting pretty hard-boiled."

"Maybe . . . no. Just realistic. I have a feeling we're headed for a lot more death and sorrow."

"Not me. As soon as we get to Stargate, I'm a civilian."

"Don't be so sure." The old familiar argument. "Those clowns who signed us up for two years can just as easily make it four or—"

"Or six or twenty or the duration. But they won't. It would be mutiny."

"I don't know. If they could condition us to kill on cue, they can condition us to do almost anything. Reenlist."

That was a chiller.

Later on we tried to make love, but both of us had too much to think about.

I got to see Marygay for the first time about a week later. She was wan, had lost a lot of weight and seemed very confused. Doc Wilson assured me that it was just the medication; they hadn't seen any evidence of brain damage.

She was still in bed, still being fed through a tube. I began to get very nervous about the calendar. Every day there seemed to be some improvement, but if she was still in bed when we hit that collapsar push, she wouldn't have a chance. I couldn't get any encouragement from Doc Wilson or Estelle; they said it depended on Marygay's resilience.

The day before the push, they transferred her from bed to Estelle's acceleration couch in the infirmary. She was lucid and was taking food orally, but she still couldn't move under her own power, not at 1-1/2 gees.

I went to see her. "Heard about the course change? We have to go through Aleph-9 to get back to Tet-38. Four more months on this damn hulk. But another six years' combat pay when we get back to Earth."

"That's good."

"Ah, just think of the great things we'll—"

"William."

I let it trail off. Never could lie.

"Don't try to jolly me. Tell me about vacuum welding, about your childhood, anything. Just don't bullshit me about getting back to Earth." She turned her face to the wall.

"I heard the doctors talking out in the corridor, one

morning when they thought I was asleep. But it just confirmed what I already knew, the way everybody'd been moping around.

"So tell me, you were born in New Mexico in 1975. What then? Did you stay in New Mexico? Were you bright in school? Have any friends, or were you too bright like me? How old were you when you first got sacked?"

We talked in this vein for a while, uncomfortable. An idea came to me while we were rambling, and when I left Marygay I went straight to Dr. Wilson.

"We're giving her a fifty-fifty chance, but that's pretty arbitrary. None of the published data on this sort of thing really fits."

"But it is safe to say that her chances of survival are better, the less acceleration she has to endure."

"Certainly. For what it's worth. The commodore's going to take it as gently as possible, but that'll still be four or five gees. Three might even be too much; we won't know until it's over."

I nodded impatiently. "Yes, but I think there's a way to expose her to less acceleration than the rest of us."

"If you've developed an acceleration shield," he said smiling, "you better hurry and file a patent. You could sell it for a considerable—"

"No, Doc, it wouldn't be worth much under normal conditions; our shells work better and they evolved from the same principles."

"Explain away."

"We put Marygay into a shell and flood—"

"Wait, wait. Absolutely not. A poorly-fitting shell was what caused this in the first place. And this time, she'd have to use somebody else's."

"I know, Doc, let me explain. It doesn't have to fit her exactly as long as the life support hookups can function. The shell won't be pressurized on the inside; it won't have to be because she won't be subjected to those thousands of kilograms-per-square-centimeter pressure from the fluid outside."

"I'm not sure I follow."

"It's just an adaptation of—you've studied physics, haven't you?"

"A little bit, in medical school. My worst courses, after Latin."

"Do you remember the principle of equivalence?"

"I remember there was something by that name. Something to do with relativity, right?"

"Uh-huh. It means that . . . there's no difference being in a gravitational field and being in an equivalent accelerated frame of—it means that when the *Anniversary* is blasting five gees, the effect on us is the same as if it were sitting on its tail on a big planet, on one with five gees' surface gravity."

"Seems obvious."

"Maybe it is. It means that there's no experiment you could perform on the ship that could tell you whether you were blasting or just sitting on a big planet."

"Sure there is. You could turn off the engines, and if—"

"Or you could look outside, sure; I mean isolated, physics-lab type experiments."

"All right. I'll accept that. So?"

"You know Archimedes' Law?"

"Sure, the fake crown—that's what always got me about physics, they make a big to-do about obvious things, and when it gets to the rough parts—"

"Archimedes' Law says that when you immerse something in a fluid, it's buoyed up by a force equal to the weight of the fluid it displaces."

"That's reasonable."

"And that holds, no matter what kind of gravitation or acceleration you're in—In a ship blasting at five gees, the water displaced, if it's water, weighs five times as much as regular water, at one gee."

"Sure."

"So if you float somebody in the middle of a tank of water, so that she's weightless, she'll still be weightless when the ship is doing five gees."

"Hold on, son. You had me going there, but it won't work."

"Why not?" I was tempted to tell him to stick to his pills and stethoscopes and let me handle the physics, but it was a good thing I didn't.

"What happens when you drop a wrench in a submarine?"

"Submarine?"

"That's right. They work by Archimedes'—"

"Ouch! You're right. Jesus. Hadn't thought it through."

"That wrench falls right to the floor just as if the submarine weren't weightless." He looked off into space, tapping a pencil on the desk. "What you describe is similar to the way we treat patients with severe skin damage, like burns, on Earth. But it doesn't give any support to the internal organs, the way the acceleration shells do, so it wouldn't do Marygay any good. . . ."

I stood up to go. "Sorry I wasted—"

"Hold on there, though, just a minute. We might be able to use your idea part-way."

"How do you mean?"

"I wasn't thinking it through, either. The way we normally use the shells is out of the question for Marygay, of course." I didn't like to think about it. Takes a lot of hypno-conditioning to lie there and have oxygenated fluorocarbon forced into every natural body orifice and one artificial one. I fingered the valve fitting imbedded above my hipbone.

"Yeah, that's obvious, it'd tear her—say . . .you mean, low pressure—"

"That's right. We wouldn't need thousands of atmospheres to protect her against five gees' straight-line acceleration; that's only for all the swerving and dodging —I'm going to call Maintenace. Get down to your squad bay; that's the one we'll use. Dalton'll meet you there."

Five minutes before injection into the collapsar field, and I started the flooding sequence. Marygay and I were the only ones in shells; my presence wasn't really vital since the flooding and emptying could be done by Control. But it was safer to have redundancy in the system and besides, I wanted to be there.

It wasn't nearly as bad as the normal routine; none of the crushing-bloating sensation. You were just suddenly filled with the plastic-smelling stuff (you never perceived the first moments, when it rushed in to replace the air in your lungs), and then there was a slight acceleration, and then you were breathing air again, waiting for the shell to pop; then unplugging and unzipping and climbing out—

Marygay's shell was empty. I walked over to it and saw blood.

"She hemorrhaged." Doc Wilson's voice echoed sepulchrally. I turned, eyes stinging, and saw him leaning in the door to the locker alcove. He was unaccountably, horribly, smiling.

"Which was expected. Doctor Harmony's taking care of it. She'll be just fine."

6.

Marygay was walking in another week, "confraternizing" in two, and pronounced completely healed in six.

Ten long months in space and it was army, army, army all the way. Calisthenics, meaningless work details, compulsory lectures—there was even talk they were going to reinstate the sleeping roster we'd had in basic, but they never did, probably out of fear of mutiny. A random partner every night wouldn't have set too well with those of us who'd established more-or-less permanent pairs.

All this crap, this insistence on military discipline, bothered me mainly because I was afraid it meant they weren't going to let us out. Marygay said I was being paranoid; they only did it because there was no other way to maintain order for ten months.

Most of the talk, besides the usual bitching about the army, was speculation about how much Earth would have changed and what we would do when we got out. We'd be fairly rich: twenty-six years' salary all at once. Compound interest, too; the $500 we'd been paid for our first month in the army had grown to over $1500.

We arrived at Stargate in late 2023, Greenwich date.

The base had grown astonishingly in the nearly seventeen years we had been on the Yod-4 campaign. It was one building the size of Tycho City, housing nearly ten thousand. There were seventy-eight cruisers, the size of the *Anniversary* or larger, involved in raids on Tauran-held portal planets. Another ten guarded Stargate itself, and two were in orbit waiting for their infantry and crew to be outprocessed. One other ship, the *Earth's Hope II,* had returned from fighting and had been waiting at Stargate for another cruiser to return.

They had lost two-thirds of their crew, and it was just not economical to send a cruiser back to Earth with only thirty-nine people aboard. Thirty-nine confirmed civilians.

We went planetside in two scoutships.

General Botsford (who had been only a major when we'd first met him on Charon, when it was only two huts and twenty-four graves) received us in an elegantly-appointed seminar room. He was pacing back and forth at the end of the room, in front of a huge holographic operations cube. I could barely make out the labels and was astonished to see how far away Yod-4 had been—but of course distance isn't important with the collapsar jump. It'd take us ten times as long to get to Alpha Centauri, which was practically next door but, of course, isn't a collapsar.

"You know—" he said, too loudly, and then more conversationally: "You know that we could disperse you into other strike forces and send you right out again. The Elite Conscription Act has been changed now, extended, five years' subjective service instead of two.

"We aren't doing that, but—damn it!—I don't see why some of you don't *want* to stay in. Another couple of years and compound interest would make you wealthy for life. Sure, you took heavy losses . . . but that was inevitable; you were the first. Things are going to be easier now. The fighting suits have been improved, we know more about the Taurans' tactics, our weapons are more effective. . . .There's no need to be afraid."

He sat down at the head of our table and looked down the long axis of it, seeing nobody. "My own memories of combat are over a half-century old. To me it was exhilarating, strengthening. I must be a different kind of person than all of you."

Or have a very selective memory, I thought.

"But that's neither here nor there. I have an alternative to offer you, one that doesn't involve direct combat.

"We're very short of qualified instructors. You might

even say we don't *have* any—because, ideally, the army would like for all of its instructors in the combat arts to be combat veterans.

"You people were taught by veterans of Vietnam and Sinai, the youngest of whom were in their forties when you left Earth. Twenty-six years ago. So we need you and are willing to pay.

"The force will offer any of you a lieutenancy if you will accept a training position. It can be on Earth, on the moon at double pay, on Charon at triple pay, or here at Stargate for quadruple pay. Furthermore, you don't have to make up your mind now. You're all getting a free trip back to Earth—I envy you. I haven't been back in twenty years, will probably never get back —and you can get the feel of being a civilian again. If you don't like it, just walk into any UNEF installation and you'll walk out an officer. Your choice of assignment.

"Some of you are smiling. I think you ought to reserve judgment. Earth is not the same place you left."

He pulled a little card out of his tunic and looked at it, half-smiling. "Most of you have on the order of four hundred thousand dollars coming to you, accumulated pay and interest. But Earth is on a war footing and, of course, it is the citizens of Earth who are supporting the war with their tax dollars. Your income puts you in a 92 percent income tax bracket. Thirty-two thousand dollars could last you about three years if you're very careful.

"Eventually you're going to have to get a job, and this is one job for which you are uniquely trained. There aren't that many others available—the population of Earth is over nine billion, with five or six billion unemployed. And all of your training is twenty-six years out of date.

"Also keep in mind that your friends and sweethearts of two years ago are now going to be twenty-six years older than you. Many of your relatives will have passed away. I think you'll find it a very lonely world.

"But to tell you more about this world, I'm going to turn you over to Sergeant Siri, who just arrived from Earth. Sergeant?"

"Thank you, General." It looked as if there was something wrong with his skin, his face; and then I realized he was wearing face powder and lipstick. His nails were smooth white almonds.

"I don't know where to begin." He sucked in his upper lip and looked at us, frowning. "Things have changed so very much since I was a boy.

"I'm twenty-three, so I wasn't even born when you people left for Aleph. . . . Well, for starts, how many of you are homosexual?" Nobody. "That doesn't really surprise me. I am, though"—no kidding— "and I guess about a third of everybody in Europe and North America is. Even more in India and the Middle East. Less in South America and China.

"Most governments encourage homosexuality—the United Nations is officially neutral—they encourage it mainly because homolife is the one sure method of birth control."

That sounded specious to me. In the army they freeze-dry and file a sperm sample and then vasectomize you. Pretty foolproof.

When I was going to school, a lot of the homosexuals on campus were using that argument. And maybe it was working, after a fashion. I'd expected Earth to have a lot more than nine billion people.

"When they told me, back on Earth, I was going to be talking to some of you I did some research, mainly reading old 'faxes and magazines.

"A lot of the things you were afraid were going to happen, didn't. Hunger, for instance. Even without using all of our arable land and sea, we manage to feed everybody and could handle twice as many. Food technology and impartial distribution of calories—when you left Earth there were millions of people slowly starving to death. Now there are none.

"You were concerned about crime. I read that you couldn't walk the streets of New York City or London or Hong Kong without a bodyguard. But with everybody better educated and better cared for, with psychometry so advanced that we can spot a potential criminal at the age of six—and give him corrective therapy that works —well, serious crime has been on the decline for twenty years. We probably have fewer serious crimes in the whole world than you used to have in one large—"

"This is all well and good," the General broke in

gruffly, making clear that it was neither, "but it doesn't completely mesh with what I've heard. What do you call serious crime? What about the rest?"

"Oh, murder, assault, rape; all the serious crimes against one's person, all are down. Crimes against property—petty theft, vandalism, illegal residence—these are still—"

"What the hell is 'illegal residence'?"

Sergeant Siri hesitated and then said primly: "One certainly shouldn't deprive others of living space by illegally acquiring property."

Alexandrov raised his hand. "You mean there's no such thing as private ownership of property?"

"Of course there is. I . . . I owned my own rooms before I was drafted." For some reason the topic seemed to embarrass him. New taboos? "But there are limits."

Luthuli: "What do you do to criminals? Serious ones, I mean. Do you still brainwipe murderers?"

He was visibly relieved to change the subject. "Oh, no. That's considered very primitive. Barbaric. We imprint a new, healthy personality on them; then they are repatterned and society absorbs them without prejudice. It works very well."

"Are there jails, prisons?" Yukawa asked.

"I suppose you could call a correction center a jail. Until they have therapy and are released, people are held there against their will. But you could say it was a malfunction of the will which led them there in the first place."

I didn't have any plans for a life of crime, so I asked him about the thing that bothered me most. "The General said that over half your population is on the dole; that we wouldn't be able to get jobs either. Well?"

"I don't know this word 'dole.' Of course you mean the government-subsidized unemployed. That's true, the government takes care of over half of us—I'd never had a job until I was drafted. I was a composer.

"Don't you see that there are two sides to this business of chronic unemployment? The world and the war could be run smoothly by a billion, certainly two billion people. This doesn't mean that the rest of us sit around idle.

"Every citizen has the opportunity for up to eighteen

years' free education—fourteen years are compulsory. This and the *freedom* from necessity of employment have caused a burgeoning of scholarly and creative activity on a scale unmatched in all of human history—there are more artists and writers working today than lived in the first two thousand years of the Christian era! And their works go to a wider and more educated audience than has ever before existed."

That was something to think about. Rabi raised his hand. "Have you produced a Shakespeare yet? A Michaelangelo? Number isn't everything."

Siri brushed hair out of his eyes with a thoroughly feminine gesture. "That's not a fair question. It's up to posterity to make comparisons like that."

"Sergeant, when we were talking earlier," the general said, "didn't you say that you lived in a huge beehive of a building, that nobody could live in the country?"

"Well, sir, it's true that nobody can live on potential farm land. And where I live, *lived*, Atlanta Complex, I had seven million neighbors in what you could technically call one building—but it's not as if we ever felt crowded. And you can go down the elevator any time, walk in the fields, walk all the way to the sea if you want. . . .

"That's something you should be prepared for. A lot of cities don't bear any resemblance to the random agglomerations of buildings they used to be. Most of the big cities were burned to the ground in the food riots in 2004, just before the UN took over the production and distribution of food. The city planners usually rebuilt along modern, functional lines.

"Paris and London, for instance, had to be rebuilt completely. Most world capitals did, though Washington survived. It's just a bunch of monuments and offices, though; almost everybody lives in the surrounding complexes, Reston, Frederick, Columbia."

Then Siri mentioned specific towns and cities—everybody wanted to know about their hometown—and, in general, things sounded a lot better than we had expected.

In response to a rude question, Siri said that he didn't wear cosmetics just because he was a homosexual; everybody did. I decided I'd be a maverick and just wear my face.

We consolidated with the survivors from *Earth's Hope II* and took that cruiser back to Earth while analysts assessed the *Anniversary*'s damage. The Commodore was scheduled for a hearing but, as far as we knew, was not going to be court-martialed.

Discipline was fairly relaxed on the way back. In seven months I read thirty books, learned how to play Go, taught an informal class in elementary—and out-of-date—physics and grew ever closer to Marygay.

7.

I hadn't given it much thought, but of course we were celebrities on Earth. At the Cape the Sec-Gen greeted each of us personally—he was a very old tiny black man named Yakubu Ojukwu—and there were hundreds of thousands, maybe millions, of spectators crowded as close as they could get to the landing field.

The Sec-Gen gave a speech to the crowd and the newsmen; then the ranking officers of *Earth's Hope II* babbled some predictable stuff, while the rest of us stood more-or-less patiently in the tropical heat.

We took a big chopper to Jacksonville, where the nearest international airport was. The city itself had been rebuilt along the lines Siri had described. You had to be impressed.

We first saw it as a solitary gray mountain, a slightly irregular cone, slipping up over the horizon and growing slowly larger. It was sitting in the middle of a seemingly endless patchwork quilt of cultivated fields, dozens of roads and rails converging on it. The eye saw these roads, fine white threads with infinitesimal bugs crawling on them, but the brain refused to integrate the information into an estimate of the size of the thing. It couldn't be that big.

We came closer and closer—updrafts making the ride a little bumpy—until finally the building seemed to be a light gray wall taking up our entire field of vision on one side. We moved closer and could barely see dots of people; one dot was on a balcony and might have been waving.

"This is as close as we can come," the pilot said over an intercom, "without locking into the city's guidance system and landing on top. Airport's to the north." We banked away, through the shadow of the city.

The airport was no great marvel, larger than any I'd ever seen before but conventional in design: a central terminal like the hub of a wheel, with monorails leading out a kilometer or so to smaller terminals where airplanes loaded and unloaded. We skipped the terminals completely, landed near a Swissair stratospheric liner and walked from the chopper to the plane. Our pathway was cordoned off and we were surrounded by a cheering mob. With six billion on relief, I didn't suppose they had any trouble rounding up a crowd for any such occasion.

I was afraid we were going to have to sit through some more speeches, but we filed straight into the plane. Stewards and stewardesses brought us sandwiches and drinks while the crowd was being dispersed. And there are no words to describe a chicken-salad sandwich and a cold beer after two years of recycled shit.

Mr. Ojukwu explained that we were going to Geneva, to the United Nations building, where tonight we'd be honored by the General Assembly. Or put on display, I thought. He said most of us had relatives waiting in Geneva.

As we climbed over the Atlantic, the water seemed unnaturally green. I was curious, made a mental note to ask the stewardess, but then the reason became apparent. It was a farm. Four large rafts (they must have been huge, but I had no idea how high up we were) moved in slow tandem across the green surface, each raft leaving a blue-black swath that slowly faded. Before we landed I found out that it was a kind of tropical algae, raised for livestock feed.

Geneva was a single building similar to Jacksonville, but seemed smaller, perhaps dwarfted by the natural mountains surrounding it. It was covered with snow, softly beautiful.

We walked for a minute through swirling snow—how

great not to be exactly at "room temperature" all the time!—to a chopper that took us to the top of the building; then down an elevator, across a slidewalk, down another elevator, another slidewalk, down a broad stationary corridor to Thantstrasse 281B, room 45, matching the address on the directions they'd given me. My finger poised over the doorbell button; I was almost afraid.

I had adjusted fairly well to the fact that my father was dead—the army had had such facts waiting for us at Stargate—and that didn't bother me as much as the prospect of seeing my mother, suddenly eighty-four. I almost ducked out to find a bar and desensitize, but went ahead and pushed the button.

The door opened quickly. She was older but not that much different, a few more lines and hair white instead of gray. We stared at each other for a second and then embraced, and I was surprised and relieved at how happy I was to see her, hold her.

She took my cape and hustled me into the living room of the suite, where I got a real shock: my father was standing there, smiling but serious, inevitable pipe in his hand. I felt a flash of anger at the army for having misled me—then realized he couldn't be my father, looking as he did, the way I remembered him from childhood.

"Michael? Mike?"

He laughed. "Who else, Willy?" My kid brother, quite middle-aged. I hadn't seen him since '93, when I went off to college. He'd been sixteen then; two years later he was on the moon with UNEF.

"Get tired of the moon?" I asked, handshaking.

"Huh? Oh . . . no, Willy, I spend a month or two every year back on terra firma. It's not like it used to be." When they were first recruiting for the moon, it was with the understanding that you got only one trip back. Fuel cost too much for commuting.

The three of us sat down around a marble coffee table and Mother passed around joints.

"Everything has changed so much," I said, before they could start asking about the war. "Tell me everything."

My brother fluttered his hands and laughed. "That's a tall enough order. Have a couple of weeks?" He was obviously having trouble figuring out how to act toward me. Was I his nephew, or what? Certainly not his older brother any more.

"You shouldn't ask Michael, anyhow," Mother said. "Loonies talk about Earth the way virgins talk about sex."

"Now, Mother . . ."

"With enthusiasm and ignorance."

I lit up the joint and inhaled deeply. It was oddly sweet.

"Loonies live a few weeks out of the year on Earth and spend half that time telling us how we ought to be running things."

"Possibly. But the other half of the time we're observing. Objectively."

"Here comes my Michael's 'objective' number." She leaned back and smiled at him.

"Mom, you *know* . . . oh hell, let's drop it. Willy's got the rest of his life to sort it out." He took a puff on the joint and I noticed he wasn't inhaling. "Tell us about the war, man. Heard you were on the strike force that actually fought the Taurans. Face to face."

"Yeah. It wasn't much."

"That's right," Mike said. "I heard they were cowards."

"Not so much . . . that." I shook my head to clear it. The marijuana was making me drowsy and lightheaded. "It was more like they just didn't get the idea. Like a shooting gallery. They lined up and we shot 'em down."

"How could that be?" Mom said. "On the news they said you lost nineteen people."

"Did they say nineteen were killed? That's not true."

"I don't remember exactly."

"Well, we did *lose* nineteen people, but only four of them were killed. That was in the early part of the battle, before we had their defenses figured out." I decided not to say anything about the way Chu died. That would get too complicated. "Of the other fifteen, one was shot by one of our own lasers. He lost an arm but lived. All of the others . . . lost their minds."

"What—some kind of Tauran weapon?" Mike asked.

"The Taurans didn't have anything to do with it! It was the army. They conditioned us to kill anything that

104

moved, once the sergeant triggered the conditioning with a few key words. When people came out of it, they couldn't handle the memory. Being a butcher." I shook my head violently a couple of times. The dope was really getting to me.

"Look, I'm sorry." I got to my feet with some effort. "I've been up some twenty—"

"Of course, William." Mother took my elbow and steered me to a bedroom and promised to wake me in plenty of time for the evening's festivities. The bed was indecently comfortable but I could've slept leaning up against a lumpy tree.

Fatigue and dope and too full a day: Mother had to wake me up by trickling cold water on my face. She steered me to a closet and identified two outfits as being formal enough for the occasion. I chose a brick-red one—the powder blue seeming a little foppish—showered and shaved, refused cosmetics (Mike was all dolled up and offered to help me), armed myself with the half-page of instructions telling how to get to the General Assembly, and was off.

I got lost twice along the way, but they had little computers at every corridor intersection that would give directions to any place, in fourteen languages.

Men's clothing, as far as I was concerned, had really taken a step backwards. From the waist up it wasn't so bad, tight high-necked blouse with a short cape; but then there was a wide shiny functionless belt, from which dangled a little jeweled dagger, perhaps adequate for opening mail; and then pantaloons that flounced out in great pleats and were tucked into shiny synthetic high-heeled boots that came almost to your knees. Give me a plumed hat and Shakespeare would've hired me on the spot.

The women fared better. I met Marygay outside the General Assembly hall.

"I feel absolutely naked, William."

"Looks good, though. Anyhow, it's the style." Most of the young women I'd passed had been wearing a similar outfit: a simple shift with large rectangular windows cut in both sides, from armpit to hem. The hem ended where your imagination began. For modesty, the outfits

105

required very conservative movements and a great faith in static electricity.

"Have you seen this place?" she said, taking my arm. "Let's go in. Conquistador."

We walked in through the automatic doors and I stopped short. The hall was so large that going into it I felt as though I'd stepped outdoors.

The floor was circular, more than a hundred meters in diameter. The walls rose a good sixty or seventy meters to a transparent dome—I remembered having seen it when we landed—on which gray drifts of snow danced and blew swirling away. The walls were done in a muted ceramic mosaic, thousands of figures representing a chronology of human achievement. I don't know how long I stared.

Across the hall, we joined the other hardy veterans for coffee. It was synthetic, but better than soya. To my dismay, I learned that tobacco was rarely grown on Earth and even, through local option, was outlawed in some areas in order to conserve arable land. What you could get was expensive and usually wretched, having been grown by amateurs on tiny backyard or balcony plots. The only good tobacco was lunar and its price was, well, astronomical.

Marijuana was plentiful and cheap. In some countries, like the United States, it was free; produced and distributed by the government.

I offered Marygay a joint and she declined. "I've got to get used to them slowly. I had one earlier and it almost knocked me out."

"Me too."

An old man in uniform walked into the lounge, his breast a riotous fruit-salad of ribbons, his shoulders weighed down with five stars apiece. He smiled benignly when half the people jumped to their feet. I was too much a civilian and remained seated.

"Good evening, good evening," he said, making a patting sit-down motion with his hands. "It's good to see you here. Good to see so many of you." Many? A little more than half the number we started out with.

"I'm General Gary Manker, UNEF Chief of Staff. In a few minutes we're going over there," he nodded in the direction of the General Assembly hall, "for a short ceremony. Then you'll be free for a well-deserved rest; put your feet up for a few months, see the world, whatever you want. So long as you can keep the reporters away.

"Before you go, though, I'd like to say a few words about what you'll want to do *after* those months, when you get tired of being on vacation, when the money starts to run low . . ." Predictably, the same spiel General Botsford had given us at Stargate. You're going to need a job, and this is the one job you can be sure of getting.

The General left after saying that an aide would be by in a few minutes to herd us over to the rostrum. We amused ourselves for several minutes, discussing the merits of re-enlistment.

The aide turned out to be a good-looking young woman who had no trouble jollying us into alphabetical order (she didn't seem to have any higher an opinion of the military than did we) and leading us over to the hall.

The first couple of rows of delegates had abandoned their desks to us. I sat in the "Gambia" place and listened uncomfortably to tales of heroism and sacrifices. General Manker had most of the facts right but used slightly wrong words.

Then they called us up one by one and Dr. Ojukwu gave each of us a gold medal that must have weighed a kilogram. Then he gave a little speech about mankind united in common cause while discreet holo cameras scanned us one by one. Inspiring fare for the folks back home. Then we filed out under waves of applause that were somehow oppressive.

I had asked Marygay, who had no living relatives, to come on up and sack with me. There was a crowd milling around the formal entrance of the hall, so we hustled the other way, took the first escalator up several stories and got totally lost on a succession of slidewalks and lifts. Then we used the little corner boxes to find our way home.

I'd told Mother about Marygay and that I'd probably be bringing her back. They greeted each other warmly and Mother settled us in the living room with a couple of drinks and went off to start dinner. Mike joined us.

"You're going to find Earth awfully boring," he said after amenities.

107

"I don't know," I said. "Army life isn't exactly stimulating. Any change has got to be—"

"You can't get a job."

"Not in physics, I know; twenty-six years is like a geologic—"

"You can't get *any* job."

"Well, I'd planned to go back and take my master's degree over, maybe go on . . ." Mike was shaking his head.

"Let him finish, William." Marygay shifted restlessly. "I think he knows something we don't."

He finished his drink and swirled the ice around in the bottom of the glass, staring at it. "That's right. You know, the moon is all UNEF, civilians and military, and we amuse ourselves by passing rumors back and forth."

"Old military pastime."

"Uh-huh. Well, I heard a rumor about you . . ." he made a sweeping gesture, "you veterans and went to the trouble to check it out. It was true."

"Glad to hear it."

"Yeah, you will be." He set down his drink, took out a joint, looked at it, put it back. "UNEF is going to do anything short of kidnapping to get you people back. They control the Employment Board, and you can be damned sure you're going to be undertrained or overtrained for any job opening that comes along. Except soldier."

"Are you sure?" Marygay asked. We both knew enough not to claim they couldn't do a thing like that.

"Sure as a Christian. I have a friend on the Luna division of the Employment Board. He showed me the directive; it's worded very politely. And it says 'absolutely no exceptions.' "

"Maybe by the time I get out of school—"

"You'll never get *into* school. Never get past the maze of standards and quotas. If you try to push, they'll claim you're too old—hell, I couldn't get into a doctoral program at *my* age, and —"

"Yeah, I get the idea. I'm two years older."

"That's it. You've got the choice of either spending the rest of your life on relief or soldiering."

"No contest," Marygay said. "Relief."

108

I agreed. "If five or six billion people can carve out a decent life without a profession, I can too."

"They've grown up in it," Mike said. "And it may not be what you would call a 'decent life.' Most of them just sit around and smoke dope and watch the holo. Get just enough to eat to balance their caloric output. Meat once a week. Even on Class I relief."

"That won't be anything new," I said. "The food part, anyhow—it's exactly the way we were fed in the army.

"As for the rest of it, as you just said, Marygay and I didn't grow up in it; we're not likely to sit around half-blown and stare at the cube all day."

"I paint," Marygay said. "I always wanted to settle down and get really good at it."

"And I can continue studying physics even if it's not for a degree. And take up music or writing or—" I turned to Marygay, "or any of those things the sergeant talked about at Stargate."

"Join the New Renaissance," he said without inflection, lighting his pipe. It was tobacco and smelled delicious.

He must have noticed my hunger. "Oh, I'm being a hell of a host." He got some papers out of his purse and rolled an expert joint. "Here. Marygay?"

"No thanks—if it's as hard to get as they say, I don't want to get back into the habit."

He nodded, relighting his pipe. "Never did anybody any good. Better to train your mind, be able to relax without it." He turned to me. "The army *did* keep up your cancer boosters?"

"Sure." Wouldn't do for you to die in so unsoldierly a fashion. I lit up the slender cigarette. "Good stuff."

"Better than anything you'll get on Earth. Lunar marijuana is better, too. Doesn't mess you up so much."

Mother came in and sat down. "Dinner'll be ready in a few minutes. I hear Michael making unfair comparisons again."

"What's unfair? Earth marijuana, a couple of j's and you're a zombie."

"Correction: *you* are. You're just not used to it."

"OK, OK. And a boy shouldn't argue with his mother."

"Not when she's right," she said, strangely without humor. "Well! Do you children like fish?"

We talked about how hungry we were, a safe enough subject, for a few minutes and then sat down to a huge broiled red snapper, served on a bed of rice. It was the first square meal Marygay and I had had in twenty-six years.

8.

Like everyone else, the next day I went to get interviewed on the cube. It was a frustrating experience.

Commentator: "Sergeant Mandella, you are one of the most-decorated soldiers in the UNEF." True, all of us had gotten a fistful of ribbons at Stargate. "You participated in the famous Aleph-null campaign, the first actual contact with Taurans, and just returned from an assault on Yod-4."

Me: "Well, you couldn't call it—"

Commentator: "Before we talk about Yod-4, I'm sure the audience would be very interested in your *personal* impression of the enemy, as one of the very few people to have met them face-to-face. They're pretty horrible looking, aren't they?"

Me: "Well, yes; I'm sure you've seen the pictures. About all they don't show is the texture of the skin. It's pebbly and wrinkled like a lizard's, but pale orange."

Commentator: "What do they smell like?" Smell?

Me: "I haven't got the faintest idea. All you can smell in a spacesuit is yourself."

Commentator: "Ha-ha, I see. What I'm trying to get, Sergeant, is how *you* felt, the first time you saw the enemy. . . . Were you afraid of them, disgusted, enraged, or what?"

"Well, I *was* afraid, the first time, and disgusted. Mostly afraid—but that was before the battle, when a solitary Tauran flew overhead. During the actual battle, we were under the influence of hate-conditioning—they conditioned us on Earth and triggered it with a phrase—and I didn't feel much except the artificial rage."

"You despised them—and showed no mercy."

"Right. Murdered them all, even though they made no attempt to fight back. But when they released us from the conditioning . . . well, we couldn't believe we had been such butchers. Fourteen people went insane and all the rest of us were on tranquilizers for weeks."

"Ah," he said absentmindedly, and glanced over to the side for a moment. "How many of them did you kill, yourself?"

"Fifteen, twenty—I don't know; as I said, we weren't in control of ourselves. It was a massacre."

All through the interview, the commentator seemed a bit dense, repetitive. That night I found out why.

Marygay and I were watching the cube with Mike. Mom was off getting fitted for some artificial teeth (the dentists in Geneva supposedly being better than American ones). My interview was on a program called "Potpourri," sandwiched between a documentary on lunar hydroponics and a concert by a man who claimed to be able to pay Telemann's *Double Fantasia in A Major* on the harmonica. I wondered whether anybody else in Geneva, in the world, was tuned in.

Well, the hydroponics thing was interesting and the harmonica player was a virtuoso, but the thing in between was pure drivel.

Commentator: "What do they smell like?"

Me (off camera): "Just horrible, a combination of rotten vegetables and burning sulfur. The smell leaks in through the suit's exhaust."

He had kept me talking and talking in order to get a wide spectrum of sounds, from which he could synthesize any kind of nonsense in response to his questions.

"How the hell can he do that?" I asked Mike when the show was over.

"Don't be too hard on him," Mike said, watching the quadruplicated musician play four different harmonicas against himself. "All the media are censored by the UNEF. It's been ten, twelve years since Earth had any objective reporting about the war. You're lucky they didn't just substitute an actor for you and feed him lines."

"Is it any better on Luna?"

"Not as far as public broadcast. But since every one

111

there is tied into UNEF, it's easy enough to find out when they're lying outright."

"He *completely* cut out the part about conditioning."

"Understandable." Mike shrugged. "They need heroes, not automatons."

Marygay's interview was on an hour later, and they had done the same thing to her. Every time she had originally said something against the war or the army, the cube would switch to a close-up of the woman interviewing her, who would nod sagely while a remarkable imitation of Marygay's voice gave out arrant nonsense.

UNEF was paying for five days' room and board in Geneva, and it seemed as good a place as any to begin exploring this new Earth. The next morning we got a map, which was a book a centimeter thick—and took a lift to the ground floor, determined to work our way up to the roof without missing anything.

The ground floor was an odd mixture of history and heavy industry. The base of the building covered a large part of what used to be the city of Geneva, and a lot of old buildings were preserved.

Mostly, though, it was all noise and hustle: big g-e trucks growling in from outside, shedding clouds of snow; barges booming against dock pilings (the Rhone River crawls through the middle of the huge expanse); even a few little helicopters beating this way and that, coordinating things, keeping away from the struts and buttresses that held up the gray sky of the next floor, forty meters up.

It was a marvel and more, and we could have watched it for hours, but we would've frozen solid in a few minutes with just light capes against the wind and cold. We decided we'd come back another day, more warmly dressed.

The floor above was called the first floor, in defiance of logic. Marygay explained that the Europeans had always numbered them that way. (Funny, I'd been a thousand light-years from New Mexico, and back, but this was the first time I'd crossed the Atlantic.) It was the brains of the organism, where the bureaucrats and the systems analysts and the cryogenic handymen hung around.

We stood in a large quiet lobby that somehow smelled of glass. One wall was a huge holo cube displaying Geneva's table of organization, a spidery orange pyramid with tens of thousands of names connected by lines, from the mayor at top to the "corridor security" people at the base. Names flicked out and were replaced by new ones as people died or were fired or promoted or demoted. Shimmering, changing shape, it looked like the nervous system of some fantastic creature. In a sense, of course, it was.

The wall opposite from the holo cube was a window overlooking a large room which a plaque identified as the *"Kontrollezimmer."* Behind the glass were hundreds of technicians in neat rows and columns, each with his own console with a semi-flat holo surrounded by dials and switches. There was an electric, busy air to the place: most of the people had on an earphone-microphone headset, and talked with some other technician while they scribbled on a tablet or fiddled with switches; others rattled away on console keyboards with their headsets dangling from their necks. A very few seats were empty, their owners striding around looking important. An automated coffee tray slid slowly up one row and down the next.

Through the glass you could hear a faint susurrus of what must have been an unholy commotion inside.

There were only two other people in the lobby, and we overheard them say they were going to look at "the brain." We followed them down a long corridor to another viewing area, rather small in comparison to the one overlooking the control room, looking down on the computers that held Geneva together. The only illumination in the viewing area was the faint cold blue light from the room below.

The computer room was also small in comparison, about the size of a baseball diamond. The computer elements were featureless gray boxes of various sizes, connected by a maze of man-sized glass tunnels which had airlocks at regular intervals. Evidently this system allowed access to one element at a time, for repair, while the rest of the room remained at a temperature near absolute zero, for superconductivity.

Though lacking the nervous activity of the control

room, and far from the exciting hurly-burly on the floor below, the computer room was more impressive in its own static way: the feeling of vast, unknowable powers under constraint; a shrine to purpose, order, intelligence.

The other couple told us there was nothing else of interest on the floor, just meeting rooms and offices and busy officials. We got back on the lift and went to the second floor, which was the main shopping arcade.

Here, the map-book was very handy. The arcade was hundreds of shops and "open-air" markets arranged in a rectangular grid pattern, with interlacing slidewalks defining blocks where related shops were grouped together. We went to the central mall, which turned out to be a whimsical reconstruction of medieval village architecture. There was a baroque church whose steeple, by holographic illusion, extended into the third and fourth floors. Smooth wall mosaics with primitive religious scenes, cobblestones laid out in intricate patterns, a fountain with water spraying from monsters' mouths . . . we bought a bunch of grapes from an open-air greengrocer (the illusion faltered when he took a caloric ticket and stamped my ration book) and walked along the narrow brick sidewalks, loving it. I was glad Earth still had time, and energy and resources, for this sort of thing.

There was a bewildering variety of objects and services for sale, and we had plenty of money, but we'd gotten out of the habit of buying things, I guess, and we didn't know how long our fortunes were going to have to last.

(We *did* have fortunes, in spite of what General Botsford had said. Rogers' father was some kind of hot-shot tax lawyer, and she'd passed the word—we only had to pay tax at the rate set for our *average* annual income. I wound up with $280,000.)

We skipped the third floor, mostly communications, because we'd crawled all over it the day before, when we went for our interviews. I was tempted to go speak to the person who'd rearranged my words, but Marygay convinced me it would be futile.

The artificial mountain of Geneva is "stepped"—like a wedding cake—the first three floors and the ground

114

level about a kilometer in diameter, rising about a hundred meters, floors four through thirty-two the same height but about half the diameter. Floors thirty-three through seventy-two make up the top cylinder, about 300 meters in diameter by 120 high.

The fourth floor, like the thirty-third, is a park: trees, brooks, little animals. The walls are transparent, open in good weather, and the "shelf" (the roof of the third floor) is planted in heavy forest. We rested for a while by a pond, watching people swim and feeding bits of grape to the minnows.

Something had been bothering me subliminally ever since we arrived in Geneva and suddenly, surrounded by all those pleasant people, I knew what it was.

"Marygay," I said. "Nobody here is unhappy."

She smiled. "Who could be glum in a place like this? All the flowers and—"

"No, no . . . I mean in all of Geneva. Have you seen anybody who looked like he might be dissatisfied with the way things are? Who—"

"Your brother . . ."

"Yeah, but he's a foreigner too. I mean the merchants and workers and the people just hanging around."

She looked thoughtful. "I haven't really been looking. Maybe not."

"Doesn't that strike you as strange?"

"It is unusual . . . but . . ." She threw a whole grape in the water and the minnows scattered. "Remember what that homosexual sergeant said? They diagnose and correct antisocial traits at a very early age. And what rational person wouldn't be happy here?"

I snorted. "Half of these people are out of work and most of the others are doing artificial jobs that are either redundant or could be done better by machine."

"But they all have enough to eat and plenty to occupy their minds. That wasn't so, twenty-six years ago."

"Maybe," I said, not wanting to argue. "I suppose you're right." Still, it bothered me.

9.

We spent the rest of that day and all of the next in the UN headquarters (essentially the capital of the world), that took up the whole top cylinder of Geneva. It would have taken weeks to see everything. Hell, it would take more than a week just to cover the Family of Man Museum. Every country had its own individual display, with a shop selling typical crafts, sometimes a restaurant with native food. I had been afraid that national identities might have been submerged, that this new world would be long on order and short on variety. Glad to have been mistaken.

Marygay and I planned a travel itinerary while we toured the UN. We decided we'd go back to the United States and find a place to stay, then spend a couple of months traveling again.

When I approached Mom for advice in getting an apartment, she seemed strangely embarrassed, the way Sergeant Siri had been. But she said she'd see what was available in Washington when she went back the next day (my father'd had a job there and Mom hadn't seen any reason to move after he died).

I asked Mike about this reluctance to talk about housing and he said it was a hangover from the chaotic years between the food riots and the Reconstruction. There hadn't been enough roofs to go around; people had had to live two families to a room even in countries that had been prosperous. It had been an unstable situation and finally the UN stepped in, first with a propaganda campaign and finally with mass conditioning, reinforcing the idea that it was virtuous to live in as small a place as possible, that it was sinful to even *want* to live alone or in a place with lots of room. And one didn't talk about it.

Most people still had some remnant of this conditioning, even though they had been detoxified over a decade before. In various strata of society it was impolite or unforgivable or rather daring to talk about such things.

Mom went back to Washington and Mike to Luna,

and Marygay and I stayed on at Geneva for a couple of days.

We got off the plane at Dulles and found a monorail to Rifton, the satellite-city where Mom lived.

It was refreshingly small after vast Geneva, even though it spread over a larger area. It was a pleasingly diverse jumble of various kinds of buildings, only a couple more than a few stories high, arranged around a lake, surrounded by trees. All of the buildings were connected by slidewalk to the largest place, a fullerdome with stores and schools and offices. There we found a directory that told us how to get to Mom's place, a duplex on the lake.

We could have taken the enclosed slidewalk but instead walked alongside it in the good cold air that smelled of fallen leaves. People slid by on the other side of the plastic, carefully not staring.

Mom didn't answer her door, but it turned out not to be locked. It was a comfortable place, extremely spacious by starship standards, full of twentieth-century furniture. Mom was asleep in the bedroom, so Marygay and I settled in the living room and read for a while.

We were startled suddenly by a loud fit of coughing from the bedroom. I raced over and knocked on the door.

"William? I didn't—" coughing "—come in, I didn't know you were . . ."

She was propped up in bed, the light on, surrounded by various nostrums. She looked ghastly, pale and lined.

She lit a joint and it seemed to quell the coughing. "When did you get in? I didn't know . . ."

"Just a few minutes ago. . . . How long has this . . . have you been . . ."

"Oh, it's just a bug I picked up in Geneva. I'll be fine in a couple of days." She started coughing again, drank some thick red liquid from a bottle. All of her medicines seemed to be the commercial, patent variety.

"Have you seen a doctor?"

"Doctor? Heavens no, Willy. They don't have . . . it's not serious . . . don't—"

"Not serious?" At eighty-four. "For Chrissake, Mother." I went to the phone in the kitchen and with some difficulty managed to get the hospital.

A plain girl in her twenties formed in the cube. "Nurse Donalson, general services." She had a fixed smile, professional sincerity. But then everybody smiled.

"My mother needs to be looked at by a doctor. She has a—"

"Name and number, please."

"Bette Mandella." I spelled it. "What number?"

"Medical services number, of course," she smiled.

I called into Mom and asked her what her number was. "She says she can't remember."

"That's all right, sir, I'm sure I can find her records." She turned her smile to a keyboard beside her and punched out a code.

"Bette Mandella?" she said, her smile turning quizzical. *"You're* her son? She must be in her eighties."

"Please. It's a long story. She really has to see a doctor."

"Is this some kind of joke?"

"What do you mean?" Strangled coughing from the other room, the worst yet. "Really—this might be very serious, you've got to—"

"But sir, Mrs. Mandella got a zero priority rating way back in 2010."

"What the hell is that supposed to mean?"

"S-i-r . . ." The smile was hardening in place.

"Look. Pretend that I came from another planet. What is a 'zero priority rating'?"

"Another—oh! I know you!" She looked off to the left. "Sonya—come over here a second. You'd never guess who . . ." Another face crowded the cube, a vapid blonde girl whose smile was twin to the other nurse's. "Remember? On the stat this morning?"

"Oh, yeah," she said. "One of the soldiers—hey, that's really max, really max." The head withdrew.

"Oh, Mr. Mandella," she said, effusive. "No wonder you're confused. It's really very simple."

"Well?"

"It's part of the Universal Medical Security System. Everybody gets a rating on their seventieth birthday. It comes in automatically from Geneva."

"What does it rate? What does it mean?" But the ugly truth was obvious.

"Well, it tells how important a person is and what level of treatment he's allowed. Class three is the same as anybody else's; class two is the same except for certain life-extending—"

"And class zero is no treatment at all."

"That's correct, Mr. Mandella." And in her smile was not a glimmer of pity or understanding.

"Thank you." I disconnected. Marygay was standing behind me, crying soundlessly with her mouth wide open.

I found a mountaineer's oxygen tank at a sporting goods store and even managed to get some black-market antibiotics through a character in a bar downtown in Washington. But Mom was beyond being able to respond to amateur treatment. She lived four days. The people from the crematorium had the same fixed smile.

I tried to get through to Mike but the phone company wouldn't let me place the call until I had signed a contract and posted a $25,000 bond. I had to get a credit transfer from Geneva. The paperwork took half a day.

I finally got through to him. Without preamble:

"Mother's dead."

For a fraction of a second, the radio waves wandered up to the moon, and in another fraction, came back. He started and then nodded his head slowly. "No surprise. Every time I've come down to Earth the past ten years, I've wondered whether she'd still be there. Neither of us had enough money to keep in very close touch." He had told us in Geneva that a letter from Luna to Earth cost $100 postage—plus $5,000 tax. It discouraged communication with what the UN considered to be a bunch of regrettably necessary anarchists.

We commiserated for a while and then Mike said, "Willy, Earth is no place for you and Marygay; you know that by now. Come to Luna. Where you can still be an individual. Where we don't throw people out the airlock on their seventieth birthday."

"We'd have to rejoin UNEF."

"True, but you wouldn't have to fight. They say they

119

need you more for training. You could study in your spare time, bring your physics up to date—maybe wind up eventually in research."

We talked some more, a total of three minutes. I got $1000 back.

Marygay and I talked about it through the night. Maybe our decision would have been different if we hadn't been staying there, surrounded by Mother's life and death, but when the dawn came the proud, ambitious, careful beauty of Rifton had turned sinister and foreboding.

We packed our bags and had our money transferred to the Tycho Credit Union and took a monorail to the Cape.

10.

"In case you're interested, you aren't the only combat veterans to have come back." The recruiting officer was a muscular lieutenant of indeterminate gender. I flipped a coin mentally and came up tails.

"Last I heard, there had been nine others," she said in her husky tenor. "All of them opted for the moon. . . . Maybe you'll find some of your friends there." She slid two simple forms across the desk. "Sign these and you're in again. Second lieutenants."

The form was a simple request to be assigned to active duty; we had never really gotten out of UNEF, since they had extended the draft law, but had just been on inactive status. I scrutinized the paper.

"There's nothing on here about the guarantees we were promised at Stargate."

"What guarantees?" She had that bland, mechanical Earthsmile.

"We were guaranteed assignment of choice and location of choice. There's nothing about that on this contract."

"That won't be necessary. The Force will . . ."

"*I* think it's necessary, Lieutenant." I handed back the form. So did Marygay.

"Let me check." She left the desk and disappeared into

120

an office. She was on a phone for a while and then we heard a printer rattle.

She brought back the same two sheets, with an addition typed under our names: GUARANTEED LOCATION OF CHOICE (LUNA) AND ASSIGNMENT OF CHOICE (COMBAT TRAINING SPECIALIST).

We got a thorough physical checkup and were fitted for new fighting suits. The next morning we caught the first shuttle to orbit, enjoyed zero-gee for a few hours while they transferred cargo to a spidery tachyon-torch shuttle, then zipped to the moon, setting down at Grimaldi base.

On the door to the Transient Officers' Billet, some wag had scratched "abandon hope all ye who enter." We found our two-person cubicle and began changing for chow.

Two raps on the door. "Mail call, sirs."

I opened the door and the sergeant standing there saluted. Just looked at him for a second and then remembered I was an officer and returned the salute. He handed me two identical 'faxes. I gave one to Marygay. Our hearts must have stopped simultaneously:

ORDERSORDERS**ORDERS**ORDERS**
ORDERS**ORDERS**ORDERS**
THE FOLLOWING NAMED PERSONNEL:
Mandella William 2LT [11 575 278] COCOMM D Co GRITRABN AND
Potter Marygay 2LT [17 386 907] COCOMM B Co GRITRABN

ARE HEREBY REASSIGNED TO:

2LT Mandella: PLCOMM 2 PL STFTHETA STARGATE
2LT Potter: PLCOMM 3 PL STFTHETA STARGATE
DESCRIPTION OF DUTIES:
command infantry platoon in Tet-2 campaign.

****

THE ABOVE NAMED PERSONNEL WILL RE-
PORT IMMEDIATELY TO GRIMALDI TRANS-
PORTATION BATTALION TO BE MANIFESTED
TO NEW ASSIGNMENT.

ISSUED   STARGATE   TACBD-1298-8684-1450/4
December 2024 SG

BY AUTH STFCOM Commander

ORDERSORDERS**ORDERS**ORDERS**
ORDERS**ORDERS**ORDERS**

"They didn't waste any time, did they?" Marygay said
bitterly.

"Must be a standing order. Strike Force Command's
light-weeks away. They can't even know we've re-upped
yet."

"What about our . . ." she let it trail off.

The guarantee. "Well, we *were* given our assignment
of choice. Nobody guaranteed we'd have the assignment
for more than an hour."

"It's so dirty."

I shrugged. "It's so army." But I had two disturbing
feelings:

That all along we knew this was going to happen.

That we were going home.

LIEUTENANT
MANDELLA
2024-2389 A. D.

"Quick and dirty." I was looking at my platoon sergeant, Santesteban, but talking to myself. And anybody else who was listening.

"Yeah," he said. "Gotta do it in the first coupla minutes or we're screwed tight." He was matter-of-fact, laconic. Drugged.

Private Collins came up with Halliday. They were holding hands unself-consciously. "Lieutenant Mandella?" Her voice broke a little. "Can we have just a minute?"

"One minute," I said, too abruptly. "We have to leave in five, I'm sorry."

Hard to watch those two together now. Neither one had any combat experience. But they knew what everybody did; how slim their chances were of ever being together again. They slumped in a corner and mumbled words and traded mechanical caresses, no passion or even comfort. Collin's eyes shone but she wasn't weeping. Halliday just looked grim, numb. She was normally by far the prettier of the two, but the sparkle had gone out of her and left a well-formed dull shell.

I'd gotten used to open female homosex in the months since we'd left Earth. Even stopped resenting the loss of potential partners. The men together still gave me a chill, though.

I stripped and backed into the clamshelled suit. The new ones were a hell of a lot more complicated, with all the new biometrics and trauma maintenance. But well worth the trouble of hooking up, in case you got blown apart just a little bit. Go home to a comfortable pension with heroic prosthesis. They were even talking about the possibility of regeneration, at least for missing arms and legs. Better get it soon, before Heaven filled up with fractional people. Heaven was the new hospital/rest-and-recreation planet.

I finished the set-up sequence and the suit closed by itself. Gritted my teeth against the pain that never came, when the internal sensors and fluid tubes poked into

125

your body. Conditioned neural bypass, so you felt only a slight puzzling dislocation. Rather than the death of a thousand cuts.

Collins and Halliday were getting into their suits now and the other dozen were almost set, so I stepped over to the third platoon's staging area. Say goodbye again to Marygay.

She was suited and heading my way. We touched helmets instead of using the radio. Privacy.

"Feeling OK, honey?"

"All right," she said. "Took my pill."

"Yeah, happy times." I'd taken mine too, supposed to make you feel optimistic without interfering with your sense of judgment. I knew most of us would probably die, but I didn't feel too bad about it. "Sack with me tonight?"

"If we're both here," she said neutrally. "Have to take a pill for that, too." She tried to laugh. "Sleep, I mean. How're the new people taking it? You have ten?"

"Ten, yeah, they're OK. Doped up, quarter-dose."

"I did that, too; try to keep them loose."

In fact, Santesteban was the only other combat veteran in my platoon; the four corporals had been in UNEF for a while but hadn't ever fought.

The speaker in my cheekbone crackled and Commander Cortez said, "Two minutes. Get your people lined up."

We had our goodbye and I went back to check my flock. Everybody seemed to have gotten suited up without any problems, so I put them on line. We waited for what seemed like a long time.

"All right, load 'em up." With the word "up," the bay door in front of me opened—the staging area having already been bled of air—and I led my men and women through to the assault ship.

These new ships were ugly as hell. Just an open framework with clamps to hold you in place, swiveled lasers fore and aft, small tachyon powerplants below the lasers. Everything automated; the machine would land us as quickly as possible and then zip off to harass the enemy. It was a one-use, throwaway drone. The vehicle that would come pick us up if we survived was cradled next to it, much prettier.

We clamped in and the assault ship cast off from the *Sangre y Victoria* with twin spurts from the yaw jets. Then the voice of the machine gave us a short countdown and we sped off at four gees' acceleration, straight down.

The planet, which we hadn't bothered to name, was a chunk of black rock without any normal star close enough to give it heat. At first it was visible only by the absence of stars where its bulk cut off their light, but as we dropped closer we could see subtle variations in the blackness of its surface. We were coming down on the hemisphere opposite the Taurans' outpost.

Our recon had shown that their camp sat in the middle of a flat lava plain several hundred kilometers in diameter. It was pretty primitive compared to other Tauran bases UNEF had encountered, but there wouldn't be any sneaking up on it. We were going to career over the horizon some fifteen klicks from the place, four ships converging simultaneously from different directions, all of us decelerating like mad, hopefully to drop right in their laps and come up shooting. There would be nothing to hide behind.

I wasn't worried, of course. Abstractedly, I wished I hadn't taken the pill.

We leveled off about a kilometer from the surface and sped along much faster than the rock's escape velocity, constantly correcting to keep from flying away. The surface rolled below us in a dark gray blur; we shed a little light from the pseudo-cerenkov glow made by our tachyon exhaust, scooting away from our reality into its own.

The ungainly contraption skimmed and jumped along for some ten minutes; then suddenly the front jet glowed and we were snapped forward inside our suits, eyeballs trying to escape from their sockets in the rapid deceleration.

"Prepare for ejection," the machine's female-mechanical voice said. "Five, four . . ."

The ship's lasers started firing, millisecond flashes freezing the land below in jerky stroboscopic motion. It was a twisted, pock-marked jumble of fissures and random black rocks, a few meters below our feet. We were dropping, slowing.

"Three—" It never got any farther. There was a too-bright flash and I saw the horizon drop away as the ship's tail pitched down—then clipped the ground, and we were rolling, horribly, pieces of people and ship scattering. Then we slid pinwheeling to a bumpy halt, and I tried to pull free but my leg was pinned under the ship's bulk: excruciating pain and a dry crunch as the girder crushed my leg; shrill whistle of air escaping my breached suit; then the trauma maintenance turned on *snick,* more pain, then no pain and I was rolling free, short stump of a leg trailing blood that froze shiny black on the dull black rock. I tasted brass and a red haze closed everything out, then deepened to the brown of river clay, then loam and I passed out, with the pill thinking *this is not so bad.* . . .

The suit is set up to save as much of your body as possible. If you lose part of an arm or a leg, one of sixteen razor-sharp irises closes around your limb with the force of a hydraulic press, snipping it off neatly and sealing the suit before you can die of explosive decompression. Then "trauma maintenance" cauterizes the stump, replaces lost blood, and fills you full of happy-juice and No-shock. So you will either die happy or, if your comrades go on to win the battle, eventually be carried back up to the ship's aid station.

We'd won that round, while I slept swaddled in dark cotton. I woke up in the infirmary. It was crowded. I was in the middle of a long row of cots, each one holding someone who had been three-fourths (or less) saved by his suit's trauma maintenance feature. We were being ignored by the ship's two doctors, who stood in bright light at operating tables, absorbed in blood rituals. I watched them for a long time. Squinting into the bright light, the blood on their green tunics could have been grease, the swathed bodies, odd soft machines that they were fixing. But the machines would cry out in their sleep, and the mechanics muttered reassurances while they plied their greasy tools. I watched and slept and woke up in different places.

Finally I woke up in a regular bay. I was strapped down and being fed through a tube, biosensor electrodes attached here and there, but no medics around. The only other person in the little room was Marygay, sleeping on the bunk next to me. Her right arm was amputated just above the elbow.

I didn't wake her up, just looked at her for a long time and tried to sort out my feelings. Tried to filter out the effect of the mood drugs. Looking at her stump, I could feel neither empathy nor revulsion. I tried to force one reaction, and then the other, but nothing real happened. It was as if she had always been that way. Was it drugs, conditioning, love? Have to wait to see.

Her eyes opened suddenly and I knew she had been awake for some time, had been giving me time to think. "Hello, broken toy," she said.

"How—how do you feel?" Bright question.

She put a finger to her lips and kissed it, a familiar gesture, reflection. "Stupid, numb. Glad not to be a soldier anymore." She smiled. "Did they tell you? We're going to Heaven."

"No. I knew it would be either there or Earth."

"Heaven will be better." Anything would. "I wish we were there now."

"How long?" I asked. "How long before we get there?"

She rolled over and looked at the ceiling. "No telling. You haven't talked to anybody?"

"Just woke up."

"There's a new directive they didn't bother to tell us about before. The *Sangre y Victoria* got orders for four missions. We have to keep on fighting until we've done all four. Or until we've sustained so many casualties that it wouldn't be practical to go on."

"How many is that?"

"I wonder. We lost a good third already. But we're headed for Aleph-7. Panty raid." New slang term for the type of operation whose main object we was to gather Tauran artifacts, and prisoners if possible. I tried to find out where the term came from, but the one explanation I got was really idiotic.

One knock on the door and Dr. Foster barged in. He fluttered his hands. "Still in separate *beds?* Marygay, I thought you were more recovered than that." Foster was all right. A flaming mariposa, but he had an amused tolerance for heterosexuality.

He examined Marygay's stump and then mine. He stuck thermometers in our mouths so we couldn't talk. When he spoke, he was serious and blunt.

"I'm not going to sugarcoat anything for you. You're both on happyjuice up to your ears, and the loss you've sustained isn't going to bother you until I take you off the stuff. For my own convenience I'm keeping you drugged until you get to Heaven. I have twenty-one amputees to take care of. We can't handle twenty-one psychiatric cases.

"Enjoy your peace of mind while you still have it. You two especially, since you'll probably want to stay together. The prosthetics you get on Heaven will work just fine, but every time you look at his mechanical leg or you look at her arm, you're going to think of how lucky the other one is. You're going to constantly trigger memories of pain and loss for each other. . . . You may be at each other's throats in a week. Or you may share a sullen kind of love for the rest of your lives.

"Or you may be able to transcend it. Give each other strength. Just don't kid yourselves if it doesn't work out."

He checked the readout on each thermometer and made a notation in his notebook. "Doctor knows best, even if he is a little weird by your own old-fashioned standards. Keep it in mind." He took the thermometer out of my mouth and gave me a little pat on the shoulder. Impartially, he did the same to Marygay. At the door, he said, "We've got collapsar insertion in about six hours. One of the nurses will take you to the tanks."

We went into the tanks—so much more comfortable and safer than the old individual acceleration shells—and dropped into the Tet-2 collapsar field already starting the crazy fifty-gee evasive maneuvers that would protect us from enemy cruisers when we popped out by Aleph-7, a microsecond later.

Predictably, the Aleph-7 campaign was a dismal failure, and we limped away from it with a two-campaign total of fifty-four dead and thirty-nine cripples bound for Heaven. Only twelve soldiers were still able to fight, but they weren't exactly straining at the leash.

It took three collapsar jumps to get to Heaven. No

ship ever went there directly from a battle, even though the delay sometimes cost extra lives. It was the one place besides Earth that the Taurans could not be allowed to find.

Heaven was a lovely, unspoiled Earth-like world; what Earth might have been like if men had treated her with compassion instead of lust. Virgin forests, white beaches, pristine deserts. The few dozen cities there either blended perfectly with the environment (one was totally underground) or were brazen statements of human ingenuity; Oceanus, in a coral reef with six fathoms of water over its transparent roof; Boreas, perched on a sheared-off mountaintop in the polar wasteland; and the fabulous Skye, a huge resort city that floated from continent to continent on the trade winds.

We landed, as everyone does, at the jungle city, Threshold. Three-fourths hospital, it's by far the planet's largest city, but you couldn't tell that from the air, flying down from orbit. The only sign of civilization was a short runway that suddenly appeared, a small white patch dwarfed to insignificance by the stately rain forest that crowded in from the east and an immense ocean that dominated the other horizon.

Once under the arboreal cover, the city was very much in evidence. Low buildings of native stone and wood rested among ten-meter-thick tree trunks. They were connected by unobtrusive stone paths, with one wide promenade meandering off to the beach. Sunlight filtered down in patches, and the air held a mixture of forest sweetness and salt tang.

I later learned that the city sprawled out over 200 square kilometers, that you could take a subway to anyplace that was too far to walk. The ecology of Threshold was very carefully balanced and maintained so as to resemble the jungle outside, with all the dangerous and uncomfortable elements eliminated. A powerful pressor field kept out large predators and such insect life as was not necessary for the health of the plants inside.

We walked, limped and rolled into the nearest building, which was the hospital's reception area. The rest of the hospital was underneath, thirty subterranean stories. Each person was examined and assigned his own room;

I tried to get a double with Marygay, but they weren't set up for that.

"Earth-year" was 2189. So I was 215 years old, God, look at that old codger. Somebody pass the hat—no, not necessary. The doctor who examined me said that my accumulated pay would be transferred from Earth to Heaven. With compound interest, I was just shy of being a billionaire. He remarked that I'd find lots of ways to spend my billion on Heaven.

They took the most severely wounded first, so it was several days before I went into surgery. Afterwards, I woke up in my room and found that they had grafted a prosthesis onto my stump, an articulated structure of shiny metal that to my untrained eye looked exactly like the skeleton of a leg and foot. It looked creepy as hell, lying there in a transparent bag of fluid, wires running out of it to a machine at the end of the bed.

An aide came in. "How you feelin', sir?" I almost told him to forget the "sir" bullshit, I was out of the army and staying out this time. But it might be nice for the guy to keep feeling that I outranked him.

"I don't know. Hurts a little."

"Gonna hurt like a sonuvabitch. Wait'll the nerves start to grow."

"Nerves?"

"Sure." He was fiddling with the machine, reading dials on the other side. "How you gonna have a leg without nerves? It'd just sit there."

"Nerves? Like regular nerves? You mean I can just think 'move' and the thing moves?"

"'Course you can." He looked at me quizzically, then went back to his adjustments.

What a wonder. "Prosthetics has sure come a long way."

"Pross-what-ics?"

"You know, artificial—"

"*Oh* yeah, like in books. Wooden legs, hooks and stuff."

How'd he ever get a job? "Yeah, prosthetics. Like this thing on the end of my stump."

"Look, sir." He set down the clipboard he'd been scribbling on. "You've been away a long time. That's gonna be a leg, just like the other leg except it can't break."

"They do it with arms, too?"

"Sure, any limb." He went back to his writing. "Livers, kidneys, stomachs, all kinds of things. Still working on hearts and lungs, have to use mechanical substitutes."

"Fantastic." Marygay would be whole again, too.

He shrugged. "Guess so. They've been doing it since before I was born. How old are you, sir?"

I told him, and he whistled. "God *damn*. You musta been in it from the beginning." His accent was very strange. All the words were right but all the sounds were wrong.

"Yeah. I was in the Epsilon attack. Aleph-null." They'd started naming collapsars after letters of the Hebrew alphabet, in order of discovery, then ran out of letters when the damn things started cropping up all over the place. So they added numbers after the letters; last I heard, they were up to Yod-42.

"Wow, ancient history. What was it like back then?"

"I don't know. Less crowded, nicer. Went back to Earth a year ago—hell, a century ago. Depends on how you look at it. It was so bad I re-enlisted, you know? Bunch of zombies. No offense."

He shrugged. "Never been there, myself. People who come from there seem to miss it. Maybe it got better."

"What, you were born on another planet? Heaven?" No wonder I couldn't place his accent.

"Born, raised and drafted." He put the pen back in his pocket and folded the clipboard up to a wallet-sized package. "Yes, sir. Third-generation angel. Best damned planet in all UNEF." He spelled it out, didn't say "youneff" the way I'd always heard it.

"Look, I've gotta run, lieutenant. Two other monitors to check, this hour." He backed out the door. "You need anything, there's a buzzer on the table there."

Third-generation angel. His grandparents came from Earth, probably when I was a young punk of a hundred. I wondered how many other worlds they'd colonized while my back was turned. Lose an arm, grow a new one?

It was going to be good to settle down and live a whole year for every year that went by.

The guy wasn't kidding about the pain. And it wasn't just the new leg, though that hurt like boiling oil. For the new tissues to "take," they'd had to subvert my body's resistance to alien cells; cancer broke out in a half-dozen places and had to be treated separately, painfully.

I was feeling pretty used up, but it was still kind of fascinating to watch the leg grow. White threads turned into blood vessels and nerves, first hanging a little slack, then moving into place as the musculature grew up around the metal bone.

I got used to seeing it grow, so the sight never repelled me. But when Marygay came to visit, it was a jolt —she was ambulatory before the skin on her new arm had started to grow; looked like a walking anatomy demonstration. I got over the shock, though, and she eventually came in for a few hours every day to play games or trade gossip or just sit and read, her arm slowly growing inside the plastic cast.

I'd had skin for a week before they uncased the new leg and trundled the machine away. It was ugly as hell, hairless and dead white, stiff as a metal rod. But it worked, after a fashion. I could stand up and shuffle along.

They transferred me to orthopedics, for "range and motion repatterning"—a fancy name for slow torture. They strap you into a machine that bends both the old and new legs simultaneously. The new one resists.

Marygay was in a nearby section, having her arm twisted methodically. It must have been even worse on her; she looked gray and haggard every afternoon, when we met to go upstairs and sunbathe in the broken shade.

As the days went by, the therapy became less like torture and more like strenuous exercise. We both began swimming for an hour or so every clear day, in the calm, pressor-guarded water off the beach. I still limped on land, but in the water I could get around pretty well.

The only real excitement we had on Heaven—excitement to our combat-blunted sensibilities—was in that carefully guarded water.

They have to turn off the pressor field for a split second every time a ship lands; otherwise it would just ricochet off over the ocean. Every now and then an animal slips in, but the dangerous land animals are too slow to get through. Not so in the sea.

The undisputed master of Heaven's oceans is an ugly customer that the angels, in a fit of originality, named the "shark." It could eat a stack of earth sharks for breakfast, though.

The one that got in was an average-sized white shark who had been bumping around the edge of the pressor field for days, tormented by all that protein splashing around inside. Fortunately, there's a warning siren two minutes before the pressor is shut down, so nobody was in the water when he came streaking through. And streak through he did, almost beaching himself in the fury of his fruitless attack.

He was twelve meters of flexible muscle with a razor-sharp tail at one end and a collection of arm-length fangs at the other. His eyes, big yellow globes, were set on stalks more than a meter out from his head. His mouth was so wide that, open, a man could comfortably stand in it. Make an impressive photo for his heirs.

They couldn't just turn off the pressor field and wait for the thing to swim away. So the Recreation Committee organized a hunting party.

I wasn't too enthusiastic about offering myself up as an hors d'oeuvre to a giant fish, but Marygay had spear-fished a lot as a kid growing up in Florida and was really excited by the prospect. I went along with the gag when I found out how they were doing it; seemed safe enough.

These "sharks" supposedly never attack people in boats. Two people who had more faith in fishermen's stories than I had gone out to the edge of the pressor field in a rowboat, armed only with a side of beef. They kicked the meat overboard and the shark was there in a flash.

This was the cue for us to step in and have our fun. There were twenty-three of us fools waiting on the beach with flippers, masks, breathers and one spear each. The spears were pretty formidable, though, jet-propelled and with high-explosive heads.

We splashed in and swam in phalanx, underwater, toward the feeding creature. When it saw us at first, it didn't attack. It tried to hide its meal, presumably so that some of us wouldn't be able to sneak around and munch on it while the shark was dealing with the others. But every time he tried for the deep water, he'd bump into the pressor field. He was obviously getting pissed off.

Finally, he just let go of the beef, whipped around and charged. Great sport. He was the size of your finger one second, way down there at the other end of the field, then suddenly as big as the guy next to you and closing fast.

Maybe ten of the spears hit him—mine didn't—and they tore him to shreds. But even after an expert, or lucky, brain shot that took off the top of his head and one eye, even with half his flesh and entrails scattered in a bloody path behind him, he slammed into our line and clamped his jaws around a woman, grinding off both of her legs before it occurred to him to die.

We carried her, barely alive, back to the beach, where an ambulance was waiting. They poured her full of blood surrogate and No-shock and rushed her to the hospital, where she survived to eventually go through the agony of growing new legs. I decided that I would leave the hunting of fish to other fish.

Most of our stay at Threshold, once the therapy became bearable, was pleasant enough. No military discipline, lots of reading and things to potter around with. But there was a pall over it, since it was obvious that we weren't out of the army; just pieces of broken equipment that they were fixing up to throw back into the fray. Marygay and I each had another three years to serve in our lieutenancies.

But we did have six months of rest and recreation coming once our new limbs were pronounced in good working order. Marygay was released two days before I was but waited around for me.

My back pay came to $892,746,012. Not in the form of bales of currency, fortunately; on Heaven they used an electronic credit exchange, so I carried my fortune around in a little machine with a digital readout. To buy something you punched in the vendor's credit number and the amount of purchase; the sum was automatically shuffled from your account to his. The machine was the size of a slender wallet and coded to your thumbprint.

Heaven's economy was governed by the continual presence of thousands of resting, recreating millionaire soldiers. A modest snack would cost a hundred bucks, a room for a night at least ten times that. Since UNEF built and owned Heaven, this runaway inflation was pretty transparently a simple way of getting our accumulated pay back into the economic mainstream.

We had fun, desperate fun. We rented a flyer and camping gear and went off for weeks, exploring the planet. There were icy rivers to swim and lush jungles to crawl through; meadows and mountains and polar wastes and deserts.

We could be totally protected from the environment by adjusting our individual pressor fields—sleep naked in a blizzard—or we could take nature straight. At Marygay's suggestion, the last thing we did before coming back to civilization was to climb a pinnacle in the desert, fasting for several days to heighten our sensibilities (or warp our perceptions, I'm still not sure), and sit back-to-back in the searing heat, contemplating the languid flux of life.

Then off to the fleshpots. We toured every city on the planet, and each had its own particular charm, but we finally returned to Skye to spend the rest of our leave time.

The rest of the planet was bargain-basement compared to Skye. In the four weeks we were using the airborne pleasure dome as our home base, Marygay and I each went through a good half-billion dollars. We gambled—sometimes losing a million dollars or more in a night—ate and drank the finest the planet had to offer, and sampled every service and product that wasn't too bizarre for our admittedly archaic tastes. We each had a personal servant whose salary was rather more than that of a major general.

Desperate fun, as I said. Unless the war changed radically, our chances of surviving the next three years were microscopic. We were remarkably healthy victims of a terminal disease, trying to cram a lifetime of sensation into a half of a year.

We did have the consolation, not small, that however short the remainder of our lives would be, we would at

137

least be together. For some reason it never occurred to me that even that could be taken from us.

We were enjoying a light lunch in the transparent "first floor" of Skye, watching the ocean glide by underneath us, when a messenger bustled in and gave us two envelopes: our orders.

Marygay had been bumped to captain, and I to major, on the basis of our military records and tests we had taken at Threshold. I was a company commander and she was a company's executive officer.

But they weren't the same company.

She was going to muster with a new company being formed right here on Heaven. I was going back to Stargate for "indoctrination and education" before taking command.

For a long time we couldn't say anything. "I'm going to protest," I said finally, weakly. "They can't make me a commander. Into a commander."

She was still struck dumb. This was not just a separation. Even if the war was over and we left for Earth only a few minutes apart, in different ships, the geometry of the collapsar jump would pile up years between us. When the second one arrived on Earth, his partner would probably be a half-century older; more probably dead.

We sat there for some time, not touching the exquisite food, ignoring the beauty around us and beneath us, only conscious of each other and the two sheets of paper that separated us with a gulf as wide and real as death.

We went back to Threshold. I protested but my arguments were shrugged off. I tried to get Marygay assigned to my company, as my exec. They said my personnel had all been allotted. I pointed out that most of them probably hadn't even been born yet. Nevertheless, allotted, they said. It would be almost a century, I said, before I even get to Stargate. They replied that Strike Force Command *plans* in terms of centuries.

Not in terms of people.

We had a day and a night together. The less said about that, the better. It wasn't just losing a lover. Marygay and I were each other's only link to real life, the Earth of the 1980s and 90s. Not the perverse grotesquerie we were supposedly fighting to preserve. When her shuttle took off it was like a casket rattling down into a grave.

I commandeered computer time and found out the orbital elements of her ship and its departure time; found out I could watch her leave from "our" desert.

I landed on the pinnacle where we had starved together and, a few hours before dawn, watched a new star appear over the western horizon, flare to brilliance and fade as it moved away, becoming just another star, then a dim star, and then nothing. I walked to the edge and looked down the sheer rock face to the dim frozen rippling of dunes half a kilometer below. I sat with my feet dangling over the edge, thinking nothing, until the sun's oblique rays illuminated the dunes in a soft, tempting chiaroscuro of low relief. Twice I shifted my weight as if to jump. When I didn't, it was not for fear of pain or loss. The pain would be only a bright spark and the loss would be only the army's. And it would be their ultimate victory over me—having ruled my life for so long, to force an end to it.

That much, I owed to the enemy.

MAJOR
MANDELLA
2458-3143

What was that old experiment they told us about in high school biology? Take a flatworm and teach it how to swim through a maze. Then mash it up and feed it to a stupid flatworm, and lo! the stupid flatworm would be able to swim the maze, too.

I had a bad taste of major general in my mouth.

Actually, I supposed they had refined the techniques since my high school days. With time dilation, that was about 450 years for research and development.

At Stargate, my orders said, I was to undergo "indoctrination and education" prior to taking command of my very own Strike Force. Which was what they still called a company.

For my education on Stargate, they didn't mince up major generals and serve them to me with hollandaise. They didn't feed me *anything* except glucose for three weeks. Glucose and electricity.

They shaved every hair off my body, gave me a shot that turned me into a dishrag, attached dozens of electrodes to my head and body, immersed me in a tank of oxygenated fluorocarbon, and hooked me up to an ALSC. That's an "accelerated life situation computer." It kept me busy.

I guess it took the machine about ten minutes to review everything I had learned previously about the martial (excuse the expression) arts. Then it started in on the new stuff.

I learned the best way to use every weapon from a rock to a nova bomb. Not just intellectually; that's what all those electrodes were for. Cybernetically-controlled negative feedback kinesthesia; I felt the weapons in my hands and watched my performance with them. And did it over and over until I did it right. The illusion of reality was total. I used a spear-thrower with a band of Masai warriors on a village raid, and when I looked down at my body it was long and black. I relearned epee from a cruel-looking man in foppish clothes, in an eighteenth-century French courtyard. I sat quietly in a tree

143

with a Sharps rifle and sniped at blue-uniformed men as they crawled across a muddy field toward Vicksburg. In three weeks I killed several regiments of electronic ghosts. It seemed more like a year to me, but the ALSC does strange things to your sense of time.

Learning to use useless exotic weapons was only a small part of the training. In fact, it was the relaxing part. Because when I wasn't in kinesthesia, the machine kept my body totally inert and zapped my brain with four millenia's worth of military facts and theories. And I couldn't forget any of it! Not while I was in the tank.

Want to know who Scipio Aemilianus was? I don't. Bright light of the Third Punic War. *War is the province of danger and therefore courage above all things is the first quality of a warrior,* von Clausewitz maintained. And I'll never forget the poetry of "the advance party minus normally moves in a column formation with the platoon headquarters leading, followed by a laser squad, the heavy weapons squad, and the remaining laser squad; the column relies on observation for its flank security except when the terrain and visibility dictate the need for small security detachments to the flanks, in which case the advance party commander will detail one platoon sergeant . . ." and so on. That's from *Strike Force Command Small Unit Leader's Handbook,* as if you could call something a handbook when it takes up two whole microfiche cards, 2,000 pages.

If you want to become a thoroughly eclectic expert in a subject that repels you, join UNEF and sign up for officer training.

One hundred nineteen people, and I was responsible for 118 of them. Counting myself but not counting the Commodore, who could presumably take care of herself.

I hadn't met any of my company during the two weeks of physical rehabilitation that followed the ALSC session. Before our first muster I was supposed to report to the Temporal Orientation Officer. I called for an appointment and his clerk said the Colonel would meet me at the Level Six Officers' Club after dinner.

I went down to Six early, thinking to eat dinner there, but they had nothing but snacks. So I munched on a fungus thing that vaguely resembled escargots and took the rest of my calories in the form of alcohol.

144

TABLE OF ORGANIZATION

Strike Force Gamma

Sade—138 Campaign

1ECHN:	*MAJ Mandella*		*COMM Antopol*
2ECHN:	*CAPT Moore*		
3ECHN:	*1LT Hilleboe*		
4ECHN:	*2LT Riland*		
	2LT Rusk		
	2LT Alsever MD		
5ECHN:	*2LT Borgstedt* *2LT Brill*	*2LT Gainor*	*2LT Heimoff*
6ECHN:	*SSgt Webster* *SSgt Gillies*	*SSgt Abrams*	*SSgt Dole*
7ECHN:	Sgt Dolins Sgt Bell	Sgt Anderson	Sgt Noyes
	Cpl Geller Cpl Kahn	Cpl Kalvin	Cpl Spraggs
8ECHN:	Pvt Boas Cpl Weiner	Pvt Miller	Pvt Conroy
	Pvt Lingeman Pvt Ikle	Pvt Reisman	Pvt Yakata
	Pvt Rosevear Pvt Schon	Pvt Coupling	Pvt Burris
	Pvt Wolfe, R. Pvt Shubik	Pvt Rostow	Pvt Cohen
	Pvt Lin Pvt. Duhl	Pvt Huntington	Pvt Graham
	Pvt Simmons Pvt Perloff	Pvt De Sola	Pvt Schoellple
	Pvt Winograd Pvt Moynihan	Pvt Pool	Pvt Wolfe, E.
	Pvt Brown	Pvt Nepala	Pvt Karkoshka
	Pvt Bloomquist Pvt Frank	Pvt Schuba	Pvt Majer
	Pvt Graubard	Pvt Ulanov	Pvt Dioujova
	Pvt Wong Pvt Orlans	Pvt Shelley	Pvt Armaing
	Pvt Louria Pvt Mayr	Pvt Lynn	Pvt Baulez
	Pvt Gross Pvt Quarton	Pvt Slaer	Pvt Johnson
	Pvt Asadi Pvt Hin	Pvt Schenk	Pvt Orbrecht
	Pvt Horman Pvt Stendahl	Pvt Deelstra	Pvt Kayibanda
	Pvt Fox Pvt Erikson	Pvt Levy	Pvt Tschudi
	Pvt Bora		

Supporting: 1LT Williams (NAV), 2LTs Jarvil (MED), Laasonen (MED), Wilber (PSY), Szydlowska (MAINT), Gaptchenko (ORD) Gedo (COMM), Gim (COMP); 1SGTs Evans (MED), Rodriguez (MED), Kostidinov (MED), Rwabwogo (PSY), Blazynski (MAINT), Turpin (ORD); SSGTs Carreras (MED), Kousnetzov (MED), Waruinge (MED), Rojas (MED), Botos (MAINT), Orban (CK), Mbugua (COMP); SGTs Perez (MED), Seales (MAINT), Anghelov (ORD) Vugin (COMP); CPLs Daborg (MED), Correa (MED), Kajdi (SEX), Valdez (SEX), Muranga (ORD); PVTs Kottysch (MAINT), Rudkoski (CK), Minter (ORD).

APPROVED STFCOM STARGATE 12 Mar 2458. FOR THE COMMANDER:

Olga Torischeva BGEN STFCOM

145

"Major Mandella?" I'd been busily engaged in my seventh beer and hadn't seen the Colonel approach. I started to rise but he motioned for me to stay seated and dropped heavily into the chair opposite me.

"I'm in your debt," he said. "You saved me from at least half of a boring evening." He offered his hand. "Jack Kynock, at your service."

"Colonel—"

"Don't Colonel me and I won't Major you. We old fossils have to . . . keep our perspective. William."

"All right with me."

He ordered a kind of drink I'd never heard of. "Where to start? Last time you were on Earth was 2007, according to the records."

"That's right."

"Didn't like it much, did you?"

"No." Zombies, happy robots.

"Well, it got better. Then it got worse, thank you." A private brought his drink, a bubbling concoction that was green at the bottom of the glass and lightened to chartreuse at the top. He sipped. "Then they got better again, then worse, then . . . I don't know. Cycles."

"What's it like now?"

"Well . . . I'm not really sure. Stacks of reports and such, but it's hard to filter out the propaganda. I haven't been back in almost two hundred years; it was pretty bad then. Depending on what you like."

"What do you mean?"

"Oh, let me see. There was lots of excitement. Ever hear of the Pacifist movement?"

"I don't think so."

"Hmn, the name's deceptive. Actually, it was a war, a guerrilla war."

"I thought I could give you name, rank and serial number of every war from Troy on up." He smiled. "They must have missed one."

"For good reason. It was run by veterans—survivors of Yod-38 and Aleph-40, I hear; they got discharged together and decided they could take on all of UNEF, Earthside. They got lots of support from the population."

"But didn't win."

"We're still here." He swirled his drink and the colors

shifted. "Actually, all I know is hearsay. Last time I got to Earth, the war was over, except for some sporadic sabotage. And it wasn't exactly a safe topic of conversation."

"It surprises me a little," I said, "well, more than a little. That Earth's population would do anything at all . . . against the government's wishes."

He made a noncommittal sound.

"Least of all, revolution. When we were there, you couldn't get anybody to say a damned thing against the UNEF—or any of the local governments, for that matter. They were conditioned from ear to ear to accept things as they were."

"Ah. That's a cyclic thing, too." He settled back in his chair. "It's not a matter of technique. If they wanted to, Earth's government could have total control over . . . every nontrivial thought and action of each citizen, from cradle to grave.

"They don't do it because it would be fatal. Because there's a war on. Take your own case: did you get any motivational conditioning while you were in the can?"

I thought for a moment. "If I did, I wouldn't necessarily know about it."

"That's true. Partially true. But take my word for it, they left that part of your brain alone. Any change in your attitude toward UNEF or the war, or war in general, comes only from new knowledge. Nobody's fiddled with your basic motivations. And you should know why."

Names, dates, figures rattled down through the maze of new knowledge. "Tet-17, Sed-21, Aleph-14. The Lazlo . . . 'The Lazlo Emergency Commission Report.' June, 2106."

"Right. And by extension, your own experience on Aleph-1. Robots don't make good soldiers."

"They would," I said. "Up to the twenty-first century. Behavioral conditioning would have been the answer to a general's dream. Make up an army with all the best features of the SS, the Praetorian Guard, the Golden Horde. Mosby's Raiders, the Green Berets."

He laughed over his glass. "Then put that army up against a squad of men in modern fighting suits. It'd be over in a couple of minutes."

"So long as each man in the squad kept his head about him. And just fought like hell to stay alive." The generation of soldiers that had precipitated the Lazlo Reports had been conditioned from birth to conform to somebody's vision of the ideal fighting man. They worked beautifully as a team, totally bloodthirsty, placing no great importance on personal survival—and the Taurans cut them to ribbons. The Taurans also fought with no regard for self. But they were better at it, and there were always more of them.

Kynock took a drink and watched the colors. "I've seen your psych profile," he said. "Both before you got here and after your session in the can. It's essentially the same, before and after."

"That's reassuring," I signaled for another beer.

"Maybe it shouldn't be."

"What, it says I won't make a good officer? I told them that from the beginning. I'm no leader."

"Right in a way, wrong in a way. Want to know what that profile says?"

I shrugged. "Classified, isn't it?"

"Yes," he said. "But you're a major now. You can pull the profile of anybody in your command."

"I don't suppose it has any big surprises." But I was a little curious. What animal isn't fascinated by a mirror?

"No. It says you're a pacifist. A failed one at that, which gives you a mild neurosis. Which you handle by transferring the burden of guilt to the army."

The fresh beer was so cold it hurt my teeth. "No surprises yet."

"If you had to kill a man, rather than a Tauran, I'm not sure you could do it. Even though you must know a thousand different ways."

I didn't know how to answer that. Which probably meant he was right.

"And as far as being a leader, you do have a certain potential. But it would be along the lines of a teacher or a minister; you would have to lead from empathy, compassion. You have the desire to impose your ideas on other people, but not your will. Which means, you're right, you'll make one hell of a bad officer unless you shape up."

148

I had to laugh. "UNEF must have known all of this when they ordered me to officer training."

"There are other parameters," he said. "For instance, you're adaptable, reasonably intelligent, analytical. And you're one of the eleven people who's lived through the whole war."

"Surviving is a virtue in a private." Couldn't resist it. "But an officer should provide gallant example. Go down with the ship. Stride the parapet as if unafraid."

He harrumphed at that. "Not when you're a thousand light years from your replacement."

"It doesn't add up, though. Why would they haul me all the way from Heaven to take a chance on my 'shaping up,' when probably a third of the people here on Stargate are better officer material? God, the military mind!"

"I suspect the bureaucratic mind, at least, had something to do with it. You have an embarrassing amount of seniority to be a footsoldier."

"That's all time dilation. I've only been in three campaigns."

"Immaterial. Besides, that's two-and-a-half more than the average soldier survives. The propaganda boys will probably make you into some kind of a folk hero."

"Folk hero." I sipped at the beer. "Where is John Wayne now that we really need him?"

"John Wayne?" He shook his head. "I never went in the can, you know. I'm no expert at military history."

"Forget it."

Kynock finished his drink and asked the private to get him—I swear to God—a "rum Antares."

"Well, I'm supposed to be your Temporal Orientation Officer. What do you want to know about the present? What passes for the present."

Still on my mind: "You've never been in the can?"

"No, combat officers only. The computer facilities and energy you go through in three weeks would keep the Earth running for several days. Too expensive for us desk-warmers."

"Your decorations say you're combat."

"Honorary. I was." The rum Antares was a tall slender glass with a little ice floating at the top, filled with pale amber liquid. At the bottom was a bright red globule about the size of a thumbnail; crimson filaments waved up from it.

"What's that red stuff?"

"Cinnamon. Oh, some ester with cinnamon in it. Quite good . . . want a taste?"

"No, I'll stick to beer, thanks."

"Down at level one, the library machine has a temporal orientation file, that my staff updates every day. You can go to it for specific questions. Mainly I want to . . . prepare you for meeting your Strike Force."

"What, they're all cyborgs? Clones?"

He laughed. "No, it's illegal to clone humans. The main problem is with, uh, you're heterosexual."

"Oh, that's no problem. I'm tolerant."

"Yes, your profile shows that you . . . think you're tolerant, but that's not the problem, exactly."

"Oh," I knew what he was going to say. Not the details, but the substance.

"Only emotionally stable people are drafted into UNEF. I know this is hard for you to accept, but heterosexuality is considered an emotional dysfunction. Relatively easy to cure."

"If they think they're going to cure *me*—"

"Relax, you're too old." He took a delicate sip. "It won't be as hard to get along with them as you might—"

"Wait. You mean nobody . . . everybody in my company is homosexual? But me?"

"William, everybody on Earth is homosexual. Except for a thousand or so; veterans and incurables."

"Ah." What could I say? "Seems like a drastic way to solve the population problem."

"Perhaps. It does work, though; Earth's population is stable at just under a billion. When one person dies or goes offplanet, another is quickened."

"Not 'born.' "

"Born, yes, but not the old-fashioned way. Your old term for it was 'test-tube babies,' but of course they don't use a test-tube."

"Well, that's something."

"Part of every creche is an artificial womb that takes care of a person the first eight or ten months after quickening. What you would call birth takes place over a period of days; it isn't the sudden, drastic event that it used to be."

O brave new world, I thought. "No birth trauma. A billion perfectly adjusted homosexuals."

"Perfectly adjusted by present-day Earth standards. You and I might find them a little odd."

"That's an understatement." I drank off the rest of my beer. "Yourself, you, uh . . . are you homosexual?"

"Oh, no," he said. I relaxed. "Actually, though, I'm not hetero any more, either." He slapped his hip and it made an odd sound. "Got wounded and it turned out that I had a rare disorder of the lymphatic system, can't regenerate. Nothing but metal and plastic from the waist down. To use your word, I'm a cyborg."

Far out, as my mother used to say. "Oh, Private," I called to the waiter, "bring me one of those Antares things." Sitting here in a bar with an asexual cyborg who is probably the only other normal person on the whole god-damned planet.

"Make it a double, please."

2.

They looked normal enough, filing into the lecture hall where we held our first muster, the next day. Rather young and a little stiff.

Most of them had only been out of the creche for seven or eight years. The creche was a controlled, isolated environment to which only a few specialists—pediatricians and teachers, mostly—had access. When a person leaves creche at age twelve or thirteen, he chooses a first name (his last name having been taken from the donor-parent with the higher genetic rating) and is legally a probationary adult, with schooling about equivalent to what I had after my first year of college. Most of them go on to more specialized education, but some are assigned a job and go right to work.

They're observed very closely and anyone who shows any signs of sociopathy, such as heterosexual leanings, is

151

sent away to a correctional facility. He's either cured or kept there for the rest of his life.

Everyone is drafted into UNEF at the age of twenty. Most people work at a desk for five years and are discharged. A few lucky souls, about one in eight thousand, are invited to volunteer for combat training. Refusing is "sociopathic," even though it means signing up for an extra five years. And your chance of surviving the ten years is so small as to be negligible; nobody ever had. Your best chance is to have the war end before your ten (subjective) years of service are up. Hope that time dilation puts many years between each of your battles.

Since you can figure on going into battle roughly once every subjective year, and since an average of 34 percent survive each battle, it's easy to compute your chances of being able to fight it out for ten years. It comes to about two one-thousandths of one percent. Or, to put it another way, get an old-fashioned six-shooter and play Russian Roulette with four of the six chambers loaded. If you can do it ten times in a row without decorating the opposite wall, congratulations! You're a civilian.

There being some sixty thousand combat soldiers in UNEF, you could expect about 1.2 of them to survive for ten years. I didn't seriously plan on being the lucky one, even though I was halfway there.

How many of these young soldiers filing into the auditorium knew they were doomed? I tried to match faces up with the dossiers I'd been scanning all morning, but it was hard. They'd all been selected through the same battery of stringent parameters, and they looked remarkably alike: tall but not too tall, muscular but not heavy, intelligent but not in a brooding way . . . and Earth was much more racially homogenous than it had been in my century. Most of them looked vaguely Polynesian. Only two of them, Kayibanda and Lin, seemed pure representatives of racial types. I wondered whether the others gave them a hard time.

Most of the women were achingly handsome, but I was in no position to be critical. I'd been celibate for over a year, ever since saying goodbye to Marygay, back on Heaven.

I wondered if one of them might have a trace of atavism, or might humor her commander's eccentricity. *It is absolutely forbidden for an officer to form sexual liaison with his subordinates*. Such a warm way of putting it. *Violation of this regulation is punishable by attachment of all funds and reduction to the rank of private or, if the relationship interferes with a unit's combat efficiency, summary execution*. If all of UNEF's regulations could be broken so casually and consistently as that one was, it would be a very easygoing army.

But not one of the boys appealed to me. How they'd look after another year, I wasn't sure.

"Tench-*hut!*" That was Lieutenant Hilleboe. It was a credit to my new reflexes that I didn't jump to my feet. Everybody in the auditorium snapped to.

"My name is Lieutenant Hilleboe and I am your Second Field Officer." That used to be "Field First Sergeant." A good sign that an army has been around too long is that it starts getting top-heavy with officers.

Hilleboe came on like a real hard-ass professional soldier. Probably shouted orders at the mirror every morning, while she was shaving. But I'd seen her profile and knew that she'd only been in action once, and only for a couple of minutes at that. Lost an arm and a leg and was commissioned, same as me, as a result of the tests they give at the regeneration clinic.

Hell, maybe she had been a very pleasant person before going through that trauma; it was bad enough just having one limb regrown.

She was giving them the usual first-sergeant peptalk, stern-but-fair: don't waste my time with little things, use the chain of command, most problems can be solved at the fifth echelon.

It made me wish I'd had more time to talk with her earlier. Strike Force Command had really rushed us into this first muster—we were scheduled to board ship the next day—and I'd only had a few words with my officers.

Not enough, because it was becoming clear that Hilleboe and I had rather disparate philosophies about how to run a company. It was true that *running* it was her job; I only commanded. But she was setting up a potential "good guy-bad guy" situation, using the chain of command to so isolate herself from the men and women

153

under her. I had planned not to be quite so aloof, setting aside an hour every other day when any soldier could come to me directly with grievances or suggestions, without permission from his superiors.

We had both been given the same information during our three weeks in the can. It was interesting that we'd arrived at such different conclusions about leadership. This Open Door policy, for instance, had shown good results in "modern" armies in Australia and America. And it seemed especially appropriate to our situation, in which everybody would be cooped up for months or even years at a time. We'd used the system on the *Sangre y Victoria,* the last starship to which I'd been attached, and it had seemed to keep tensions down.

She had them at ease while delivering this organizational harangue; pretty soon she'd call them to attention and introduce me. What would I talk about? I'd planned just to say a few predictable words and explain my Open Door policy, then turn them over to Commodore Antopol, who would say something about the *Masaryk II.* But I'd better put off my explanation until after I'd had a long talk with Hilleboe; in fact, it would be best if she were the one to introduce the policy to the men and women, so it wouldn't look like the two of us were at loggerheads.

My executive officer, Captain Moore, saved me. He came rushing through a side door—he was always rushing, a pudgy meteor—threw a quick salute and handed me an envelope that contained our combat orders. I had a quick whispered conference with the Commodore, and she agreed that it wouldn't do any harm to tell them where we were going, even though the rank and file technically didn't have the "need to know."

One thing we didn't have to worry about in this war was enemy agents. With a good coat of paint, a Tauran might be able to disguise himself as an ambulatory mushroom. Bound to raise suspicions.

Hilleboe had called them to attention and was dutifully telling them what a good commander I was going to be; that I'd been in the war from the beginning, and if they intended to survive through their enlistment they had better follow my example. She didn't mention that I was a mediocre soldier with a talent for getting missed. Nor that I'd resigned from the army at the earliest opportunity and only got back in because conditions on Earth were so intolerable.

"Thank you, Lieutenant." I took her place at the podium. "At ease." I unfolded the single sheet that had our orders, and held it up. "I have some good news and some bad news." What had been a joke five centuries before was now just a statement of fact.

"These are our combat orders for the Sade-138 campaign. The good news is that we probably won't be fighting, not immediately. The bad news is that we're going to be a target."

They stirred a little bit at that, but nobody said anything or took his eyes off me. Good discipline. Or maybe just fatalism; I didn't know how realistic a picture they had of their future. Their lack of a future, that is.

"What we are ordered to do . . . is to find the largest portal planet orbiting the Sade-138 collapsar and build a base there. Then stay at the base until we are relieved. That will be two or three years, probably.

"During that time we will almost certainly be attacked. As most of you probably know, Strike Force Command has uncovered a pattern in the enemy's movements from collapsar to collapsar. They hope eventually to trace this complex pattern back through time and space and find the Taurans' home planet. For the present, they can only send out intercepting forces, to hamper the enemy's expansion.

"In a large perspective, this is what we're ordered to do. We'll be one of several dozen strike forces employed in these blocking maneuvers, on the enemy's frontier. I won't be able to stress often enough or hard enough how important this mission is—if UNEF can keep the enemy from expanding, we may be able to envelope him. And win the war."

Preferably before we're all dead meat. "One thing I want to be clear: we may be attacked the day we land, or we may simply occupy the planet for ten years and come on home." Fat chance. "Whatever happens, every one of us will stay in the best fighting trim all the time. In transit, we will maintain a regular program of calisthenics as well as a review of our training. Especially construction techniques—we have to set up the base and its defense facilities in the shortest possible time."

God, I was beginning to sound like an officer. "Any questions?" There were none. "Then I'd like to introduce Commodore Antopol. Commodore?"

The Commodore didn't try to hide her boredom as she outlined, to this room full of ground-pounders, the characteristics and capabilities of *Masaryk II*. I had learned most of what she was saying through the can's force-feeding, but the last thing she said caught my attention.

"Sade-138 will be the most distant collapsar men have gone to. It isn't even in the galaxy proper, but rather is part of the Large Magellanic Cloud, some 150,000 light years distant.

"Our voyage will require four collapsar jumps and will last some four months, subjective. Maneuvering into collapsar insertion will put us about three hundred years behind Stargate's calendar by the time we reach Sade-138."

And another seven hundred years gone, if I lived to return. Not that it would make that much difference; Marygay was as good as dead and there wasn't another person alive who meant anything to me.

"As the major said, you mustn't let these figures lull you into complacency. The enemy is also headed for Sade-138; we may all get there the same day. The mathematics of the situation is complicated, but take our word for it; it's going to be a close race.

"Major, do you have anything more for them?"

I started to rise. "Well . . ."

"Tench-*hut!*" Hilleboe shouted. Had to learn to expect that.

"Only that I'd like to meet with my senior officers, echelon 4 and above, for a few minutes. Platoon sergeants, you're responsible for getting your troops to Staging Area 67 at 0400 tomorrow morning. Your time's your own until then. Dismissed."

I invited the five officers up to my billet and brought out a bottle of real French brandy. It had cost two

156

months' pay, but what else could I do with the money? Invest it?

I passed around glasses but Alsever, the doctor, demurred. Instead she broke a little capsule under her nose and inhaled deeply. Then tried without too much success to mask her euphoric expression.

"First let's get down to one basic personnel problem," I said, pouring. "Do all of you know that I'm not homosexual?"

Mixed chorus of yes sirs and no sirs.

"Do you think this is going to . . . complicate my situation as commander? As far as the rank and file?"

"Sir, I don't—" Moore began.

"No need for honorifics," I said, "not in this closed circle; I was a private four years ago, in my own time frame. When there aren't any troops around, I'm just Mandella, or William." I had a feeling that was a mistake even as I was saying it. "Go on."

"Well, William," he continued, "it might have been a problem a hundred years ago. You know how people felt then."

"Actually, I don't. All I know about the period from the twenty-first century to the present is military history."

"Oh. Well, it was, uh, it was, how to say it?" His hands fluttered.

"It was a crime," Alsever said laconically. "That was when the Eugenics Council was first getting people used to the idea of universal homosex."

"Eugenics Council?"

"Part of UNEF. Only has authority on Earth." She took a deep sniff at the empty capsule. "The idea was to keep people from making babies the biological way. Because, *A*, people showed a regrettable lack of sense in choosing their genetic partner. And *B*, the Council saw that racial differences had an unnecessarily divisive effect on humanity; with total control over births, they could make everybody the same race in a few generations."

I didn't know they had gone quite that far. But I suppose it was logical. "You approve? As a doctor."

"As a doctor? I'm not sure." She took another capsule from her pocket and rolled it between thumb and forefinger, staring at nothing. Or something the rest of us couldn't see. "In a way, it makes my job simpler. A lot of diseases simply no longer exist. But I don't think they know as much about genetics as they think they do. It's not an exact science; they could be doing something very wrong, and the results wouldn't show up for centuries."

She cracked the capsule under her nose and took two deep breaths. "As a woman, though, I'm all in favor of it." Hilleboe and Rusk nodded vigorously.

"Not having to go through childbirth?"

"That's part of it." She crossed her eyes comically, looking at the capsule, gave it a final sniff. "Mostly, though, it's not . . . having to . . . have a man. Inside me. You understand. It's disgusting."

Moore laughed. "If you haven't tried it, Diana, don't—"

"Oh, shut up." She threw the empty capsule at him playfully.

"But it's perfectly natural," I protested.

"So is swinging through trees. Digging for roots with a blunt stick. Progress, my good major; progress."

"Anyway," Moore said, "it was only a crime for a short period. Then it was considered a, oh, curable . . ."

"Dysfunction," Alsever said.

"Thank you. And now, well, it's so rare . . . I doubt that any of the men and women have any strong feelings about it, one way or the other."

"Just an eccentricity," Diana said, magnanimously. "Not as if you ate babies."

"That's right, Mandella," Hilleboe said. "I don't feel any differently toward you because of it."

"I—I'm glad." That was just great. It was dawning on me that I had not the slightest idea of how to conduct myself socially. So much of my "normal" behavior was based on a complex unspoken code of sexual etiquette. Was I suppose to treat the men like women, and vice versa? Or treat everybody like brothers and sisters? It was all very confusing.

I finished off my glass and set it down. "Well, thanks for your reassurances. That was mainly what I wanted to ask you about . . . I'm sure you all have things to do, goodbyes and such. Don't let me hold you prisoner."

They all wandered off except for Charlie Moore. He and I decided to go on a monumental binge, trying to hit every bar and officer's club in the sector. We managed twelve and probably could have hit them all, but I decided to get a few hours' sleep before the next day's muster.

The one time Charlie made a pass at me, he was very polite about it. I hoped my refusal was also polite—but figured I'd be getting lots of practice.

3.

UNEF's first starships had been possessed of a kind of spidery, delicate beauty. But with various technological improvements, structural strength became more important than conserving mass (one of the old ships would have folded up like an accordian if you'd tried a twenty-five-gee maneuver), and that was reflected in the design: stolid, heavy, functional-looking. The only decoration was the name MASARYK II, stenciled in dull blue letters across the obsidian hull.

Our shuttle drifted over the name on its way to the loading bay, and there was a crew of tiny men and women doing maintenance on the hull. With them as a reference, we could see that the letters were a good hundred meters tall. The ship was over a kilometer long (1036.5 meters, my latent memory said), and about a third that wide (319.4 meters).

That didn't mean there was going to be plenty of elbow-room. In its belly, the ship held six large tachyon-drive fighters and fifty robot drones. The infantry was tucked off in a corner. *War is the province of friction*, Chuck von Clausewitz said; I had a feeling we were going to put him to the test.

We had about six hours before going into the acceleration tank. I dropped my kit in the tiny billet that would be my home for the next twenty months and went off to explore.

Charlie had beaten me to the lounge and to the privi-

159

lege of being first to evaluate the quality of *Marsaryk II*'s coffee.

"Rhinocerous bile," he said.

"At least it isn't soya," I said, taking a first cautious sip. Decided I might be longing for soya in a week.

The officers' lounge was a cubicle about three meters by four, metal floor and walls, with a coffee machine and a library readout. Six hard chairs and a table with a typer on it.

"Jolly place, isn't it?" He idly punched up a general index on the library machine. "Lots of military theory."

"That's good. Refresh our memories."

"Sign up for officer training?"

"Me? No. Orders."

"At least you have an excuse." He slapped the on-off button and watched the green spot dwindle. "I signed up. They didn't tell me it'd feel like this."

"Yeah." He wasn't talking about any subtle problem: burden of responsibility or anything. "They say it wears off, a little at a time." All of that information they force into you; a constant silent whispering.

"Ah, there you are." Hilleboe came through the door and exchanged greetings with us. She gave the room a quick survey, and it was obvious that the Spartan arrangements met with her approval. "Will you be wanting to address the company before we go into the acceleration tanks?"

"No, I don't see why that would be . . . necessary." I almost said "desirable." The art of chastising subordinates is a delicate art. I could see that I'd have to keep reminding Hilleboe that she wasn't in charge.

Or I could just switch insignia with her. Let her experience the joys of command.

"You could, please, round up all platoon leaders and go over the immersion sequence with them. Eventually we'll be doing speed drills. But for now, I think the troops could use a few hours' rest." If they were as hungover as their commander.

"Yes, sir." She turned and left. A little miffed, because what I'd asked her to do should properly have been a job for Riland or Rusk.

Charlie eased his pudgy self into one of the hard

160

chairs and sighed. "Twenty months on this greasy machine. With her. Shit."

"Well, if you're nice to me, I won't billet the two of you together."

"All right. I'm your slave forever. Starting, oh, next Friday." He peered into his cup and decided against drinking the dregs. "Seriously, she's going to be a problem. What are you going to do with her?"

"I don't know." Charlie was being insubordinate, too, of course. But he was my XO and out of the chain of command. Besides, I had to have *one* friend. "Maybe she'll mellow, once we're under weigh."

"Sure." Technically, we were already under weigh, crawling toward the Stargate collapsar at one gee. But that was only for the convenience of the crew; it's hard to batten down the hatches in free fall. The trip wouldn't really start until we were in the tanks.

The lounge was too depressing, so Charlie and I used the remaining hours of mobility to explore the ship.

The bridge looked like any other computer facility; they had dispensed with the luxury of viewscreens. We stood at a respectful distance while Antopol and her officers went through a last series of checks before climbing into the tanks and leaving our destiny to the machines.

Actually, there was a porthole, a thick plastic bubble, in the navigation room forward. Lieutenant Williams wasn't busy, the pre-insertion part of his job being fully automated, so he was glad to show us around.

He tapped the porthole with a fingernail. "Hope we don't have to use this, this trip."

"How so?" Charlie said.

"We only use it if we get lost." If the insertion angle was off by a thousandth of a radian, we were liable to wind up on the other side of the galaxy. "We can get a rough idea of our position by analyzing the spectra of the brightest stars. Thumbprints. Identify three and we can triangulate."

"Then find the nearest collapsar and get back on the track," I said.

"That's the problem. Sade-138 is the only collapsar we know of in the Magellanic Clouds. We know of it

161

only because of captured enemy data. Even if we could find another collapsar, assuming we got lost in the cloud, we wouldn't know how to insert."

"That's great."

"It's not as though we'd be actually lost," he said with a rather wicked expression. "We could zip up in the tanks, aim for Earth and blast away at full power. We'd get there in about three months, ship time."

"Sure," I said. "But 150,000 years in the future." At twenty-five gees, you get to nine-tenths the speed of light in less than a month. From then on, you're in the arms of Saint Albert.

"Well, that is a drawback," he said. "But at least we'd find out who'd won the war."

It made you wonder how many soldiers had gotten out of the war in just that way. There were forty-two strike forces lost somewhere and unaccounted for. It was possible that all of them were crawling through normal space at near-lightspeed and would show up at Earth or Stargate one-by-one over the centuries.

A convenient way to go AWOL, since once you were out of the chain of collapsar jumps you'd be practically impossible to track down. Unfortunately, your jump sequence was pre-programmed by Strike Force Command; the human navigator only came into the picture if a miscalculation slipped you into the wrong "wormhole," and you popped out in some random part of space.

Charlie and I went on to inspect the gym, which was big enough for about a dozen people at a time. I asked him to make up a roster so that everyone could work out for an hour each day when we were out of the tanks.

The mess area was only a little larger than the gym —even with four staggered shifts, the meals would be shoulder-to-shoulder afairs—and the enlisted men and women's lounge was even more depressing than the officers'. I was going to have a real morale problem on my hands long before the twenty months were up.

The armorer's bay was as large as the gym, mess hall and both lounges put together. It had to be, because the great variety of infantry weapons that had evolved over the centuries. The basic weapon was still the fighting suit, though it was much more sophisticated than that first model I had been squeezed into, just before the Aleph-Null campaign.

Lieutenant Riland, the armory officer, was supervising his four subordinates, one from each platoon, who were doing a last-minute check of weapons storage. Probably the most important job on the whole ship, when you contemplate what could happen to all those tons of explosives and radioactives under twenty-five gees.

I returned his perfunctory salute. "Everything going all right, Lieutenant?"

"Yessir, except for those damned swords." For use in the stasis field. "No way we can orient them that they won't be bent. Just hope they don't break."

I couldn't begin to understand the principles behind the stasis field; the gap between present-day physics and my master's degree in the same subject was as long as the time that separated Galileo and Einstein. But I knew the effects.

Nothing could move at greater than 16.3 meters per second inside the field, which was a hemispherical (in space, spherical) volume about fifty meters in radius. Inside, there was no such thing as electromagnetic radiation; no electricity, no magnetism, no light. From inside your suit, you could see your surroundings in ghostly monochrome—which phenomenon was glibly explained to me as being due to "phase transference of quasi-energy leaking through from an adjacent tachyon reality," so much phlogiston to me.

The result of it, though, was to make all conventional weapons of warfare useless. Even a nova bomb was just an inert lump inside the field. And any creature, Terran or Tauran, caught inside the field without the proper insulation would die in a fraction of a second.

At first it looked as though we had come upon the ultimate weapon. There were five engagements where whole Tauran bases were wiped out without any human ground casualties. All you had to do was carry the field to the enemy (four husky soldiers could handle it in Earth-gravity) and watch them die as they slipped in through the field's opaque wall. The people carrying the generator were invulnerable except for the short periods when they might have to turn the thing off to get their bearings.

The sixth time the field was used, though, the Taurans were ready for it. They wore protective suits and were armed with sharp spears, with which they could breach the suits of the generator-carriers. From then on the carriers were armed.

Only three other such battles had been reported, although a dozen strike forces had gone out with the stasis field. The others were still fighting, or still enroute, or had been totally defeated. There was no way to tell unless they came back. And they weren't encouraged to come back if Taurans were still in control of "their" real estate—supposedly that constituted "desertion under fire," which meant execution for all officers (although rumor had it that they were simply brainwiped, imprinted and sent back into the fray).

"Will we be using the stasis field, sir?" Riland asked.

"Probably. Not at first, not unless the Taurans are already there. I don't relish the thought of living in a suit, day in and day out." Neither did I relish the thought of using sword, spear, throwing knife; no matter how many electronic illusions I'd sent to Valhalla with them.

Checked my watch. "Well, we'd better get on down to the tanks, Captain. Make sure everything's squared away." We had about two hours before the insertion sequence would start.

The room the tanks were in resembled a huge chemical factory; the floor was a good hundred meters in diameter and jammed with bulky apparatus painted a uniform, dull gray. The eight tanks were arranged almost symmetrically around the central elevator, the symmetry spoiled by the fact that one of the tanks was twice the size of the others. That would be the command tank, for all the senior officers and supporting specialists.

Sergeant Blazynski stepped out from behind one of the tanks and saluted. I didn't return his salute.

"What the hell is that?" In all that universe of gray, there was one spot of color.

"It's a cat, sir."

"Do tell." A big one, too, and bright calico. It looked ridiculous, draped over the sergeant's shoulder. "Let me rephrase the question: what the hell is a cat doing here?"

"It's the maintenance squad's mascot, sir." The cat raised its head enough to hiss half-heartedly at me, then returned to its flaccid repose.

I looked at Charlie and he shrugged back. "It seems kind of cruel," he said. To the sergeant: "You won't get much use of it. After twenty-five gees, it'll be just so much fur and guts."

"Oh no, sir! Sirs." He ruffed back the fur between the creature's shoulders. It had a fluorocarbon fitting imbedded there, just like the one above my hipbone. "We bought it at a store on Stargate, already modified. Lots of ships have them now, sir. The Commodore signed the forms for us."

Well, that was her right; maintenance was under both of us equally. And it was her ship. "You couldn't have gotten a dog?" God, I hated cats. Always sneaking around.

"No, sir they don't adapt. Can't take free fall."

"Did you have to make any special adaptations? In the tank?" Charlie asked.

"No, sir. We had an extra couch." Great; that meant I'd be sharing a tank with the animal. "We only had to shorten the straps.

"It takes a different kind of drug for the cell-wall strengthening, but that was included in the price."

Charlie scratched it behind an ear. It purred softly but didn't move. "Seems kind of stupid. The animal, I mean."

"We drugged him ahead of time." No wonder it was so inert; the drug slows your metabolism down to a rate barely adequate to sustain life. "Makes it easier to strap him in."

"Guess it's all right," I said. Maybe good for morale. "But if it starts getting in the way, I'll personally recycle it."

"Yes, sir!" he said, visibly relieved, thinking that I couldn't really do anything like that to such a cute bundle of fur. Try me, buddy.

So we had seen it all. The only thing left, this side of the engines, was the huge hold where the fighters and drones waited, clamped in their massive cradles against the coming acceleration. Charlie and I went down to take a look, but there were no windows on our side of the airlock. I knew there'd be one on the inside, but the chamber was evacuated, and it wasn't worth going through the fill-and-warm cycle merely to satisfy our curiosity.

I was starting to feel really supernumerary. Called Hilleboe and she said everything was under control. With an hour to kill, we went back to the lounge and had the computer mediate a game of *Kriegspieler*, which was just starting to get interesting when the ten-minute warning sounded.

The acceleration tanks had a "half-life-to-failure" of five weeks; there was a fifty-fifty chance that you could stay immersed for five weeks before some valve or tube popped and you were squashed like a bug underfoot. In practice, it had to be one hell of an emergency to justify using the tanks for more than two weeks' acceleration. We were only going under for ten days, this first leg of our journey.

Five weeks or five hours, though, it was all the same as far as the tankee was concerned. Once the pressure got up to an operational level, you had no sense of the passage of time. Your body and brain were concrete. None of your senses provided any input, and you could amuse yourself for several hours just trying to spell your own name.

So I wasn't really surprised that no time seemed to have passed when I was suddenly dry, my body tingling with the return of sensation. The place sounded like an asthmatics' convention in the middle of a hay field: thirty-nine people and one cat all coughing and sneezing to get rid of the last residues of fluorocarbon. While I was fumbling with my straps, the side door opened, flooding the tank with painfully bright light. The cat was the first one out, with a general scramble right behind him. For the sake of dignity, I waited until last.

Over a hundred people were milling around outside, stretching and massaging out cramps. Dignity! Surrounded by acres of young female flesh, I stared into their faces and desperately tried to solve a third-order differential equation in my head, to circumvent the gallant reflex. A temporary expedient, but it got me to the elevator.

Hilleboe was shouting orders, getting people lined up, and as the doors closed I noticed that all of one platoon had a uniform light bruise, from head to foot. Twenty pairs of black eyes. I'd have to see both Maintenance and Medical about that.

After I got dressed.

4.

We stayed at one gee for three weeks, with occasional periods of free fall for navigation check, while the *Masaryk II* made a long, narrow loop away from the collapsar Resh-10, and back again. That period went all right, the people adjusting pretty well to ship routine. I gave them a minimum of busy-work and a maximum of training review and exercise—for their own good, though I wasn't naive enough to think they'd see it that way.

After about a week of one gee, Private Rudkoski (the cook's assistant) had a still, producing some eight liters a day of 95 percent ethyl alcohol. I didn't want to stop him—life was cheerless enough; I didn't mind as long as people showed up for duty sober—but I was damned curious both how he managed to divert the raw materials out of our sealed-tight ecology, and how the people paid for their booze. So I used the chain of command in reverse, asking Alsever to find out. She asked Jarvil, who asked Carreras, who sat down with Orban, the cook. Turned out that Sergeant Orban had set the whole thing up, letting Rudkoski do the dirty work, and was aching to brag about it to a trustworthy person.

If I had ever taken meals with the enlisted men and women, I might have figured out that something odd was going on. But the scheme didn't extend up to officers' country.

Through Rudkoski, Orban had juryrigged a ship-wide economy based on alcohol. It went like this:

Each meal was prepared with one very sugary desert —jelly, custard or flan—which you were free to eat if you could stand the cloying taste. But if it was still on your tray when you presented it at the recycling window, Rudkoski would give you a ten-cent chit and scrape the sugary stuff into a fermentation vat. He had two twenty-liter vats, one "working" while the other was being filled.

The ten-cent chit was at the bottom of a system that allowed you to buy half-liter of straight ethyl (with your choice of flavoring) for five dollars. A squad of five people who skipped all of their desserts could buy about a liter a week, enough for a party but not enough to constitute a public health problem.

When Diana brought me this information, she also brought a bottle of Rudkoski's Worst—literally; it was a flavor that just hadn't worked. It came up through the chain of command with only a few centimeters missing.

Its taste was a ghastly combination of strawberry and caraway seed. With a perversity not uncommon to people who rarely drink, Diana loved it. I had some ice water brought up, and she got totally blasted within an hour. For myself, I made one drink and didn't finish it.

When she was more than halfway to oblivion, mumbling a reassuring soliloquy to her liver, she suddenly tilted her head up to stare at me with childlike directness.

"You have a real problem, Major William."

"Not half the problem you'll have in the morning, Lieutenant Doctor Diana."

"Oh not really." She waved a drunken hand in front of her face. "Some vitamins, some glu . . . cose, an eensy cc of adren . . . aline if all else fails. You . . . you . . . have . . . a real . . . problem."

"Look, Diana, don't you want me to—"

"What you need . . . is to get an appointment with that nice Corporal Valdez." Valdez was the male sex counselor. "He has empathy. Itsiz job. He'd make you—"

"We talked about this before, remember? I want to stay the way I am."

"Don't we all." She wiped away a tear that was probably one percent alcohol. "You know they call you the Old C'reer. No they don't."

She looked at the floor and then at the wall. "The Ol' Queer, that's what."

I had expected names worse than that. But not so

168

soon. "I don't care. The commander always gets names."

"I know but." She stood up suddenly and wobbled a little bit. "Too much t' drink. Lie down." She turned her back to me and stretched so hard that a joint popped. Then a seam whispered open and she shrugged off her tunic, stepped out of it and tiptoed to my bed. She sat down and patted the mattress. "Come on, William. Only chance."

"For Christ's sake, Diana. It wouldn't be fair."

"All's fair," she giggled. "And 'sides, I'm a doctor. I can be clin'cal; won't bother me a bit. Help me with this." After five hundred years, they were still putting brassiere clasps in the back.

One kind of gentleman would have helped her get undressed and then made a quiet exit. Another kind of gentleman might have bolted for the door. Being neither kind, I closed in for the kill.

Perhaps fortunately, she passed out before we had made any headway. I admired the sight and touch of her for a long time before, feeling like a cad, I managed to gather everything up and dress her.

I lifted her out of the bed, sweet burden, and then realized that if anyone saw me carrying her down to her billet, she'd be the butt of rumors for the rest of the campaign. I called up Charlie, told him we'd had some booze and Diana was rather the worse for it, and asked him whether he'd come up for a drink and help me haul the good doctor home.

By the time Charlie knocked, she was draped innocently in a chair, snoring softly.

He smiled at her. "Physician, heal thyself." I offered him the bottle, with a warning. He sniffed it and made a face.

"What is this, varnish?"

"Just something the cooks whipped up. Vacuum still."

He set it down carefully, as if it might explode if jarred. "I predict a coming shortage of customers. Epidemic of death by poisoning—she actually drank that vile stuff?"

"Well, the cooks admitted it was an experiment that didn't pan out; their other flavors are evidently potable. Yeah, she loved it."

"Well . . ." He laughed. "Damn! What, you take her legs and I take her arms?"

"No, look, we each take an arm. Maybe we can get her to do part of the walking."

She moaned a little when we lifted her out of the chair, opened one eye and said, "Hello Charlee." Then she closed the eye and let us drag her down to the billet. No one saw us on the way, but her bunkmate, Laasonen, was sitting up reading.

"She really drank the stuff, eh?" She regarded her friend with wry affection. "Here, let me help."

The three of us wrestled her into bed. Laasonen smoothed the hair out of her eyes. "She said it was in the nature of an experiment."

"More devotion to science than I have," Charlie said. "A stronger stomach, too."

We all wished he hadn't said that.

Diana sheepishly admitted that she hadn't remembered anything after the first drink, and talking to her, I deduced that she thought Charlie had been there all along. Which was all for the best, of course. But oh! Diana, my lovely latent heterosexual, let me buy you a bottle of good scotch the next time we come into port. Seven hundred years from now.

We got back into the tanks for the hop from Resh-10 to Kaph-35. That was two weeks at twenty-five gees; then we had another four weeks of routine at one gravity.

I had announced my open door policy, but practically no one ever took advantage of it. I saw very little of the troops and those occasions were almost always negative: testing them on their training review, handing out reprimands, and occasionally lecturing classes. And they rarely spoke intelligibly, except in response to a direct question.

Most of them either had English as their native tongue or as a second language, but it had changed so drastically over 450 years that I could barely understand it, not at all if it was spoken rapidly. Fortunately, they had all been taught early twenty-first century English during their basic training; that language, or dialect, served as a temporal *lingua franca* through which a

170

twenty-fifth century soldier could communicate with someone who had been a contemporary of his nineteen-times-great-grandparents. If there had still been such a thing as grandparents.

I thought of my first combat commander, Captain Stott—whom I had hated just as cordially as the rest of the company did—and tried to imagine how I would have felt if he had been a sexual deviate and I'd been forced to learn a new language for his convenience.

So we had discipline problems, sure. But the wonder was that we had any discipline at all. Hilleboe was responsible for that; as little as I liked her personally, I had to to give her credit for keeping the troops in line.

Most of the shipboard graffiti concerned improbable sexual geometries between the Second Field Officer and her commander.

From Kaph-35 we jumped to Samk-78, from there to Ayin-129 and finally to Sade-138. Most of the jumps were no more than a few hundred light years, but the last one was 140,000—supposedly the longest collapsar jump ever made by a manned craft.

The time spent scooting down the wormhole from one collapsar to the next was always the same, independent of the distance. When I'd studied physics, they thought the duration of a collapsar jump was exactly zero. But a couple of centuries later, they did a complicated wave-guide experiment that proved the jump actually lasted some small fraction of a nanosecond. Doesn't seem like much, but they'd had to rebuild physics from the foundation up when the collapsar jump was first discovered; they had to tear the whole damned thing down again when they found out it took time to get from A to B. Physicists were still arguing about it.

But we had more pressing problems as we flashed out of Sade-138's collapsar field at three-quarters of the speed of light. There was no way to tell immediately whether the Taurans had beat us there. We launched a pre-programmed drone that would decelerate at 300 gees and take a preliminary look around. It would warn us if it detected any other ships in the system, or evidence of Tauran activity on any of the collapsar's planets.

The drone launched, we zipped up in the tanks and the computers put us through a three-week evasive maneuver while the ship slowed down. No problems except that three weeks is a hell of a long time to stay frozen in the tank; for a couple of days afterward everybody crept around like aged cripples.

If the drone had sent back word that the Taurans were already in the system, we would immediately have stepped down to one gee and started deploying fighters and drones armed with nova bombs. Or we might not have lived that long: sometimes the Taurans could get to a ship only hours after it entered the system. Dying in the tank might not be the most pleasant way to go.

It took us a month to get back to within a couple of AUs of Sade-138, where the drone had found a planet that met our requirements.

It was an odd planet, slightly smaller than Earth but more dense. It wasn't quite the cryogenic deepfreeze that most portal planets were, both because of heat from its core and because S Doradus, the brightest star in the cloud, was only a third of a light year away.

The strangest feature of the planet was its lack of geography. From space it looked like a slightly damaged billiard ball. Our resident physicist, Lieutenant Gim, explained its relatively pristine condition by pointing out that its anomalous, almost cometary orbit probably meant that it had spent most of its life as a "rogue planet," drifting alone through interstellar space. The chances were good that it had never been struck by a large meteor until it wandered into Sade-138's bailiwick and was captured—forced to share space with all the other flotsam the collapsar dragged around with it.

We left the *Masaryk II* in orbit (it was capable of landing, but that would restrict its visibility and getaway time) and shuttled building materials down to the surface with the six fighters.

It was good to get out of the ship, even though the planet wasn't exactly hospitable. The atmosphere was a thin cold wind of hydrogen and helium, it being too cold even at noon for any other substance to exist as a gas.

"Noon" was when S Doradus was overhead, a tiny, painfully bright spark. The temperature slowly dropped at night, going from twenty-five degrees Kelvin down to seventeen degrees—which caused problems, because just before dawn the hydrogen would start to condense out of the air, making everything so slippery that it was useless to do anything other than sit down and wait it out. At dawn a faint pastel rainbow provided the only relief from the black-and-white monotony of the landscape.

The ground was treacherous, covered with little granular chunks of frozen gas that shifted slowly, incessantly in the anemic breeze. You had to walk in a slow waddle to stay on your feet; of the four people who would die during the base's construction, three would be the victims of simple falls.

The troops weren't happy with my decision to construct the anti-spacecraft and perimeter defenses before putting up living quarters. That was by the book, though, and they got two days of shipboard rest for every "day" planetside—which wasn't overly generous, I admit, since ship days were 24 hours long, and a day on the planet was 38.5 hours from dawn to dawn.

The base was completed in just less than four weeks, and it was a formidable structure indeed. The perimeter, a circle one kilometer in diameter, was guarded by twenty-five gigawatt lasers that would automatically aim and fire within a thousandth of a second. They would react to the motion of any significantly large object between the perimeter and the horizon. Sometimes when the wind was right and the ground damp with hydrogen, the little ice granules would stick together into a loose snowball and begin to roll. They wouldn't roll far.

For early protection, before the enemy came over our horizon, the base was in the center of a huge mine field. The buried mines would detonate upon sufficient distortion of their local gravitational fields: a single Tauran would set one off if he came within twenty meters of it; a small spacecraft a kilometer overhead would also detonate it. There were 2800 of them, mostly 100-microton nuclear bombs. Fifty of them were devastatingly powerful tachyon devices. They were all scattered at random in a ring that extended from the limit of the lasers' effectiveness, out another five kilometers.

Inside the base, we relied on individual lasers, microton grenades, and a tachyon-powered repeating rocket

173

launcher that had never been tried in combat, one per platoon. As a last resort, the stasis field was set up beside the living quarters. Inside its opaque gray dome, as well as enough paleolithic weaponry to hold off the Golden Horde, we'd stashed a small cruiser, just in case we managed to lose all our spacecraft in the process of winning a battle. Twelve people would be able to get back to Stargate.

It didn't do to dwell on the fact that the other survivors would have to sit on their hands until relieved by reinforcements or death.

The living quarters and administration facilities were all underground, to protect them from line-of-sight weapons. It didn't do too much for morale, though; there were waiting lists for every outside detail, no matter how strenuous or risky. I hadn't wanted the troops to go up to the surface in their free time, both because of the danger involved and the administrative headache of constantly checking equipment in and out and keeping track of who was where.

Finally I had to relent and allow people to go up for a few hours every week. There was nothing to see except the featureless plain and the sky (which was dominated by S Doradus during the day, and the huge dim oval of the galaxy at night), but that was an improvement over staring at the melted-rock walls and ceiling.

A favorite sport was to walk out to the perimeter and throw snowballs in front of the laser; see how small a snowball you could throw and still set the weapon off. It seemed to me that the entertainment value of this pastime was about equal to watching a faucet drip, but there was no real harm in it, since the weapons would only fire outward and we had power to spare.

For five months things went pretty smoothly. Such administrative problems as we had were similar to those we'd encountered on the *Masaryk II*. And we were in less danger as passive troglodytes than we had been scooting from collapsar to collapsar, at least until the enemy showed up.

I looked the other way when Rudkoski reassembled his still. Anything that broke the monotony of garrison duty was welcome, and the chits not only provided booze for the troops but gave them something to gamble with. I only interfered in two ways: nobody could go outside unless they were totally sober, and nobody could sell sexual favors. Maybe that was the Puritan in me, but it was, again, by the book. The opinion of the supporting specialists was split. Lieutenant Wilber, the psychiatric officer, agreed with me; the sex counselors Kajdi and Valdez didn't. But then, they were probably coining money, being the resident "professionals."

Five months of comfortably boring routine, and then along came Private Graubard.

For obvious reasons, no weapons were allowed in the living quarters. The way these people were trained, even a fistfight could be a duel to the death, and tempers were short. A hundred merely normal people would probably have been at each other's throats after a week in our caves, but these soldiers had been hand-picked for their ability to get along in close confinement.

Still, there were fights. Graubard had almost killed his ex-lover Schon when that worthy made a face at him in the chow line. He had a week of solitary detention (so did Schon, for having precipitated it) and then psychiatric counseling and punitive details. Then I transferred him to the fourth platoon, so he wouldn't be seeing Schon every day.

The first time they passed in the halls, Graubard greeted Schon with a savage kick to the throat. Diana had to build him a new trachea. Graubard got a more intensive round of detention, counseling and details—hell, I couldn't transfer him to another *company*—and then he was a good boy for two weeks. I fiddled their work and chow schedules so the two would never be in the same room together. But they met in a corridor again, and this time it came out more even: Schon got two broken ribs, but Graubard got a ruptured testicle and lost four teeth.

If it kept up, I was going to have at least one less mouth to feed.

By the Universal Code of Military Justice I could have ordered Graubard executed, since we were technically in a state of combat. Perhaps I should have, then and there. But Charlie suggested a more humanitarian solution, and I accepted it.

We didn't have enough room to keep Graubard in solitary detention forever, which seemed to be the only humane yet practical thing to do, but they had plenty of room aboard the *Masaryk II,* hovering overhead in a stationary orbit. I called Antopol and she agreed to take care of him. I gave her permission to space the bastard if he gave her any trouble.

We called a general assembly to explain things, so that the lesson of Graubard wouldn't be lost on anybody. I was just starting to talk, standing on the rock dias with the company sitting in front of me, and the officers and Graubard behind me—when the crazy fool decided to kill me.

Like everybody else, Graubard was assigned five hours per week of training inside the stasis field. Under close supervision, the soldiers would practice using their swords and spears and whatnot on dummy Taurans. Somehow Graubard had managed to smuggle out a weapon, an Indian chakra, which is a circle of metal with a razor-keen outer edge. It's a tricky weapon, but once you know how to use it, it can be much more effective than a regular throwing knife. Graubard was an expert.

All in a fraction of a second, Graubard disabled the people on either side of him—hitting Charlie in the temple with an elbow while he broke Hilleboe's kneecap with a kick—and slid the chakra out of his tunic and spun it toward me in one smooth action. It had covered half the distance to my throat before I reacted.

Instinctively I slapped out to deflect it and came within a centimeter of losing four fingers. The razor edge slashed open the top of my palm, but I succeeded in knocking the thing off course. And Graubard was rushing me, teeth bared in an expression I hope I never see again.

Maybe he didn't realize that the *old queer* was really only five years older than he; that the *old queer* had combat reflexes and three weeks of negative feedback kinesthesia training. At any rate, it was so easy I almost felt sorry for him.

His right toe was turning in; I knew he would take one more step and go into a savage leap. I adjusted the distance between us with a short *ballestra* and, just as both his feet left the ground, gave him an ungentle side-kick to the solar plexus. He was unconscious before he hit the ground.

If you had to kill a man, Kynock had said, *I'm not sure you could do it.* Over 120 people in that small room, and the only sound was the steady drip of blood from my clenched fist to the floor. *Even though you must know a thousand different ways.* If I had kicked him a few centimeters higher and at a slightly different angle, it would have killed him instantly. But Kynock had been right; I didn't have the instinct for it.

If I'd merely killed him in self-defense, my troubles would have been over instead of suddenly being multiplied.

A simple psychotic troublemaker a commander can lock up and forget about. But not a failed assassin. And I didn't have to take a poll to know that executing him was not going to improve my relationship with the troops.

I realized that Diana was on her knees beside me, trying to pry open my fingers. "Check Hilleboe and Moore," I mumbled, and to the troops: "Dismissed."

5.

"Don't be an ass," Charlie said. He was holding a damp rag to the bruise on the side of his head.

"You don't think I have to execute him?"

"Stop twitching!" Diana was trying to get the lips of my wound to line up together so she could paint them shut. From the wrist down, the hand felt like a lump of ice.

"Not by your own hand, you don't. You can detail someone. At random."

"Charlie's right," Diana said. "Have everybody draw a slip of paper out of a bowl."

I was glad Hilleboe was sound asleep on the other cot. I didn't need her opinion. "And if the person so chosen refuses?"

"Punish him and get another," Charlie said. "Didn't you learn anything in the can? You can't abrogate your

177

authority by publicly doing a job . . . that obviously should be detailed."

"Any other job, sure. But for this . . . nobody in the company has ever killed. It would look like I was getting somebody else to do my moral dirty work."

"If it's so damned complicated," Diana said, "why not just get up in front of the troops and tell them how complicated it is. Then have them draw straws. They aren't children."

There had been an army in which that sort of thing was done, a strong quasi-memory told me. The Marxist POUM militia in the Spanish Civil War, early twentieth. You obeyed an order only after it had been explained in detail; you could refuse if it didn't make sense. Officers and men got drunk together and never saluted or used titles. They lost the war. But the other side didn't have any fun.

"Finished." Diana set the limp hand in my lap. "Don't try to use it for a half-hour. When it starts to hurt, you can use it."

I inspected the wound closely. "The lines don't match up. Not that I'm complaining."

"You shouldn't. By all rights, you ought to have just a stump. And no regeneration facilities this side of Stargate."

"Stump ought to be at the top of your neck," Charlie said. "I don't see why you have any qualms. You should have killed the bastard outright."

"I know that, goddamnit!" Both Charlie and Diana jumped at my outburst. "Sorry, shit. Look, just let me do the worrying."

"Why don't you both talk about something else for a while." Diana got up and checked the contents of her medical bag. "I've got another patient to check. Try to keep from exciting each other."

"Graubard?" Charlie asked.

"That's right. To make sure he can mount the scaffold without assistance."

"What if Hilleboe—"

"She'll be out for another half-hour. I'll send Jarvil down, just in case." She hurried out the door.

"The scaffold . . ." I hadn't given that any thought. "How the hell are we going to execute him? We can't do it indoors: morale. Firing squad would be pretty grisly."

"Chuck him out the airlock. You don't owe him any ceremony."

"You're probably right. I wasn't thinking about him." I wondered whether Charlie had ever seen the body of a person who'd died that way. "Maybe we ought to just stuff him into the recycler. He'd wind up there eventually."

Charlie laughed. "That's the spirit."

"We'd have to trim him up a little bit. Door's not very wide." Charlie had a few suggestions as to how to get around that. Jarvil came in and more-or-less ignored us.

Suddenly the infirmary door banged open. A patient on a cart; Diana rushing alongside pressing on the man's chest, while a private pushed. Two other privates were following, but hung back at the door. "Over by the wall," she ordered.

It was Graubard. "Tried to kill himself," Diana said, but that was pretty obvious. "Heart stopped." He'd made a noose out of his belt; it was still hanging limply around his neck.

There were two big electrodes with rubber handles hanging on the wall. Diana snatched them with one hand while she ripped his tunic open with the other. "Get your hands off the cart!" She held the electrodes apart, kicked a switch, and pressed them down onto his chest. They made a low hum while his body trembled and flopped. Smell of burning flesh.

Diana was shaking her head. "Get ready to crack him," she said to Jarvil. "Get Doris down here." The body was gurgling, but it was a mechanical sound, like plumbing.

She kicked off the power and let the electrodes drop, pulled a ring off her finger and crossed to stick her arms in the sterilizer. Jarvil started to rub an evil-smelling fluid over the man's chest.

There was a small red mark between the two electrode burns. It took me a moment to recognize what it was. Jarvil wiped it away. I stepped closer and checked Graubard's neck.

"Get out of the way, William, you aren't sterile." Diana felt his collarbone, measured down a little ways and made an incision straight down to the bottom of his

179

breastbone. Blood welled out and Jarvil handed her an instrument that looked like big chrome-plated bolt-cutters. I looked away but couldn't help hearing the thing crunch through his ribs. She asked for retractors and sponges and so on while I wandered back to where I'd been sitting. With the corner of my eye I saw her working away inside his thorax, massaging his heart directly.

Charlie looked the way I felt. He called out weakly, "Hey, don't knock yourself out, Diana." She didn't answer. Jarvil had wheeled up the artificial heart and was holding out two tubes. Diana picked up a scalpel and I looked away again.

He was still dead a half-hour later. They turned off the machine and threw a sheet over him. Diana washed the blood off her arms and said, "Got to change. Back in a minute."

I got up and walked to her billet, next door. Had to know. I raised my hand to knock but it was suddenly hurting like there was a line of fire drawn across it. I rapped with my left and she opened the door immediately.

"What—oh, you want something for your hand." She was half-dressed, unself-conscious. "Ask Jarvil."

"No, that's not it. What happened, Diana?"

"Oh. Well," she pulled a tunic over her head and her voice was muffled. "It was my fault, I guess. I left him alone for a minute."

"And he tried to hang himself."

"That's right." She sat on the bed and offered me the chair. "I went off to the head and he was dead by the time I got back. I'd already sent Jarvil away because I didn't want Hilleboe to be unsupervised for too long."

"But, Diana . . . there's no mark on his neck. No bruise, nothing."

She shrugged. "The hanging didn't kill him. He had a heart attack."

"Somebody gave him a shot. Right over his heart."

She looked at me curiously. "I did that, William. Adrenaline. Standard procedure."

You get that red dot of expressed blood if you jerk away from the projector while you're getting a shot. Otherwise the medicine goes right through the pores, doesn't leave a mark. "He was dead when you gave him the shot?"

"That would be my professional opinion." Deadpan. "No heartbeat, pulse, respiration. Very few other disorders show these symptoms."

"Yeah. I see."

"Is something . . . what's the matter, William?"

Either I'd been improbably lucky or Diana was a very good actress. "Nothing. Yeah, I better get something for this hand." I opened the door. "Saved me a lot of trouble."

She looked straight into my eyes. "That's true."

Actually, I'd traded one kind of trouble for another. Despite the fact that there were several disinterested witnesses to Graubard's demise, there was a persistent rumor that I'd had Doc Alsever simply exterminate him —since I'd botched the job myself and didn't want to go through a troublesome court-martial.

The fact was that, under the Universal Code of Military "Justice," Graubard hadn't deserved any kind of trial at all. All I had to do was say "You, you and you. Take this man out and kill him, please." And woe betide the private who refused to carry out the order.

My relationship with the troops did improve, in a sense. At least outwardly, they showed more deference to me. But I suspected it was at least partly the cheap kind of respect you might offer any ruffian who had proved himself to be dangerous and volatile.

So *Killer* was my new name. Just when I'd gotten used to *Old Queer*.

The base quickly settled back into its routine of training and waiting. I was almost impatient for the Taurans to show up, just to get it over with one way or the other.

The troops had adjusted to the situation much better than I had, for obvious reasons. They had specific duties to perform and ample free time for the usual soldierly anodynes to boredom. My duties were more varied but offered little satisfaction, since the problems that percolated up to me were of the "the buck stops here" type; those with pleasing, unambiguous solutions were taken care of in the lower echelons.

I'd never cared much for sports or games, but found

181

myself turning to them more and more as a kind of safety valve. For the first time in my life, in these tense, claustrophobic surroundings, I couldn't escape into reading or study. So I fenced, quarterstaff and saber, with the other officers, worked myself to exhaustion on the exercise machines and even kept a jump-rope in my office. Most of the other officers played chess, but they could usually beat me—whenever I won it gave me the feeling I was being humored. Word games were difficult because my language was an archaic dialect that they had trouble manipulating. And I lacked the time and talent to master "modern" English.

For a while I let Diana feed me mood-altering drugs, but the cumulative effect of them was frightening—I was getting addicted in a way that was at first too subtle to bother me—so I stopped short. Then I tried some systematic psychoanalysis with Lieutenant Wilber. It was impossible. Although he knew all about my problems in an academic kind of way, we didn't speak the same cultural language; his counseling me about love and sex was like me telling a fourteenth-century serf how best to get along with his priest and landlord.

And that, after all, was the root of my problem. I was sure I could have handled the pressures and frustrations of command; of being cooped up in a cave with these people who at times seemed scarcely less alien than the enemy; even the near-certainty that it could lead only to painful death in a worthless cause—if only I could have had Marygay with me. And the feeling got more intense as the months crept by.

He got very stern with me at this point and accused me of romanticizing my position. He knew what love was, he said; he had been in love himself. And the sexual polarity of the couple made no difference—all right, I could accept that; that idea had been a cliché in my parents' generation (though it had run into some predictable resistance in my own). But love, he said, love was a fragile blossom; love was a delicate crystal; love was an unstable reaction with a half-life of about eight months. Bullshit, I said, and accused him of wearing cultural blinders; thirty centuries of prewar society taught that love was one thing that could last to the grave and even beyond *and if he had been born instead*

of hatched he would know that without being told!
Whereupon he would assume a wry, tolerant expression
and reiterate that I was merely a victim of self-imposed
sexual frustration and romantic delusion.

In retrospect, I guess we had a good time arguing
with each other. Cure me, he didn't.

I did have a new friend who sat in my lap all the
time. It was the cat, who had the usual talent for hiding
from people who like cats and cleaving unto those who
have sinus trouble or just don't like sneaky little animals. We did have something in common, though, since
to my knowledge he was the only other heterosexual
male mammal within any reasonable distance. He'd
deen castrated, of course, but that didn't make much
difference under the circumstances.

6.

It was exactly 400 days since the day we had begun
construction. I was sitting at my desk not checking out
Hilleboe's new duty roster. The cat was on my lap, pur-
ring loudly even though I refused to pet it. Charlie was
stretched out in a chair reading something on the view-
er. The phone buzzed and it was the Commodore.

"They're here."

"What?"

"I said they're here. A Tauran ship just exited the collapsar field. Velocity .80c. Deceleration thirty gees. Give
or take."

Charlie was leaning over my desk. "What?" I dumped
the cat.

"How long? Before you can pursue?" I asked.

"Soon as you get off the phone." I switched off and
went over to the logistic computer, which was a twin to
the one on *Masaryk II* and had a direct data link to it.
While I tried to get numbers out of the thing, Charlie fiddled with the visual display.

The display was a hologram about a meter square by
half a meter thick and was programmed to show the positions of Sade-138, our planet, and a few other chunks

of rock in the system. There were green and red dots to show the positions of our vessels and the Taurans'.

The computer said that the minimum time it could take the Taurans to decelerate and get back to this planet would be a little over eleven days. Of course, that would be straight maximum acceleration and deceleration all the way; we could pick them off like flies on a wall. So, like us, they'd mix up their direction of flight and degree of acceleration in a random way. Based on several hundred past records of enemy behavior, the computer was able to give us a probability table;

Days to Contact	Probability
11	.000001
15	.001514
20	.032164
25	.103287
30	.676324
35	.820584
40	.982685
45	.993576
50	.999369

MEDIAN

28.9554	.500000

Unless, of course, Antopol and her gang of merry pirates managed to make a kill. The chances of that, I had learned in the can, were slightly less than fifty-fifty.

But whether it took 28.9554 days or two weeks, those of us on the ground had to just sit on our hands and watch. If Antopol was successful, then we wouldn't have to fight until the regular garrison troops replaced us here and we moved on to the next collapsar.

"Haven't left yet." Charlie had the display cranked down to minimum scale; the planet was a white ball the size of a large melon and *Masaryk II* was a green dot off to the right some eight melons away; you couldn't get both on the screen at the same time.

While we were watching a small green dot popped out of the ship's dot and drifted away from it. A ghostly number 2 drifted beside it, and a key projected on the display's lower left-hand corner identified it as 2—*Pursuit Drone*. Other numbers in the key identified the *Masaryk II*, a planetary defense fighter and fourteen planetary defense drones. Those sixteen ships were not yet far enough away from one another to have separate dots.

The cat was rubbing against my ankle; I picked it up and stroked it. "Tell Hilleboe to call a general assembly. Might as well break it to everyone at once."

The men and women didn't take it very well, and I couldn't blame them. We had all expected the Taurans to attack much sooner—and when they persisted in not coming, the feeling grew that Strike Force Command had made a mistake and that they'd never show up at all.

I wanted the company to start weapons training in earnest; they hadn't used any high-powered weapons in almost two years. So I activated their laser-fingers and passed out the grenade and rocket launchers. We couldn't practice inside the base for fear of damaging the external sensors and defensive laser ring. So we turned off half the circle of bevawatt lasers and went out about a klick beyond the perimeter, one platoon at a time, accompanied by either me or Charlie. Rusk kept a close watch on the early-warning screens. If anything approached, she would send up a flare, and the platoon would have to get back inside the ring before the unknown came over the horizon, at which time the defensive lasers would come on automatically. Besides knocking out the unknown, they would fry the platoon in less than .02 second.

We couldn't spare anything from the base to use as a target, but that turned out to be no problem. The first tachyon rocket we fired scooped out a hole twenty meters long by ten wide by five deep; the rubble gave us a multitude of targets from twice-man-sized on down.

The soldiers were good, a lot better than they had been with the primitive weapons in the stasis field. The best laser practice turned out to be rather like skeet-shooting: pair up the people and have one stand behind the other, throwing rocks at random intervals. The one who was shooting had to gauge the rock's trajectory and zap it before it hit the ground. Their eye-hand coordination was impressive (maybe the Eugenics Council had done something right). Shooting at rocks down to pebble-size, most of them could do better than nine out of ten. Old non-bioengineered me could hit maybe seven out of ten, and I'd had a good deal more practice than they had.

They were equally facile at estimating trajectories with the grenade launcher, which was a more versatile weapon than it had been in the past. Instead of shooting one-microton bombs with a standard propulsive charge, it had four different charges and a choice of one-, two-, three- or four-microton bombs. And for really close infighting, where it was dangerous to use the lasers, the barrel of the launcher would unsnap, and you could load it with a magazine of "shotgun" rounds. Each shot would send out an expanding cloud of a thousand tiny flechettes that were instant death out to five meters and turned to harmless vapor at six.

The tachyon rocket launcher required no skill whatsoever. All you had to do was to be careful no one was standing behind you when you fired it; the backwash from the rocket was dangerous for several meters behind the launching tube. Otherwise, you just lined your target up in the crosshairs and pushed the button. You didn't have to worry about trajectory; the rocket traveled in a straight line for all practical purposes. It reached escape velocity in less than a second.

It improved the troops' morale to get out and chew up the landscape with their new toys. But the landscape wasn't fighting back. No matter how physically impressive the weapons were, their effectiveness would depend on what the Taurans could throw back. A Greek phalanx must have looked pretty impressive, but it wouldn't do too well against a single man with a flamethrower.

And as with any engagement, because of time dilation, there was no way to tell what sort of weaponry they would have. They might have never heard of the stasis field. Or they might be able to say a magic word and make us disappear.

I was out with the fourth platoon, burning rocks, when Charlie called and asked me to come back in, urgent. I left Heimoff in charge.

"Another one?" The scale of the holograph display

186

was such that our planet was pea-sized, about five centimeters from the *X* that marked the position of Sade-138. There were forty-one red and green dots scattered around the field; the key identified number *41* as *Tauran Cruiser* (*2*).

"You called Antopol?"

"Yeah." He anticipated the next question. "It'll take almost a day for the signal to get there and back."

"It's never happened before," but of course Charlie knew that.

"Maybe this collapsar is especially important to them."

"Likely." So it was almost certain we'd be fighting on the ground. Even if Antopol managed to get the first cruiser, she wouldn't have a fifty-fifty chance on the second one. Low on drones and fighters. "I wouldn't like to be Antopol now."

"She'll just get it earlier."

"I don't know. We're in pretty good shape."

"Save it for the troops, William." He turned down the display's scale to where it showed only two objects: Sade-138 and the new red dot, slowly moving.

We spent the next two weeks watching dots blink out. And if you knew when and where to look, you could go outside and see the real thing happening, a hard bright speck of white light that faded in about a second.

In that second, a nova bomb had put out over a million times the power of a gigawatt laser. It made a miniature star half a click in diameter and as hot as the interior of the sun. Anything it touched it would consume. The radiation from a near miss could botch up a ship's electronics beyond repair—two fighters, one of ours and one of theirs, had evidently suffered that fate, silently drifting out of the system at a constant velocity, without power.

We had used more powerful nova bombs earlier in the war, but the degenerate matter used to fuel them was unstable in large quantities. The bombs had a tendency to explode while they were still inside the ship. Evidently the Taurans had the same problem—or they had copied the process from us in the first place—because they had also scaled down to nova bombs that used less than a hundred kilograms of degenerate matter. And they deployed them much the same way we did, the warhead separating into dozens of pieces as it approached the target, only one of which was the nova bomb.

They would probably have a few bombs left over after they finished off *Masaryk II* and her retinue of fighters and drones. So it was likely that we were wasting time and energy in weapons practice.

The thought did slip by my conscience that I could gather up eleven people and board the fighter we had hidden safe behind the stasis field. It was pre-programmed to take us back to Stargate.

I even went to the extreme of making a mental list of the eleven, trying to think of eleven people who meant more to me than the rest. Turned out I'd be picking six at random.

I put the thought away, though. We did have a chance, maybe a damned good one, even against a fully-armed cruiser. It wouldn't be easy to get a nova bomb close enough to include us inside its kill-radius.

Besides, they'd space me for desertion. So why bother?

Spirits rose when one of Antopol's drones knocked out the first Tauran cruiser. Not counting the ships left behind for planetary defense, she still had eighteen drones and two fighters. They wheeled around to intercept the second cruiser, by then a few light-hours away, still being harassed by fifteen enemy drones.

One of the drones got her. Her ancillary crafts continued the attack, but it was a rout. One fighter and three drones fled the battle at maximum acceleration, looping up over the plane of the ecliptic, and were not pursued. We watched them with morbid interest while the enemy cruiser inched back to do battle with us. The fighter was headed back for Sade-138, to escape. Nobody blamed them. In fact, we sent them a farewell-good luck message; they didn't respond, naturally, being zipped up in the tanks. But it would be recorded.

It took the enemy five days to get back to the planet and be comfortably ensconced in a stationary orbit on the other side. We settled in for the inevitable first phase of the attack, which would be aerial and totally automated: their drones against our lasers. I put a force of fifty men and women inside the stasis field, in case one of the drones got through. An empty gesture, really; the enemy could just stand by and wait for them to turn off the field, fry them the second it flickered out.

Charlie had a weird idea that I almost went for.

"We could boobytrap the place."

"What do you mean?" I said. "This place *is* booby-trapped, out to twenty-five klicks."

"No, not the mines and such. I mean the base itself, here, underground."

"Go on."

"There are two nova bombs in that fighter." He pointed at the stasis field through a couple of hundred meters of rock. "We can roll them down here, booby-trap them, then hide everybody in the stasis field and wait."

In a way it was tempting. It would relieve me from any responsibility for decision-making, leave everything up to chance. "I don't think it would work, Charlie."

He seemed hurt. "Sure it would."

"No, look. For it to work, you have to get every single Tauran inside the kill-radius before it goes off—but they wouldn't all come charging in here once they breached our defenses. Least of all if the place seemed deserted. They'd suspect something, send in an advance party. And after the advance party set off the bombs—"

"We'd be back where we started, yeah. Minus the base. Sorry."

I shrugged. "It was an idea. Keep thinking, Charlie." I turned my attention back to the display, where the lop-sided space war was in progress. Logically enough, the enemy wanted to knock out that one fighter overhead before he started to work on us. About all we could do was watch the red dots crawl around the planet and try to score. So far the pilot had managed to knock out all the drones; the enemy hadn't sent any fighters after him yet.

I'd given the pilot control over five of the lasers in our defensive ring. They couldn't do much good, though. A gigawatt laser pumps out a billion kilowatts per second at a range of a hundred meters. A thousand klicks up,

189

though, the beam was attenuated to ten kilowatts. Might do some damage if it hit an optical sensor. At least confuse things.

"We could use another fighter. Or six."

"Use up the drones," I said. We did have a fighter, of course, and a swabbie attached to us who could pilot it. It might turn out to be out only hope, if they got us cornered in the stasis field.

"How far away is the other guy?" Charlie asked, meaning the fighter pilot who had turned tail. I cranked down the scale, and the green dot appeared at the right of the display. "About six light-hours." He had two drones left, too near to him to show as separate dots, having expended one in covering his getaway. "He's not accelerating any more, but he's doing point nine gee."

"Couldn't do us any good if he wanted to." Need almost a month to slow down.

At that low point, the light that stood for our own defensive fighter faded out. "Shit."

"Now the fun starts. Should I tell the troops to get ready, stand by to go topside?"

"No . . . have them suit up, in case we lose air. But I expect it'll be a little while before we have a ground attack." I turned the scale up again. Four red dots were already creeping around the globe toward us.

I got suited up and came back to Administration to watch the fireworks on the monitors.

The lasers worked perfectly. All four drones converged on us simultaneously; were targeted and destroyed. All but one of the nova bombs went off below our horizon (the visual horizon was about ten kilometers away, but the lasers were mounted high and could target something at twice that distance). The bomb that detonated on our horizon had melted out a semicircular chunk that glowed brilliantly white for several minutes. An hour later, it was still glowing dull orange, and the ground temperature outside had risen to fifty degrees Absolute, melting most of our snow, exposing an irregular dark gray surface.

The next attack was also over in a fraction of a second, but this time there had been eight drones, and four of them got within ten klicks. Radiation from the glowing craters raised the temperature to nearly 300 degrees. That was above the melting point of water, and I was starting to get worried. The fighting suits were good to over a thousand degrees, but the automatic lasers depended on low-temperature superconductors for their speed.

I asked the computer what the lasers' temperature limit was, and it printed out *TR 398-734-009-265, "Some Aspects Concerning the Adaptability of Cryogenic Ordnance to use in Relatively High-Temperature Environments,"* which had lots of handy advice about how we could insulate the weapons if we had access to a fully-equipped armorer's shop. It did note that the response time of automatic-aiming devices increased as the temperature increased, and that above some "critical temperature," the weapons would not aim at all. But there was no way to predict any individual weapon's behavior, other than to note that the highest critical temperature recorded was 790 degrees and the lowest was 420 degrees.

Charlie was watching the display. His voice was flat over the suit's radio. "Sixteen this time."

"Surprised?" One of the few things we knew about Tauran psychology was a certain compulsiveness about numbers, especially primes and powers of two.

"Let's just hope they don't have 32 left." I queried the computer on this; all it could say was that the cruiser had thus far launched a total of 44 drones and that some cruisers had been known to carry as many as 128.

We had more than a half-hour before the drones would strike. I could evacuate everybody to the stasis field, and they would be temporarily safe if one of the nova bombs got through. Safe, but trapped. How long would it take the crater to cool down, if three or four—let alone sixteen—of the bombs made it through? You couldn't live forever in a fighting suit, even though it recycled everything with remorseless efficiency. One week was enough to make you thoroughly miserable. Two weeks, suicidal. Nobody had ever gone three weeks, under field conditions.

Besides, as a defensive position, the stasis field could be a death-trap. The enemy has all the options since the dome is opaque; the only way you can find out what

191

they're up to is to stick your head out. They didn't have to wade in with primitive weapons unless they were impatient. They could keep the dome saturated with laser fire and wait for you to turn off the generator. Meanwhile harassing you by throwing spears, rocks, arrows into the dome—you could return fire, but it was pretty futile.

Of course, if one man stayed inside the base, the others could wait out the next half-hour in the stasis field. If he didn't come get them, they'd know the outside was hot. I chinned the combination that would give me a frequency available to everybody echelon 5 and above.

"This is Major Mandella." That still sounded like a bad joke.

I outlined the situation to them and asked them to tell their troops that everyone in the company was free to move into the stasis field. I would stay behind and come retrieve them if things went well—not out of nobility, of course; I preferred taking the chance of being vaporized in a nanosecond, rather than almost certain slow death under the gray dome.

I chinned Charlie's frequency. "You can go, too. I'll take care of things here."

"No, thanks," he said slowly. "I'd just as soon . . . Hey, look at this."

The cruiser had launched another red dot, a couple of minutes behind the others. The display's key identified it as being another drone. "That's curious."

"Superstitious bastards," he said without feeling.

It turned out that only eleven people chose to join the fifty who had been ordered into the dome. That shouldn't have surprised me, but it did.

As the drones approached, Charlie and I stared at the monitors, carefully not looking at the holograph display, tacitly agreeing that it would be better not to know when they were one minute away, thirty seconds . . . And then, like the other times, it was over before we knew it had started. The screens glared white and there was a yowl of static, and we were still alive.

But this time there were fifteen new holes on the horizon—or closer!—and the temperature was rising so fast that the last digit in the readout was an amorphous blur.

The number peaked in the high 800s and began to slide back down.

We had never seen any of the drones, not during that tiny fraction of a second it took the lasers to aim and fire. But then the seventeenth one flashed over the horizon, zig-zagging crazily, and stopped directly overhead. For an instant it seemed to hover, and then it began to fall. Half the lasers had detected it, and they were firing steadily, but none of them could aim; they were all stuck in their last firing position.

It glittered as it dropped, the mirror polish of its sleek hull reflecting the white glow from the craters and the eerie flickering of the constant, impotent laser fire. I heard Charlie take one deep breath, and the drone fell so close you could see spidery Tauran numerals etched on the hull and a transparent porthole near the tip— then its engine flared and it was suddenly gone.

"What the hell?" Charlie said, quietly.

The porthole. "Maybe reconnaissance."

"I guess. So we can't touch them, and they know it."

"Unless the lasers recover." Didn't seem likely. "We better get everybody under the dome. Us, too."

He said a word whose vowel had changed over the centuries, but whose meaning was clear. "No hurry. Let's see what they do."

We waited for several hours. The temperature outside stabilized at 690 degrees—just under the melting point of zinc, I remembered to no purpose—and I tried the manual controls for the lasers, but they were still frozen.

"Here they come," Charlie said. "Eight again."

I started for the display. "Guess we'll—"

"Wait! They aren't drones." The key identified all eight with the legend *Troop Carrier*.

"Guess they want to take the base," he said. "Intact."

That, and maybe try out new weapons and techniques. "It's not much of a risk for them. They can always retreat and drop a nova bomb in our laps."

I called Brill and had her go get everybody who was in the stasis field, set them up with the remainder of her platoon as a defensive line circling around the northeast and northwest quardrants. I'd put the rest of the people on the other half-circle.

"I wonder," Charlie said. "Maybe we shouldn't put everyone topside at once. Until we know how many Taurans there are."

That was a point. Keep a reserve, let the enemy underestimate our strength. "It's an idea. . . . There might be just 64 of them in eight carriers." Or 128 or 256. I wished our spy satellites had a finer sense of discrimination. But you can only cram so much into a machine the size of a grape.

I decided to let Brill's seventy people be our first line of defense and ordered them into a ring in the ditches we had made outside the base's perimeter. Everybody else would stay downstairs until needed.

If it turned out that the Taurans, either through numbers or new technology, could field an unstoppable force, I'd order everyone into the stasis field. There was a tunnel from the living quarters to the dome, so the people underground could go straight there in safety. The ones in the ditches would have to fall back under fire. If any of them were still alive when I gave the order.

I called in Hilleboe and had her and Charlie keep watch over the lasers. If they came unstuck, I'd call Brill and her people back. Turn on the automatic aiming system again, then sit back and watch the show. But even stuck, the lasers could be useful. Charlie marked the monitors to show where the rays would go; he and Hilleboe could fire them manually whenever something moved into a weapon's line-of-sight.

We had about twenty minutes. Brill was walking around the perimeter with her men and women, ordering them into the ditches a squad at a time, setting up overlapping fields of fire. I broke in and asked her to set up the heavy weapons so that they could be used to channel the enemy's advance into the path of the lasers.

There wasn't much else to do but wait. I asked Charlie to measure the enemy's progress and try to give us an accurate count-down, then sat at my desk and pulled out a pad, to diagram Brill's arrangement and see whether I could improve on it.

The cat jumped up on my lap, mewling piteously. He'd evidently been unable to tell one person from the other, suited up. But nobody else ever sat at this desk. I reached up to pet him and he jumped away.

The first line that I drew ripped through four sheets of paper. It had been some time since I'd done any delicate work in a suit. I remembered how in training, they'd made us practice controlling the strength-amplification circuits by passing eggs from person to person, messy business. I wondered if they still had eggs on Earth.

The diagram completed, I couldn't see any way to add to it. All those reams of theory crammed in my brain; there was plenty of tactical advice about envelopment and encirclement, but from the wrong point of view. If you were the one who was being encircled, you didn't have many options. Sit tight and fight. Respond quickly to enemy concentrations of force, but stay flexible so the enemy can't employ a diversionary force to divert strength from some predictable section of your perimeter. *Make full use of air and space support,* always good advice. Keep your head down and your chin up and pray for the cavalry. Hold your position and don't contemplate Dienbienphu, the Alamo, the Battle of Hastings.

"Eight more carriers out," Charlie said. "Five minutes. Until the first eight get here."

So they were going to attack in two waves. At least two. What would I do, in the Tauran commander's position? That wasn't too far-fetched; the Taurans lacked imagination in tactics and tended to copy human patterns.

The first wave could be a throwaway, a kamikaze attack to soften us up and evaluate our defenses. Then the second would come in more methodically, and finish the job. Or vice versa: the first group would have twenty minutes to get entrenched; then the second could skip over their heads and hit us hard at one spot—breach the perimeter and over-run the base.

Or maybe they sent out two forces simply because two was a magic number. Or they could launch only eight troop carriers at a time (that would be bad, implying that the carriers were large; in different situations they had used carriers holding as few as 4 troops or as many as 128).

"Three minutes." I stared at the cluster of monitors that showed various sectors of the mine field. If we were lucky, they'd land out there, out of caution. Or maybe pass over it low enough to detonate mines.

I was feeling vaguely guilty. I was safe in my hole, doodling, ready to start calling out orders. How did those seventy sacrificial lambs feel about their absentee commander?

Then I remembered how I had felt about Captain Stott that first mission, when he'd elected to stay safely in orbit while we fought on the ground. The rush of remembered hate was so strong I had to bite back nausea.

"Hilleboe, can you handle the lasers by yourself?"

"I don't see why not, sir."

I tossed down the pen and stood up. "Charlie , you take over the unit coordination; you can do it as well as I could. I'm going topside."

"I wouldn't advise that, sir."

"Hell no, William. Don't be an idiot."

"I'm not taking orders, I'm giv—"

"You wouldn't last ten seconds up there," Charlie said.

"I'll take the same chance as everybody else."

"Don't you hear what I'm saying. *They'll* kill you!"

"The troops? Nonsense. I know they don't like me especially, but—"

"You haven't listened in on the squad frequencies?" No, they didn't speak my brand of English when they talked among themselves. "They think you put them out on the line for punishment, for cowardice. After you'd told them anyone was free to go into the dome."

"Didn't you, sir?" Hilleboe said.

"To punish them? No, of course not." Not consciously. "They were just up there when I needed . . . Hasn't Lieutenant Brill said anything to them?"

"Not that I've heard," Charlie said. "Maybe she's been too busy to tune in."

Or she agreed with them. "I'd better get—"

"There!" Hilleboe shouted. The first enemy ship was visible in one of the mine field monitors; the others appeared in the next second. They came in from random directions and weren't evenly distributed around the base. Five in the northeast quadrant and only one in the southwest. I relayed the information to Brill.

But we had predicted their logic pretty well; all of them were coming down in the ring of mines. One came close enough to one of the tachyon devices to set it off. The blast caught the rear end of the oddly streamlined craft, causing it to make a complete flip and crash nose-first. Side ports opened up and Taurans came crawling out. Twelve of them; probably four left inside. If all the others had sixteen as well, there were only slightly more of them than of us.

In the first wave.

The other seven had landed without incident, and yes, there were sixteen each. Brill shuffled a couple of squads to conform to the enemy's troop concentration, and he waited.

They moved fast across the mine field, striding in unison like bowlegged, top-heavy robots, not even breaking stride when one of them was blown to bits by a mine, which happened eleven times.

When they came over the horizon, the reason for their apparently random distribution was obvious: they had analyzed beforehand which approaches would give them the most natural cover, from the rubble that the drones had kicked up. They would be able to get within a couple of kilometers of the base before we got any clear line-of-sight of them. And their suits had augmentation circuits similar to ours, so they could cover a kilometer in less than a minute.

Brill had her troops open fire immediately, probably more for morale than out of any hope of actually hitting the enemy. They probably were getting a few, though it was hard to tell. At least the tachyon rockets did an impressive job of turning boulders into gravel.

The Taurans returned fire with some weapon similar to the tachyon rocket, maybe exactly the same. They rarely found a mark, though; our people were at and below ground level, and if the rocket didn't hit something, it would keep going on forever, amen. They did score a hit on one of the bevawatt lasers, though, and the concussion that filtered down to us was strong enough to make me wish we had burrowed a little deeper than twenty meters.

The gigawatts weren't doing us any good. The Taurans must have figured out the lines of sight ahead of time, and gave them wide berth. That turned out to be fortunate, because it caused Charlie to let his attention wander from the laser monitors for a moment.

"What the hell?"

"What's that, Charlie?" I didn't take my eyes off the monitors. Waiting for something to happen.

"The ship, the cruiser—it's gone." I looked at the holograph display. He was right; the only red lights were those that stood for the troop carriers.

"Where did it go?" I asked inanely.

"Let's play it back." He programmed the display to go back a couple of minutes and cranked out the scale to where both planet and collapsar showed on the cube. The cruiser showed up, and with it, three green dots. Our "coward," attacking the cruiser with only two drones.

But he had a little help from the laws of physics.

Instead of going into collapsar insertion, he had skimmed *around* the collapsar field in a slingshot orbit. He had come out going nine-tenths of the speed of light; the drones were going .99c, headed straight for the enemy cruiser. Our planet was about a thousand light-seconds from the collapsar, so the Tauran ship had only ten seconds to detect and stop both drones. And at that speed, it didn't matter whether you'd been hit by a nova-bomb or a spitball.

The first drone disintegrated the cruiser, and the other one, .01 second behind, glided on down to impact on the planet. The fighter missed the planet by a couple of hundred kilometers and hurtled on into space, decelerating with the maximum twenty-five gees. He'd be back in a couple of months.

But the Taurans weren't going to wait. They were getting close enough to our lines for both sides to start using lasers, but they were also within easy grenade range. A good-size rock could shield them from laser fire, but the grenades and rockets were slaughtering them.

At first, Brill's troops had the overwhelming advantage; fighting from ditches, they could only be harmed by an occasional lucky shot or an extremely well-aimed grenade (which the Taurans threw by hand, with a range of several hundred meters). Brill had lost four, but it looked as if the Tauran force was down to less than half its original size.

Eventually, the landscape had been torn up enough so that the bulk of the Tauran force was able to fight from holes in the ground. The fighting slowed down to individual laser duels, punctuated occasionally by heavier weapons. But it wasn't smart to use up a tachyon rocket against a single Tauran, not with another force of unknown size only a few minutes away.

Something had been bothering me about that holographic replay. Now, with the battle's lull, I knew what it was.

When that second drone crashed at near-lightspeed, how much damage had it done to the planet? I stepped over to the computer and punched it up; found out how much energy had been released in the collision, and then compared it with geological information in the computer's memory.

Twenty times as much energy as the most powerful earthquake ever recorded. On a planet three-quarters the size of Earth.

On the general frequency: "Everybody—topside! Right now!" I palmed the button that would cycle and open the airlock and tunnel that led from Administration to the surface.

"What the hell, Will—"

"Earthquake!" How long? "Move!"

Hilleboe and Charlie were right behind me. The cat was sitting on my desk, licking himself unconcernedly. I had an irrational impulse to put him inside my suit, which was the way he'd been carried from the ship to the base, but knew he wouldn't tolerate more than a few minutes of it. Then I had the more reasonable impulse to simply vaporize him with my laser-finger, but by then the door was closed and we were swarming up the ladder. All the way up, and for some time afterward, I was haunted by the image of that helpless animal, trapped under tons of rubble, dying slowly as the air hissed away.

"Safer in the ditches?" Charlie said.

"I don't know," I said. "Never been in an earthquake." Maybe the walls of the ditch would close up and crush us.

I was surprised at how dark it was on the surface. S Doradus had almost set; the monitors had compensated for the low light level.

An enemy laser raked across the clearing to our left, making a quick shower of sparks when it flicked by a gigawatt mounting. We hadn't been seen yet. We all decided yes, it would be safer in the ditches, and made it to the nearest one in three strides.

There were four men and women in the ditch, one of them badly wounded or dead. We scrambled down the ledge and I turned up my image amplifier to log two, to inspect our ditchmates. We were lucky; one was a grenadier and they also had a rocket launcher. I could just make out the names on their helmets. We were in Brill's ditch, but she hadn't noticed us yet. She was at the opposite end, cautiously peering over the edge, directing two squads in a flanking movement. When they were safely in position, she ducked back down. "Is that you, Major?"

"That's right," I said cautiously. I wondered whether any of the people in the ditch were among the ones after my scalp.

"What's this about an earthquake?"

She had been told about the cruiser being destroyed, but not about the other drone. I explained in as few words as possible.

"Nobody's come out of the airlock," she said. "Not yet. I guess they all went into the stasis field."

"Yeah, they were just as close to one as the other." Maybe some of them were still down below, hadn't taken my warning seriously. I chinned the general frequency to check, and then all hell broke loose.

The ground dropped away and then flexed back up; slammed us so hard that we were airborne, tumbling out of the ditch. We flew several meters, going high enough to see the pattern of bright orange and yellow ovals, the craters where nova bombs had been stopped. I landed on my feet but the ground was shifting and slithering so much that it was impossible to stay upright.

With a basso grinding I could feel through my suit, the cleared area above our base crumbled and fell in.

Part of the stasis field's underside was exposed when the ground subsided; it settled to its new level with aloof grace.

Well, minus one cat. I hoped everybody else had time and sense enough to get under the dome.

A figure came staggering out of the ditch nearest to me and I realized with a start that it wasn't human. At that range, my laser burned a hole straight through his helmet; he took two steps and fell over backward. Another helmet peered over the edge of the ditch. I sheared the top of it off before he could raise his weapon.

I couldn't get my bearings. The only thing that hadn't changed was the stasis dome, and it looked the same from any angle. The gigawatt lasers were all buried, but one of them had switched on, a brilliant flickering searchlight that illuminated a swirling cloud of vaporized rock.

Obviously, though, I was in enemy territory. I started across the trembling ground toward the dome.

I couldn't raise any platoon leaders. All of them but Brill were probably inside the dome. I did get Hilleboe and Charlie; told Hilleboe to go inside the dome and roust everybody out. If the next wave also had 128, we were going to need everybody.

The tremors died down and I found my way into a "friendly" ditch—the cooks' ditch, in fact, since the only people there were Orban and Rudkoski.

"Looks like you'll have to start from scratch again, Private."

"That's all right, sir. Liver needed a rest."

I got a beep from Hilleboe and chinned her on. "Sir . . .there were only ten people there. The rest didn't make it."

"They stayed behind?" Seemed like they'd had plenty of time.

"I don't know, sir."

"Never mind. Get me a count, how many people we have, all totalled." I tried the platoon leaders' frequency again and it was still silent.

The three of us watched for enemy laser fire for a couple of minutes, but there was none. Probably waiting for reinforcements.

Hilleboe called back. "I only get fifty-three, sir. Some may be unconscious."

"All right. Have them sit tight until—" Then the second wave showed up, the troop carriers roaring over the horizon with their jets pointed our way, decelerating. *"Get some rockets on those bastards!"* Hilleboe yelled to everyone in particular. But nobody had managed to stay attached to a rocket launcher while he was being tossed around. No grenade launchers, either, and the range was too far for the hand lasers to do any damage.

These carriers were four or five times the size of the ones in the first wave. One of them grounded about a kilometer in front of us, barely stopping long enough to disgorge its troops. Of which there were over 50, probably 64—times 8 made 512. No way we could hold them back.

"Everybody listen, this is Major Mandella." I tried to keep my voice even and quiet. "We're going to retreat back into the dome, quickly but in an orderly way. I know we're scattered all over hell. If you belong to the second or fourth platoon, stay put for a minute and give covering fire while the first and third platoons, and support, fall back.

"First and third and support, fall back to about half your present distance from the dome, then take cover and defend the second and fourth as they come back. They'll go to the edge of the dome and cover you while you come back the rest of the way." I shouldn't have said "retreat"; that word wasn't in the book. Retrograde action.

There was a lot more retrograde than action. Eight or nine people were firing, and all the rest were in full flight. Rudkoski and Orban had vanished. I took a few carefully aimed shots, to no great effect, then ran down to the other end of the ditch, climbed out and headed for the dome.

The Taurans started firing rockets, but most of them seemed to be going too high. I saw two of us get blown away before I got to my half-way point; found a nice big rock and hid behind it. I peeked out and decided that only two or three of the Taurans were close enough to be even remotely possible laser targets, and the better part of valor would be in not drawing unnecessary attention to myself. I ran the rest of the way to the edge of the field and stopped to return fire. After a couple of shots, I realized that I was just making myself a target; as far as I could see there was only one other person who was still running toward the dome.

A rocket zipped by, so close I could have touched it. I flexed my knees and kicked, and entered the dome in a rather undignified posture.

7.

Inside, I could see the rocket that had missed me drifting lazily through the gloom, rising slightly as it passed through to the other side of the dome. It would vaporize the instant it came out the other side, since all of the kinetic energy it had lost in abruptly slowing down to 16.3 meters per second would come back in the form of heat.

Nine people were lying dead, face-down just inside of the field's edge. It wasn't unexpected, though it wasn't the sort of thing you were supposed to tell the troops.

Their fighting suits were intact—otherwise they wouldn't have made it this far—but sometime during the past few minutes' rough-and-tumble, they had damaged the coating of special insulation that protected them from the stasis field. So as soon as they entered the field, all electrical activity in their bodies ceased, which killed them instantly. Also, since no molecule in their bodies could move faster than 16.3 meters per second, they instantly froze solid, their body temperature stabilized at a cool 0.426 degrees Absolute.

I decided not to turn any of them over to find out their names, not yet. We had to get some sort of defensive position worked out before the Taurans came through the dome. If they decided to slug it out rather than wait.

With elaborate gestures, I managed to get everybody collected in the center of the field, under the fighter's tail, where the weapons were racked.

There were plenty of weapons, since we had been prepared to outfit three times this number of people.

After giving each person a shield and short-sword, I traced a question in the snow: GOOD ARCHERS? RAISE HANDS. I got five volunteers, then picked out three more so that all the bows would be in use. Twenty arrows per bow. They were the most effective long-range weapons we had; the arrows were almost invisible in their slow flight, heavily weighted and tipped with a deadly sliver of diamond-hard crystal.

I arranged the archers in a circle around the fighter (its landing fins would give them partial protection from missiles coming in from behind) and between each pair of archers put four other people: two spear-throwers, one quarterstaff, and a person armed with battleax and a dozen throwing knives. This arrangement would theoretically take care of the enemy at any range, from the edge of the field to hand-to-hand combat.

Actually, at some 600-to-42 odds, they could probably walk in with a rock in each hand, no shields or special weapons, and still beat the shit out of us.

Assuming they knew what the stasis field was. Their technology seemed up to date in all other respects.

For several hours nothing happened. We got about as bored as anyone could, waiting to die. No one to talk to, nothing to see but the unchanging gray dome, gray snow, gray spaceship and a few identically gray soldiers. Nothing to hear, taste or smell but yourself.

Those of us who still had any interest in the battle were keeping watch on the bottom edge of the dome, waiting for the first Taurans to come through. So it took us a second to realize what was going on when the attack did start. It came from above, a cloud of catapulted darts swarming in through the dome some thirty meters above the ground, headed straight for the center of the hemisphere.

The shields were big enough that you could hide most of your body behind them by crouching slightly; the people who saw the darts coming could protect themselves easily. The ones who had their backs to the action, or were just asleep at the switch, had to rely on dumb luck for survival; there was no way to shout a warning, and it only took three seconds for a missile to get from the edge of the dome to its center.

We were lucky, losing only five. One of them was an

archer, Shubik. I took over her bow and we waited, expecting a ground attack immediately.

It didn't come. After a half-hour, I went around the circle and explained with gestures that the first thing you were supposed to do, if anything happened, was to touch the person on your right. He'd do the same, and so on down the line.

That might have saved my life. The second dart attack, a couple of hours later, came from behind me. I felt the nudge, slapped the person on my right, turned around and saw the cloud descending. I got the shield over my head, and they hit a split-second later.

I set down my bow to pluck three darts from the shield and the ground attack started.

It was a weird, impressive sight. Some three hundred of them stepped into the field simultaneously, almost shoulder-to-shoulder around the perimeter of the dome. They advanced in step, each one holding a round shield barely large enough to hide his massive chest. They were throwing darts similar to the ones we had been barraged with.

I set up the shield in front of me—it had little extensions on the bottom to keep it upright—and with the first arrow I shot, I knew we had a chance. It struck one of them in the center of his shield, went straight through and penetrated his suit.

It was a one-sided massacre. The darts weren't very effective without the element of surprise—but when one came sailing over my head from behind, it did give me a crawly feeling between the shoulder blades.

With twenty arrows I got twenty Taurans. They closed ranks every time one dropped; you didn't even have to aim. After running out of arrows, I tried throwing their darts back at them. But their light shields were quite adequate against the small missiles.

We'd killed more than half of them with arrows and spears, long before they got into range of the hand-to-hand weapons. I drew my sword and waited. They still outnumbered us by better than three to one.

When they got within ten meters, the people with the chakram throwing knives had their own field day. Although the spinning disc was easy enough to see and took more than a half-second to get from thrower to target, most of the Taurans reacted in the same ineffective way, raising up the shield to ward it off. The razor-sharp, tempered heavy blade cut through the light shield like a buzz-saw through cardboard.

The first hand-to-hand contact was with the quarter-staffs, which were metal rods two meters long that tapered at the ends to a double-edged, serrated knife blade. The Taurans had a cold-blooded—or valiant, if your mind works that way—method for dealing with them. They would simply grab the blade and die. While the human was trying to extricate his weapon from the frozen death-grip, a Tauran swordsman, with a scimitar over a meter long, would step in and kill him.

Besides the swords, they had a bolo-like thing that was a length of elastic cord that ended with about ten centimeters of something like barbed wire, and a small weight to propel it. It was a dangerous weapon for all concerned; if they missed their target it would come snapping back unpredictably. But they hit their target pretty often, going under the shields and wrapping the thorny wire around ankles.

I stood back-to-back with Private Erikson, and with our swords we managed to stay alive for the next few minutes. When the Taurans were down to a couple of dozen survivors, they just turned around and started marching out. We threw some darts after them, getting three, but we didn't want to chase after them. They might turn around and start hacking again.

There were only twenty-eight of us left standing. Nearly ten times that number of dead Taurans littered the ground, but there was no satisfaction in it.

They could do the whole thing over, with a fresh 300. And this time it would work.

We moved from body to body, pulling out arrows and spears, then took up places around the fighter again. Nobody bothered to retrieve the quarterstaffs. I counted noses: Charlie and Diana were still alive (Hilleboe had been one of the quarterstaff victims), as well as two supporting officers, Wilber and Szydlowska. Rudkoski was still alive but Orban had taken a dart.

After a day of waiting, it looked as though the enemy had decided on a war of attrition rather than repeating the ground attack. Darts came in constantly, not in swarms anymore, but in twos and threes and tens. And from all different angles. We couldn't stay alert forever; they'd get somebody every three or four hours.

We took turns sleeping, two at a time, on top of the stasis field generator. Sitting directly under the bulk of the fighter, it was the safest place in the dome.

Every now and then, a Tauran would appear at the edge of the field, evidently to see whether any of us were left. Sometimes we'd shoot an arrow at him, for practice.

The darts stopped falling after a couple of days. I supposed it was possible that they'd simply run out of them. Or maybe they'd decided to stop when we were down to twenty survivors.

There was a more likely possibility. I took one of the quarterstaffs down to the edge of the field and poked it through, a centimeter or so. When I drew it back, the point was melted off. When I showed it to Charlie, he rocked back and forth (the only way you can nod in a suit); this sort of thing had happened before, one of the first times the stasis field hadn't worked. They simply saturated it with laser fire and waited for us to go stir-crazy and turn off the generator. They were probably sitting in their ships playing the Tauran equivalent of pinochle.

I tried to think. It was hard to keep your mind on something for any length of time in that hostile environment, sense-deprived, looking over your shoulder every few seconds. Something Charlie had said. Only yesterday. I couldn't track it down. It wouldn't have worked then; that was all I could remember. Then finally it came to me.

I called everyone over and wrote in the snow:

GET NOVA BOMBS FROM SHIP.
CARRY TO EDGE OF FIELD.
MOVE FIELD.

Szydlowska knew where the proper tools would be aboard ship. Luckily, we had left all of the entrances open before turning on the stasis field; they were electronic and would have been frozen shut. We got an assortment of wrenches from the engine room and climbed up to the cockpit. He knew how to remove the access plate that exposed a crawl space into the bomb-bay. I followed him in through the meter-wide tube.

Normally, I supposed, it would have been pitch-black. But the stasis field illuminated the bomb-bay with the same dim, shadowless light that prevailed outside. The bomb-bay was too small for both of us, so I stayed at the end of the crawl space and watched.

The bomb-bay doors had a "manual override" so they were easy; Szydlowska just turned a hand-crank and we were in business. Freeing the two nova bombs from their cradles was another thing. Finally, he went back down to the engine room and brought back a crowbar. He pried one loose and I got the other, and we rolled them out the bomb-bay.

Sergeant Anghelov was already working on them by the time we climbed back down. All you had to do to arm the bomb was to unscrew the fuse on the nose of it and poke something around in the fuse socket to wreck the delay mechanism and safety restraints.

We carried them quickly to the edge, six people per bomb, and set them down next to each other. Then we waved to the four people who were standing by at the field generator's handles. They picked it up and walked ten paces in the opposite direction. The bombs disappeared as the edge of the field slid over them.

There was no doubt that the bombs went off. For a couple of seconds it was hot as the interior of a star outside, and even the stasis field took notice of the fact: about a third of the dome glowed a dull pink for a moment, then was gray again. There was a slight acceleration, like you would feel in a slow elevator. That meant we were drifting down to the bottom of the crater. Would there be a solid bottom? Or would we sink down through molten rock to be trapped like a fly in amber —didn't pay to even think about that. Perhaps if it happened, we could blast our way out with the fighter's gigawatt laser.

Twelve of us, anyhow.

HOW LONG? Charlie scraped in the snow at my feet.

That was a damned good question. About all I knew

was the amount of energy two nova bombs released. I didn't know how big a fireball they would make, which would determine the temperature at detonation and the size of the crater. I didn't know the heat capacity of the surrounding rock, or its boiling point. I wrote: ONE WEEK, SHRUG? HAVE TO THINK.

The ship's computer could have told me in a thousandth of a second, but it wasn't talking. I started writing equations in the snow, trying to get a maximum and minimum figure for the length of time it would take for the outside to cool down to 500 degrees. Anghelov, whose physics was much more up-to-date, did his own calculations on the other side of the ship.

My answer said anywhere from six hours to six days (although for six hours, the surrounding rock would have to conduct heat like pure copper), and Anghelov got five hours to 4-1/2 days. I voted for six and nobody else got a vote.

We slept a lot. Charlie and Diana played chess by scraping symbols in the snow; I was never able to hold the shifting positions of the pieces in my mind. I checked my figures several times and kept coming up with six days. I checked Anghelov's computations, too, and they seemed all right, but I stuck to my guns. It wouldn't hurt us to stay in the suits an extra day and a half. We argued good-naturedly in terse shorthand.

There had been nineteen of us left the day we tossed the bombs outside. There were still nineteen, six days later, when I paused with my hand over the generator's cutoff switch. What was waiting for us out there? Surely we had killed all the Taurans within several klicks of the explosion. But there might have been a reserve force farther away, now waiting patiently on the crater's lip. At least you could push a quarterstaff through the field and have it come back whole.

I dispersed the people evenly around the area, so they might not get us with a single shot. Then, ready to turn it back on immediately if anything went wrong, I pushed.

8.

My radio was still tuned to the general frequency; after more than a week of silence my ears were suddenly assaulted with loud, happy babbling.

We stood in the center of a crater almost a kilometer wide and deep. Its sides were a shiny black crust shot through with red cracks, hot but no longer dangerous. The hemisphere of earth that we rested on had sunk a good forty meters into the floor of the crater, while it had still been molten, so now we stood on a kind of pedestal.

Not a Tauran in sight.

We rushed to the ship, sealed it and filled it with cool air and popped our suits. I didn't press seniority for the one shower; just sat back in an acceleration couch and took deep breaths of air that didn't smell like recycled Mandella.

The ship was designed for a maximum crew of twelve, so we stayed outside in shifts of seven to keep from straining the life support systems. I sent a repeating message to the other fighter, which was still over six weeks away, that we were in good shape and waiting to be picked up. I was reasonably certain he would have seven free berths, since the normal crew for a combat mission was only three.

It was good to walk around and talk again. I officially suspended all things military for the duration of our stay on the planet. Some of the people were survivors of Brill's mutinous bunch, but they didn't show any hostility toward me.

We played a kind of nostalgia game, comparing the various eras we'd experienced on Earth, wondering what it would be like in the 700-years-future we were going back to. Nobody mentioned the fact that we would at best go back to a few months' furlough and then be assigned to another strike force, another turn of the wheel.

Wheels. One day Charlie asked me from what country my name originated; it sounded weird to him. I told him it originated from the lack of a dictionary and that if it were spelled right, it would look even weirder.

I got to kill a good half-hour explaining all the peripheral details to that. Basically, though, my parents were "hippies" (a kind of subculture in the late-twentieth-century America, that rejected materialism and embraced a broad spectrum of odd ideas) who lived with a group of other hippies in a small agricultural community. When my mother got pregnant, they wouldn't be so conventional as to get married: this entailed the woman taking the man's name, and implied that she was his property. But they got all intoxicated and sentimental and decided they would both change their names to be the same. They rode into the nearest town, arguing all the way as to what name would be the best symbol for the love-bond between them—I narrowly missed having a much shorter name—and they settled on Mandala.

A mandala is a wheel-like design the hippies had borrowed from a foreign religion, that symbolized the cosmos, the cosmic mind, God, or whatever needed a symbol. Neither my mother nor my father knew how to spell the word, and the magistrate in town wrote it down the way it sounded to him.

They named me William in honor of a wealthy uncle, who unfortunately died penniless.

The six weeks passed rather pleasantly: talking, reading, resting. The other ship landed next to ours and did have nine free berths. We shuffled crews so that each ship had someone who could get it out of trouble if the pre-programmed jump sequence malfunctioned. I assigned myself to the other ship, in hopes it would have some new books. It didn't.

We zipped up in the tanks and took off simultaneously.

We wound up spending a lot of time in the tanks, just to keep from looking at the same faces all day long in the crowded ship. The added periods of acceleration got us back to Stargate in ten months, subjective. Of course, it was 340 years (minus seven months) to the hypothetical objective observer.

There were hundreds of cruisers in orbit around Stargate. Bad news: with that kind of backlog we probably wouldn't get any furlough at all.

I supposed I was more likely to get a court-martial than a furlough, anyhow. Losing 88 percent of my company, many of them because they didn't have enough confidence in me to obey the direct earthquake order. And we were back where we'd started on Sade-138; no Taurans there, but no base either.

We got landing instructions and went straight down, no shuttle. There was another surprise waiting at the spaceport. Dozens of cruisers were standing around on the ground (they'd never done that before for fear that Stargate would be hit)—and two captured Tauran cruisers as well. We'd never managed to get one intact.

Seven centuries could have brought us a decisive advantage, of course. Maybe we were winning.

We went through an airlock under a "returnees" sign. After the air cycled and we'd popped our suits, a beautiful young woman came in with a cartload of tunics and told us, in perfectly-accented English, to get dressed and go to the lecture hall at the end of the corridor to our left.

The tunic felt odd, light yet warm. It was the first thing I'd worn besides a fighting suit or bare skin in almost a year.

The lecture hall was about a hundred times too big for the twenty-two of us. The same woman was there and asked us to move down to the front. That was unsettling; I could have sworn she had gone down the corridor the other way—I *knew* she had; I'd been captivated by the sight of her clothed behind.

Hell, maybe they had matter transmitters. Or teleportation. Wanted to save herself a few steps.

We sat for a minute and a man, clothed in the same kind of unadorned tunic the woman and we were wearing, walked across the stage with a stack of thick notebooks under each arm.

The woman followed him on, also carrying notebooks.

I looked behind me and she was still standing in the aisle. To make things even more odd, the man was virtually a twin to both of them.

The man riffled through one of the notebooks and cleared his throat. "These books are for your convenience," he said, also with perfect accent, "and you don't

212

have to read them if you don't want to. You don't have to do anything you don't want to do, because . . . you're free men and women. The war is over."

Disbelieving silence.

"As you will read in this book, the war ended 221 years ago. Accordingly, this is the year 220. Old style, of course, it is 3138 A.D.

"You are the last group of soldiers to return. When you leave here, I will leave as well. And destroy Stargate. It exists only as a rendezvous point for returnees and as a monument to human stupidity. And shame. As you will read. Destroying it will be a cleansing."

He stopped speaking and the woman started without a pause. "I am sorry for what you've been through and wish I could say that it was for good cause, but as you will read, it was not.

"Even the wealth you have accumulated, back salary and compound interest, is worthless, as I no longer use money or credit. Nor is there such a thing as an economy, in which to use these . . . things."

"As you must have guessed by now," the man took over, "I am, we are, clones of a single individual. Some two hundred and fifty years ago, my name was Kahn. Now it is Man.

"I had a direct ancestor in your company, a Corporal Larry Kahn. It saddens me that he didn't come back."

"I am over ten billion individuals but only one consciousness," she said. "After you read, I will try to clarify this. I know that it will be difficult to understand.

"No other humans are quickened, since I am the perfect pattern. Individuals who die are replaced.

"There are some planets, however, on which humans are born in the normal, mammalian way. If my society is too alien for you, you may go to one of these planets. If you wish to take part in procreation, I will not discourage it. Many veterans ask me to change their polarity to heterosexual so that they can more easily fit into these other societies. This I can do very easily."

Don't worry about that, Man, just make out my ticket.

"You will be my guest here at Stargate for ten days, after which you will be taken wherever you want to go," he said. "Please read this book in the meantime. Feel free to ask any questions, or request any service." They both stood and walked off the stage.

Charlie was sitting next to me. "Incredible," he said. "They let . . . they encourage . . . men and women to do *that* again? Together?"

The female aisle-Man was sitting behind us, and she answered before I could frame a reasonably sympathetic, hypocritical reply. "It isn't a judgment on your society," she said, probably not seeing that he took it a little more personally than that. "I only feel that it's necessary as a eugenic safety device. I have no evidence that there is anything wrong with cloning only one ideal individual, but if it turns out to have been a mistake, there will be a large genetic pool with which to start again."

She patted him on the shoulder. "Of course, you don't have to go to these breeder planets. You can stay on one of my planets. I make no distinction between heterosexual play and homosexual."

She went up on the stage to give a long spiel about where we were going to stay and eat and so forth while we were on Stargate. "Never been seduced by a computer before," Charlie muttered.

The 1143-year-long war had been begun on false pretenses and only continued because the two races were unable to communicate.

Once they could talk, the first question was "Why did you start this thing?" and the answer was "Me?"

The Taurans hadn't known war for millenia, and toward the beginning of the twenty-first century it looked as though mankind was ready to outgrow the institution as well. But the old soldiers were still around, and many of them were in positions of power. They virtually ran the United Nations Exploratory and Colonization Group, that was taking advantage of the newly-discovered collapsar jump to explore interstellar space.

Many of the early ships met with accidents and disappeared. The ex-military men were suspicious. They armed the colonizing vessels, and the first time they met a Tauran ship, they blasted it.

They dusted off their medals and the rest was going to be history.

You couldn't blame it all on the military, though. The

evidence they presented for the Taurans' having been responsible for the earlier casualties was laughably thin. The few people who pointed this out were ignored.

The fact was, Earth's economy needed a war, and this one was ideal. It gave a nice hole to throw buckets of money into, but would unify humanity rather than dividing it.

The Taurans relearned war, after a fashion. They never got really good at it, and would eventually have lost.

The Taurans, the book explained, couldn't communicate with humans because they had no concept of the individual; they had been natural clones for millions of years. Eventually, Earth's cruisers were manned by Man, Kahn-clones, and they were for the first time able to get through to each other.

The book stated this as a bald fact. I asked a Man to explain what it meant, what was special about clone-to-clone communication, and he said that I *a priori* couldn't understand it. There were no words for it, and my brain wouldn't be able to accommodate the concepts even if there were words.

All right. It sounded a little fishy, but I was willing to accept it. I'd accept that up was down if it meant the war was over.

Man was a pretty considerate entity. Just for us twenty-two, he went to the trouble of rejuvenating a little restaurant-tavern and staffing it at all hours (I never saw a Man eat or drink—guess they'd discovered a way around it). I was sitting in there one evening, drinking beer and reading their book, when Charlie came in and sat down next to me.

Without preamble, he said, "I'm going to give it a try."

"Give what a try?"

"Women. Hetero." He shuddered. "No offense . . . it's not really very appealing." He patted my hand, looking distracted. "But the alternative . . . have you tried it?"

"Well . . . no, I haven't." Female Man was a visual treat, but only in the same sense as a painting or a piece of sculpture. I just couldn't see them as human beings.

215

"Don't." He didn't elaborate. "Besides, they say—he says, she says, it says—that they can change me back just as easily. If I don't like it."

"You'll like it, Charlie."

"Sure that's what *they* say." He ordered a stiff drink. "Just seems unnatural. Anyway, since, uh, I'm going to make the switch, do you mind if . . . why don't we plan on going to the same planet?"

"Sure, Charlie, that'd be great." I meant it. "You know where you're going?"

"Hell, I don't care. Just away from here."

"I wonder if Heaven's still as nice—"

"No." Charlie jerked a thumb at the bartender. "He lives there."

"I don't know. I guess there's a list."

A man came into the tavern, pushing a cart piled high with folders. "Major Mandella? Captain Moore?"

"That's us," Charlie said.

"These are your military records. I hope you find them of interest. They were transferred to paper when your strike force was the only one outstanding, because it would have been impractical to keep the normal data retrieval networks running to preserve so few data."

They always anticipated your questions, even when you didn't have any.

My folder was easily five times as thick as Charlie's. Probably thicker than any other, since I seemed to be the only trooper who'd made it through the whole duration. Poor Marygay. "Wonder what kind of report old Stott filed about me." I flipped to the front of the folder.

Stapled to the front page was a small square of paper. All the other pages were pristine white, but this one was tan with age and crumbling around the edges.

The handwriting was familiar, too familiar even after so long. The date was over 250 years old.

I winced and was blinded by sudden tears. I'd had no reason to suspect that she might be alive. But I hadn't really known she was dead, not until I saw that date.

"William? What's—"

"Leave me be, Charlie. Just for a minute." I wiped my eyes and closed the folder. I shouldn't even read the damned note. Going to a new life, I should leave the old ghosts behind.

But even a message from the grave was contact of a sort. I opened the folder again.

11 Oct 2878

William—

All this is in your personnel file. But knowing you, you might just chuck it. So I made sure you'd get this note.

Obviously, I lived. Maybe you will, too. Join me.

I know from the records that you're out at Sade-138 and won't be back for a couple of centuries. No problem.

I'm going to a planet they call Middle Finger, the fifth planet out from Mizar. It's two collapsar jumps, ten months subjective. Middle Finger is a kind of Coventry for heterosexuals. They call it a "eugenic control baseline."

No matter. It took all of my money, and all the money of five other old-timers, but we bought a cruiser from UNEF. And we're using it as a time machine.

So I'm on a relativistic shuttle, waiting for you. All it does is go out five light years and come back to Middle Finger, very fast. Every ten years I age about a month. So if you're on schedule and still alive, I'll only be twenty-eight when you get here. Hurry!

I never found anybody else and I don't want anybody else. I don't care whether you're ninety years old or thirty. If I can't be your lover, I'll be your nurse.

—Marygay.

"Say, bartender."

"Yes, Major?"

"Do you know of a place called Middle Finger? Is it still there?"

"Of course it is. Where would it be?" Reasonable question. "A very nice place. Garden planet. Some people don't think it's exciting enough."

217

"What's this all about?" Charlie said.

I handed the bartender my empty glass. "I just found out where we're going."

9. EPILOGUE

From *The New Voice,* Paxton, Middle Finger 24-6

14/2/3143

OLD-TIMER HAS FIRST BOY

Marygay Potter-Mandella (24 Post Road, Paxton) gave birth Friday last to a fine baby boy, 3.1 kilos.

Marygay lays claim to being the second-"oldest" resident of Middle Finger, having been born in 1977. She fought through most of the Forever War and then waited for her mate on the time shuttle, 261 years.

The baby, not yet named, was delivered at home with the help of a friend of the family, Dr. Diana Alsever-Moore.